REUNION

"I missed you so much," Shocaw whispered. "Those long nights without you, wondering what you were doing, remembering you, your warmth, the feel of your skin."

Showcaw's hands moved over her and her body sang a response to him. Above them the starry night seemed closer, enclosing them in a privacy that was theirs alone. Bree's own hands moved with urgent need over his strong, hard physique, craving him, eager and ready for him to repeat again and again his every movement of love and passion.

Later, in the exquisite aftermath of ecstasy, Bree's fingertips tingled as she brushed across his sweaty brow and stroked the thick black locks. Her lips were tender as she rubbed them lightly across his chin. She was more alive with this man than she'd ever been in her life. . . .

RENEGADE
HEART

Peggy Hanchar

AN ONYX BOOK

NEW AMERICAN LIBRARY

Onyx is a trademark of New American Library

SIGNET, SIGNET CLASSIC, MENTOR, ONYX, PLUME,
MERIDIAN and NAL BOOKS are published by
New American Library, 1633 Broadway,
New York, New York 10019

First Printing, January, 1987

1 2 3 4 5 6 7 8 9

PRINTED IN THE UNITED STATES OF AMERICA

To Elsa, my dear mother, who early on instilled in me the first tool a writer needs, curiosity, and to Eileen Bertelli, whose encouragement with this book will always be appreciated.

Chapter 1

It's not the same, Bree thought, not the same at all! One slim hand pushed at the mass of golden curls that clung damply to the back of her neck. The afternoon heat lay heavy and languid over the land.

Drawing in a breath of the moist tropical air, Brittany Rikkar slowly expelled it and looked around. Everything still looked the same. The rolling lawn and flower garden and the lush fields beyond the stables were still the same tumble of growth that defeated the most diligent efforts to tame it. The white columns of the magnificent plantation house rose behind her, regally guarding their domain, while people moved freely about, safe and secure within the gracious walls.

Greenwood was as beautiful and impressive within as it was without. Its spacious rooms were filled with treasures from other lands, brought here by her father's own merchant ships. There were thickly woven rugs from the Orient, fine crystal and china from France and England, exquisite lace from Belgium, gilt-edged and ornate furniture from France and fine-grained mahoganies from England.

Over it all—from the choice of rugs on the

darkly polished floors to the precise placement of a Chippendale basin stand in some back guest room—was her mother's sure hand. All of Greenwood reflected the care and wealth of its owners.

Pausing in the shade of the deep veranda, Bree's gaze moved once again to the green fields of cotton and tobacco that sustained the rich plantation. Beyond the acres of crops immediately available to the eye, she knew there were more crops of sugarcane and citrus orchards in the loamy, black soil of the lowlands. David Rikkar was as vigorous and successful as a planter as he was at everything else he tried.

Bree strolled along the veranda, her eyes thoughtful as she studied the landscape. How beautiful was her homeland of Florida. Flower, the Spaniards had named it, and aptly so. No gentle dew-misted French countryside was this. The earth seemed to explode with a raw vibrancy, wild and untamable. It called to her own unbridled spirit in a poignant, familiar rhythm. How she had missed this, how she'd longed to return from her exile in France.

Five long years she'd spent there at school and she might be there yet if not for Aunt Elsa's intervention. It wasn't that Lainie hadn't wanted her daughter back, but Bree had been sent to France for safety from the menace of the warring Seminole Indians. At first it was to have been only for a year, until the Indians were once again defeated, but the war was still raging and no end seemed in sight. It gave Bree little comfort that Jared had spent the years at school in the North. Although their parents had visited them frequently, Bree had longed to return to Greenwood. The years had passed and it became obvious that desperate measures were needed.

Only a letter from Aunt Elsa telling her mother of her sudden fascination for a decadent and penniless Frenchman had caused Lainie Rikkar to relent and arrange for Bree's return. In spite of the dangers posed by the hated Seminoles, it was better in Lainie's estimation to have her daughter home than lose her forever to some dandified, wastrel Frenchman who would only break her heart. So Bree had returned triumphantly. Her ploy had worked.

She smiled to herself now as she thought of Mama's hasty reaction. Bree had never meant to marry such a lecherous drunk as the Comte Giles Davey. Her destiny lay here in this green enchanted land. She was home where she wanted to be, and regardless of the Seminole threat, she had no intentions of ever leaving Greenwood again.

Yet she sensed things were not the same as they'd been when she'd left. Even her father, one of the leaders in Florida politics, showed signs of that same tension. He seemed torn between concern for his land holdings here in central Florida and sympathy for the unfortunate Seminoles.

Her mother felt no such division of loyalties. She'd hated the Seminoles ever since they'd attacked Greenwood when she was just a bride here. Helplessly Lainie had watched as Metoo, her dearest friend, had been cut down and her infant brother, Jean Pierre, kidnapped. Only once had Bree questioned her mother and listened to the anguished voice recall that horror-filled night. Bree had never asked again, but the images her mother's words had conjured up stayed with her. Images of Greenwood burning, the flames dancing wildly against the dark sky while painted figures twirled and danced in the fire's eerie glow, bringing death with the swing of a tomahawk. Those images had haunted Bree's childhood dreams long after she'd been sent to France.

But that war had ended. The Indians had been driven deep into the swamps. Greenwood had been rebuilt. The grief for Metoo had been spent, but never forgotten. For years there had been peace, then war had flared again, and this time the Seminoles had not been so easily put down.

Bree's gaze moved to the dark outline of forest beyond the fields. On the other side of that majestic stand of pines the Green swamp began. It stretched for miles, dominating the interior of central Florida, a mysterious and shadowy otherworld. Its dark, sullen presence had always lurked there just out of reach, forbidding and alluring at the same time, and it was there within the vast semitropical swampland that the soldiers and Seminoles fought to their deadly end.

Sighing, Bree moved still deeper into the shade and wandered past white-painted wicker tables and chairs where the socially prominent of the budding community of Tampa sat chatting and sipping tall cool drinks. The battle against the Seminoles seemed far removed from the gaiety around her. Lainie Rikkar was giving a garden party. It was only one of many Bree had attended during the past few weeks and it would not be the last. Her mother loved to entertain and well she might. She was loved and pampered by all. The admiration was well deserved, for Lainie was generous and openhearted with people, so they were drawn to her as much by her kindness as by her beauty.

House servants moved silently on bare feet among the guests, replenishing drinks and filling dainty, painted china plates with food from the heaped tables in the dining room. Other servants worked quietly and discreetly, moving chairs and tables and making sure all was ready for the ball that would begin as soon as the sun set. Bree could tell by the lilt of voices and the gentle echo of laughter on the hot afternoon air that the reputation of Greenwood and its beautiful mistress had been upheld.

A languorous mood had fallen over the party and Bree noted that some of the ladies were already signaling to their maids to follow them inside and up the sweeping stairs to the bedrooms that awaited them above. They would loosen their corsets and rid themselves of their stays while they took a short nap and rested for the ball. The men were already making their way to her father's study, where they would spend the lazy afternoon talking about crops and politics while they drank their host's fine whiskey. Such was the pattern of life the rich planters had made for themselves in this semitropical paradise.

Bree left the veranda and strolled along the flower-strewn path of the garden, nodding her head as she passed old neighbors and friends. They had all been a part of her life for as long as she could remember.

"Miss Brittany, I hope you'll do me the honor of a dance at the ball tonight?" a handsome young man with brown eyes and a nice smile asked.

"I was hoping you would ask me, Wesley," she answered, giving him a heart-stopping smile over her shoulder.

"Brittany, this is Lieutenant Robert Whitlock. His family is a branch of the Virginia Whitlocks."

"How do you do, Lieutenant?" Bree said graciously. "I do hope you'll like it down here. Florida must seem so different from the North."

"Yes, it is, but the people are most friendly," he said, and smiled. He was tall and slim with pale silvery-blond hair and blue eyes that didn't quite warm with the smile on his lips.

"It's good of your mother to invite me," he

said. The cool blue eyes were assessing as his gaze moved across her face.

"Bree honey," someone called, "you've just got to join us and tell us about Paris."

"Excuse me, Lieutenant," she said with a gracious smile.

"Certainly, Miss Rikkar," he replied mildly.

"It's so nice to have you home, Bree," someone called out, reaching out a hand to draw her closer to their tables.

"I just love that dress, Bree," Sarah Jackson cooed. "Is it from Paris?"

"Yes ma'am, it is." Bree smiled and stood chatting about her afternoon party gown of white batiste when in reality she cared little about the dainty rows of buttons, lace, and satin ribbon. It mattered not at all that the deep cut of the neckline showed her long, slender throat and slim shoulders to perfection, or that the full skirt seemed to enhance the smallness of her waist and the soft mounds of her breasts. She wished instead that she were in her old cotton riding habit, astride Windfire, the new mare her father had given her for her birthday.

"My, you've grown into a beauty, just like your mama," Sarah said, and Bree flushed at her frankness. Compliments meant little to Bree. Most of the time she gave little thought to her good looks.

"I remember when yo'r mama was carryin' you," Mavis Cooper said, weak blue eyes gazing at the young girl's face in near wonderment, "and now here you are, all grown up. How old are you, child?"

"Nineteen, ma'am," Bree answered, trying not to fidgit as Mavis's gnarled old hand took hold of hers, patting it affectionately.

"Oh my, Bree, those were the days back then," said the old woman, "and yo'r mama was a sight to see. She was about yo'r age, I reckon, when she first came to Greenwood. She was so delicate and pretty, just a little slip of a thing with that French accent when she got too angry."

"She was tough, though, had a lot more strength than most folks gave her credit for," Sarah Jackson said.

"That's a fact," Mavis said. "Why, I remember"—Bree suppressed a sigh—"I remember how she took over the plantation and kept it going while yo'r daddy was away and how she fought those Seminoles that took off with her brother, and she was already pregnant with yo'r brother Jared. Where is Jared?" The old woman interrupted her reminiscing to peer about as if expecting Jared to be within her eyesight.

"I don't know, ma'am, I was just about to go look for him," Bree said, and backed away a step or two in spite of the hand still clutching hers.

"You tell him to come by here and see me, you hear?" Mavis instructed. "Just 'cause these young folks grow up is no sign they cain't come greetin' their elders. I remember seein' Jared runnin' round this yard with his britches off, and May chasing after him. He ain't too big to come see an old lady."

"Yes, ma'am. I'll tell him," Bree said, and made her escape. Mavis Cooper had always been partial to Jared. She and her husband had no children of their own, and had doted on Lainie and David Rikkar's offspring. Bree would make a special point to give him the message. In the meantime she hurried across the lawn.

"Young lady, yo' bettah git this here hat on. Yo' mama's goin' ta whip yo' breeches," May, her mother's maid, scolded as she hobbled toward Bree. With a smile Bree watched her approach. She could never remember her mother without the old Negress at her side. May had tended them when they were children and hadn't hesitated to plant a firm hand on their bottoms when she felt it was deserved.

Bree had been painfully aware since returning home of just how much May had aged. That was one of the things that was wrong, she thought as she watched May's slow painful approach. She didn't want May to be so old and fragile. For if May were to grow older, then someday soon her mother and father would begin to look the same way. Bree couldn't imagine it happening.

"Put this on, afore yo'r mama sees you," May instructed, and making a pretty pout with her lips, Bree complied. As she tied the long satin ribbons under her chin, she looked at the fragile figure and scowling face of the old black woman.

"Mama wouldn't whip mah breeches, May," she said, forcing herself to gaiety as she gently mocked the old slave's words. "Ah'm too big."

"Yo' nevah too big when yo' need a whuppin'," May answered, pulling her eyebrows down in a fierce scowl that brought a real chuckle from Bree. "Don' yo' laugh, young lady, yo' not too fine a lady fo' ole May to give yo' what fo' when yo' need it."

"I know I'm not," Bree said, suddenly giving the aging and arthritic servant a hug. Fiercely, May's thin old arms came up to return the embrace.

"Oh, May, I—I'm so glad to be home." Bree stopped and swallowed hard against the lump in her throat.

"I loves yo', girl," May said, and Bree felt the tears spring to her eyes.

"I love you too, May," she said. "I don't know who I missed most, you or Mama, while I was in France."

"Shh, don't yo' be sayin' that now." May drew back. "Yo' mama be hurt she hear yo' talk lak dat."

"I don't think she would, May. She would understand." Bree took the old Negress's arm and helped her back toward the house.

"Brittany, darling," Lainie said, approaching the two of them. Her cheeks were flushed and there was a breathless quality to her that made her seem girlish in spite of her years. Looking at Lainie, it was hard for Bree to realize she was at least as old as Aunt Elsa. The golden hair was without a touch of gray and the lithe figure was as willowy as a girl's.

"Mrs. Southfield is looking for you," Lainie told her daughter. "She says she hasn't seen you all afternoon, and Denise Payne asked about you."

"I'll be sure to say hello," Bree said, although she couldn't repress a small grimace of distaste. Denise Payne was the old-maid daughter of Commander Payne, who had been in charge of Fort Brooks many years before. He had long since retired and settled comfortably into civilian life here in the territory he'd once protected. His daughter lived with him.

"I know how you feel, darling," Lainie was saying in one of her surprising displays of insight. "Denise is a difficult woman to talk to, but just remember she's all alone save for her father and she's very unhappy."

"I don't know how you can be so charitable toward her, Mama. She says the most dreadful things about people," Bree exclaimed in exasperation.

"That's true, but her unkind words hurt her more than anyone," Lainie said with a soft light in her dark eyes. Bree was about to mention her suspicion that Denise Payne was in love with her father, but held back. What did it really matter anyway? David Rikkar had eyes only for his beautiful wife.

Bree moved across the lawn to the side ve-

randa, where Denise Payne was engaged in
conversation with old Millicent Southfield. Might
as well kill two birds with one stone, she thought
with resignation, and steeled herself to walk
toward the two women. Climbing the steps she
pulled the wide-brimmed straw bonnet from her
head and with the back of her hand wiped at the
dampness that had already formed at her temples. She hadn't adjusted yet to the warm Florida temperatures.

She paused for a moment, gripping the ornate
railing that ran along the veranda, dreading the
encounter with the two women. Somehow they
each made her feel young and insignificant, even
now after all her schooling and social polish.

Like a reprieve, the sound of male laughter
drew her through the French doors and into one
of the side parlors. Beyond was her father's study,
and even from here she could tell that the smoke-
filled room was crowded with men. Slowly she
approached the half-opened door and peered in.
The men had made themselves comfortable, lounging on chairs and stools in shirt-sleeves, their
coats flung carelessly over the backs of their
chairs. They were intent upon their conversa-
tions and the fine imported whiskey and Cuban
cigars their host had provided, and didn't notice
Bree.

Through the swirl of smoke Bree's gaze met
her father's and he wagged an eyebrow to acknowledge her presence. It was a secret invitation used since early childhood. She might enter
her father's study at such times as long as she
remained inconspicuous. With an impish grin,
Bree sidled along the wall, much as she had as a
child, and sat down in the bay window, drawing
her long, slender legs up on the seat beside her.
She was half hidden by the heavy formal draper-

ies and the lighter, gauzy curtains that hung
between them.

Once she'd fit here easily with lots of room
left over for her favorite dolls and books, but
now she was forced to bend her knees and pull
them up toward her chest. The long skirt of her
gown and the ruffled petticoats beneath took up
much of the room and she felt trapped. It was
just one more reminder of how much things had
changed while she'd been away.

Bree leaned her head back against the wooden
panel. She could smell the lemon oil and laven-
der even here, a fragrant reminder from her
childhood of her mother's careful attention to
their comfort. Beyond the glazed windows the
brilliantly flowered gardens and rich verdant
fields stretched away as far as the eye could see.
Soon the slender green stalks of cotton would
offer up their yield of white fluffy heads for the
slaves to pick.

Ladies moved along the bricked garden paths,
chatting easily, exchanging bits of gossip, their
colorful, afternoon party gowns looking like delicate butterflies hovering among the greenery.
There was a sense of continuity, of permanence
in everything around Greenwood. She felt safe
and secure here, as if nothing could touch her.
Yet underneath was that nagging little worry
that something was about to threaten her world.

Despite the open window, her haven was hot
and stuffy. She could feel the sweat roll down
between her breasts and fervently hoped it would
not dampen her gown. Mama would be appalled
if she showed evidence of perspiring in such an
intimate place. The voices of the men caught her
attention and she momentarily forgot her discomfort.

"General Armistead hasn't really changed
things; it's an uneasy peace at best," one man

was saying. "Look at what happened to the treaty old Rough and Ready Taylor got for us last year. The Indians agreed in July that they'd stay within the boundaries set for them, and by fall they were killing and burning just like always."

"Come on, Les, you've got to agree that a bounty of two hundred dollars for every Indian scalp brought in had a lot to do with ending that peace attempt," David Rikkar spoke up, and a smile curved Bree's soft lips. Her father was easily the most handsome man there and he was brave and kind as well. No wonder she loved him so much.

"Men were out beating the bushes for any Indian they could find," Rikkar went on, "and it didn't matter if it was a brave or a woman or child."

"I heard tell a few dog pelts got put in as well," Ulcie Thompson spoke up. " 'Course, they really ain't much difference between an Injin an' a mongrel dog." His words were greeted by a chorus of agreement as well as hot denial. Some men like her father advocated a more humane approach to the Indian problem.

"Gentlemen." A tall, young officer stepped away from the mantel where he'd been lounging. The afternoon sun streaking through the French doors was reflected in the bright gold buttons of his uniform and the pale blond of his hair. From her perch Bree craned forward and recognized Lieutenant Whitlock, whom she'd met earlier. His icy blue eyes, alert and assessing, captured each man's gaze, and they fell silent, waiting for him to continue.

"If you're interested in becoming a state," he said, casting a measuring look around the room, "you're going to have to rid Florida of the Seminoles. It's as simple as that."

"I don't agree," David Rikkar spoke up again. "Florida will become a state, even if there are

Seminoles here. To take them from their home-land seems cruel and unnecessary."

"This territory was meant for the white men," the lieutenant said. "The Spaniards cleaned out the Indians that lived here once and then these Seminoles, these wanderers, renegades from the Creek nation, wandered down from Georgia and settled here. General Jackson did a lot for this territory, taming the Seminoles, pushing them into the swamps. Now it's up to you men of Florida to help the army rid these lands of the Indians once and for all."

"They have more right to stay here than we do!" a young, impassioned voice cried, and Bree peered through the curtains, looking for her brother. Jared had been standing quietly at one end of the room. Now he moved forward to challenge the lieutenant's words. Once again Bree marveled at the height and breadth of shoulders he'd attained during her absence.

"They lost their rights, boy, when they started killing innocent people," the lieutenant asserted. "When people go to bed at night, they want to know they'll be getting up in the morning with their hair in place."

"That's right," a man raised his voice in angry agreement. "My brother said some of his neighbors came back to try and resettle their farms and the Seminoles attacked and killed them before they could even get cabins built to shelter their families."

"I recall that incident," the lieutenant was quick to press his point. "The Seminoles killed women and children too. They bashed a baby's head against a tree and laid him back in his dead mother's arms." The lieutenant stopped speaking and leaned back against the mantel once more, his eyes gauging the shocked reactions of the men in the room.

Bree shrank back in the window seat, her stomach roiling with nausea at the thought of the mutilated baby and his dead mother. Fervently she wished herself out of her stuffy hiding place and back outside in the serene coolness of the gardens. The terror she was hearing didn't belong to the world she knew. She remembered the starving, ragged Indians she'd seen in her childhood. When they'd wandered onto Greenwood property, her father'd ordered them fed. How pitiable and helpless they'd looked, stoically accepting their lot. Could these destitute people have committed these atrocities she was hearing?

"It's true the Indians have murdered and burned," her father acknowledged. Bree sat forward and peered through the curtains again. Her brother stood beside his father, a younger version of the dark-haired master of Greenwood. Jared's fists were clenched in barely suppressed fury as he glared at the young lieutenant, who had so callously condemned the Seminoles. Pride welled within Bree at the sight of the two men she loved most standing shoulder to shoulder, their proud heads thrown back in the same graceful way, their weight balanced on long, muscular legs in a stance so similar it was eloquent testimony of their kinship.

"It's true we've suffered at the Seminoles' hands, but we must look with fair eyes at this war," her father was saying. "The Indians have been badly abused by the white man."

"They brought it on themselves," Ulcie cried.

"Did they?" Jared swung around to glare at him. "How would you respond if your home had been taken from you and you were shoved into the meanest, poorest bit of swampland possible, made to eke out a living on scant hammocks, dodging poisonous snakes and man-eating alligators?" he cried. "Wouldn't you feel hatred for the men who'd done that to you?"

The men shuffled their feet and dropped their eyes. Only the lieutenant continued to face the two men who championed the Indians' rights. The young officer's smile was little more than an arrogant curl of his lips.

"Your son has some strange ideas, Rikkar,' he said softly.

"Not so strange," Rikkar said. "Have you family in the North, Lieutenant Whitlock? Wouldn't you feel anger and rage if you saw them hungry and driven from their homes?"

"Are you comparing a white man to a dirty, lazy Indian?" the lieutenant snapped, straightening away from the mantel. His blue eyes had turned cold.

"Is the idea so farfetched?" Rikkar asked mildly. "Don't forget, gentlemen, that the Seminoles once had prosperous farms and cattle ranches right where many of our richest plantations are now sitting. No, Lieutenant, it is not the Seminole who've brought about this war. Why don't we discuss the real issue here? The wealthy slave owners of Georgia and Mississippi are concerned that the Seminoles offer their runaway slaves a haven. Here in Florida we are fighting for the wealthy slave owners, and at what cost to ourselves?"

"'I have observed, Captain Rikkar," the lieutenant said smoothly, only his eyes giving away his anger at being contradicted by this man, "that you are yourself a slave owner. Aren't we fighting for you as well as every other land holder struggling to make it here in Florida?"

"Yes, by God, you are and we be grateful to you for it," a voice cried.

"Besides, we aren't driving the Seminoles off their land. You've said yourself the swamp is an unfit place for man or beast to live. We're taking the Indians out west and giving them land they can work." Listening to the lieutenant's reasoning, Bree wondered for a moment if he might be right. Then her brother spoke again.

"The Arkansas Territory," he said with disgust. "It's barren wasteland where the Seminole'll have to exist on government handouts. Perhaps they feel it's better to starve and die in their own homeland than in a strange, hostile one."

"If that's to be his choice," said the lieutenant, "then he's chosen death." Jared's face reddened and he bristled at the officer's words. Rikkar stepped forward and placed an arm around his son's shoulders, a subtle reminder that the conversation had turned too heated and should be changed.

"The war has dragged on too long," Rikkar said. "There's not a man here who doesn't want to see it end."

"I don't know about that, Rikkar," Ulcie spoke up. "All those federal funds pouring into the territory have been a boon to the economy down here."

"There's talk that the war is affecting our national economy," Rikkar replied. "Some fear it'll throw the country into a depression. It's only a matter of time before we'll feel it. This is a false prosperity we're enjoying."

The men looked warily at each other. There was a low murmur as they discussed this latest bit of war news.

"Seems like the federal government's poured enough money and men into this war to've wiped the last Seminole out of Florida," a man observed to the lieutenant. "They've made some costly mistakes, like bringing those bloodhounds in from Cuba to track down the Seminoles. Why, any fool'd know you can't track over water."

Horrified, Bree listened. Surely they hadn't tracked down human beings with dogs, but the lieutenant was speaking again and he wasn't denying it.

"Yes, we've made some errors of judgment," the lieutenant admitted uncomfortably. "The bloodhounds were a good idea, if they'd worked. But we've made headway otherwise. There are just a handful of Indians left out there to lead this resistance. If we could get them, we could end this war."

"Who's left?" Ulcie asked, and the men turned attentive faces to the officer. Sure of his audience, the lieutenant paused for effect, then walked to the Pembroke table which held bottles of her father's whiskey. With studied casualness he poured himself a drink and turned to face the other men.

"One of them is Coacoochee," he began. "Wildcat, as we know him, and aptly named. He's smart and he's slippery. Then there's Halleck Tustenuggee, or Tiger Tail. He hates the whites worse than any of the others. We've heard he killed his own sister because she favored compromising with us."

The lieutenant downed the whiskey in one neat swallow and set his glass down with a precise snap against the mahogany tabletop. All eyes were riveted to him. "There's also Billy Bolecks, or Billy Bowlegs as we call him. He's got his whole tribe hidden out there in the swamps somewhere, and then there's Shocaw Hadjo the half-breed."

"I thought he was dead," Rikkar said. "The rumor was that Osceola killed him back at the start of the war because he betrayed his people."

"That was his uncle on his mother's side somewhere. He was just a young buck when his uncle was killed but he's one of their best chiefs now.

Emathla is his title as a war chief. He's mean and he's tough and he's smart."

"Some say he's Osceola all over again," Ulcie Thompson interjected.

"He's a lot like him," the lieutenant agreed. "His father was white. He was adopted by a white man when he was about ten but he got into trouble with the law over a white woman when he was a young man and ran away to live with his mother's people. Don't be fooled by his light skin and education though. He hates the white man."

"Some say he don't take scalps or kill women and children," Ulcie spoke up again.

"So they say," Whitlock said doubtfully. "But would you trust your wives and children with him?" He looked about the room at the men. Their answer was plain on their faces.

"If you ever see Shocaw Hadjo," he continued, "shoot first and palaver later. Otherwise you'll be dead. He's the Seminole I want more than any of the others." The intensity of his voice made Bree shiver behind her curtain as she visualized the fierce Indian Shocaw Hadjo.

"Did I ever tell you about the Lesley family?" a man asked. "Wooee! Those Indians were blood-thirsty. Not a head of hair left in the place and you shoulda seen how them bodies was carved up."

Before the man could go further with his grisly tale, Bree slipped out of her window hideaway and moved toward the door. A quick flash of her father's eyes and she knew he had seen her go and applauded her discretion.

Bree made her way to the cool, deep shade of the veranda. She felt faint and slightly nauseous and wasn't sure if it was caused by the heat or the tales she'd heard. She looked out across the fields of Greenwood and the image of a baby with a pitifully bashed-in head nestled in his dead mother's arms swam across her vision. For a moment she feared she might fall down with the vapors, but the sound of a voice made her draw in her breath and square her shoulders.

"Are you all right, Miss Rikkar?" Lieutenant Whitlock had followed her out onto the porch and now stood closer to her than she cared for. His bright blue eyes were alert as he watched her pale face.

"I'm fine, Lieutenant. Thank you," she said, and took a step backward away from him. She could feel the porch railing against her hips. Fumbling with her fan, she opened it and began to wave it quickly back and forth in front of her flushed face.

"You aren't used to the heat yet," he said, and it seemed to her he'd stepped forward. Once again she felt smothered and hemmed in by him. She wished him away, but he seemed inclined to stay, settling himself on the railing.

"We met earlier," he said, giving a slight bow.

"Yes, I remember," Bree said faintly.

"I wasn't sure you would." Robert Whitlock smiled. His words were at odds with his air of assurance. It was obvious he considered himself a man not easily forgotten, especially by the ladies.

"I'm sorry you heard all that talk in there, Miss Rikkar," he said, now affecting an air of sympathy. "It wasn't meant for ladies' ears or their tender sensibilities."

"Why not, Lieutenant," she challenged, "wasn't it true?"

"Unfortunately, it was true, every word and then some."

"I had no idea how bad things really were here," Bree said, beginning to understand finally the tension she'd sensed in those around her.

"Ah, but you've just returned from France.

You can't be expected to involve yourself in what's happening here." His pale eyes raked over her face in a bold gaze.

"This is my homeland, Lieutenant," Bree said, irritated by his condescending manner. He perceived her as little more than a bit of empty-headed fluff. "I intend to involve myself with everything that happens here." So saying, she edged her away down the railing. There was something about the man she didn't like. Perhaps she was prejudiced because of the scene she'd witnessed between him and her brother in the study. She glanced back at his thin, aristocratic face. How different he seemed now as he subtly wooed her.

"Have you been able to see much of Florida yet, Lieutenant Whitlock," she asked, taking a few more steps away from him under the pretense of picking one of the hibiscus blossoms growing near the railing.

"None that's been worth seeing," he replied. "Just mostly swamps and hammocks." Something in his tone made her turn and look at him again.

"You don't like our territory," she observed.

"It's kind of hard to like a country when you're struggling to stay alive and dry," he answered. "We're either dodging Indian bullets or poisonous snakes and God knows what else in those hellish swamps."

"The Seminoles must do it all the time," Bree said without thinking. Jared's words came back to her.

"That's their choice, ma'am," Whitlock began angrily, then caught himself. Bree studied him for a moment.

"It isn't really their choice, Lieutenant. As we've just heard, Andrew Jackson pushed them into the swamps so the white settlers could have their lands."

"Of which it seems your father has a mighty big chunk," the lieutenant shot back. Angrily Bree turned away from him, caught between her loyalty to her own people and sympathy for the Seminoles. Whitlock looked at the delicate profile of the girl and tried again.

"You'll have to excuse me, Miss Rikkar, if I'm less than enthusiastic about Florida. I'm from Boston and took my training at West Point. Your territory is quite a change from what I'm used to. If not for the beauty and hospitality of lovely ladies like yourself and your mother—"

"And Denise Payne," Bree said, knowing it was a breach of manners. Already rumors had begun to circulate about the young officer and the aging beauty. It was unladylike for her to make reference to it, no matter how oblique, but the smugness of the man rankled.

Whitlock paused for a moment, his pale eyes steady on hers as he thought about her words. He'd arrived with Denise and Commander Payne. He could hardly deny his association with her.

"—and Miss Payne," he continued smoothly, "it would be unbearable here, indeed." Taking her soft, white hand in his, he placed a moist kiss on it. Quickly, Bree drew her hand away, barely repressing the urge to wipe it on the skirts of her gown. Her distaste was obvious in the expression of her lovely face. She let the silence stretch between them. Perhaps he'd take the hint and go away. She saw his eyes darken and knew she'd offended him. He drew himself up, his smile thin, the glint of his eyes colder still. He would not easily forgive this slight.

Robert Whitlock freely claimed a link to the Virginia Whitlocks, but he was all too aware they claimed no such kinship. He'd been born a bastard and grown up in middle-class obscurity, supported by a uncaring uncle who'd provided only enough for their most basic needs and nothing for their higher aspirations. His mother's festering resentment over his denied birthright and her high expectations had become his own. With the reluctant help of the same uncle who'd doled out his pittance, Robert had received an appointment at West Point and a warning that nothing more would be forthcoming. He was on his own. Spurred on by his anger, dogged by a fear of failing, he'd struggled to excel. His views were narrow, his pride easily offended as it had been now.

"Your brother seems uncommonly fond of the Seminoles," he said, his tone baiting now. Anger and injured pride flared behind his bland expression.

"My brother hates to see anyone unfairly treated," Bree explained. "He feels sorry for the way the Seminoles must live."

"He should save his sympathy for his own kind," Whitlock retorted derisively. "Folks around here won't take kindly to an Indian lover." His tone was scathing. Anger flared within Bree. How dare this outsider condemn her brother's views.

"Nor do we take kindly to others who come down here and try to take over when they know nothing of the real situation," she snapped. "I've heard tales of the incompetence of the commanding officers and the atrocities they've allowed their men to commit."

"There've been no acts of cruelty on my men's parts, Miss Rikkar, which wasn't deserved by those savages." His arrogant smile had vanished and he was no longer lounging against the railing. "It's too bad your thinking has become so influenced by your brother's viewpoints."

"I do my own thinking, Lieutenant, and form my own opinions, and I think it's men like you who've caused this war to drag on like it has."

"What do you know about this war?" Whitlock demanded. "You've been away to school in France, sent there, I'd wager, by your parents so you'd be safe from the very Seminoles you champion."

"I—I know more than you think," Bree sputtered, angry that he'd come so close to the truth. "Jared wrote to me every week." she said hotly.

"Jared," the lieutenant scoffed. "Once again, you offer the ravings of a rebellious child still wet behind the ears. He's probably never even been off this plantation and has little more education than one of your ignorant Florida crackers."

"Sir, I take offense at your words and your attitude toward my brother. I must ask you to leave our home," Bree flared. The lieutenant stared at her bright beauty, heightened now by her anger, and his eyes narrowed speculatively. This spoiled, pampered girl would be a welcome diversion from the overblown charms he'd found thus far in Denise Payne. He looked at the arch of her eyebrow, the flare of her nostrils, the pale translucent quality of her skin, and wondered how her slender body would feel against his own. He'd started out badly, he saw. He'd have to make amends.

"My apologies, Miss Rikkar," he said easily. The words came too quickly to his lips, Bree thought, and had little meaning to him. His teeth flashed as he turned his most charming smile on her. He was not without experience in charming women and had enjoyed great success back in Boston.

Bree stared at him, unbending in her anger and unwilling to forgive and forget as good manners dictated she should. Again Robert Whitlock smiled at her and reached out and caught her hand in his.

"I'm sorry if I've offended you," he said softly,

his hands gripping hers in a touch much more intimate than it should have been.

"You've offended me as well!" Jared said, stepping forward from the shadowed interior of the study. By the tight line of his mouth, Bree could tell he'd overheard Whitlock's words and was itching for a fight.

"Then it seems I must apologize to you as I have to your sister," the lieutenant said, and the tone itself was a sneering insult to the younger man. "I'm sorry if you've taken offense at my words."

"I take offense at you, sir," Jared said, moving toward the officer, his fists clenched.

"You should behave yourself, boy." Whitlock grinned nastily. "Or I'll have to take you out back and give you a whipping."

"Not by yourself." Jared stepped forward, his fists held chest high now as he glared at him.

"Go cool off, youngster, before I have to teach you what a real man is all about." Whitlock gave him a shove, sending him backward across the veranda.

"Jared," Bree screamed, and hurried to help her brother, who had fallen with a jarring sound against the wall of the house. Jared straightened himself, shaking his head to get his breath. With a snarl, he launched himself across the veranda.

"Jared." David Rikkar's voice cracked on the air, stopping his enraged son in his tracks. Jared drew himself up, breathing heavily while his eyes never left the lieutenant's face. "What's going on here?" Rikkar demanded. Other people had come from the study and the garden to stare with avid curiosity at the three young people on the veranda.

"We were having a disagreement—" Jared began.

"And your son tripped and fell backward," Whitlock interjected smoothly. His smile at Jared was one of condescension and indulgence for an incompetent boy. Bree could sense Jared bristling beside her at the lie, but she could see the wisdom of accepting the lieutenant's words, as belittling as they were to her brother.

"I'm afraid it's partly my fault, Father," she said with a bright smile, and put a supportive, almost protective hand at her brother's elbow. A light squeeze admonished him to wipe the angry scowl from his face. The lieutenant, she noticed, was still smiling, the curve of his lips arrogant, the flash of his eyes derisive as he watched Jared.

"Lieutenant Whitlock was just telling me he has to leave," she said with a regretful smile. She was pleased to see his own smile fade. He'd had no intention of absenting himself from one of the major social events the area had to offer, but he'd been neatly outmaneuvered by this slim young girl.

"I'm sorry to hear you can't stay, but I understand the need for you to fulfill your duties." Rikkar's words sealed the end of the lieutenant's visit. It was obvious Rikkar hadn't quite believed the innocence of what had occurred between the three of them, but as a good host he was prepared to ignore it for the moment.

"Good day, Lieutenant," he said, and thus dismissed, Whitlock had no choice but to bid goodbye to his hostess and leave. He cast a last look back over his shoulders at the trio standing on the veranda. Strikingly handsome, each of them, they were totally absorbed in each other, chatting easily, happy and secure in their positions. The lieutenant perceived they had given no further thought to him than if he'd been one of their slaves.

Clamping his hat over his pale hair, he made his way to the stables, where he roundly cursed the stablehand for his slowness in bringing his

horse. Swinging into his saddle, he started the
long ride back to the fort, his mind filled with
bitterness toward the Rikkars of this world.

Alone again, Bree drifted along the garden paths,
trying to forget the scene on the veranda and the
things she'd heard in her father's study. She was
troubled by visions of the Seminoles, ragged and
starving, desperately making a stand against the
white men who had already taken too much and
now sought to break their last tenuous hold on
this beautiful land.

How would they survive in the desert after
living here in the swamplands and waterways of
Florida? Her heart wrenched with pity for them.

And yet, unbidden came the image of the people the Indians had killed, their scalped, mutilated heads, the women and children, the baby
in his mother's arms, and she was forced to stop
and cling to the branch of a tree, waiting for the
bile to settle again and the sweating, trembling
malaise to leave her.

She'd been right. Things weren't the same anymore. The war had never touched her before,
had, in fact, seemed hardly to exist, but now all
the things she'd overheard made her painfully
aware of the horrible realities behind the languorous, pampered world she'd known. It wounded
her to think that in her beautiful Florida such
atrocities could occur, might be happening even
now as she stood in her frilly white party gown.

A breeze sprang up and Bree held her feverish
face up so she might feel it against her cheeks.
From the stable Windfire issued a challenge and
a complaint, her whinny loud and plaintive. With
a chuckle Bree opened the gate and moved across
the stableyard. Here was the diversion she needed
to take her thoughts from the things she'd heard.
Grabbing up a sugar cube from the supply near
the stable door, she entered and made her way

toward Windfire's stall. She could hear the high-spirited horse snorting and stamping her feet.

"Here you are, girl," Bree crooned, allowing the mare to take the cube from her hand. The horse's nose was warm and silky against the palm of her hand. Bree stroked the satiny neck, listening as Windfire uttered her objections to being shut in.

"I know how you feel, girl," Bree whispered, and on a sudden impulse turned to the stablehand."

"Rasmus, saddle up Windfire for me," she ordered.

"But Miss Bree, they's not no one 'round to ride wif yo'," he protested, his dark eyes wide and uncertain. Her father had decreed that she not ride without an escort.

"That's all right, Rasmus," she reassured him. "I'll ride alone and stay in sight of the plantation. Windfire and I both need some exercise. Hurry now."

"Yas'm," Rasmus said, and hurried to do as she bade. In no time at all his nimble fingers had harnessed and saddled the impatient horse. When she was led out to the mounting block, Windfire reared and tossed her head, sending her silky white mane flying. Bree laughed in understanding. She felt that way too.

"Yo' goin' ridin' dressed lak that?" Rasmus asked in disbelief when she climbed up on the mounting block. Bree looked down at her dainty dress with its ribbons and lace and the white satin slippers.

"Yes, I am," she answered defiantly, and mounted. Hooking her knees over the leaping horn, she tossed her head, sending her long golden curls flying much as Windfire had done. She was feeling better already. Rasmus guided her daintily shod foot to the stirrup, then she was leaning

forward in the saddle, urging the mare forward
with whispered words that were little needed.
The impatient horse sprang away, as eager for
this ride as she.

They didn't take time for the gate, electing
instead to jump it, sailing over its wooden slats
with ease, then they were thundering away down
the path, the wind blowing Bree's hair behind
her in a wild golden tangle of curls.

She let the horse have its head as it raced flat
out, its long legs reaching out for more ground
beneath its flying hooves. Greenwood and its stables disappeared behind them and the fields
passed by on either side in a white and green
blur. Up ahead the road disappeared into the
forests. Common sense told Bree they should
return to the stableyard. Rasmus would be worried, but when she sought to turn the little
mare, Windfire resisted, trumpeting her displeasure at the pressure of the bit. With a laugh Bree
let her have her way and they left behind the
searing heat of the afternoon sun and entered
the cool greenness of the forest.

At first the mare's speed went unchecked, then,
as if affected by the quietness of this place, she
slowed to a canter. Her hooves hardly made a
sound on the thick cushion of fallen pine needles
and Bree drew in a deep breath, reveling in the
cool peacefulness of the place. Now that Windfire
had run herself out, Bree let the reins hang loosely
in her hands. The mare seemed to know to move
slowly and easily.

Bree let her mind float free, leaving behind
the death and horror she'd overheard. Instead
she thought of the beauty of the green forests,
the music of the pine trees soughing in the breeze,
the trill of a bird and its answering mate. They
traveled deeper into the woods and drew near a
stream where Bree had often come as a child to

sit on its mossy banks and stare with delight and wonderment into its tumbling waters. Here she had picked wildflowers and fished unsuccessfully for the silvery fish darting beneath the clear waters.

She loved the rich, earthy smells and the delicious taste of the cold water on a hot afternoon. Her gaze followed the familiar arch of branches over her head. The sunlight streamed downward, diffused and softened by the leaves.

Suddenly the cathedral-like stillness was shattered by the raucous call of a bird and Windfire pranced restlessly beneath her. A note of alarm shivered along Bree's spine and she peered into the dark shadows beyond the clearing.

Was it only her imagination or had she caught a glimpse of a shadow moving beyond those dense tree trunks? The birdcall sounded again, shrill and insistent, behind her now, and Bree's head swung around, her hair swirling about her shoulders. A shiver ran along her bare arms. Suddenly the forest seemed deadly and menacing.

Windfire whinnied a warning, tossing her head, her hooves striking against the forest floor in growing panic. Instinctively Bree pulled the reins to turn the horse but she was already too late. Silent shadows had moved from the trees and now hands reached out for her, grasping at her legs and arms. Strong fingers bit cruelly into her tender flesh.

Windfire screamed again, rearing back from the strange shadows, her nostrils flaring at their unfamiliar odor. She lunged away across the clearing toward freedom, but the foreign shapes and smells were there as well so she wheeled and pranced sideways, searching for a way clear of this enemy. Bree clung to the reins with one hand and lashed out blindly at the grasping hands. Seminoles, she thought, and remembered the things she'd just heard about them. She was about to become one of their victims.

"No," she cried out, and her scream rent the air, startling the birds nesting in a nearby tree. They rose with a flutter on silvered wings and flew away. She felt the reins being wrenched from her hands and was aware of expert hands and a gentle voice calming the frightened mare, bringing her to a standstill.

"No," Bree cried again, and tried to kick her heels into Windfire's belly, but now the hands caught her foot and dragged her from the saddle. She fell, landing heavily on the floor of the dark forest, and lay still.

Chapter 2

She lay stunned, feeling the spongy ground beneath, seeing the green filtered sunlight above. Within her view came large bodies and faces made fierce by streaks of paint. Black eyes, intimidating in their intensity, stared at her impassively.

A whimper escaped her lips as she pushed up on her elbows and stared back at the Indian warriors. There were three of them, but their tall, broad bodies seemed to crowd in on her. They made no further move to touch her. Their smell filled her nostrils, alien and therefore frightening.

Her heart pounded in her chest and she feared she might faint, then welcomed the thought of such oblivion. But the roaring left her ears and the swirling, green-gold, sunlit clearing righted itself. She lay very still, not sure of the consequences if she moved. Her gray eyes were wide with fright. Finally when none of the warriors made a move to touch her, she began to inch backward, dragging the torn, white ruffled skirt of her dress across the damp black ground.

Windfire had been gentled now, her reins held by a young warrior. If only Bree could get back to

the mare, she could escape. She was sure of it.
Once she set her heels to Windfire's belly no one
could catch them.

Suddenly the Indians stiffened and looked
around expectantly. Bree had heard nothing, but
now another Indian emerged from the shadowy
woods. He was taller than the other braves, with
a regal bearing and like them wore only moccasins and leather leggings. His dark hair was held
away from his face with a twisted rawhide band.
His upper torso was bare and like his face was
covered with vermilion paint. He stood out in
brilliant relief against the black-green of the pine
forest. He looked like some tropical bird, yet
Bree sensed he was a far more deadly force.
Involuntarily she shrank back.

Even under the paint, she could see the noble
planes and angles of his face and sensed the
power in his lean body. It was obvious by the
way he carried himself and the deferential attitude of the other braves that he was their leader.

Instinctively Bree scrambled to her feet, keeping the three braves between herself and the new
arrival. Her knees were bent and quivering in
anticipation of flight. Her movements brought
the Indian leader's attention to her and now he
halted in his tracks and studied her. The black
eyes pinned her where she stood as they swept
over her tousled curls to the muddy slippers on
her feet, then back over her face to the long
golden strands that lay across her shoulders and
breasts.

During his perusal his face remained impassive and Bree felt a helpless kind of fear run
down her spine. The fact that she was a woman
would mean nothing to this man. They scalp
men and women alike, Bree thought, remembering the conversation she'd overheard in her fa-

ther's study. They even kill babies. There was no hope for her. She was doomed. Well, she wouldn't die like a coward, she thought, raising her chin. She clasped her trembling hands in front of her and all the emotions she felt—terror, fear, and a strange fatalism—were plain on her face.

The war chief's black gaze caught and held hers, giving her little cause to hope. What would they do with her, she wondered.

"Shocaw," a voice called. It was harsh and guttural. Another Indian stepped out of the forest, followed by other Seminole braves. Bree's discerning eye caught a movement in the green shadows and she guessed there were other Indians hidden among the trees. The new arrival was short and stocky, and he swaggered across the clearing as if he were in charge. Something about him sparked even greater fear in Bree. The cruel lines of his mouth were highlighted by the white and black paint he wore and the whites of his eyes were yellow and bloodshot.

The evil-looking man spoke again. Uneasily, Bree stood where she was. She couldn't know what he had said, but she guessed it had to do with her.

"Munks-chay," the vermilion-painted leader said abruptly, and the other warrior's face contorted in surprise and anger as he spoke again. The other braves moved so they stood side by side, acting as a shield in front of Bree, but their attention was riveted on the two men who argued. Tension was heavy in the air and Bree sensed that the hostility between the two was not new.

Even the young brave watching Windfire had dropped one of the reins as he listened. Now was her chance, Bree realized, if she were ever going to make a break. Fear lent her speed and strength, carrying her across the short space to Windfire.

Before the startled youth knew what she was
about, she had placed one satin slipper in the
stirrup and sought to pull herself into the saddle.

Startled by her sudden movement, Windfire
reared, her front hooves pawing the air, her wild
scream bringing the heads of the warriors around.
They shouted and ran toward the rearing mare.
Bree clung to the leaping horn with all her
strength, one leg flying out like a rag doll's. She
must not let go. As long as she clung to Windfire,
she had a chance, even if she had to let the mare
half drag her back to Greenwood.

"Home, Windfire," she screamed. "Go home,
girl." Her voice was lost in the whinny and pounding hooves of the horse and she had no air to call
out any more orders. Windfire came down with a
jarring slam that nearly tore her arm from its
socket. Still she clung to the horn, ignoring the
pain of her foot caught in the stirrup, desperate
to escape. Hands tore at her shoulder and she was
wrenched away from the mare and thrown to the
ground. Once again the youth grabbed the bridle
and held the mare captive, speaking to it in low
musical tones. Windfire quieted and stood snorting and blowing, the muscles in her legs twitch-
ing nervously.

Bree leaped to her feet, fighting against the
hands that held her. These hands were rough,
hurting her, ripping the delicate material of her
dress. Blindly she struck out at her attacker,
feeling her small fists connect with hard flesh.
There was only one attacker now, and her heart
fluttered frantically within her chest when she
realized it was the squat, evil-looking Indian. A
blow at her temple stunned her and she fell once
more to the ground.

She could smell the sweat on his body as he
stepped forward and straddled her, his hands
reaching out to grasp the long, blond strands of

her hair. Cruelly he pulled her head up and backward. Her eyes stared into his face. Viewed close up, he was even more frightening. Through half-closed lashes she could see him reaching for his knife.

He's going to scalp me, she thought in amazement, and wondered how she would look with her head all bald. Like old Millicent Southfield, no doubt. For an insane moment she felt like giggling. Instead she opened her mouth and screamed as loud and long as she could before she was forced to pull air back into her lungs.

As if from outside herself, she saw the warrior's large dirty hand descending toward her again, felt the explosion of pain inside her head, and fell sideways across his knee, too stunned to offer any further resistance. Once again the Indian reached for his knife, his lips drawing back from blackened teeth in a macabre grin of satisfaction. Any moment now she would feel the sharp edge of his knife at her hairline, and her lashes fluttered weakly down so she might not see it coming.

She sought to close her mind to the horror of what was happening to her. Neither Papa nor Jared could rescue her now. Tears squeezed from between her tightly closed lids and coursed down her cheeks.

"Munks-chay! Hal-wuk!" a voice said. Her eyes fluttered open and she glimpsed the vermilion-painted war chief. He stood nearby, angrily shaking his head from side to side, his dark eyes blazing in anger at the short Indian. Her captor tightened his grip on her hair and gestured angrily at Bree.

"Chi-yot-chee." Violently he shook the long curls, roughly pulling her hair and causing her to cry out. *"Sup-pa-lo es-chay!"* he proclaimed, slamming his closed fist against his chest.

"Munks-chay!" the Seminole leader repeated, and this time his voice was deadly and low. His fist hit against the hard wall of his chest.

"Shocaw's hoke-tee," he uttered in the same quiet voice that brooked no further opposition. His lips were a thin, angry line in his painted face and his eyes were dark and unwavering as they stared at the warrior crouched over Bree.

For a long moment the warrior kept his grip on Bree's hair, uncertain of whether to back down and possibly lose face in front of the watching braves or defy the young war chief. Finally, with a low grunt, he released his hold on Bree and rose. The two Indians stood facing one another, each measuring the strength of the other, trying to decide whether to continue the argument between them.

With a quivering, gasping intake of breath, Bree looked from one to the other, then scrambled to her feet. The squat warrior looked at her with fury before making a dismissive gesture with his hands. Turning his back on her, he stalked away.

Now Bree was left facing the Indian with the vermilion paint. His dark eyes were pitiless as they stared at her disheveled beauty. She was unaware of the appealing picture she made as she studied his face with tearful eyes, searching for some sign of mercy where she knew there was none. One hand went out in an unconscious gesture of entreaty as she silently pleaded for her life.

"Shocaw," one of the three braves called softly, and the tall Indian spun to look at him. Dimly Bree perceived that this was his name. It echoed in her mind for a moment as if she'd heard it before, but the past few minutes had been too filled with terror for her to concentrate.

The Seminoles stood absolutely still, their bodies stiff and tense, only their eyes moving as they listened. Bree listened too, but heard nothing.

"I-wox-chee!" the Indian named Shocaw said softly, and with a slashing gesture directed the warriors toward the trees. Bree's gaze darted from one figure to another as they melted soundlessly back into the shadows of the forest and disappeared. It was as if they'd never been. Only the leader stood before her now.

Suddenly her own ears picked up the sound of horse's hooves pounding on the forest path. Her face lit with hope. Someone was coming, riding fast and hard. There was more than one. Relief surged through her as she drew a deep breath and opened her mouth to scream. Her father was nearby. He had come to rescue her and he had brought help.

Her cry was cut off before it had begun. A large, strong hand closed over her half-opened mouth and nose and she felt herself being lifted effortlessly, pinned against the rock-hard wall of the Indian's chest. Silently he moved toward the concealing forest.

Windfire had been left behind and now the little mare pranced nervously, sensing the danger and tension. Uneasily she whinnied her concern.

Wildly Bree kicked out at the Indian holding her, her arms flailing helplessly. He simply adjusted his hold and now her arms were imprisoned behind her, pinned between her body and his. Her soft fingertips brushed against the smooth, warm skin of his sides before she clenched her hands tightly into fists.

With the clearing left behind them, the light dimmed, filtered by the thick leaves overhead. It cast an eerie green glow over the moving figures. The semitropical forest was hushed and still, its quietness broken only by the pounding of hooves as the riders entered the clearing the Indians had just left. Bree heard Windfire's welcoming cry and her father's frantic voice calling out her name.

"Bree! Bree!" Her name rang through the forest and echoed back from the dense wall of trees. A sob rose in Bree's chest and her nostrils flared as she sought to draw in air, straining to answer her father's call, but the hand clamped over her mouth allowed no sound to escape. Tears of frustration welled and rolled down her cheeks and over the brown fingers that held her silent.

Papa! Papa! she screamed silently in response to the cries that grew fainter by the moment. She could hear the crash of bodies through the tangled undergrowth and knew her father and his men were trying vainly to follow them. If Calusa, her father's Indian friend, were with them, they could track the Indians. They could still catch them. She might yet be rescued. She tried to keep a ray of hope alive.

The Seminoles moved swiftly through the green twilight, and the sounds of pursuit grew fainter. Finally she could hear nothing save the twitter of birds nestling in the trees. Her father had either given up and gone back to get more help, or his men had fallen too far behind to ever catch them. Hope died and she slumped against the Indian's body, not caring that their bare skin touched briefly with each step he took.

Tirelessly Shocaw pushed his warriors. The white man was too close to them now, having lost one of their women to the Indians, they would be relentless in their pursuit, tracking deep into the swamps before giving up. Still he couldn't have left her behind to give away their number and the path they had taken, nor did he want to kill her.

As he ran through the tangled underbrush,

Shocaw made little sound, his strong legs churning, his moccasined feet landing unerringly in the best place before springing ahead. The burden of the white woman against his side was nothing to him. From a boy of twelve he had learned to run long distances with a deer slung across his back. Even as a youth he'd excelled as a leader among his people.

The warriors moved through the flickering shadows of the forest, emerging on the other side where the pine-needle carpet gave way to the spongy mud of the swamp. They moved silently, pausing now and then to listen intently before moving forward again. And still Shocaw carried the white captive, his hand clamped over her mouth. He was taking no chance that her cry might yet carry through the forest and lead her rescuers to them.

Shocaw did not ask himself why he hadn't killed the white woman and left her behind. He never killed women or children. The thought was repugnant. Even those soldiers who had fallen before him and lay helpless and pleading were shown mercy. Perhaps they could use her as barter for the return of some of their Seminole chiefs. The glimmer of fading sunlight on golden strands of hair caught his eye and he glanced down at the girl.

She was given to tears more than the women of his people, but that was the way of the white women. Yet she had proven to be surprisingly courageous, fighting back when she'd thought it might bring her people to her rescue. She was very beautiful, even with the dirt smudging her tearstained face.

Shocaw remembered the anger he'd felt when he'd seen Lopochee about to take her scalp. For a moment there had been a murderous rage in his heart to think that something of such beauty

could be so mutilated. He looked down at the
silky strands spilling across his arm and chest and
thought of how close Lopochee had come to hanging it at his belt as a trophy.

Shocaw's lips tightened grimly. He was tired
of the bloodletting and the savagery. He wanted
peace for his people. He wanted time to enjoy
the beauty of his land and his people and, yes, of
the white man's women. He became aware of the
softness of her breasts against his skin as she
rested wearily against him. The ripped bodice of
her dress barely covered the smooth white mounds.
Shocaw felt a stirring in his loins and pushed it
away. She was only a woman and he must keep
his mind on the danger that still existed for
them. He was Seminole, he reminded himself,
and he no longer had desire for the white man's
woman. He walked on, wondering why the Great
Spirit had put such a woman in his path. Perhaps he was being tested.

They came to a murky, slime-covered stream
of water and turned to follow along its banks.
The tall Indian leader known as Shocaw had
allowed her to walk now. Obviously he thought
all danger of pursuit was past, although he still
followed closely behind. Bree kept alert to any
possibility of escape.

The terrain was different from any she'd seen
before. Vines and moss hung from knobby, strangely distorted tree trunks, and the earth and still
black waters smelled rank.

Now and then there was a low baying sound
not at all like the domesticated animals on the
plantation, and she felt a shiver of fear run up
her spine. Brilliantly plumed tropical birds, some
of which she recognized, flitted into view. Once
she glimpsed an ugly snake twining itself about a
tree branch to stare down on her with evil eyes.
A gasp escaped her lips and her body stiffened

in fear, but Shocaw seemed not to notice, urging her relentlessly onward. He moved easily, familiarly, through the swamp.

They came to a halt beside the sluggish, muddy stream, and roughly hewn dugouts were pulled from their hiding place behind the clumps of palmetto and sawgrass. The braves got into them and with long poles pushed themselves out into the middle of the stream. Picking her up, Shocaw placed Bree into one of the dugouts and prepared to push off.

"Wait," she cried piteously. She sensed that the canoes would carry them deeper into the swamp and all hope of escaping would be gone.

Shocaw waited, his hands braced on either side of the dugout, his dark eyes staring into hers. Bree nearly fell silent under his fierce gaze, but gathered her courage and appealed to him.

"Please, let me go," she begged. "Leave me here on shore where my father will find me. I won't tell him which way you've gone. Please!" The warrior remained silent, his black gaze moving over her face.

"You probably don't even understand me," Bree lamented. "You're just a savage. How can I make you understand? It will do you no good to kill me." Her voice broke and tears filled her eyes.

"We will not kill you." His voice was deep and strong. Startled, Bree met his gaze. In the half-light of the swamp forest she thought she saw shadows of compassion in his eyes, then he shifted and the look was gone.

"You understood, you speak English," Bree cried, and when he would have pushed away from shore, her plea unanswered, she cried out again and put a soft hand on one of the red-streaked, muscular arms that held the canoe steady.

"Leave me here," she urged. "There's no reason to take me with you. I can walk back to meet my father."

"It is too dangerous to leave you," he replied, sitting back on his haunches. "We have come many miles from your home and the swamp paths take many false turns."

"I'm not afraid. Let me try," she cried, leaping to her feet as if she would flee now. Shocaw's hands held the boat steady.

"It is too late," he said. "You are a prisoner of the Seminoles." Quickly he pushed against the dugout and it floated into the stream, Shocaw perched on its side. Then he clambered in and took up the pole, and with long, powerful strokes pushed the craft downstream in the direction the other warriors had taken. Bree had no choice but to sit down lest she fall overboard into the murky water.

Under Shocaw's mighty thrusts, the clumsy craft moved swiftly through the water with surprising grace. Shocaw towered above her, the muscles of his arms flexing with each stroke of the pole. Bree sat in abject misery and looked about her.

Except for Shocaw and the squat evil Indian who had tried to scalp her, she'd thought the others looked alike. Now she watched with curiosity the Indians in the dugout ahead. The youth who had held Windfire's reins leaned over the edge of the canoe and scooped up water to wash away the paint on his face and body. Startled, Bree saw that he was white. His skin was deeply tanned from his days in the hot Florida sun, but it was obvious he had no Indian blood. His dark hair and eyes suggested he might be of Spanish or French origin. He was a good-looking young man only a few years older than she. How had he come to be with the Seminoles, she wondered.

The youth felt her gaze and turned to look back at her, smiling openly, his dark eyes lighting with natural good humor. Bree turned away. Beyond the youth, Bree sensed the evil Indian's eyes on her and, encountering his gaze, gasped with sudden fear at the murderous rage she found there. Quickly she averted her eyes and studied the shoreline.

There was no comparison between the well-tended fields and gardens of Greenwood and the jumble of vines and moss-covered trees that spilled over the shoreline and threatened to clog the already narrow stream. Little wonder the Indians had taken to the waterways. It would be nearly impossible for any man to penetrate the thick growth. At some point, in the dreary, late afternoon, Bree lay down in the canoe and slept. The bumping of the canoe against the bank brought her awake, frightened and disoriented.

She could sense the movement of the other Indians as they climbed out of the dugouts and pulled them onto shore.

"Come," Shocaw said, holding out a hand to her. There was a strangely gentle note to his voice. Grasping his strong hand, she stepped from the canoe and looked around the dark clearing. Shafts of moonlight penetrated the thick, moss-draped branches, giving a little light as the Indians moved about setting up camp.

"Cooee," Shocaw called, and the sound was soft and musical upon his lips. In answer the young brave who had held Windfire came forward. In a rapid fire of words that were strangely pleasant to the ear, Shocaw spoke to the youth.

"Ho!" the young brave said, and turned to Bree. The tall Indian leader melted away into the darkness.

"Do not be afraid, we wish you to come and

rest," Cooee said, smiling at her shyly. He was only a shadow against the moonlit water, but she sensed his gentleness and her fears were mollified somewhat.

"You speak English," she cried, glad she wasn't dependent on Shocaw. He was too diffident. Cooee, she sensed, would speak to her freely.

"I learn good English from slaves in our village," the youth said proudly. Did they have other white people who were slaves, Bree wondered.

"Can you help me?" Bree asked desperately. "Please." Her voice broke on the last word.

"There is nothing I can do. You must obey Shocaw. We all must obey him. He is our war chief."

"But what is he going to do with me?" Bree cried. "Is he going to kill me?"

"He saved you from Lopochee, who wished to scalp you," Cooee said, surprised that she had not understood what had transpired back in the clearing. "Many times Lopochee challenge Shocaw and each time Shocaw claim you for his. Shocaw has that right since he is the war chief."

"Why won't he let me go?" Bree pleaded.

"That cannot be done," the young brave answered, "but perhaps he will trade you back to the white man."

"When?" Bree demanded, hope springing up again. She might be ransomed for some of their leaders or for money. "When?"

"I do not know," Cooee answered. "Perhaps soon. It is up to the council and to Shocaw." He turned away and Bree knew he would say no more about the subject.

"I will bring you food," he said instead. "Shocaw is preparing a place for you to sleep. When we travel, we do not make a fire," he explained in his low musical voice as he settled her on a nearby log and handed her some pieces of food. Bree looked at them. She'd never seen food like this before.

"Eat!" Cooee urged. "It is dried meat and coontie bread prepared by the women of Chillocotee."

"Chillo—" Bree began hesitantly.

"Chillocotee," Cooee repeated. "You may call it Horse Creek Village. It is the village of our tribe. That is where we go now."

"Is it very far?" Bree asked.

Cooee smiled. "It is deep in the swamp. That is why the soldiers have not found us yet." His words made Bree's spirit sink even more. Cooee watched her face, and she sensed he sympathized with her.

"Eat," he advised her. "You will feel better then. It will make you stronger, and when you are stronger, you don't feel afraid." Valiantly, Bree took a small bite. It did not taste bad. There was a nutlike flavor to the bread, although the meat was tough and stringy.

"The coontie flour comes from a root that grows here in the swamp. Without it, our people would have starved many years ago," Cooee explained. He passed her a gourd of warm, brackish-tasting water and gratefully she drank.

"You know my name," Cooee said, "but I do not know yours."

"I am Brittany Marie Rikkar," she said, and remembered how Lieutenant Whitlock had pronounced her name in full only that afternoon. Somehow, it seemed years away from her now.

"Brit-ey?" Cooee said hesitantly.

"Just call me Bree," she said, and tried to swallow back the desire to put her head on her knee and bawl.

"Like the evening breeze?" Cooee asked, and his smile made her feel a little better.

"No, just Bree," she repeated the name for him.

"Bree." The low musical voice came from behind her and she swung around to see Shocaw smiling down at them. From the pale light of the moon she could see he had washed the paint from his body and she was surprised at how pleasing his features were. An aquiline nose and high cheekbones proclaimed his Indian heritage and lent a haughty sensitivity to his face. The powerful shoulders and chest were ridged with hard muscles and she remembered how tirelessly he'd carried her. His black eyes were in shadows, but she could see the flash of white teeth against the dark bronze of his skin.

"Bree," he repeated softly, and put out a hand to touch one of the pale curls that lay upon her shoulder. With a barely perceptible gasp she drew back, but the strand of hair still clung to his finger as if with a will of its own.

Shocaw stood as if entranced by it, then he glanced at her face and saw the fear in her eyes. Reluctantly, he let go of the curl, watching as it pulled away from his finger in fine silken threads of spun gold.

"Come," he said, turning away and walking swiftly across the clearing. Bree got to her feet and hurried to catch up with him. Cooee followed behind.

Shocaw led her to a small lean-to of sticks covered with palmetto leaves which had been set up on a slight swell of ground. Inside the lean-to a bed of leaves and dried Spanish moss had been placed. A similar cover sat beside the first one and it was obvious to her anxious eyes that only one person could sleep in each shelter. Other such structures were scattered about the small clearing and some of the braves had already crawled inside to sleep.

"Rest now," he said gently. "Tomorrow we will rise early." Bree crawled inside and settled herself. It was surprisingly comfortable. The wide thick palm leaves kept off the cold dampness of the night and the thick pad of Spanish moss cushioned her tired muscles.

For a moment Shocaw hovered outside the lean-to, then one hand reached forward to grasp hers. Startled, Bree cried out and jerked backward, but he held it fast. A leather cord was slipped over her hands and tightened about her wrists, binding them together. Briefly the rope bit into her flesh, causing her to cry out again, then strong, nimble fingers loosened the rope a little. His hands were warm against the sensitive skin of her wrists. Her pulse leaped beneath his fingertips and for a moment he glanced at her. Her lashes were lowered against the curve of her soft cheek. Her full lower lip pouted a little. She did not like the rope, he guessed, but he had little choice.

Taking the other end of the rope back to his own shelter, Shocaw tied it to the main pole of his lean-to. If she tried to escape during the night, he would know it. He crawled inside the shelter and prepared himself for sleep that long eluded him.

In her own makeshift tent, Bree had stopped struggling against the confines of her rope and lay thinking of her captivity. If only she had gained better footing and swung herself into the saddle, she and Windfire could have escaped, she mourned. The moment was behind her, she must not dwell on it anymore. Still, she wondered what Papa and Mama were doing. Were they searching for her even now? Somehow she knew they were. Her father would not rest until she was safely back at Greenwood.

By the time the sun was casting its orange red
light over the trees and black waters, the line of
dugouts was already moving down the stream.
They paused at midday for dried venison and a
few sips of the warm water from the gourd.

Sometime in the afternoon, she heard the trill
of a bird much like that she'd heard in the clearing when she'd been captured. She was startled
to see the Indian's response. They ducked low in
the canoe and froze. Without the constant pressure applied by the poles, the canoes drifted to a
standstill.

Along the banks, a few feet deep in the dense
jungle growth, men and horses moved, making
an inordinate amount of noise, it seemed to Bree.
Slowly the realization came to her that these
might be soldiers and she had only to scream to
draw their attention to the Indians and herself.
Before she could even draw a breath, Shocaw
was beside her. His hand clamped firmly over
her mouth and nose, allowing her little room to
breathe.

She grew faint from lack of air and lay swooning, pinned against the hard cypress sides of the
canoe and the equally hard body of Shocaw as he
lay across her. One breast was crushed by his
rocklike chest and she raised mute eyes to his.
His eyes were hard and alert as he listened intently for the soldiers to pass by.

It seemed to Bree that they lay like that for
hours. Her muscles screamed in protest against
the cramped position. When she tried to shift
her weight, Shocaw's glance flew to meet hers in
a silent warning and she lay still. At last the
pressure of his hand against her mouth loosened,
and she was able to draw in more air.

His head dipped to hers and he placed his
mouth against her ear. His hot breath fanned

across her cheek, disturbing the tendrils of hair. His other hand came up to her throat, and in it he held a knife. Placing the point against the soft skin, he made a soft hissing sound in her ear and loosened his hand a bit more.

The message was all too clear. If she made a sound, he would kill her. Bree drew in air. Shocaw applied a slight pressure on the knife and the point threatened to break the skin. Eyes filled with fear swung to the implacable face of the Indian as mutely she telegraphed her acquiescence. She would not cry out.

The soldiers moved away through the swamp and still the Indians waited, silent and alert. At last Shocaw removed his knife from her throat and Bree was able to sit up.

Involuntarily, her hand went to the spot where his knife had pressed. A tiny drop of blood stained her fingertips when she brought it away. Shocaw's eyes still stared into hers, reinforcing his threat, then lithely he rose to his feet and began to pole the canoe down the stream.

They seemed to move in a dream. The Indians made no sound or movement except the men who pushed against the long poles. Silently the canoes glided along the narrow stream, barely disturbing its quiet surface.

For a moment she considered calling out, despite her captor's threat. One look at his stony face and she knew he would keep his word. The cry would hardly have left her throat before she felt the plunge of his knife. It would do her little good to be rescued if she were dead when the soldiers finally got to her.

Tears of hopelessness filled her eyes and rolled unheeded down her cheeks. She would never see her mother or father again, never talk to Jared or be teased by him, never even have the chance to talk to poor old Millicent Southfield. She would never dance again with the young men who had flocked around her at parties, returning their innocent flirtations with carefree abandon. She would never be married or have children or be the mistress of a great plantation like Greenwood someday.

All those years at school, years she might have spent at Greenwood, were wasted. Her life was ended before she'd had a chance to do anything with it. What good did French and Italian do her now? What did it matter if she could sew a straight, dainty stitch or read Latin or pour tea with graceful precision or converse as a genteel lady should. There was no one for her to converse with except a youth who'd accepted his lot with the Seminoles and a half-breed who threatened to kill her.

Hysteria bubbled up, causing sobs to build deep within her and force their way from her throat. She was unaware of the sounds she'd made as she gave way to her misery until Shocaw knelt beside her, his knife brought within inches of her throat. Once again his dark eyes bored into hers, repeating his terrible unspoken message. Mindless of the smudges she left as she wiped at her wet cheeks, she swallowed back the sobs that shook her body. Her hand clamped over her mouth in an attempt to silence the straggling cries. Shocaw's dark gaze held hers, hypnotic, demanding, as he went back to poling the dugout. Mutely Bree stared back at him, as anguished, silent tears rolled down her cheeks.

It seemed hours before they stopped. Bree's tears had long before dried, although her throat felt tight and raw at the sobs she'd swallowed.

Shocaw poled the dugout to the bank and, leaping out, pulled Bree out. As she stepped onto the muddy bank, her foot slipped and she half slid into the murky water, the remnants of her skirt turning a muddy brown. Remembering some of the slimy life forms she'd seen slithering about in the dirty waters, Bree screamed, clutching frantically at Shocaw's hand. Instantly she was out of the water and against his hard chest as his free hand went to her mouth.

So they were still not safe.

How far away were the soldiers, she wondered, peering into the dark jungle of trees. Docilely she waited until the Indians hid the canoes, all the while darting her eyes about the clearing, looking for a means of escape. Ironically, it was Lopochee, the squat Indian who appeared to hate her the most, who provided her opportunity. As they turned to follow the other braves down the path, Lopochee fell back from the others and spoke to Shocaw, his voice once again challenging. His words were angry and venemous sounding.

Shocaw shook his head and answered Lopochee furiously. As he turned away, Lopochee leaped forward, a knife clutched in his hand, his evil, yellow eyes gleaming with rage. Shocaw moved aside and drew his own knife, half crouching as his feet automatically sought more advantageous footing. The two adversaries circled, their eyes intent as they looked for an opening.

Bree's heart hammered wildly in her chest. Now was her chance to escape. Hesitantly she looked about her. The other warriors had gone ahead on the path and were out of sight. Only the three of them remained and both men were too intent upon each other to notice her. Quickly Bree crept backward toward the path that led away from the other braves.

Drawing a trembling breath, she cast one last look at the two Indians. Lopochee had leaped toward Shocaw. Bree saw the flash of his blade and the bright spurt of blood. She must flee now

If Lopochee killed Shocaw, she would have no one to protect her. Whirling, she ran through the forest, terror lending speed to her feet. She paid no heed to the rough, jutting coral that ripped through the soles of her shoes and cut her feet. She must get away. She must. The words beat like a wild refrain in her terrified mind. Bree ran full out, the skirt of her tattered gown clutched high above her knees, leaping mud puddles and ravines. Vines and branches snatched at her, impeding her progress, ripping at her clothes and hair, and still she plunged on blindly until she was forced to halt and draw a breath, a hand gripping her aching side.

Was there someone back there pursuing her, she wondered, and held her breath so she could listen better. Was it Shocaw or Lopochee coming after her? In terror she ran, fell, got up, and ran again until she could run no more. She stumbled from one supporting tree trunk to another as she tried to draw air into her aching chest.

Suddenly a hard, dirty hand bit into her shoulder while another closed over her mouth, cutting short her startled cry.

"Well, Jed, lookee here what we found," a nasal voice said, and in surprise Bree jerked her head around to look at her captor. It was a white man. She was saved!

"She shore is a pretty thang," said another voice, and Bree's wildly darting eyes picked out his companion in the green gloom. Both men wore wide-brimmed hats, spotted dark with sweat and dirt. Their shirts and britches were in little better repair, and both men wore beards. One man's beard was scraggly and long and incredibly filthy, while the younger man's was short and stubby and thin in places. Both men eyed her greedily. When she was sure it wasn't a Seminole who held her, Bree ceased her struggling and now the man removed his hand from her mouth.

"Where'd you come from, girl," he asked in a fast, hard voice. Bree swallowed and raised grateful eyes to his.

"Thank God, I found you," she cried. "The Seminoles captured me, but I got away. I'm afraid they're still out there."

"Seminoles." Instantly both men dropped to their knees in the brush, their rifles at the ready. Bree crouched down beside them.

"How far back did you leave them?" Jed demanded.

"I—I don't know." Bree put a trembling hand to her forehead as she tried to think. "Maybe a mile back. We were by a stream."

"How many were they?" the foul-smelling man who'd grabbed her asked.

"Nearly twenty, I think," Bree answered. "They went ahead on the path and the last two were fighting, so I ran."

"Right smart of you," Jed said, eyeing her. "Don't too many git away from them Seminoles, on'st they git caught."

"Reckon we best not use rifles, Caleb," Jed ordered, putting his down and drawing a wicked-looking, long-bladed knife.

"What do you mean?" Bree asked. "Surely you aren't going to try to kill them. We passed some soldiers earlier this afternoon. Let's try to get to them."

"We don't need no soldiers for this, little leddy. In fact, we don't want 'em. They'd jest claim the reward. Caleb, I'll work my way down to the left there and you take the right."

"Shouldn't we get away while we can," she tried again.

"First, we goin' t'git us some Indian scalps. They still worth a couple hunnerd apiece," Caleb said. His eyes rolled back to look at Bree. "Then we'll have us some fun," he offered. One dirty hand came out to touch the bare skin above her breast. With a cry, Bree drew back. "Yessir, I ain't had me a woman in a while. Mighty nice you jest came along out here when I was gittin' to needin' one real bad." Panic welled in Bree.

"First things first, Caleb," Jed admonished. "Let's go git us some Indians."

"Should be easy this time," Caleb said. "We got us some bait."

"Yeah," Jed said, eyeing Bree. "That's kind of the way I figured it." In terror Bree looked from one man to the other. She'd thought herself free of the nightmare, but she was in a worse one.

"You," Caleb said to her. "Get on back out there on that path and jest walk back the way you come, real nice and easy."

"No," Bree cried, springing to her feet. "I won't. I'm getting away while I can. You're worse than the Indians."

"You're gonna do's you're told," Caleb said, grabbing her arm and slinging her around and back toward the path she'd run down before. "Get goin', gel, or I'll slit you out quicker'n a possum going up a tree." He brandished his knife at her.

Shocked, Bree looked from one man to the other, unable to comprehend that they were not going to save her. She was in worse danger than before.

"Get going," Jed shouted at her. Frightened by the wild look in his eyes, she turned and stumbled back the way she'd come. All around her the swamp seemed to lie silent and deadly. No birdsong filled the air, no small animal scurried through the underbrush. A breathless hush had settled over the swamp, while its creatures waited for death to strike and pass on its way. Gasping back a sob, Bree walked slowly, her eyes darting from side to side on the path. Suddenly to her right, there was a rustle in the brush, then a half-strangled cry and once again the eerie stillness.

"Jed?" Caleb called out softly. "That you, Jed? D'you get one?" An ominous silence answered.

"Answer me, Jed, dad burn it, don't play possum with me. Aaigh!" His scream was high-pitched and plaintive and ended abruptly. Chills started up Bree's spine and she hugged her arms about her chest trying to fight down the panic. Light had faded now and the shadows lay all around her, black and menacing. A flock of birds started from a bush and flew away into the evening sky as Bree began to run. Unable to see the path in the enveloping darkness, she ran wildly, blindly, ignoring the pain of branches whipping at her face and body, the hysteria bubbling up within her until it escaped in shrill shrieks of terror.

She was stopped by a wall, a human wall that was hard and immovable. Arms wrapped around her, pinning her down. Her terrified screams echoed in the moist night air and the Indian made no move to check them, letting her give voice to her fright until she fell against his chest weak and trembling, too breathless to cry out anymore, too tired and defeated to offer resistance. One strong hand held the back of her head in a grip that was oddly comforting and reassuring while his other hand half patted, half stroked her back. Bree lay quivering and silent against Shocaw's broad chest, thankful it was he who had found her.

"Come," he said at last. "You are safe with me." Strangely she believed him and followed docilely as he led her back down the path his braves had taken.

After some time, she was aware that Lopochee joined them, was aware too of the two grisly new trophies that hung at his belt. Her numbed mind closed away the horror of it. Mutely she followed after Shocaw, keeping in view his broad back lest he disappear and leave her alone again in the swamp. When her feet were too sore to walk farther, Shocaw tended them and gave her moccasins to wear. And thus it was that the three of them arrived at the village of Chillocotee on Horse Creek, one of the last strongholds of the Seminole nation.

Chapter 3

The villagers gathered around the returning warriors, their faces smiling in welcome. Their voices were low and musical as they greeted each one. As it became apparent that some of the warriors would not be returning, sounds of weeping could be heard.

Bree followed Shocaw as he led his band of warriors to the center of the square and came to a halt before a raised platform with a thatched roof. As she stepped into the firelight, some of the villagers made hissing sounds while others reached out to touch her bright hair. Frightened by their touches, tentative and gentle though they were, Bree pulled the tattered remnants of her filthy gown about her and stared back at the strange dark faces.

She was struck first of all by the black eyes, lively and curious, then her attention moved to their colorful dress. Unlike the Indians in the northern part of the country, the Seminoles did not dress in buckskins. The weather was far too hot and muggy in Florida for leather to be comfortable. Only the men wore leggings of rawhide, much as Shocaw and his men wore. In addition they wore long cotton shirts of one piece which

fell nearly to their knees and were belted about
their waists with intricately beaded sashes.
Around their necks they wore bandannas and
large flat gorgets of hammered silver and coins.
Some of the Seminole men wore twisted bandannas tied about their foreheads as Shocaw's
men did and some of them wore brightly colored
turbans decorated with plush plumes.

The women were no less colorful, dressed in
skirts that reached to the ground, nearly hiding
their bare feet. Intricate designs pieced from cloth
bordered the hems of the skirts. Their blouses
were capelike affairs and each woman sported
many strands of beads about her neck.

In contrast to the men, who were nearly all tall
and well built like Shocaw, the women were
shorter and of a small frame with many of them
on the plump side.

Hesitantly Bree smiled at the women, but their
dark eyes were unresponsive; some even displayed
hostility. One young Indian girl about her age
shyly returned her smile. Strangely Bree did
not feel fearful of the villagers and reassured
herself she would be safe. Young children ran
freely in and out among the tolerant adults. It
was obvious by the indulgent smiles that children were loved and appreciated. The villagers
reminded her of her father's slaves back at Greenwood and the thought gave her comfort.

The people milled about the warriors, touching them and laughing quietly, exchanging com-
ments with each other, and Bree thought of the
way her own people greeted new arrivals. Some
of the men approached the warriors and shook
hands with them, only their hands gripped each
other's elbows, a far warmer greeting, Bree
thought.

Suddenly the people grew silent and moved

back, making room for a very old man. Once he
too had been tall like his young warriors, but
now his body was gnarled and bent with the
weight of his years. He walked slowly and with
difficulty. Obviously the people accorded him
much respect, several addressing him as Micco
Onnitchee.

Two men walked beside him, one a man of
some years who bore himself with great dignity
and pride. The other was the medicine man. The
markings of his dress and headpiece as well as
the pouches at his waist gave evidence of his
position. They helped the elderly chief mount
the platform and take a seat, then seated themselves on the floor beside him. With a wave of a
snowy white feather mounted on a stick, the
elderly chief indicated the warriors were to speak.
Shocaw stepped forward and the people pressed
closer.

He spoke well. She didn't understand his
words, but she understood the expressions on
the people's faces as they listened to him with
rapt attention. At first the villagers smiled,
then frowned as Shocaw spoke. They clicked
their tongues in displeasure and one woman
wailed loudly. Others tore at their clothes and
hair.

Bree was startled by the noise and realized
that the village was by contrast very quiet. Even
the children did not raise their voices as they
played nearby. They glanced over at their parents
now and then, their large eyes curious and
intelligent.

For the first time, Bree looked about the village. She'd been too anxious to look before. Houses
on stilts, the phrase jumped into her mind. She
remembered her father describing the Seminole
houses to her as a child, and he had instructed

Razzy, the slave carpenter, to make one for her for a Chirstmas present. It was stored in some forgotten corner in the attic now.

The houses were built about three feet off the ground with thatched roofs of palmetto leaves and sawgrass. Huge cypress trunks formed the corner posts of the houses and the stilts upon which they rested. There were no walls to the homes so the cooling breezes could blow through. The houses were chickees, she recalled. She loved the sound of the name and had wondered as a child what it would be like to live in one. It seemed she was about to find out.

Behind the chickees Bree caught a glimpse of small gardens with corn and neatly staked rows of beans and pumpkin vines growing up nearby tree trunks. The small pumpkins hung from the vines like green apples. Before each chickee was a small fire pit, although a larger fire pit dominated one end of the square. Eight uncut logs radiating from the center provided light, warmth, and a cooking area. Pots of food sat bubbling over the coals or were kept warm between the huge trunks, while children perched on the other end. The women had left their cooking pots when the warriors arrived and were now listening intently to the speakers.

Shocaw had spoken calmly and with the authority that accompanied his position as war chief, but now Lopochee stepped forward. His words were guttural and excited. Sometimes he shouted and pointed an accusing finger at Bree. In sudden fear she cringed from him.

The women turned fierce, hostile faces to glare at her and the men looked at her with the same flat, inscrutable eyes Shocaw and his men had. Lopochee's voice rose in fury as he talked, stirring up the feeling of the people, and even the children halted in their play and drew near again. The squat Indian ended his passionate tale with a mighty thump of a closed fist against his chest and stood back, his arms folded once more over his chest, a smile of satisfaction on his face.

Now Shocaw moved forward to speak again and his voice was again dispassionate and calm. He too gestured toward Bree as he talked, but she didn't feel frightened of his intentions. When he finished, he also clamped a closed fist against his chest and stepped backward. The people looked at one another with consternation. Then the chief, who had sat listening to it all with great attention, got slowly and painfully to his feet, assisted by his advisers. The murmurs of the people fell silent as he prepared to speak, their faces filled with respect for his age and wisdom.

Raising both hands, he made a gesture over the crowd with the white feather, then he spoke, his voice high and reedy in his tired old body. The villagers listened quietly, some of them shaking their heads in agreement as he spoke. When he had finished, he made another sign with the white plume and turned back to his advisers. Immediately they rose and led him from the platform.

Apprehensively Bree looked toward Shocaw. His face was closed and unreadable. The villagers had begun to move away from the square and go back to their tasks. Something drew her glance to Lopochee and she gasped as she noted the flash of triumph in his malevolent eyes. Foreboding washed over her.

"Toschee," the menacing warrior called to one of the women who had glared at her with such hostility earlier. Immediately the short plump woman left her friends and hurried toward her husband. The two Indians approached her, their eyes gleaming cruelly, and fear fluttered in Bree's heart. She began to inch backward, looking about wildly for a way to escape.

Obviously she'd been given to Lopochee and she had little doubt about her fate. He had expressed his hatred for her many times during their journey to the village. Frantically, Bree's eyes darted about the square, looking for a place to run. Finding none, she glanced with frightened eyes back at Shocaw who had already turned and was moving away. He had been her protector once; would he be again?

"Shocaw," she screamed out, and at the sound of his name, he spun around, his dark gaze meeting hers over the distance. There was surprise on his face at her use of his name and a flash of something else—pity, she thought—then his dark eyes became as unreadable as ever.

"Shocaw, please help me," she cried as Lopochee and his wife took hold of her arms and began to pull her away. For a moment it looked as if Shocaw were about to speak again, but he turned and walked away. Lopochee and Toschee yanked her along, their grip painful.

"Shocaw!" Bree's frantic cry rang out in the square and the villagers gathered around to watch. Bree drew breath into her lungs to cry out again, while she twisted about in her captors' grasp, then she felt Lopochee's fist slam against her face and her knees gave beneath her.

Unceremoniously they dragged her across the square and dumped her on the ground at the foot of a ladder leading into a chickee. Lopochee began to speak to her in a rapid flow of words. Bewildered, Bree got to her feet and stood looking at him blankly. The Indian waited for her response, and when she did nothing, his nostrils flared in anger. Raising a fist, he brought it down on the side of her face again. The blow was so fierce she was knocked to the ground and lay there stunned. Lopochee looked at her with a pleased expression on his evil face. Giving rapid-fire instructions to his wife, he strutted away. He would leave the disobedient prisoner to the attentions of his wife and the other women. He would attend the black drink ceremony in triumph tonight, which would be all the sweeter for his victory over his enemy, Shocaw.

Bree gratefully watched the warrior leaving and raised her eyes mutely to his wife. Perhaps, being a woman herself, she would show more mercy. The thought quickly died as she looked into the woman's cold, hostile face. Although Lopochee's wife had been obsequious and meek before him, her lips curled now in cruel anticipation as she looked at the helpless girl before her.

Bree raised herself into a half-sitting position and looked around in despair. Was there no help for her, she wondered dazedly. The women of the village had followed them and now made a circle around her, hemming her into a small space before the chickee.

"*Ot-som-ka-taw,*" the woman called Toschee ordered, using the same imperious tones her husband had. "*Ot-som-ka-taw!*" Slowly Bree got to her feet and stood staring into the open chickee.

"*Lopko!*" the woman demanded, and pushed Bree. What was expected of her now, Bree wondered and stayed where she was.

"Ah!" the woman said in disgust and uttered a string of words, then turned to the other women and spoke. At once the women began to advance on Bree and from their pouches they took out dried animal claws and bone needles. Fearfully Bree backed away from them until her back was against the raised floor of the chickee.

Whimpers welled in her throat as her eyes swung wildly around the circle of advancing women. She was trapped! Then she felt the sharp edge of the raised platform and realized there was an open space beneath it. Quickly she ducked under the floor of the chickee, going down on her hands and knees to crawl to the other side. If she could just get there, she could run into the forest and perhaps escape them, she thought. But even now she could hear the excited yells of the women and see the hems of their colorful skirts as they raced around the chickee to head her off.

She was trapped beneath the chickee and huddled miserably, trying to decide what to do next. Suddenly from behind, her foot was seized, throwing her face forward into the dirt, and she was dragged kicking and struggling back into the open. Now the women fell upon her, using their claws and needles to scratch long furrows into her cheeks, arms and legs. In the melee there was much kicking and punching, so Bree was forced to roll herself into a ball, her arms cradling her head in an attempt to escape their punishment. At last the assault ended and the women stepped back. Once again Toschee stood before her.

"*Ot-som-ka-taw,*" she ordered imperiously. Bree raised a tearstained, blood-smeared face and looked about the circle of women. At one side she saw the young girl who had smiled at her. There was sympathy on her face and Bree was sure she hadn't participated in the attack upon her.

"*Ot-som-ka-taw!*" Toschee repeated, and knelt to hold an animal claw menacingly close to Bree's face. Bree shrank away.

"Go, chickee," the young girl said softly, and Bree's tearful gaze flew to her face. She fought to bring her sobs under control as she looked around at her attackers. What did they have in store for her now, she wondered fearfully. To her surprise she saw that most of them had left and were walking back to the fire pit in the center of the square. Now that the newcomer had been properly chastised, they must see to preparing the evening meal. Bree's gaze moved back to the young girl.

"Do you speak English?" she asked, but the girl only looked at her in puzzlement. Bree's hopes sank. "Get Cooee, please," she cried, hoping the girl would understand at least that much.

"Cooee?" The girl repeated the name softly and might have said more but Toschee turned on her, spitting out a string of words. The girl listened wide eyed, then bowed her head in acquiescence and turned away.

"Don't go," Bree cried, getting to her feet, but the girl was already disappearing across the square. Perhaps she was going to get Cooee. Bree prayed she would.

Toschee spoke again, her voice harsh and threatening as she shoved Bree toward the ladder to the chickee. Obediently Bree stumbled up the steps and waited docilely as Toschee took down a piece of rope and tied it about Bree's neck. The other end was secured above Bree's head well out of her reach.

Toschee motioned again and Bree hurried to sit down in the corner as indicated, although she felt the rope tighten about her neck. It was not long enough to allow her to move about freely or even to lie down. Gratefully, Bree leaned back against the thick trunk, trying to calm her pounding heart.

A movement at the steps brought her gaze around. Lopochee had once again entered the chickee. With an evil grin he approached the

captive girl. One large, dirty hand yanked her to
her feet by her hair. With a cry, Bree struggled
to stand.

Looking at her ravaged face, Lopochee began to
laugh. His tones were full of mockery as he spoke
to his wife and she began to laugh. Lopochee
released his captive's hair and spoke curtly to
his wife. Carefully Toschee listened, her shoulders curved inward in an obsequious manner,
and when he was finished, she bobbed her head
and hurried away.

Bree squeezed back against the log pillar. She
was alone with this maniacal man. Lopochee
turned back to her, standing so close she could
smell the stench of his body. Slowly, his eyes
watching hers for any flicker of fear, he withdrew his knife from its sheath. His hand grasped
her hair once again, forcing her head backward
as he raised the knife before her face.

Bree struggled to hide her fear, knowing how
much pleasure Lopochee gained from it. She
would not scream or cry out, she resolved. She
would not give him the satisfaction, but now the
blade crept closer to her hairline and pressed
against the skin and terror crawled along her
spine. Her scream was high and long in the night
air.

In his chickee across the square, Shocaw heard
it and clenched his fist. It was best if he did not
interfere, he told himself. Lopochee was trying
to goad him into a fight. Now was not the time.
They must save their energies to fight the white
man. He must believe the old chief's warnings
were holding Lopochee's cruelty in check. Still
his hand trembled near his knife and he longed
to dash across the square and rescue the white
girl.

He'd seen what the women of his village had

done and was not surprised. They often had scratching rites, which were thought to drive the evil spirits from the body. The girl would be frightened and have some discomfort, but her life was not in danger from the women.

How fiercely she'd fought against the women, giving them chase under the chickee. She was wily and brave. Shocaw's eyes darkened. With Lopochee such bravery could bring about her death. Do not fight so, my little *chofee,* he thought and was surprised at the endearment that sprang to his mind. Angry with himself and his thoughts, he flung himself from the chickee and walked toward the fire pit. The girl's scream had died away but he heard her sobs, low and filled with terror. She was alive, her fears would pass, and Lopochee would pay for this moment of pleasure, Shocaw vowed.

Lopochee's wild laughter filled the chickee. Blood from the small cut he'd made on Bree's forehead dribbled into her eyes.

"Lopochee!" Toschee had returned. She stood at the top of the ladder, two shell bowls filled with food in her hands, her eyes dark and apprehensive as she spoke urgently to her husband. Angrily Lopochee answered and, with a last look at Bree's terror-filled face, replaced the knife at his waist. With a dismissive grunt he turned his back on his helpless prisoner and settled himself on the mat that Toschee had spread.

The two Indians sat cross-legged, and deferentially Toschee served her husband then began to eat herself. They ate noisily, grunting as they chewed, and Lopochee spoke to his wife about the prisoner, laughing as he imitated her scream. Toschee laughed obligingly, although there was a note of unease about her as she glanced at Bree.

None of the food was offered to Bree, but she

hadn't the stomach for it. Her whole body trembled with fear and shock. She huddled against the post trying to remain calm and not think of her fate at the hands of Lopochee and his wife. She hardly felt the sting of insects on her tender, exposed flesh or the scrape of rope about her neck.

When the two Indians had finished eating, Lopochee rose and left the chickee, casting a last derisive look over his shoulders at the prisoner. On stocky legs he stalked across the square and disappeared into the forest, where even now sounds of revelry could be heard. Toschee scraped the remains of the two bowls together and brought it to Bree, setting it on the floor beside the prisoner before she too left the chickee and headed toward the fire pit. There would be many new things to discuss tonight and she would have a prominent part in the discussions about the prisoner.

Bree looked at the remains of the food congealing in the bottom of the shell bowl and knew she would never be able to eat it, no matter how hungry she might become. She pushed it away with her foot and leaned back against the cypress pillar, too miserable even to cry.

"Bree," a voice called softly from the darkness behind the chickee, and she turned her head to peer into the shadows.

"Cooee," she cried.

"I am here," he said softly, and stepped from the darkness.

Happily she greeted him. Standing on the ground as he was, the level of his eyes fell a few inches below her.

"Shocaw sent food for you," Cooee said, and passed over a shell bowl much like the one Lopochee's wife had left. This one was full of a thick stew. Large chunks of meat and vegetables made up the savory-smelling dish. Still Bree was too excited to eat.

"What has happened?" she cried. "Why am I with Lopochee? I'm afraid he is going to kill me."

"He will not kill you," Cooee said with such certainty that Bree sat silently and stared at him. "Lopochee claims you for his slave and Shocaw claims you for his. Now it is for the council to decide."

"But I am not a slave," Bree said indignantly.

"You have been captured by Shocaw and his men. Lopochee claims he saw you first, therefore you are his." Bree shuddered. "Shocaw and the warriors must travel to Fort Brooke and will be gone for several days. You are to stay with Lopochee—"

"No," Bree cried.

"Lopochee's wife." Cooee finished. "Toschee will guard you so you don't escape. She'll see that no one harms you."

"But she and the other women attacked me," Bree cried, rubbing at the scratches on her hand and arms.

"They do not mean you harm," Cooee said, and Bree bit back her retort of disbelief. "It is the custom of my people to scratch one so the evil spirits can be let out."

Bree looked at him in dismay, thinking of what he said. It might well be an Indian custom but she'd found it frightening and disgusting. Some of the women had done their job with far too much zeal. Her ribs ached from their kicks.

"I will try to bring something for your injuries," Cooee said. "Now you must eat." He pushed the bowl toward her and Bree picked it up. She took a bite, at first to please him since he had come to comfort her and then out of hunger as she tasted the rich stew. She'd had nothing hot in her stomach since the Indians had taken her.

When she'd emptied the bowl, Cooee pushed a palm leaf toward her. On it were pieces of delicately flavored fish and a meat she couldn't identify but which tasted like chicken. She grew full but still she ate until she'd devoured everything on the palm leaf. Licking her fingers, she sat back and smiled her gratitude at Cooee.

He gathered up the bowl and palm leaf and at the sound of voices ducked down. At first Bree was surprised at his action, then surmised he didn't want Lopochee to know he had come to help.

"Shocaw say the council will meet in a few days. Be brave, little *chofee*," Cooee whispered, and was gone, melting away into the dark shadows of the night.

Toschee and another Indian woman mounted the ladder to the chickee and Bree leaned back against the trunk, feigning sleep. Toschee approached and, taking up the shell bowl of food she'd left for the girl, turned to her companion, gesturing and talking in a shrill, outraged voice. Food was not to be easily refused among the Seminoles. Toschee cast a disapproving glance at the white captive and set the bowl aside. She would eat it herself, if she became hungry.

The other Indian woman left and Toschee took down the rolled bed mats stored beneath the thatched roof. She also took down blankets and soft deer hides and made a pallet for her husband and herself. Lopochee would not return until late into the night, but his bed must be ready for him.

With a grunt, Toschee settled herself in the warm, comfortable-looking bed, while Bree hud-

dled miserably where she was, perceiving that
no such bedding would be given to her, nor would
the rope be lengthened so she could lie down.
She shivered in the chill dampness that had settled over the land once the warmth of the sun
was gone. It would be a long uncomfortable night,
Bree thought, and wrapped her arms about her
knees, which she'd drawn close to her chest in
an attempt to preserve body heat. Longingly she
thought of the shelter Shocaw had built for her
the night before, with the soft moss beneath her
and the wide palm leaves above to shield her
from the dew.

Restlessly she dozed, awakened now and then
by the unfamiliar night sounds. She heard the
sounds of war cries from the men's secret meeting place. It rose high and bloodcurdling on the
air. There was a baying sound like she'd heard
the night before and which Cooee had said was
the baying of an alligator. A rabbit screamed. His
cry, high and pitiful, was drowned by the sudden shrill cry of birds; then all was silent. Once
more the swamp slept.

Bree fought against the desire to cry out herself in loneliness and despair as she gazed with
wide, fearful eyes into the dark shadows of the
jungle night. Later she was awakened by the
stumbling steps of Lopochee as he returned to
the chickee and then by the rustle of bedclothes
and the animal-like grunts of the two people as
they coupled and fell apart. Lopochee, she surmised, was as callous toward his own wife as he
had been toward everyone else. She clamped her
hands over her ears so she wouldn't hear the
sounds of their coupling.

She awoke the next morning with the rope
cutting into her throat as she slumped down in
sleep. Hastily she straightened and pulled at the

cord to ease its gagging pressure. Lopochee, she
saw, had already left the chickee, and Toschee
was tying their bedding back in its place under
the roof. With a quick hostile glance at Bree, she
left the chickee and walked toward the fire pit,
where other women had gathered to cook their
meals in the large pots. Bree looked about, hoping to catch a glimpse of Shocaw or Cooee, but
there were no men in the village. They must
have already left for Fort Brooks.

Why hadn't she asked Cooee to persuade Shocaw
to return her to her people. The fort was only a
few miles from Greenwood.

Her despair turned to hope as another thought
came to her. Perhaps Shocaw had gone to barter
with the white soldiers for her return. The
thought gave her strength to sit up and push her
untidy hair back from her face.

Toschee returned to the chickee with a bowl of
food, and Bree decided she would even eat it this
morning, for she must keep up her strength. She
might be going home very soon. But Toschee did
not offer her the bowl of food. Instead she sat
cross-legged on the floor of the chickee and ate it
herself. Once again when she was finished, she
brought the leftovers to Bree.

"Hum-pux-chay-hum-pee-taw!" The woman
sneered and set the cold leftover food down beside Bree. When Bree only sat and looked at the
bowl, Toschee shouted at her and made a fierce
gesture, and quickly Bree picked up the bowl,
holding it in her hand until Toschee had left the
chickee. Sickened, she looked down at the food.
So great was her dislike for Toschee and Lopochee
that the thought of eating after either of them
was repugnant. She'd seen how they reached into
the bowl with their unclean hands. Hastily she
set the bowl back on the floor. After the food

Cooee had brought her the night before, she really wasn't so hungry after all.

The women gathered in the square of the village, hoes and makeshift shovels clasped in their hands. Together they left the village, disappearing through the trees as silently and effortlessly as the warriors had done. Bree sat where she was, looking at the spot where they had disappeared. There was no sign of a trail. Finally she sat back and looked around the square.

Only the children had been left in the village, and a young girl of ten or twelve had been assigned the task of watching them. She bustled about, a fat brown baby perched on one slender hip.

The sun rose in the sky, drying away the moistness of the early dew and no one came near Bree. She became thirsty and licked at her swollen lips, tasting the dried blood left by the women's attack upon her the night before. No one came at midday as Bree had hoped. She could hear the quiet sounds of the children playing at the other end of the square. She tried to call to them, to ask for water, but her voice was a hoarse croak in her throat. No one heard and no one came.

She dozed, sitting with her head back against the pillar to relieve the pressure of the rope, jerked awake, and dozed again. The afternoon passed in torturous slowness. She awoke hot and sweaty, with the drone of flies in her ears. Sitting up, she brushed through the air about her head trying to send them away. Persistently they stayed, intent on settling on the scratches on her face and arms.

Her thirst was unbearable and she looked around with little hope of getting anyone's attention. The sun had dipped downward in the sky and the shadows were lengthening when she finally

caught a glimpse of someone. Bree scrambled to
her feet and peered at the approaching figure. It
was the young Indian girl who'd smiled and spoken to her the night before when the women
attacked her.

Across her shoulders was balanced a long pole
and suspended from either end were several large
gourds. They were obviously freshly filled with
water, for now and then some spilled out, the
drops silvery in the bright sunlight.

"Hello," Bree called; her voice came out in a
croak and she feared the girl had not heard her,
but she halted in her footsteps and turned her
face toward the chickee where Bree sat. "Please,"
Bree called again, "some water. Wa-ter." Her
voice cracked in her effort to be heard and
understood.

Slowly the Indian girl approached the chickee;
her bare feet silently kicked up little puffs of
sand as she walked. Pausing near the chickee,
she looked at Bree with friendly eyes.

"Nock-a-tee?" she asked, her voice lilting upward.

"Please, may I have some water?" Bree asked,
and when the girl continued to stand there smiling
blankly, she repeated her request, gesturing toward
the water gourds.

"Water, Wa-ter!" she said slowly and distinctly.

"We-wa?" the Indian girl asked, looking at her
with puzzled eyes. Then her dark gaze glanced
at the gourds she carried and back at Bree with
bright understanding. *"We-wa,"* she said, and
mounted the ladder.

Comprehension dawned on Bree and gratefully
she shook her head, reaching out eagerly for the
gourd the girl offered. *"We-wa,"* she said, and
drank deeply, not minding the spill of water
down her chin and bodice. She had never tasted

anything so wonderful in her life. She lowered
the gourd for a quick breath, then raised it to her
lips again. Patiently the girl waited until Bree's
thirst was slaked.

"Thank you," Bree whispered, handing the
gourd back to the girl. How she longed to keep
one of the gourds at her side for when she was
next thirsty, but she sensed that would not be
allowed. Even now the girl was casting a quick
look over her shoulder as she reattached the
gourd to the pole and rose and left the chickee.
She cast one last bright glance over her shoulder,
and it comforted Bree.

The girl was barely away from the chickee
when Toschee and the other women returned
to the village, appearing suddenly out of the forest. Had the young Indian girl been able to hear
their approach? Bree wondered. She herself had
heard nothing.

No one came near Bree that evening. Toschee
stayed at the fire pit with the other women until
darkness fell. When she returned to the chickee,
she brought no food or water for Bree. Silently
she unrolled her sleeping mat and settled herself
beneath the warm furs. Silent and miserable, Bree
huddled against the post for a second night.

"Toschee, *we-wa*," Bree said urgently the next
morning when the Indian woman prepared to leave
the chickee. She couldn't go a second day without water to drink, Bree thought. Toschee cast her
a triumphantly evil smile and left without saying
a single word to her. Helplessly Bree watched as
the women left the village. She must have water.
She could do without food, but already her tongue
felt swollen and dried in her mouth.

"We-wa," she called after the women, but no
one turned to look at her. Not even the young
Indian girl who had befriended her the night
before came to help her.

The day dragged as the one before had. The sun was relentless as it pounded down on the thatched roof of the chickee. Heat waves shimmered up from the hot sands of the village square. There was no sound of children at play. They had been taken into the cool, shaded woods near where their mothers were working.

Bree kept in the shade provided by the roof as much as the short rope allowed her to, but the chickee became a hot box and there was no way to escape the heat. Her head grew heavy, too heavy to hold up, and she lolled against the post, gasping for breath. Her eyes felt hot and scratchy and she kept them closed to ease the burning irritation. She dozed, escaping her misery in dreams of Greenwood and the cool comfort she'd taken for granted there.

Clouds moved across the face of the sun, blotting its relentless light. The air grew sullen and muggy. Insects seemed to become even more persistent as they droned about her face, but Bree slept on. Only the distant rumble of thunder aroused her, and she opened her eyes to see that the women and children had returned early to the village.

"*We-wa!*" Bree called, but no one paid any attention to her. They were too busy putting things away against the coming storm.

The first raindrops fell hesitantly, as if uncertain of their reception by the dry earth, then seeming to gain more confidence, they fell in uniform thickness like a gray curtain over the village. The women gathered under the protective roof of the fire pit and began preparations for the evening meal. Gleefully their children ran in and about, challenging the falling rain in some game of their own.

At first Bree lay as she had all day, listening to

the soothing sounds of the rainfall and the subdued laughter of the children. Slowly the sound
invaded her dulled senses, and with a jerk she
sat up.

There was water, water she could drink and
splash on herself. In her eagerness, she forgot
about the short binding rope about her neck and
tried to jump to the ground. For one terrifying
moment she hung by her neck, gagging and gasping for breath as her feet frantically sought the
edge of the platform again. With her feet once
more beneath her, she stood clinging to the post,
drawing in air. She could have hanged herself!

Frustration permeated her very soul. There
was water, water she so badly needed, and she
couldn't get to it. The overhanging thatched roof,
designed to protect the chickee's inhabitants from
the weather, kept the rain from her. Clinging to
the cypress post, Bree leaned out as far as she
dared, holding out a cupped hand to catch what
water she could. She could feel the rain pelt
against her palm, cold and wet. Eagerly she lapped
at the water and caught more to splash over her
face and neck. She couldn't seem to get enough
and held out her hand again and again to catch
the precious drops.

So preoccupied was she with her task, she
didn't notice the tall warrior who had stepped
out of the trees and stood staring at her. Bree
stood sipping the water from her dirty hand,
tipping her head back so it ran cool and silvery
down her parched throat.

A shout from one of the children as he ran to
greet the returning men made her turn her head
and catch sight of Shocaw. He was back, she
thought joyfully, a smile lighting her grimy face,
then she caught sight of Shocaw's face and shrank
back against the pole, her eyes wide and uncertain. Was she doing something she shouldn't have,

she wondered. Why was there such disapproval on his face? Perhaps he would come and speak to her, but Shocaw merely gathered up the carcass of a deer and turned toward the fire pit.

Bree stood where she was, disappointment washing over her, and unaccountably she thought of how she must look. Her hair was matted, her dress filthy and torn. Her face and hands were covered with dried blood and festering bites and scratches. She'd never before felt ugly, but now she did and the thought distressed her.

Chapter 4

That evening Lopochee returned to the chickee briefly, and once again Bree's life seemed to be filled with terror. At his belt hung fresh scalps, and she turned away in sickened horror when she saw them. Lopochee threw back his head and laughed maniacally. Its sound swept through her, chilling her to the very marrow of her bone. She sat trembling long after he'd left the chickee and strode away to the men's secret gathering place in the swamp.

When darkness fell and Toschee was occupied at the fire pit with the other women, Cooee came slipping out of the dark shadows at the back of the chickee. Once more he brought food and a gourd of water. Eagerly Bree drank the water and wolfed down the food, barely taking time to breathe between bites. She didn't stop until her empty stomach protested and she lost all the food she'd gulped down so greedily.

"You must eat more slowly and a little bit at a time, until your stomach is used to food once again," Cooee told her, and weakly Bree shook her head in agreement.

"Drink some more water," Cooee urged, and held the gourd to her lips. When she'd finished drinking, he gathered up the shell bowl and gourd and prepared to leave.

"Can't you leave some water with me?" Bree asked.

"If Lopochee discovered I'd helped you, he would take it out on you," Cooee said. "Besides, it is only until tomorrow. The council will meet and you will be given to Shocaw."

"Shocaw," Bree gasped. "Why don't they just return me to my people?"

"Perhaps they will," Cooee said, and smiled encouragingly. Voices approached and quickly he ducked down. "I will see you in the morning," he whispered, and was gone into the shadows.

No one else came to the chickee. Toschee and the other women were busy working over the deer and game the men had brought. The meat would not keep in the heat, so they must begin at once to preserve what they could and cook up that which they could not preserve. In the firelight Bree could see the women at work, their talk cheerful. There was food for their pots. No one would go hungry for a while.

Watching them, Bree felt a great loneliness invade her soul. She longed to be home among her own people. Clemmy, the cook, would be bustling in the kitchen cooking up some of her favorite foods, and Mama would be overseeing the setting of the table, making sure everything was perfect for Papa and them when he came in from his ride about the plantation.

Perhaps there would be an extra guest or two. There often were and Jared and she would sit listening to the talk about Tampa or some of the other plantations. The lamps would soon be lit and the slaves would have cooking fires lit in front of their cabins as they prepared their own evening meals.

A peacefulness not unlike that of the village

would have settled over the great plantation, which housed more people within its many buildings than this poor village did. Bree felt a sadness wash over her and bit her lips to hold back the tears.

Once again the warriors were not in evidence in the village that evening, and Bree could hear their long, drawn-out war wails from deep in the swamp. The children, tired now from their day of playing and the excitement of the return of the warriors, finished their evening meal and unprotestingly went off to bed. The fire burned down and still the women worked on until at last their fatigue drove them back to their chickees. The rest of the meat could wait for morning before it was finished.

Toschee returned to the chickee and, as before, silently took down her bed mat and rolled herself into the warm furs, ignoring her prisoner.

Bree sat huddled against the trunk, seeking warmth where there was none. Her stomach, having rejected the food earlier, now rumbled emptily. She sat listening to the hoot of the owls and the other strange sounds of the swamp. They were becoming familiar to her now. Finally she lay her head back against the post and dozed. Somewhere in the distance she heard a man's voice raised in a war cry.

"*Yo-he-lo!*" it echoed on the night air, fierce and defiant. A shiver pushed up Bree's spine.

Once again she awakened stiff, cold, and sore from her cramped position during the night. How she yearned for her soft featherbed at Greenwood. She ran her tongue around her cracked lips and thought of the water Cooee had brought her the night before. How long would it be until she was given water again, she wondered.

Looking about, her gaze fell on the droplets of dew and rain that still clung to the leaves at the edge of the roof. Reaching out a hand, she coaxed the droplets onto her finger and quickly brought it to her mouth, sucking greedily at the pitiful amount of moisture. Eagerly she looked up but there were no more droplets. She sat nursing her disappointment, wondering what was to become of her.

Some movement made her raise her tearful gaze to the edge of the square. Once again Shocaw stood there, his dark gaze fastened on her, his expression disapproving and angry as it swept over her. Bree sat staring back at him.

Well he might disapprove of the way she looked, she thought rebelliously. She was all too aware of her filthy appearance. He had not been starved and made to go without adequate water these past days. In fact, he had even been able to bathe this morning. She could tell, for his hair was wet and his skin still glistened with droplets of water upon its smooth brown surface. For a moment Bree had a vision of putting her lips to the cool moist skin and licking away the beads of water. Aghast at her thoughts, she drew back against the corner post, her head spinning dizzily.

It was her intense need for water that prompted such thoughts, she told herself. Still her eyes strayed to the Indian brave as he turned away and strode with long, purposeful steps toward the other end of the square.

Depressed more than she'd ever thought possible, Bree lowered herself to the floor of the chickee, crouching against the huge trunk. It seemed to have become her haven during the past few days. She lay her swimming head back against it, wondering how long it would take a person to starve to death or whether she'd die of thirst.

She'd heard her father's cronies say that was the thing that got you first. She believed it. She

closed her eyes against the brightness of the sunshine and listened to the droning insects. She no
longer bothered to swat them away when they
landed on her. She ignored their sting. She hardly
felt them anymore.

Shocaw was angry. It showed in the way he
held his shoulders and his long-legged steps. The
villagers recognized his anger and turned away,
grateful when he stalked on by. His anger was
not aimed at them.

Shocaw had observed the way Lopochee and
his wife had treated the captive and now this
morning the sight of her striving to catch the
pitiful drops of water tore at his heart. The
white men called them savages and it was little
wonder when every encounter brought about this
kind of treatment. It was true that the white
man was every bit as savage as the Seminole, but
somehow someone would have to begin to understand and show mercy.

He intended to ask the council for the captive.
She could be very valuable to them if they wished
to barter with the white man, but she would be
of no value if she were dead. Shocaw had sat on
the council himself for many years and he knew
that as the old chief grew feeble and weak, the
others looked to him for leadership and wisdom.
He would make them see the wisdom of keeping
the hostage alive and of giving her to him for
safekeeping. Shocaw felt confidence and strength
flow through him. He would convince the council to accept his decision. He had to. He didn't
want to see the girl put to death.

He entered his chickee and took down his special clothes, which he wore when he participated
in council business. First he donned a brightly
colored shirt like the other men wore caught at
the waist by a colorful beaded sash. He tied

bright bandannas about his neck. An amulet of beaten silver was placed about his neck so it hung low over his chest. Lastly, Shocaw put on a turban, which the Seminole men wore when not in battle. At last he was satisfied with his appearance and climbed down the ladder of his chickee and made his way across the square toward the council platform.

Even among a race of tall, well-built men, Shocaw stood out. His broad shoulders and well-shaped head were carried proudly and his walk was graceful, soft as the tread of a panther through the swampy jungle, yet surefooted and deliberate. Shocaw carried himself with an air of authority that encouraged his people to turn to him. One day he would be a great chief to his people, just as he was now a great war chief.

The other men on the platform greeted Shocaw, and as he looked about the gathering he knew the men would listen to him about the prisoner and heed his advice, all save one. Lopochee's black eyes were full of hatred as they met his.

Bree must have dozed, for when a noise awakened her, she was surprised to see that many of the villagers were standing before Lopochee's chickee and Lopochee himself was climbing the ladder, his face a study in fury. He moved toward Bree and untied the thong that had kept her pegged to the cypress trunk. Jerking angrily at the rope, he indicated she was to get up and follow him. Again he jerked cruelly and the rope bit into her neck.

What was going to happen, Bree wondered, getting to her feet as he had bidden. Was this it, then? Was she about to be killed? A moment of fear made her pull back, then she remembered what it had been like for the last few days sitting here and slowly starving to death. A fast death would be preferable. Her glance went to the fresh scalps at his belt. Soon hers would be added there, she thought fatalistically, and cringed for a moment before straightening her shoulders and raising her chin. Stepping forward toward the ladder, her eyes were fearless as they met the avid gaze of the other villagers. She would be brave, she vowed, and began to climb down the ladder, but Lopochee was bent on denying her any dignity. He gave a vicious jerk on the rope and she was pulled down, gagging and clawing at the cutting thong at her throat as she landed on the ground at his feet.

"Lopochee," a voice called out, and Bree looked up to see Shocaw standing above her. His fists were clenched as he faced Lopochee. His voice carried a warning that could not be denied, and with an angry grimace Lopochee let go of the rope. With the tautness gone, Bree was able to loosen its choking tightness. Drawing in deep breathfuls of air, she glanced up gratefully at Shocaw, who still stood facing the older Indian. With a barely perceptible gesture of his hand, he motioned to Cooee, who sprang forward and helped her to her feet.

"The council has met this morning and you are to be Shocaw's slave," Cooee said, and smiled at her happily. Bree turned to look at the two warriors, who still glared at each other. The stiff stance of Lopochee declared his unhappiness with the decision, and suddenly Bree perceived just how fortunate she was to be out from under his protection. Between his barbarous savagery and Toschee's cruel neglect she would surely have died. She looked back at Shocaw and some instinct told her she was safe with him. He would not kill her. Yet again he had saved her life.

"Come, we will go to Shocaw's chickee." Cooee removed the noose from around her neck and let

it fall on the ground beside her. For a moment
Bree hesitated, uncertain if she could walk across
the square, but Shocaw turned a dark commanding gaze upon her.

"*Aw-lock-chay,*" he said, and turned away.

"Come," Cooee translated, motioning to her,
and with one last look at the faces around her,
she followed after them, forcing her stiff, sore
legs to move one step after the other. As she
shuffled across the bright square of sand to the
chickee that belonged to Shocaw she was aware
of the other Seminoles trailing along behind them.
A glance over her shoulder confirmed her suspicions. Their faces were bright with curiosity.

Under this escort they arrived at a chickee
where the tall Indian paused at the ladder leading up and turned to Bree.

"*Pish-wa-chi-us-chee!*" he commanded, folding
his arms across his chest and looking out over
the heads of the onlookers. Bree cast a quick
glance at Cooee.

"He said he wants meat," Cooee said. "You
must go to the fire and bring him back food to
eat. You must answer him like so. '*Ho,* Shocaw.' "
Cooee bent his head slightly toward the warrior
and turned back to Bree. "You must do it now, to
show you are a good, obedient slave, otherwise
Shocaw will have to beat you to show the village
he has made a good slave of you."

"But I'm not a slave," Bree said indignantly.
She looked at Shocaw in outrage. She would not
be a slave to this savage. He was little better
than Lopochee and his wife. Her father owned
more slaves than the number of people in this
village and she would not humble herself so this
man could save face before his people.

"*Lop-ko!*" Shocaw said imperiously, and pointed
toward the fire pit.

"He said to make haste," Cooee said. "It would be wise to—"

"Munks-chay!" Bree interrupted, her temper exploding from her in that one word. A silence fell upon the onlookers and the gaze Shocaw turned upon her was terrible in its intimidation. She had, she realized, gone too far. It had been foolhardy for her to act thus. Being Shocaw's slave was infinitely better than being Lopochee's, but she couldn't recall her hasty words.

Shocaw's face was closed and angry as he stepped forward and seized her arm. In a deliberate display of physical superiority, he pulled her arm forward, his dark eyes boring into hers unrelentingly. Turning her hand over, her reached for his knife while the villagers looked on impassively.

"No! *Munks-chay!*" Bree cried out, trying to draw back her arm, but Shocaw held it fast. With a quick downward motion of his arm, his knife sliced across the fleshy underside of her forearm well above the wrist.

So quickly and neatly was it done that she hardly felt the sharp blade. Only the blood welling from her arm assured her of what had happened. She cast a quick glance at the Seminole's face and once again found it expressionless, his eyes black and flat as they stared into hers.

Again she tried to wrench her arm out of his grasp, but he held it fast, watching as the blood gathered on her arm and began to drip onto the sand at their feet.

In disbelief Bree watched the droplets fall, then turned her horrified gaze back to Shocaw. She had thought she would be safer with him than with Lopochee. How foolish she'd been. He was just as savage as the other Indian. Suddenly, Shocaw let go of her hand, almost flinging it from him as he stepped backward away from her.

"Pish-wa-chi-us-chee," he ordered once again, raising a muscular arm and pointing to the fire pit. For a moment Bree stood, not sure of what to do. Her gaze moved from Shocaw's stern face to Cooee's silently pleading one.

She had no other choice, she realized. She looked again at the cut on her arm. The bleeding had already slowed. It had not been a deep cut after all. A shifting of feet among the Indians who watched made her aware of Shocaw's position in this. His cut had been shallow; her punishment could have been worse, and in all likelihood would be if she continued to resist him. The hot sun beat down on her head, reminding her of her thirst, and she licked her dried, cracked lips. She had no choice, she reminded herself again, and with a quick movement bobbed her head in acquiescence.

"Ho, Shocaw," she said, and sensed his expulsion of breath. Cooee smiled, delighted at her, and behind them, the villagers murmured softly among themselves. Somehow she sensed they were glad she had given in. She was probably too valuable a slave to be multilated, she thought cynically, and caught a glimspe of Lopochee and Toschee's faces. They were not glad to see her behaving so compliantly. Averting her gaze, she made her way toward the fire pit.

The men gathered about Shocaw, clapping him on the back for his actions with his slave, and the women meandered in curiosity toward the fire pit. Bree paused and looked about. Should she just help herself to the food in the pots or should she ask permission? A short Indian woman came forward and, handing Bree a palm leaf, began to heap it with food. There was a large hunk of venison and a fat rear leg from a rabbit. A coontie flour cake was added and a bowl of corn mush.

"Th-thank you," Bree said, but the woman made no answer and her eyes remained hooded. Holding the palm leaf carefully so no food would fall from it, Bree walked slowly back to Shocaw's chickee.

As she came to a halt before the warrior, her eyes lowered meekly, he uttered some words and made a dismissive gesture to the men who still clustered about him. One by one they began to move away back to their own chickees. Only when the last man had left did Shocaw turn his eyes back to his new slave. He made no move to take the food from her.

"You have done well," he said, smiling down at her. The harshness was gone from his features and his eyes were warm and friendly. "Welcome to my chickee," he said, gesturing toward the ladder. Slowly she turned toward the ladder and placed one foot on the bottom rung.

"Cooee," Shocaw said softly, and the youth sprang forward and took the food from her. Bree offered him a smile of gratitude and hastily climbed the ladder. Cooee scrambled up behind her, expertly balancing the palm leaf.

"Shocaw say you take this and eat," Cooee replied, and Bree stared at him in astonishment. The food had not been for Shocaw after all. Then why had he ordered it and why had he cut her arm when she'd refused? Her good hand went to cover the slash. It no longer bled. Still, anger surged through her and she glared down at the warrior who stood watching her. His dark eyes held her gaze for a moment, then moved over her face and down her raggedly clad figure. He spoke a few rapid words to Cooee, then spun on his heels and walked away. Bree resisted the urge to call him back.

"Come and eat now," Cooee said, leading her to the back of the chickee where a thick mat had been placed. "I will explain everything to you." He handed Bree the food and waited until she had begun to eat before he spoke.

"It is very good that you obeyed Shocaw. Lopochee and Toschee say you are not a good slave and should be put to death. Shocaw say he can make you a good slave. So he show everyone you are a good, obedient slave. You may live and be his slave."

"But I have no wish to be anyone's slave," Bree cried, then turned silent while she thought of everything Cooee had said. How very near she'd come to death without knowing it, she thought. Suddenly the tensions she lived with for so many days seemed overwhelming and she set aside the bowl and gave herself up to weeping. Wisely Cooee let her cry.

Her sobs were hoarse and guttural, coming from deep inside, and the tears flowed freely over her dirty, scratched cheeks. Not having seen women cry as this one did, except when some member of their family was killed, Cooee didn't know what to make of her sobs. Silently he waited. Finally the wild sobbing stilled and she drew in hiccuping breaths of air. She wiped away the tears, unaware of the ugly smear they made through the dirt and blood on her face, aware only of the sting of salt penetrating her open scratches. She sat up and turned on apologetic smile on Cooee, who was enchanted by her clear gray eyes, still shiny with moisture. None of the Indian women had eyes such as these, he thought, not even Milakee.

"Do you wish to eat first?" he asked, greatly distracted. "Then I will tend your wounds. In his eyes were such dancing lights of friendship that Bree suddenly felt lighthearted. She was not entirely friendless, she told herself, and picked up the bowl and began to eat. Suddenly she was ravenous.

"Cooee," she said, taking great care to eat slowly. She remembered the night before too well. "You are not Seminole. Why do you live with them? Why don't you run away, go back to your own people?"

"The Seminole are my people," he said. "I was captured as a baby and I know no other people."

"Don't you want to know who your real people are?" Perhaps she could persuade him to return to the white world and take her with him.

"I am with my real people," he replied patiently.

"But—"

"Bree, don't talk anymore," he said, and she realized she had offended him.

"I'm sorry," she said softly, and was rewarded with a quick, forgiving smile. He turned back to his task of mixing some white powder with a dirtlike mixture. Silently she ate, refraining from asking him any more questions. She would learn what he was about soon enough, she guessed. At last she pushed aside her empty bowl.

Cooee stirred the contents of the shell bowl and turned to her. Taking some upon his finger, he smeared it on her face. At first Bree jerked backward but the mud pack felt soothing to her skin and she leaned forward again, sitting silent while Cooee covered her face and arms with the mixture. When all her exposed skin had been covered, he sat back and looked at her with a grunt of satisfaction.

She could well imagine how she looked, she thought, holding her mud-encrusted arms out in front of her. Her wide gray eyes looked even larger and lighter, giving her an owlish look, and an impish grin appeared on Cooee's face. Bree glared at him, her brows drawing together, and the effect was even more comical under the heavy layer of mud. Cooee tried to curb his laughter, and although he managed to hold his lips straight, his dark eyes twinkled merrily.

Suddenly the humor of it hit Bree and a chuckle escaped her lips. Cooee looked at her in surprise, then his own laughter burst forth. The sound seemed to feed Bree's need to laugh and she opened her lips and gave way to the merriment she felt. It wasn't so bad, she thought to herself. She was still alive, her stomach was full, and her wounds had been attended to even if in such a ridiculous manner. There was someone to whom she could talk and she had been rescued from an Indian who had meant to do her great harm. Hope rose within her again. As long as she remained alive, she could hope that she would be rescued. Her relief was great and her laughter bubbled forth light and musical.

Cooee was the first to notice Shocaw, and his laughter slowed and stopped. He sprang to his feet and stood before the warrior. Bree fell silent and stared up at him, aware once again of how very tall and broad-shouldered he was.

Shocaw watched her for a moment, his gaze roaming over the mud-smeared face and arms, the tangled mass of hair, its golden glory tarnished by dirt and mud. She looked a sad, bedraggled creature in her dirty, tattered dress, and he thought of her arrogant beauty as she had ridden through the forest on her beautiful horse. It was good to see her thus, he thought. Her beauty had haunted his sleep too much during the past few nights. This would make him remember she was just a woman and not deserving of a warrior's thoughts.

Bright lights danced in the dark depths of his eyes and Bree realized he was amused by her. She didn't want him to find her an object of mirth. She was sorry he had seen her this way.

"Lie back and try to rest now," Shocaw said

gently. "You are safe." Bree sensed he spoke the truth. Obediently she lay back and looked at the figure towering above her. His dark gaze raked over her body.

She lay still, barely breathing, and watched the changing lights in his eyes. There was little left to her delicate gown. The material had been torn away, leaving one long slim leg exposed. Only thin shreds of gauze held the gown over one shoulder while the skimpy front drooped over her young breasts, giving a glimpse now and then of the soft curves beneath.

Self-consciously she pulled the tattered wisps about her legs and bodice, and as if he understood her embarrassment, Shocaw turned away and left the chickee. Bree lay for a long time, thinking of the warrior and the way he affected her, trying to still the thump of her heart and the rapid intaking of breath. He was a savage, for all his handsomeness, she reminded herself.

True, he was a virile and imposing figure here in the rough village where his people looked up to him, but how would he seem in her mother's drawing room? She had a feeling he would be just as impressive there, and thought of Denise Payne flirting shamelessly with the handsome half-breed.

The heat of the afternoon settled around her, and with thoughts of Shocaw flitting about in her mind, she dozed off into the first real sleep she'd had in days. For once she was free of the stinging insects. They seemed not to like the mud pack any better than she did.

When she awoke, it was late afternoon and the sun was already nearing the tops of the tall palms. The women had returned from their day in the fields and were at the fire pit preparing the evening meal. Bree sat up and watched them as they worked.

Some were busy pounding corn in the end of a hollowed-out stump. They worked rhythmically, talking and laughing softly as they went about their labors. Other women were busy cleaning fish or skinning a rabbit, while others cut up vegetables into an iron kettle. The men were not about.

Feeling well rested for the first time in days, Bree scrambled up and tidied the chickee as she had seen Toschee do, tying the bed mat back in place and sweeping away the leaves and dirt that had settled in the corners. When all was tidied, she sat down with folded hands to wait for the return of Cooee or Shocaw. A soft sound made her look toward the ladder of the chickee.

"Shocaw's *hoke-tee*," the voice called gently, and she saw the young Indian girl who had brought her water poke her head over the edge of the platform.

"Aw-lock-chay," she said in her gentle voice. Her eyes were bright and friendly as she motioned to Bree.

Bree remembered those words had been said to her before and with the same motion. She understood now that they meant she was to come or follow. Casting one last look about for Cooee, Bree scrambled to the ladder and climbed down.

"Milakee," the girl said, pointing to herself and Bree understood she was introducing herself.

"Ho, Milakee!" she acknowledged. Then patting her own chest, she gave her name.

"Bree," Milakee said, drawing out the syllables so the name sounded musical, like a soft wind through the trees. *"Aw-lock-chay,"* the girl said again, and turned away from the village.

Bree hurried to follow her. Where was she taking her? she wondered. They moved down a path barely discernible to the eyes, but which the girl seemed to know well.

They soon left the sounds of the village behind. Once the trees and vines had closed in around them, it was as if the village did not exist. Bree heard no sound of children playing or of the women softly talking and laughing.

No wonder the soldiers had so much trouble finding the villages, Bree thought. She took care to stay close to Milakee. She had no wish to become lost in the vast greenness of the swamp.

Very soon they came to a small clearing and Bree could see a pool, shiny and still in the late sun. Several Seminole maidens were swimming in the clear water while others stood on shore, rewinding their long, black hair into knots on top of their heads. As Bree and Milakee approached the pond, one maiden raised her head and, looking at Bree, began to laugh loudly and mockingly. Other girls looked at Bree and joined in the laughter.

"*Hoke-tee-li-tee.*" The girl sneered. She arranged her features in a grotesque grimace, and shuffled about as Bree had done that morning when she'd first tried to walk on her sore legs. Milakee walked past the girl without a flicker of acknowledgment on her immobile face and Bree contrived to do the same.

Miffed at being ignored, the mocking girl moved in front of Bree, wagging her head and sneering. Her hands flashed out and she would have raked her nails down Bree's cheeks if Milakee had not cried out.

"*Munks-chay,*" she commanded, and the Indian woman's nails halted just inches from Bree's face. "Shocaw's *hoke-tee,*" Milakee said, and there was a deliberate note of satisfaction in her voice. At her words the Indian woman's eyes widened in anger and her lips thinned.

"She not Shocaw's woman," she said, glaring at Bree. "She too ugly."

Bree gasped with surprise. "You speak English," she cried, her face lighting up.

"I speak white man's tongue," the woman said haughtily.

"I'm so glad," Bree cried. Someone else with whom she could communicate. "We can talk, you can tell me things," she began eagerly, but the other woman's face was rigid with dislike.

"I not talk you," she said. "I not talk white-man words.'

"You're speaking it now. Why can't you continue? I need—"

"Munks-chay, hoke-tee-li-tee," she said. "You are old woman, ugly to look at. Shocaw not want you, he want me." She patted her chest with an open hand while she glared into Bree's eyes, then she took a handful of Bree's curls, their gold reflecting the setting sun, and spat into it. Bree recoiled in disgust.

"Hal-wuk," Milakee said, pushing the older Indian girl away. With a final sneering glance at Bree, the woman picked up her bundle of clothes and moved toward the path they had taken earlier. Why had she been so hostile? Bree wondered, looking after the Seminole woman. She thought of the words the woman had hurled at her in anger. Obviously she thought Bree was a threat to her claim on Shocaw!

"Katcalani, bad," Milakee said, and Bree turned back to her.

"Milakee, do you speak English?" Bree asked, but the little maiden only motioned her to follow and, stripping off her clothes, waded into the pool. She seemed to feel no embarrassment over her naked brown body. She turned with an open smile and motioned to Bree to join her.

Bree stood on shore undecided. Although several other girls stood about waiting for their skin to dry before donning their clothes, Bree was reluctant to undress.

In the hope that some of the girls might leave, she stalled. She sat down on the bank and removed the moccasins Shocaw had placed on her feet when they traveled. It had been many days since her wounds had been tended, and although her soles were not sore, she was sure they would be red and infected. She was surprised when she pulled the leaves away to find they were nearly healed.

She had no more excuses now for not going into the water and in truth she didn't want to stay on shore. She longed to jump into the bright pool and wash away the mud that had begun to itch unbearably. She could go in with her dress on, she thought. It could use a good washing but she was fearful the delicate material would give way and she would have nothing left to wear once she came out. Taking a deep breath, she quickly stripped the material from her body and plunged into the pool.

The water was heavenly, just as she had imagined it. She reveled in its silken coolness, lying on her back and floating about while she stared up at the sky where the shadow of a new moon waited for darkness to welcome its glow.

Milakee swam to the other end of the pool and back, then came to stand beside Bree in the shallow water. From her pouch she produced a broken stem of a plant and, peeling its reedy stalk open, squeezed out the soft milky-white center of it. With a smile of reassurance she applied the creamy substance to Bree's hair and began rubbing it briskly into her scalp, working it into a fragrant lather. She handed Bree more of the soaplike plant and motioned to her to use it on her arms and body. Bree did as instructed and was pleased to see the rest of the mud wash

away from her skin, revealing the scratches and
gouges, which had greatly diminished. Even the
slash on her arm was beginning to heal.

Whatever was in the mud mixture Cooee had
smeared on her had amazing healing powers. Once
again Bree slathered the creamy soap over her
skin, feeling absurdly pampered just to have clean
skin once again. How many days had it been, she
thought, then put her memories of those desperate days lashed to Lopochee's chickee behind
her. She was free of him at last and she was
giving herself a lovely bath, even if it were *au
natural*.

She kicked away from the shallow shoreline
and swam down the length of the pool as Milakee
had done. Her slender arms flashed in and out,
spraying the water behind her like silvery wings.
At last she swam back to shore where she'd left
her clothes and climbed out. She'd never felt so
exhilarated. Her skin tingled and glowed, yet
was even softer to the touch.

There were no linen towels for her to dry herself, so she gently wrung out her golden strands
and wiped at the droplets on her skin with her
hands. Then just as the other girls had done she
stood naked on the shore and combed through
her hair with her fingers, trying to work out the
tangles.

Milakee had also come on shore and now she
reached into her pouch and brought out a comb
decorated in a lovely pattern with colorful shells.
Gratefully, Bree took the comb and set to work
on her hair, grimacing with pain when a snarl
proved too stubborn, yet determined to restore
her hair to its former glory. When she'd finished,
it hung in long wet strands to her hips.

The other young maidens stared at her with
open curiosity. Her slim figure, so pale that many
of them thought it unattractive, and the long

golden strands of her hair captivated them. They had never seen a white woman unclothed before and they compared their bodies to hers unashamedly.

Shyly Bree reached for her dress and began to fit it about herself, but again Milakee was there, and this time, she handed Bree one of the long colorful skirts and capelike blouses worn by the other women. Grateful to have clean clothes, Bree put them on, trying not to think of the drawers and chests back at Greenwood crammed full of silken petticoats and corsets trimmed with ribbon and the finest of laces from Europe. She pushed aside the memory of white silk stockings and dainty slippers as she laced up the moccasins Shocaw had given her. She should be grateful for those, she thought. Most of the Seminole women seemed to go barefoot.

When she'd tied the moccasins in place, she rose, and Milakee led her back to the village, where Shocaw and Cooee were waiting.

"How do you say 'thank you,' in your language?" Bree asked the young brave.

"Mot-to," Cooee responded, and Bree repeated it back softly then turning to Milakee smiled warmly.

"Mot-to, Milakee," she said, extending her hand as she'd seen Shocaw and his braves do. Milakee looked blankly at the proffered hand. Raising her eyes in perplexity, she smiled tentatively, then as an idea came to her, she delved into her pouch and brought out the beautiful shell comb she had allowed Bree to use at the pond.

"Mot-to," she said, and laid the comb in Bree's outstretched hand.

"Oh no, I didn't mean you should give me your comb," Bree said, shaking her head from side to side as she stared at the Indian girl.

"It is a gift, you must keep it now," Cooee said, "or you will offend Milakee."

"But I only meant to shake hands with her to show my appreciation," Bree said lamely.

"The women of our village do not shake hands," Cooee said. "She did not understand."

"Then you must explain," Bree appealed to him.

Her words were cut off as Shocaw moved to the front of the chickee and spoke. Bree had been aware of his dark presence and now she stood back a little, purposefully avoiding his gaze. For some reason the pulse in her throat leaped spasmodically. Cooee nodded his head in understanding and turned back to her.

"Shocaw say you must keep the comb. It is a gift from Milakee and she will be much offended if you do not take it." Cooee translated and Bree stared at the warrior in silence. He had made his wishes clear. She bowed her head in acquiescence.

"There is food for you to eat," Cooee said, gesturing to the chickee.

"*Mot-to,* Cooee," Bree said softly, trying out the new word again, but Cooee, who was normally so attentive to her needs, was preoccupied, his dark eyes going again and again to the pretty young Indian girl who stood with demurely lowered lashes. There was about Cooee at this moment an awkwardness the youth seldom possessed. Bree cast a quick glance at Milakee and noted the rosy blush on her brown cheeks.

For some reason, Bree's glance few to Shocaw where he still lounged near the ladder. He had also noted the blushing awareness between the two and his dark eyes gleamed with sudden humor.

"*Ah-es-chay,*" he said, suddenly giving the younger brave a push. Cooee's face registered a myriad of emotions, surprise at Shocaw's action, uncertainty, embarrassment, and a flare of hope. Shyly he turned toward Milakee and held out his hand. The maiden's dark eyes were bright with pleasure as she took Cooee's hand. Together they walked away across the village square. Bree watched them for a moment, suddenly feeling lonely and melancholy. The young couple's innocence was touching. Would she ever return to her home again, where handsome young men with admiring eyes might woo her?

Suddenly, she was aware of Shocaw's dark gaze lingering on her. Her heart was thumping in her chest so hard she thought it must be visible to the Indian's observant eyes, but he simply motioned her into the chickee and toward the food Cooee had left. Hesitantly Bree climbed the short ladder and seated herself on the mat provided. She took up the bowl of food but found she had no appetite. Swallowing nervously, she looked up with wide eyes at the silent warrior. She wished Cooee could have stayed longer. The chickee, which had seemed so spacious and roomy this afternoon, seemed small and overwhelmingly crowded now. Silently she looked down at her bowl of food.

Shocaw watched her for a moment, trying to sort out his emotions. From the moment he'd seen her walking across the square with Milakee, he'd once again fallen captive to her beauty. What a fool he'd been to think it could be diminished in any way.

She looked like a shiny star, bright and blinding in the intensity of light she emanated. He'd thought he could forget the fragile paleness of her face and hair, until she returned from her bath. Even the innocence of her wide gray eyes cut through him. He could never betray the trust she'd begun to have toward him by taking her against her will, yet it was unlikely she would ever choose to give herself to a man who was her enemy. Desire, insistent and intense, seared through him. Even now as she sat looking demurely down at her bowl of food, he longed to throw aside the bowl and rip the covering blouse and skirt from the lovely limbs.

How quietly she sat. Where were the smiles she gave so readily to Cooee? Had it bothered her to see Cooee with Milakee? Cooee was not Seminole. Did he find favor in the white girl's eyes? Setting his bowl on the floor of the chickee with a resounding thunk, Shocaw sprang to his feet and left the chickee, striding on long legs across the sandy square. Where was Katcalani, he wondered. He would take her to him this very night. Other men took maidens. It was permitted. The strict laws governing such things occurred after marriage. Shocaw strode to the chickee were Katcalani lived.

Bree had been startled by Shocaw's abrupt departure and sat tensely waiting for his return before putting down her bowl of uneaten food. Somehow she felt his leaving had been her fault. She should have made some friendly overture to him. After all, he had tried to protect her. He had saved her life. Sighing, she stood up and began taking down the sleeping blankets and furs.

She was sure she would never be able to get to sleep again. She'd slept all afternoon. When she had the bedding prepared, she lay down anyway. Beyond the edge of the roof she could see the new moon arching above the trees. Its bright light pushed back some of the fearsome darkness of the swamp.

A soft breeze blew through the chickee, caressing her cheek and stirring the tendrils of hair at her temple. Close by an owl gave his familiar call and she lay listening expectantly to the other sounds of the swamp, trying to sort them out.

Surprisingly, she grew drowsy and realized how relaxed and unafraid she felt compared to the

nights in Lopochee's chickee. It was surprising
what a full belly and a warm blanket did for
one's morale, she told herself, and knew full well
the real comfort lay in knowing she was in
Shocaw's chickee. He might be a savage, but she
did not believe he was evil or unnecessarily cruel
as Lopochee and Toschee were.

A slight noise at the ladder told her the warrior had returned. Slowly his footsteps moved
across the floor and came to a stop beside her
mat. Suddenly her heart was pounding and the
pulse leaped in her throat. Where is all your
bravery now, she mocked herself. Should she
feign sleep?

Then the memory of all Shocaw had done for
her this day made her turn toward him and sit
up. At once, the Indian knelt beside her, his face
and eyes in shadows as he stared at her. She
could feel the intensity of his gaze and the rhythm
of her wild heartbeat changed. The blood sang
through her veins in a different tempo that was
far more frightening than her feelings before.

She could hear Shocaw's breathing; it was fast
and slightly irregular. She'd never heard him
breathe like that even when he was carrying her
through the swamp. Her cheeks blanched, then
the color came sweeping back as her face grew
hot. What was he thinking, she wondered, this
half-breed with the penetrating eyes.

"Mot-to," she said softly, her tongue stumbling
over the words, thanking him for his kindness.
She had no knowledge of the decision he had
made while wandering out in the village square,
so she couldn't know how her simple words
touched him, killing his desire and determination. Her face was filled with trust as she looked
at him. How could he betray that trust?

"Som-mus-ka-lar-nee-sha-maw-lin," he said. Bree
didn't know he had uttered the Seminole's tradi-

tional words of best wishes for her, but she sensed the mood of what he said and her fears eased even more.

For a long moment, Shocaw sat looking at her, regret coursing through him. She was so beautiful. A hand reached out to touch the softness of her cheek and trace the line of bone down to her rounded chin. One long finger moved across the full, soft lips, feeling their texture.

The touch of his fingers was not unpleasant. Bree sat rigid, unsure of what he would do next, but Shocaw's hands moved to her hair and he stroked down through the long, golden strands, his hand grazing the mound of her breasts and eliciting a small gasp. For a moment his hand paused, his gaze fixed on her face, and Bree drew in a shaky breath. Once again his hands moved downward through her hair, pausing deliberately at her breast, the large palm closing softly about its rounded contour, while his dark eyes watched her face as if for some sign, some invitation.

But that was silly, Bree thought. She would never invite him to— No never. Her lips trembled and her eyes widened as she stared back at him. Suddenly, she wanted to push him away and run into the swamp, crashing through vines and trees as she strove to escape him. Instead she sat as she was, quivering beneath his touch.

"Chee cho-fee," he said softly, and the words were like a husky caress, yet it held another note that Bree's frantic ear caught. There was comfort and reassurance in his tone, and she sensed how close she'd come to being taken by the Indian—and felt regret sweep through her.

Regret? Don't be foolish, she scolded silently. How can you feel regret that he isn't going to force himself upon you? Yet her wide eyes searched the shadows of his face, knowing in-

stinctively that this was a man who did not take
women against their will. He would simply bend
their will to his, so that she would desire his
touch. Was that what had happened to her? Had
he bewitched her, so she desired him too?

Once again Bree gasped and lay back abruptly
against her mat, pulling the blankets and furs
high beneath her chin, while her eyes stared back
at the crouching warrior. From this angle the
moon lit his face and she could see the slight
smile curving his firm lips and the humor reflected in his dark eyes. Lithely, he rose to his
feet and moved across the chickee to his own bed
and she was left lying alone beneath her covers,
wondering what it would have been like to have
the bronzed giant make love to her.

The thought invaded her mind and she could
not push it away. Would he have been like the
worshipful, gallant men of the Southern gentry
she'd observed at Greenwood, treating her as if
she were a delicate Dresden doll who must be
protected from man's baser nature? Some instinct told her he would have treated her as a
passionate woman. Making love with him would
no doubt be like skimming a fence on Windfire's
back with the wind in her hair. It would have
been rich with exhilarating sensations of motion
and fire and a sweet, sweet wildness.

Bree turned on her hard bed, not knowing that
across the chickee, Shocaw wrestled with his
passions, cursing himself for weakening and not
taking her, when even now, he could imagine the
feel of her beneath him.

Chapter 5

Bree dreamed of green foliage and bright flowers the color of the rainbow and of sunlight pouring into a clearing, where she knelt beside a still pond. She leaned forward and looked into the clear, mirrorlike water, seeing her reflection, laughing with delight at the golden curls that danced about her shoulders. Childlike, she put out her hand and touched the image, and it spun away from her, losing itself in ripples that spread away from her touch in ever-widening circles.

When the water was still again, she saw her image had changed. The long blond curls were gone, and behind her, an evil man with blackened teeth and bloodshot eyes held his grisly trophy aloft and laughed. Bree screamed and tried to run away, but the sawgrass and other foliage caught at her, ripping her dress, scratching her face and arms. Vines twined about her ankles, tripping her and holding her fast.

Bree cried out again and struck at the dark shadows that filled her dreams. The vines had turned to hands and their grasp upon her shoulders was too real.

A deep guttural voice cut through the darkness and slowly the shadowy nightmares receded.

She awoke to see Shocaw crouched over her, his strong hands gripping her. At first her fear made her shrink away from him, but Shocaw held her fast and spoke to her reassuringly. His tone comforted her, chasing away the demon of her dreams. She ceased struggling and her shoulders slumped as she sat silent and submissive beneath his touch.

Pity stirred the warrior's heart. Her tears were no less real than those of his own people, he thought. Her pain was the same as theirs. She cried for the loss of a world she'd known and the people she loved. A gentle hand stroked the bowed head.

Bree raised tear-filled eyes to him, strangely comforted by his presence. His face was in shadows, but his silhouette stood in bold relief in the wash of moonlight. She drew in a quivering breath, very much aware of the strong muscular body beside her. Her body telegraphed its awareness and its churning responses.

Bree sensed the latent strength, the utterly masculine power of his body. His clean, musky smell seemed to envelop her, acting as a spur to her enflamed senses, and with all these new sensations came a new kind of fear. A fear that told her she was in danger of losing far more than her virginity or her life, she was in danger of losing her very being, her heart and soul to this man.

Her eyes were wide as they stared into the darkness that shadowed the Indian's face, and somehow she sensed he looked at her with the same intensity and confused emotions that she felt. For a moment, it seemed as if all things disappeared from them and they were in a world of another kind, a world where only they existed. A man and a woman, with the promise of much between them, with no fears or reservations. Someday, they would belong to each other. There would be pain between them and joy, mis-

understandings and doubts, and love and passion
and yes, even hate. They would be bound to each
other, would never know freedom from the other,
not in thought or need.

The unspoken promises were too much, the
moment too fraught with demands neither wanted
to meet, so Bree blinked and lay back against the
covers and Shocaw stood up abruptly and moved
away. She heard him leave the chickee and knew
he would not be back that night.

She lay upon her pallet and stared beyond the
uneven line of the thatched roof to the star-
strewn, velvety black sky. Her heart raced within
her chest and her mind whirled around in confusion as she thought of that moment just past.

It hadn't been her imagination. Shocaw had
felt it too. That was why he was wandering somewhere out there in the dark of the night. This
was madness. This could not be. He was a savage, of a world totally alien to her own.

And what of Shocaw? If he and his people
seemed strange and cruel to her, how must the
white man seem to them. What had the girl by
the river called her, an old woman with no
color, and she had spat into Bree's hair. Perhaps
to the Indians with their dark coloring and vivid
dress, such light color as Bree's might seem ugly.
Yet she remembered the way Shocaw had held
her hair, marveling at its fine texture as the
moon shone on it. He did not find her ugly, she
knew, and was confused at the surge of happiness she felt in knowing he found her attractive.

What was wrong with her? She was the captive of a savage people and Shocaw was one of
them. They had captured her as they returned
from a raid, a raid against her own people. She
could feel nothing for this savage, nothing. She
must try to escape. Her mind and will had been

affected by the swamp. She'd heard some of her
father's slaves say it happened.

Perhaps that was the reason for these confusing thoughts about Shocaw. Perhaps she was delirious with swamp fever. She hoped so, then
uttered a hopeless, sighing laugh as she thought of
what she'd wished on herself. People died from
swamp fever. Was that what she was wishing on
herself?

Yes, a thousand times yes, rather than submit
to a filthy Indian who had committed all manner
of atrocities against her people. Deliberately, she
judged Shocaw with Lopochee's deeds, although
she'd never known anything but kindness and
consideration from him. She felt too frightened
and hemmed in to be fair. Tomorrow she would
escape, she vowed. Somehow she would make
her way through the jungle and back to her father. Getting away should be easy. She remembered how quickly the swamp seemed to hide
any evidence of the village once they had moved
away from it. The swamp could work for her as
well. She would simply walk away when no one
was looking and melt into the shadows and disappear as the Indians did.

She lay staring into the black night, planning
her escape, picturing herself back at Greenwood,
and she refused to think of the dangers of the
swamp or the tall Seminole, who by his very
presence, was unknowingly driving her away
from the village.

Shocaw did not return to the chickee that night
and Bree slept no more. She lay watching the
dark shadows of night give way before the eastern
light streaking the horizon. When the pearly-
gray light was stained with rose and she knew
the sun would soon rise above the dark silhouette of trees, she rose and put the chickee to
rights as she had the day before. When all was in

place, she sat down to wait for someone to come,
her hands folded tranquilly in her lap, her mind
blank of all thoughts of Shocaw.

She watched as the village came to life. First
the men rose and gathered at the end of the
square, their rifles and pouches at the ready.
They would go into the swamp and hunt for food
this day. Bree looked for the tall figure of Shocaw
and, when she'd found him, turned quickly away.

When the men had gone, the women and children rose. The women threw handfuls of ground
cornmeal into pots of water and put them on the
fire to simmer. Later vegetables and chunks of
meat would be added and the whole mixture
would cook slowly over the coals. The men would
be hungry when they returned from their hunting.

Coontie flour cakes left over from the night
before were given to the children; then taking up
their hoes and rakes, the women prepared to
leave the village. The children would be left in
the care of Sofangee, the young girl Bree had observed before.

"*Aw-lock-chay*," Milakee called to Bree, and
motioned to her to join them. Bree hurried down
the steps of Shocaw's chickee and across the
square toward the women. Was she to go to the
fields with them? Perhaps they didn't trust her
to be alone in the village all day. She could have
made good her vows to escape, but suddenly,
returning Milakee's warm smile, she was glad
she wouldn't be given the opportunity. The village and its people seemed a haven from the dark
dangers of the swamp.

They left the village behind them, and once
again, evidence of its presence was lost to them
after they'd traveled only a few feet. Bree kept
her eyes open, looking for any sign of a trail that
led away from the Indian village. There seemed

not to be one. Yet with complete assurance the women moved forward.

They walked side by side until the path narrowed and they were forced to go single file, walking carefully along a narrow strip of land or a log as they crossed streams and green-scummed backwaters. They seemed to be going ever deeper into the swamp, where the land grew more and more scarce. Bree was surprised when suddenly the trail widened and they entered a glade, a clearing on a hillock. Here the tangle of brush and jungle vines had been cleared and the Seminoles had planted corn, beans, and pumpkins.

The field was quite large and immediately the women moved down the rows and busied themselves with chopping at the weeds around the tender young plants. Bree stood watching them, thinking of the fields back at Greenwood. The Seminoles, she realized, were not so different from the white man who planted and tended his crops. Except here everyone seemed to be responsible for tending the fields.

"Chee-yi-chee-e-sho-e-caw?" Milakee asked, holding out a hoe not all that unlike the ones used by the slaves at Greenwood. Bree's eyes widened in amazement as she realized Milakee meant for her to use the hoe as the other women were doing. Wordlessly she took a step backward, shaking her head from side to side.

She had never worked in the fields in her life and had no idea of how to do so. The thought was ludicrous. Vigorously she shook her head at Milakee, who looked at her helplessly then cast a worried look at the other women who were working nearby.

Lopochee's wife, Toschee, scowled at the white girl who disdained work. She made some comment to the other women, who stopped their work and turned their attention to the white

captive. Katcalani smirked with satisfaction as
she looked at Bree. Not only was she ugly, but she
was lazy as well, the Indian girl thought with
satisfaction. This captive would not take Shocaw
from her.

The worry on Milakee's face transmitted itself
to Bree, and looking about at the scowling faces
of the women, she took a step forward and reached
for the hoe which Milakee still held. Milakee
smiled encouragingly and, taking up another hoe
for herself, led the way down a row. She hoped
the white slave was a good worker. It would go
easier for her with the other women if she were.

Silently Bree followed Milakee, all too aware
of the stoic stares of the other women. The Indian girl led her to an untended place where the
weeds threatened to choke out the tender shoots.
Smiling at the white girl, Milakee spoke to her
and began to chop away the weeds.

Although Bree didn't understand the words,
she knew Milakee was trying to show her what
was expected of her, but the sun beat down on
their heads and Bree was hot and thirsty and
most of all tired from the long trek through the
swamp. They had walked for at least two miles
and she needed to rest before she was expected
to work in the hot sun.

Yet there was Milakee, who had walked the
same two miles, hard at work, her head down,
her shoulders swinging rhythmically. Bree glanced
around at the other women and was surprised
to see that Toschee and some of the others still
stood leaning on their hoes, watching her cur-
iously. Toschee had moved closer under the pretense of chopping away some of the weeds and
Bree could see the cruel sneer of anticipcation
on her face.

Toschee had once incited the women to attack
her, and the fear that she might do so yet again

made Bree quell her rebellious thoughts and bend to her task. When the other women saw she was working, they returned to their work. Only Toschee seemed disappointed, her face dark as she cast black glances at the girl.

Ineffectively, Bree pulled the hoe through the tangle of weeds, her inexperience all too evident. Time after time the hoe bit too deeply into the black earth, causing her to tug at it harder than she had to, or else she missed altogether and the hoe leaped forward to strike her in the shin. Quickly she tired and the soft, tender skin of her palms grew red and sore and blistered.

Still she worked on, trying valiantly to do what was expected of her as her mind planned her escape. The sun moved higher in the sky. Perspiration rolled down her forehead and into her eyes, making them sting, and still she was expected to work on. More often now the hoe slipped through the weeds and struck her in the shins, each time setting her legs to aching. If not for the moccasins, her legs would have been lashed and bleeding.

With each stroke now, anger boiled within her. She was no slave, no field hand, she thought rebelliously as she slashed away at the stubborn weeds and plants. Why should she have to stand here in the hot sun tending their fields for them? Let the weeds grow around the plants; she cared not. She would escape, running through the cool, green swamp until she found the trail back to Greenwood and there she would once again sit on the veranda and let May or Cassie bring her tall cool drinks while she chatted idly with Mama or Millicent Southfield. She jerked the hoe through a tangle of weeds and felt it strike her shin harder than it ever had before.

"Ahhh!" she cried, dropping the hoe and sitting down in the dirt to nurse her injured leg.

Pain laced up the shin to her knee. Behind her she heard Toschee's voice raised in shrill anger as she waved her arms and complained about the white girl.

Although she could hear Toschee clumping through the dirt toward her, Bree began to unlace her moccasin to see how bad the cut was on her leg. At this rate there would soon be nothing left of her, she thought, and bit back a little sob of self-pity as she peeled away the leather.

To her surprise there was no blood and no cut. Once again the deer-hide moccasin had saved her from the sharp edge of the hoe. However, there was a red spot that was already beginning to swell. Her legs would be covered with bruises by tomorrow. Bree cupped her hand around her injured leg and sat rocking back and forth. She could smell Toschee as she came closer.

"Hal-wuk," Toschee said, snatching up the severed plants and holding them up for all to see. A murmur of dismay passed among the women as they looked at the row where Bree had worked. For a moment Bree stared at them, nonplussed. So she had accidently cut down a plant, she thought. She wasn't used to doing this kind of work; surely they allowed for mistakes. She looked back along the row and her heart sank. In her anger she had cut down nearly all the cornstalks in the row.

Regret washed over her. She hadn't meant to destroy the plants. She'd just been so uncomfortable and angry. Quickly she looked at Milakee, but Milakee looked away, unable to offer any help. The worried look on her face told Bree of the seriousness of her crime more than any words could have.

"Look, I'm sorry. I didn't mean to cut down so many of the stalks," she said, looking up at the Indian women, but there was no softening in

their expressions. Slowly they advanced toward
her and in alarm Bree sprang to her feet.

"I'm sorry," she cried again. "I don't know
how to hoe your fields. I've never done it before." The women's faces were angry as they
advanced toward her. Whirling, Bree turned and
ran down the long row back toward the path
they had taken earlier. This time she would run
into the swamp and escape, she resolved, but at
the edge of the field the women caught her. She
could feel their hands and nails along the skin of
her arms as they grabbed her. She would fight
back, Bree thought, and turned to meet them.
She would not stand meekly while they attacked
her again. Blindly she struck out at them, feeling
her fists connect with flesh and hearing a grunt
of pain, but she was outnumbered and they soon
had her arms held fast, while Toschee and some
of the other women drew their knives and moved
toward her.

"Toschee." Bree could hear Milakee's voice.
"Shocaw's *hoke-tee*," she said several times until
the women stopped and stood back to stare at the
young Indian woman in anger. "Shocaw's *hoke-
tee*," Milakee repeated, and moved to stand in
front of Bree. Bree didn't know what the words
meant, but she remembered that Milakee had
used them at the pond the night before when the
other Indian girl had meant to attack her. The
words had produced the same effect as now. The
women drew away from her, all save Toschee
and Katcalani, who still stood glaring at her.

Toschee stepped closer to Milakee, her eyes
flashing as she spewed out angry words. Calmly
Milakee stood her ground in the face of the woman's anger and gratefully Bree acknowledged the
bravery of the young Indian woman. Bree was
almost as frightened of Toschee as she was of her

husband, Lopochee, yet Milakee seemed unmoved by the woman's wrath.

The women behind Toschee listened intently while she spoke, nodding their heads in agreement and calling out encouragement. Milakee stepped forward and began to speak, her voice low and musical. Bree could tell the women did not like what she had to say but they would follow her instructions. Casting baleful glances over their shoulders, they returned to the field and, picking up their hoes, began to work once again.

Toschee stood where she was, glaring in rage at Bree and Milakee until the last Indian woman returned to work, then she turned away, spitting a final expletive.

"*Aw-lock-chay,*" Milakee said, turning back toward the village, and Bree followed, rubbing the scratches on her arm. They were nothing like the ones she had received her first day in the Indian village. Milakee led her back through the swamp to the village and Shocaw's chickee. With a small reassuring smile, the Indian girl turned back toward the swamp.

Surprised at being left alone, Bree was uncertain of what to do with herself. The chickee was in order and Sofangee, the young girl, was caring for the children. Finally Bree sat forlornly on the floor, her feet dangling over the edge of the chickee. The afternoon sun was hot and she wandered to the gourd that held the water, then plodded through the hot sand back to the chickee. At least it afforded her some shade from the merciless sun. She leaned against the post of the chickee, gasping in the afternoon heat that danced mockingly in waves on the yellow sand of the square.

I must run away from here, she thought, but first she must rest a little. Taking out a sleeping pad, she spread it out and lay down. Lethargy crept over her, pinning her to the soft mat, weighting down her long lashes so they closed and she slept. After she'd rested a bit, she would leave the village, run away while she had the chance.

She was awakened by the sound of voices and opened her eyes to see that the Indians had returned. Even the men were back from their hunting. Sleepily she sat up and rubbed at her eyes, then pushed her tangled hair away from her face. The rough texture of the sleeping mat had left its print on her soft cheek and she rubbed it absently as she watched the Seminoles.

They were gathered in front of the platform where the old Indian chief had sat the first night she'd been brought to the village, and as then, the villagers were voicing their complaints. Bree felt a chill of alarm as she watched the women talking excitedly. Now and then one of them pointed to the chickee where she sat.

Hesitantly Bree got to her feet and moved to the ladder, searching through the crowd for Milakee. She was relieved when she saw that Shocaw stood on the ledge with the other men of the council and Cooee stood slightly behind him. Shocaw's eyebrows were pulled downward in a fierce scowl and his lips were tight and angry looking.

After the women had spoken, Shocaw turned to the old chief and spoke himself. His words met with the disapproval of the people, for they called out angrily at him. The old chief listened patiently to Shocaw, then looked into the distance; his watery old eyes seemed to look far into the future of his people. At last he raised his feathered stick and struck it against the floor. Although his voice was weak, his words rang out with authority upon the evening air. When he had finished speaking, Shocaw motioned Cooee to follow him and strode purposefully toward his chickee. The look on his face was one of terrible anger.

In sudden fear, Bree backed across the chickee until she felt one of the posts behind her. With a bound, Shocaw was up the stairs and standing before her, his black eyes accusing as they looked into hers. For a moment he stared at her, noting the lovely tangle of golden hair, the soft, trembling mouth, and the wide eyes darting fearfully from him to Cooee and back again. He perceived her fear, and it made her guilt even more real to him.

He did nothing to soften the looming intimidation of his presence. She was their enemy and she had committed an act that might cause some of them to go hungry in the winter months ahead. She was weak, even for a woman, giving way to the tears and mewings of a puppy whenever the mood struck her. Why had he not let Lopochee take her scalp or at least have her for his slave, he wondered, and tried to ignore the answer that was written deep within his heart.

She was of little value to anyone, he thought, unsuited to work in the fields or even to take care of herself. Unlike the Seminole maidens who were trained from early childhood, this girl had not been taught and her stubborn nature defied all efforts to teach her. Yet something about her tugged at him and he could not relinquish her to his people's justice. He had seen her spirit and beauty and sensed her passion.

"*Hal-wuk,*" he said, and his dark eyes bored into hers, crushing her will with his own. "It is bad, this thing you have done," he continued in his own language. "Like the white soldiers who invade our sacred grounds, you have destroyed

some of our crops, and although the amount is
small, it may be that amount which will feed a
small child and keep him from death or give the
warrior the strength to go into battle."

Silently he waited while Cooee translated the
words for her. He watched her face for the
expressions of feelings he saw there. At first he
saw fear and concern for herself, then contrition
for her actions and shame as she thought of a
small child going hungry for her deed, then anger blazed in her eyes. Jutting her small chin
out, Bree took a step forward and, tipping back her
head, glared into the warrior's dark eyes.

"I am glad," she said in a low, even voice, "if
my deed makes one warrior unable to go into
battle. You do battle with my own people and I
cannot be sorry if I've helped stop your killing of
them." She stopped speaking and glared up at
him as fiercely as he had glared at her. Shocaw
felt anger rise within him. She was so small and
dainty he could crush her with one blow, yet
here she stood, openly defying him. Didn't she
know her life was in danger?

"When the soldiers destroy our crops, we kill
them so they may destroy no more," Shocaw
said, and this time he spoke in the white man's
tongue, watching as the fear flickered across her
eyes. "Even now, my people wait for the decision of the old chief to put you to death." Again
he waited and saw that she didn't want to die,
yet after only a moment's hesitation, she raised
her chin and spoke.

"Then kill me," she said quietly. Then passion
flared within her and she struck her chest with
one small fist. "If you must kill me, then do so. I
did not set out to cut away the corn. I do not
wish your people to die from hunger. If I am to
die, I will not beg for mercy, for I perceive there
is none among the Seminoles. Kill me, if that is

your wish." Her voice broke on the brave words and she stood before him, her slight body trembling as she drew in breath. Her gray eyes, so like the sky before a summer storm, were glistening with unshed tears, yet still her chin was high.

"Why have you done this to our people?" Shocaw asked. "Do you hate us so much?"

"Oh no!" Bree cried. "I bear no hatred for your people. I want to understand them and their ways. I want to help them." She raised a trembling hand. Tears glistened in her eyes. "I was angry. I've never worked in the fields. I don't know how. In my anger and ignorance I just chopped at everything." She paused and looked up at Shocaw.

"I didn't think of the importance of one stalk of corn when the field was filled with so many," she said simply. "I don't know your ways or understand the reason for them. I'm sorry."

It seemed to Shocaw her words, uttered with simple dignity, included more than the mere act of cutting down the cornstalks. She had recognized the sufferings of his people at the hands of the white man and the need for understanding between the two worlds. He felt his heart move within him.

There was so much ignorance and hatred between the two races, and it was those very emotions that fanned the flames of the war that was slowly strangling the Seminole nation. It was not because of the destroyed corn that his people wished to punish this white girl, it was because of their hatred and their need to seek vengeance against her people. This terrible hatred was destroying one race of people and deeply staining the honor of another.

All these thoughts passed through Shocaw's mind as he stood looking down at Bree's set face. Abruptly making up his mind, he turned back to the ladder, indicating to Cooee he was to bring the prisoner.

"You must walk very carefully if you wish to live," Cooee told her as he took one arm and led her across the square. "There are many who wish to see you dead."

"I don't care anymore," Bree answered numbly. "I would rather be dead than be a prisoner." She stumbled after him to the trampled ground in front of the raised platform. She could hear the angry buzz of the women as they talked among themselves. Shocaw mounted the platform once again while Cooee remained below with Bree.

Bewildered, Bree listened as Shocaw spoke. It was obvious he was bidding for her life. The angry murmur of the women rose as they too listened, but the faces of the men on the platform remained stoic and unreadable.

"These are the men of our council. They will decide what must happen to you," Cooee explained. Bree studied their faces, dismay filling her when she saw Lopochee was among the men on the platform. She knew what his decision would be. Helplessly she looked at the other men. Was her crime so serious that she must lose her life over a few stalks of corn? Her father would gladly give them ten times the amount they'd lost if she were returned. Impulsively she stepped forward and, gripping the edge of the platform, began to speak to the men of the council.

"Return me to my people," she called to them, "and my father will give you much grain and corn. He—he will give you potatoes and cattle and chickens and many other things so your people need not go hungry this winter."

Shocaw stopped speaking and the men stared down at her silently. Their expressions were unreadable, but they appeared to be listening to her. Hopefully Bree continued.

"My father feeds many more people than there are here in your village every day," she said, waving her arm to take in all the Indians in the square. "To feed all of you would be very easy for him. We have much food on our plantation. He would be grateful if you took me back there and he would give you some of his food." The Indians sat unmoving, their eyes staring back at her. "Greenwood is a very prosperous plantation. There are many cattle and chickens, the lands are rich, and our crops are heavy and abundant." The Indians' eyes seemed dark and angry as they listened to her. Bree took a step backward, unsure of what she had said to anger them. Then an Indian warrior leaped to his feet and, walking to the end of the platform, spat on her. Bree recoiled in disgust, moving backward, but now the women surged forward, pushing her back to the platform. Another member of the council rose to his feet and, walking to the edge, spat on her as well.

Horrified, Bree felt the warm spittle hit her brow and cheeks and slide down her face as one by one each warrior of the council repeated the act, all save Shocaw. Gleefully the women held her arms, their hands grasping her hair to hold her face upward so she could not avoid the defilement.

At last the old chief rose to his feet and, raising an arm above his head, motioned his people to release her. His wavering voice rose on the evening air, at once guttural and musical as Bree dabbed at her face with the hem of her skirt.

The low murmur of the Seminoles made her pause in her frantic actions and look up at the old chief. The sound of his words seemed to hang on the air long after he'd finished speaking and she perceived he had just passed sentence on her. Was she to be put to death then? she wondered, and her eyes flew to Shocaw's face.

She could tell nothing of his thoughts as he stood gazing over her head, his arms folded over his chest. Wildly she looked about for Cooee and saw him standing at the corner of the platform.

"Cooee," she called softly, urgently, but he looked away and did not answer. The old chief continued speaking, then halted abruptly and lowered his hand and the feathered stick. His shoulders slumped as if he were tired of all that had occurred here. She was to be put to death, Bree thought frantically. The thought rose within her with a certainty that could not be denied.

She, Brittany Rikkar, fresh from one of Europe's finest finishing schools, able to speak and read in five different languages, an heir of one of the most prosperous plantations in central Florida, the pampered daughter of one of Florida's most powerful men, was about to die here in this swamp clearing at the hands of a few ignorant savages, simply because she had cut down a few stalks of corn. Suddenly the magnitude of it was too much to bear.

"No," she screamed, her cry long and startlingly loud, echoing across the quiet square. A roaring filled her head and she slumped to the ground. Instantly Cooee was at her side, then Shocaw was there, his hands impersonal as he raised her to her feet. His dark eyes flashed with anger and contempt as he looked down upon her, and Bree resisted the impulse to whimper and cringe away from him. Where was her bravery now?

Shocaw's voice was cold and deadly sounding as he turned to Cooee and barked out instructions. With a nod of understanding the young brave took her arm and led her away. Docilely Bree followed. She was about to die, she thought. How would they go about it? Would the death be quick or would it be so lingering and painful that she would pray to die? Would they torture her first?

Cooee led her to an abandoned chickee set back from the rest of the village. The thatch on the roof was old and thin and the floor unswept. There he tethered her to a post much as Lopochee had done.

"Why are they going to kill me?" Bree cried in despair as Cooee prepared to leave her. For a moment the youth looked at her in surprise, then came to squat down beside her.

"You are not to be killed, although Toschee and Lopochee spoke strongly for your death. Shocaw has made the council protect you. However, you must be punished so you remember our ways and not disregard them again."

"I'm not going to die?" Bree cried, disbelief mingling with a glimmer of hope. Despite her earlier disclaimer, she realized she very much wanted to live. Her gray eyes glistened as she stared at Cooee. "Cooee, thank you," she cried fervently as she clasped his arm. "Thank you for saving my life."

"I did not save your life, Shocaw did," Cooee said.

"No, it was you. You told the council I didn't mean to cut down the corn," Bree cried gratefully, but the young Seminole shook his head.

"Shocaw told the council you have great value, but if you are dead you have no value. He said if they kill you it would be the same as cutting down the cornstalks. Both destroy the Seminole's chance to survive."

Bree backed away and stared at Cooee, digesting his words.

"What did Shocaw mean by that?" she asked. Could he be planning to trade her after all?

"I do not know," Cooee said, and turned away. A sudden thought made Bree call out to him.

"Cooee, wait." He turned and waited. "You said I am to be punished for cutting down the corn. What is my punishment to be?"

"I do not know." Cooee paused as Shocaw climbed the ladder into the chickee and stood glaring at his prisoner. Bree was hard put to return his level gaze. The bright turban he wore seemed to shadow his dark eyes and make him appear even taller than he really was.

"Th-thank you for saving my life," she said hesitantly. "I—I was asking Cooee what my punishment is to be." She tried to control the tremor in her voice.

Shocaw looked at her a moment more before speaking. His voice was low and flat sounding and he spoke in the Seminole tongue. In alarm Bree looked at Cooee.

"You are to be without food for three days so you may see how it is to go hungry," Shocaw said.

"I already know what it is to go hungry. I am hungry now. I've eaten very little since my capture. I have not yet eaten today," she answered. She was relieved to hear the punishment was to be no worse.

"You will go three days without food. You will be given only water to drink. No one will speak to you in those three days so you may think of your act and what pain it can bring upon the Seminoles who are your host.

"My host? My host?" Bree's voice fairly shrieked as she looked at Shocaw. Anger washed through her as she thought again of the insult she'd suffered from the men of the council. Even now their spittle was drying on her face.

"I am not a guest here. I am a prisoner, a captive. I've begged you to return me to my people but you refuse. I have been scratched and beaten and starved and made to go without water to drink or to bathe myself. No one punished the women who attacked me, but I am to be punished for cutting down a few stalks of corn. Your justice and hospitality are sadly lacking." Bree's voice rose in indignation while she talked. "You are all savages, without honor or manners. It is no wonder the white man wishes to throw you out of this land."

"Please do not say more," Cooee said, interrupting her tirade.

"Why not?" she demanded. "Everything I say is true. Your great war chief is like a tree, without ears or a mind. He brings me here against my will to this godforsaken, filthy hole and expects me to be grateful while his people spit on me and revile me."

"At least you are alive and you have not been violated as our women have been," Shocaw answered coldly.

"I do not doubt even that will come," Bree said bitterly.

"The things that happened in the square, you brought upon yourself. You brag of the rich lands and food of your people, but these lands once belonged to the Seminole nation. Once we too had plenty of food and could feed many more than we number now, but the white man took it from us. Do not speak of the white man's wealth again."

"I did not do these things to your people," Bree cried. "Why must I be made to pay? Before I submit myself to more of the Seminole's torture, I prefer to die. Kill me now and be done with it."

"Starvation is a very slow, painful way to die," Shocaw replied. "You will not starve to death in three days, you will only think about it." Motioning to Cooee, he turned and left the chickee. The line of his shoulders and back expressed all too well his contempt for the white man, who was too used to his comforts and too lacking in understanding of the Indian's most basic needs for survival.

Quickly Cooee hurried after him. Bree stood staring after them until they disappeared, then she sat down on the platform and thought of what they'd said. Had her words seemed like bragging? She hoped not. She'd seen how the pots of the village depended upon the game the hunters brought in each day. What happened on those days when there was no game or when the crops were destroyed?

She was very lucky, she realized. Some of the Indians had wanted to kill her, but once again Shocaw had fought for her life. She would live. She could do without food for three days, and what did it matter if no one spoke to her? She couldn't understand any of them and they couldn't understand her. She already felt isolated and set apart.

She would survive better than Shocaw and the others thought she could. She would show them a white woman could be just as strong and noble as a Seminole.

She felt buoyed by her resolution. It was important to her that the Seminoles see her as something other than a bragging, spoiled daughter of the men who had stolen their lands. Squaring her shoulders, she settled herself on the dirty floor of the chickee. Three days were not so long, but by the time Milakee brought a gourd of water and walked away without any acknowledgment that she existed, Bree was already feeling lonely. She was growing to like the young Indian girl and longed to go to the bathing pond with her again.

Through the trees she could see the women working around the fire pit, preparing the evening meal, and the smell of their cooking wafted on the evening air, reminding her she'd eaten nothing that day. Her shoulders slumped and she couldn't stop the tears of self-pity that filled her eyes and rolled down her cheeks.

Chapter 6

Shocaw slept fitfully that night. It had been a day too fraught with tension for him to throw it off. It had been much harder than he'd anticipated to persuade the council to save Bree. The warriors, hunting for game deeper in the swamp than ever before, had been surprised by a detail of soldiers and had escaped only by leaving behind what game they had taken. As it was, several men had been wounded and the villagers were angry.

They wanted to take out their revenge on the white prisoner who had defiantly tried to destroy some of the crops. Only with great skill had he been able to bring them around to his way of thinking. She must be kept alive. Only then was she of value to his people.

Shocaw tried to tell himself it was for this purpose alone that he had fought so hard for her life. Tomorrow he would seek out the white soldiers and send them a message that he would trade the white girl for one of the captured Seminole chiefs. When she was back with her own people, maybe then he would forget her.

Too often his thoughts had turned to this golden-haired girl with the stormy gray eyes and

soft breasts. Even now in his half dreams she
came to him, mocking him, enticing him with
her long, white limbs and soft pink mouth, and
he felt the ache in his loins. Restlessly he turned
on his pallet and sought the comfort of the little
death of sleep.

Shocaw awoke early the next morning, and
taking a few hand-picked men—Lopochee included so he could keep an eye on him—he left
the camp. They would be gone for three days,
and during that time the old chief had assured
him no one would harm the captive.

They had traveled only a short distance when
Shocaw heard his name called and turned back
to see Katcalani running toward them. She was a
tall, willowy girl with lively brown eyes that
flashed invitingly beneath the straight line of
her bangs. Her long dark hair fanned behind as
she ran, then settled about her shoulders like a
silken curtain when she came to a stop before
him.

Katcalani was one of the prettiest girls in the
village and was sought after by many of the un-
wed braves. Now, as she called his name, Shocaw
walked back to meet her while his men moved
discreetly ahead on the trail.

Shocaw knew Katcalani was courted by many
but had set her mind on him and he had not
discouraged her. There had even been speculation among some of the women that the two
would wed at the next Green Corn Dance ceremony. Shocaw looked at her dark loveliness as
she smiled up at him and wished he felt the
same way about her as he did about the captive.
Katcalani, he perceived, was vain and often
treated others as if she considered them beneath
her. Shocaw had seen the same mannerisms among
the spoiled rich white women who had once pursued him.

RENEGADE HEART   137

"Shocaw." Katcalani made her voice soft and breathless as she spoke his name. Once again she smiled at him, letting him see the bold invitation in her eyes. "I have made this shirt for you." She held out a bundle to him and Shocaw stood staring blankly down at it.

It was the custom of a maiden to offer a shirt to the man she hoped to marry, and suddenly he felt trapped. He remembered all too clearly that he'd brought a deer to the doorstep of Katcalani's family, demonstrating his ability to be a good provider, but he had been only half serious, knowing the young maiden was enjoying her conquests with the vying warriors. Now it appeared she had indeed chosen him and he stood staring down at the shirt she offered and felt a reluctance to carry their courtship further.

"I go on a trip to the white man," he said haltingly.

"Shocaw may have need of a fine shirt when he goes before the white man. It will give him more stature among his enemy when they see how finely he is dressed."

"I might lose the shirt in the swamp and the little raccoon might wear it. It is much too fine for the raccoon." Shocaw saw uncertainty in her eyes. Was he rejecting her or did he truly not desire harm to come to her offering? She chose to think the latter and smiled back at him.

"I will keep the shirt until Shocaw returns," she said. "I will take great care that it is kept safe for you." She took a step forward, allowing her body to brush against his, and smiled to herself as she saw his eyes widen at the contact. He was aware of her as a woman. No matter what Milakee said about the white captive, Shocaw was hers.

Perhaps, when Shocaw returned, she would give herself to him. It was the custom of her people for young maidens to mate with the young brave of her choice although they were not husband and wife. She had not done so because she'd enjoyed the attention she'd received from the other young men of the village. She would do so now. She would choose Shocaw. He was a chief among her people and she would be his wife. She would gain great stature among the other women.

The lights in Shocaw's eyes darkened as he read the promise in her seductive gaze and full pouting lips. With a quick movement, he captured her waist and pulled her toward him. His lips settled on her mouth in a hard kiss that left her breathless. He released her as quickly as he had seized her but the imprint of his mouth still blazed on her lips.

With a triumphant smile Katcalani stepped backward and watched as Shocaw strode off after his men. Now his thoughts would be of her, Katcalani, and not of the captive. The white girl was no match for her. Katcalani made her way back to the village. She was the most beautiful and desirable of maidens. Hadn't many of the warriors whispered that in her ears? She could have any brave she wanted and she wanted Shocaw. She meant to have him. Still, her self-assurance was needled by the remembrance that Shocaw had not taken the shirt, whatever his reason.

Bree woke hot and thirsty with the rays of the hot sun piercing the thatched roof. It burned down on her fiercely. Moaning for no other reason than that it relieved her sense of misery, she brushed ineffectually at the flies that clung to her sweaty skin. Wearily she reached for the gourd of tepid water. It was nearly empty again and she hoped Milakee remembered to bring her a fresh one. She had been here for three days now without food and with only water to sustain her. No one had approached her or spoken to her in all that time. Even Milakee had kept her eyes averted and remained silent as she brought fresh water.

Bree took another swallow and lay down again. It was easier, she'd found, if she didn't stir around a lot. The first day she'd fought against her bonds, trying to loosen them so she might flee into the swamp and escape, but her efforts had been useless. The second day she had sat huddled against the post, her knees drawn up to her chest, in an effort to relieve the hunger pains of her stomach, and today she had lain quietly, unresisting against the vivid dreams that haunted her.

She could begin to understand the Indians' belief in dreams, for hers had seemed all too real as her body made its need for nourishment evident. Her dreams had been peopled by all her loved ones who stood before her urging her to partake of the wonderful, succulent dishes of food they held in their hands. They wheedled and cajoled until she reached for the food, then withdrew it with a loving smile. "It is for your own good," they said. "It is to help you understand." One by one they disappeared from her dream, taking the food with them, a sad smile upon their faces.

Bree whimpered and turned over. Now into her dreams came the figure of an Indian; his great shoulders were covered by a robe of deer hide and he wore a turban with a large plume in it. He was a Seminole chief. He pointed his finger at Bree and she recoiled in fright. Behind him, Indian women pressed close, their hands curled into claws as they reached for Bree. Again she drew back. She was very frightened and cried as she ran into the swamp. The Indians followed her.

Finally she came to the edge of a great stream whose waters were black and seemed to lead off into the shadows of another world. Bree stepped into a dugout and began to pole her way across the stream. She'd left the Indians on the shore behind her. They called to her, and when she looked back, she saw they had changed. Now her mother and father and Jared stood on the shore. Even May was there and the old Negress held out her arms. They all cried out her name, urging her back to the shore, but Bree was unable to turn the dugout in the current and it drifted away.

Looking ahead of her, she could see into the shadows of the other world and there she saw Milakee and Cooee. Shocaw was there, his dark eyes bright as he smiled and beckoned to her. Their hands were empty, but their faces shone with laughter. They were not angry with her anymore. Once again Bree heard her mother call to her, but the sound was faint and she pushed the pole deep into the stream and sent the dugout down the stream toward the Indians. For a moment she felt frightened until she saw Shocaw's face. He held out a hand to her and now she saw he held the golden grains of corn she'd once destroyed. Bree was happy. Now she and her people would not go hungry through the winter. She poled the dugout toward shore and Shocaw was there to take her hand as she stepped out.

For a moment she looked back at the distant shore, but it was empty. Her mother and father were gone. Only a majestic white ibis rose from the water, filling the air with the whir of its wings, graceful and majestic as it swept across the sky and disappeared. The Seminole called it hi-lo-lo. Bree called after the bird, "hi-lo-lo," and watched it fly into the sun.

She awoke, her clothes wet with sweat and clinging to her. Taking a deep steadying breath, she wiped at the wet tendrils of hair about her face. She was surprised to see she had fallen asleep sitting up, almost as if she'd been in a trance. Yet her mind was sharp and clearer than ever before, open to all things. A well of understanding sprang into being within her and she felt a kinship with all men.

The world she'd left behind seemed unimportant now. The real value of life lay not in the turn of a petticoat, the fineness of a lace, but in the depths of her very soul.

On the plantation she was pampered and protected from all that was unpleasant in life. She'd never been tested except in her capacity to flirt from behind a fan and chatter gaily. Thoughtlessly she'd moved through life, never knowing herself or her capacity to feel, never understanding her place as a being in God's universe.

Now she sensed she was being tested by a greater power than the Seminoles. She had met her first test and survived. She was stronger than she'd ever thought possible. She had been afraid and would be again, but now she knew her fears could not defeat her. She had only to look within herself to draw strength.

They were all one with the earth and the trees and animals that dwelled side by side with man. They were all part of those who had gone before and those who would follow. Death was no longer frightening to her, for it was an extension of life itself.

All past notions seemed to fall away from her like an old skin, once protective and comfortable, now outgrown. She could never move backward from this moment. She had gone beyond it. With that thought came a sense of freedom she'd never known before.

Slowly an awareness of her surroundings, of the Indian village and the flicker of the cooking fires came to her. She became aware, too, of two men, Cooee and Lopochee, who stood before her.

"Your punishment has ended," Cooee said, coming to loosen her bonds and set her free. "You are wanted at the council platform."

"Lop-ko!" Lopochee said imperiously and glared at her. Once Bree would have shrunk before his fierceness, but now she felt no fear of the cruel warrior. She was untouched by his anger and intimidation.

Lopochee seemed to sense the change in her and raised his arm to deliver a blow, then slowly lowered it again. He remembered the look on her face when they'd first come to the chickee. There had been a look of the other world about her pale features. Now she moved across the chickee to the ladder with a proud dignity that hadn't been there before. Thoughtfully Cooee watched her. She seemed different. Her face carried the same look as some of the warriors when they had purged themselves with the black drink and received a vision.

It was not the warriors who took Bree across the sandy square to the platform. It was she who led them, walking unhurriedly with such simple dignity that the Seminoles were struck at once by her poise. Her eyes were clear and direct as she looked at them, with none of the fear or evil spirits of madness they had seen there when she was first brought to the village. They fell back from her as she walked past them.

When Shocaw first saw her, his lips tightened in anger as they did when he saw a wild bird caught in the white man's traps left to flounder and drown in the swamp waters or to injure its great beautiful wings as it sought to escape. Her golden hair was matted and dirty, her face filthy, still carrying the marks of the spittle that had rained on her three days before. Her pale skin seemed almost translucent and he perceived that the three-day ordeal had taken much of her strength, yet she stood before them with more pride than he'd seen in any being, man or woman, Indian or white.

This was a woman who stood out among others. He remembered her as he had seen her that first day as she rode into the forest on her white horse. She had seemed like a vision to him then, incredibly lovely, but now she seemed more flesh and blood and he sensed a new strength within her.

A remembrance of the dream that had come to him the night before returned and desire for the woman warred with his duty to his people. He had made arrangements for her to go back to her own kind, and in return, Chief Tahullah and his families would be released to them. It was no longer in his hands. He had already related his dream to his people and its must be fulfilled.

Shocaw thought back over his dream. Could there have been some other interpretation of it, he wondered. No, it had been too clear. He had seen his people on one shore surrounded by the blue coats of the soldiers. His people were without weapons and food and the soldiers were approaching, ready to kill the Seminoles, when a great white ibis had swooped out of the sky, coming between the soldiers and the Seminoles. When it had passed by, the soldiers were gone. The great white bird circled above the Indians, then with one last call turned and flew away after the soldiers. Shocaw had known the great spirit meant for the white woman to return unharmed to her people.

The Micanopy, the old chief, stood up on his feeble legs and addressed the people of the village and the prisoner. His wavery old voice sounded weak and tired. Soon he would go to the great heaven, the Intoketa, where he would once again be young and hunt the deer and wild turkey, which would be plentiful there. Now he must try to guide his people through this evil made by the white man. Shocaw had found a way to help return some of the Seminoles to their homeland. The way was with the white captive they held.

Bree listened to his words, trying to discern her fate. Whatever happened to her now seemed not to matter as much as it once had. She thought of her dreams, once again seeing herself in the dugout floating between two worlds before the vessel took her to the distant shore with Shocaw and his people.

If this must be her life, so be it. She would survive. It would not matter. She would make these people her people. Above her, she heard the Indian chief speak and was aware of the other people of the village behind her. She must tell them she understood, she thought, but her head felt too light and dizzy. She must tell them she would not feel anger at being a captive of the Seminoles. She would learn their ways and obey them. The ground dipped and swayed in front of her and she stayed where she was, fighting to stand erect.

The Indian chief stopped speaking. The people of the village had heard Shocaw's dream, the medicine man had interpreted it, and he, Micco Onnitchee, had told them his will. Still the council must decide. Lopochee would object, but perhaps the others had listened and would decide wisely.

Micco Onnitchee looked at his people, and in

the silence that fell, the prisoner staggered forward and, gripping the edge of the platform, raised her wide gray eyes to the men seated there. In frozen silence everyone watched her. If she spoke unwisely now, she would be lost, the old chief thought, while Shocaw clenched his teeth in an effort not to cry out a warning to her. It seemed as if every member of the village held their breath, their eyes riveted on the girl.

"Hi-lo-lo," Bree said, and her voice rang out with electrifying clearness in the night air. "Hi-lo-lo." Her gray eyes closed and slowly she slid to the sand, her arms flung out gracefully, her long hair fanning around her head. A murmur ran through the villagers. The memory of Shocaw's dream of the great white ibis, who turned away the soldiers and chased them from Seminole lands, made them gasp in alarm.

She had walked among them with strength and pride, in spite of her punishment, the name of the great bird upon her lips, and now she lay crushed and still, her slender arms flung outward like broken wings. With a murmur they drew away and looked at their leaders. They hoped they had not offended the Mighty Ishtohollo, the Breath Maker, the two-sided god whose second name was Yohewah or Evil Spirit. This two-sided god brought all good things to man, but if angered, he could also bring evil. If they had offended him in some way, his wrath could be great, greater than they had ever felt.

Shocaw leaped from the edge of the platform and knelt above the still form, raising one eyelid to look at her eyes and bending an ear near her still chest to catch some slight sound or movement of life. At last he swooped her up into his arms and carried her to his chickee. Over his shoulder he called to Milakee and Cooee to follow and they hurried after him, their faces mir-roring their own concern for the prisoner.

The medicine man was summoned and he came, wearing his special robes and turban with its snow-white plumes. He brought his pouches of herbs, collected only from the north and east sides of special plants. He mixed them together while singing the age-old chants of his people. The herbs were placed over a small fire built on the edge of the platform and the medicine man blew through the reed while it brewed.

At last it was ready and could be administered to the patient. The medicine man stood and called upon all the spirits of nature to help draw back the ghost of the slight form before him. He walked from one corner of the platform to another call-ing upon the forces of the wind, the storms, and other gods and ghosts that wandered around the world. With his chants he wooed the ghost of the white captive so it would not escape on great wings into the night sky, and when he could do no more, he waited to see if his medicine would work.

The rest of the people waited with him. Shocaw crouched in one corner of the chickee watching the small pale face and remembered the anima-tion and joy he'd seen on it as she had ridden her horse. How proudly she'd carried herself, the wind whipping through her hair, spinning it be-hind her like a golden fan, while she had laughed with abandon. Now her laughter was stilled. Si-lently they waited.

The face was fierce. The black eyes, snapping beneath the white turban with the large white plumes, invaded her peaceful dreams. She bid the image go away. She wished only to rest, but the face would not allow her to sink back into darkness. She heard its chants floating around her, filling the air until there was no peace for her, no chance to slip away into the void that beckoned to her so enticingly.

She felt a great rush of wind as if wings were beating the air and she followed the sound to the light. When she opened her eyes, there were pine torches lit all around her bed. The disembodied head had a body and from the robes and pouches he carried she recognized the medicine man. Her eyelids fluttered down and opened again as she looked at him and saw the face was not so fierce after all.

"I'm hungry," she said in a clear voice, and those who had kept vigil over her sighed collectively. There was a sound of murmuring and laughter in the background. Over the shoulder of the medicine man, Bree could see Shocaw as he crouched in the corner of the chickee. His black eyes reflected the light of the torches and instinctively she knew he had worried over her. Tremulously she smiled at him, little aware of how it transformed her lovely face.

Shocaw felt the jolt of her beauty from where he sat. Her smile was like a sunrise after a storm, and he felt moved by it. Quickly he stood and slipped away into the darkness. Bree's gaze followed him until he disappeared from her line of view, then with a sigh, she allowed Cooee to help her sit up and Milakee to feed her from a bowl of hot stew. She was especially conscious of the rich yellow kernels of corn cooked plump and tender in the sofkee.

Her face was luminous, her eyes deep with the mystical secrets she'd seen. Every villager who looked at her face sensed she'd seen a vision. They'd heard her words, had seen the sign as she fell to the sand. But it was the look on her face that convinced them. They'd seen the same look on the faces of their holy men and their young warriors who were tested and so honored by the

Gods. Their hatred and suspicions were forgotten for the moment as they pressed forward to look at the white captive.

After she'd eaten, she rested again, her sleep dreamless, and awoke feeling refreshed and strong. As she walked to the fire pit for a bowl of sofkee for her breakfast, she was surprised at the deferential treatment the other women showed her. Each walked forward to touch her arm or hair with a gentle hand. Their faces smiled shyly at her. She was startled to realize she'd gained a new status among the people of the village. She was the object of a great warrior chief's vision and had had a vision herself. Such visions did not normally come to women, only to those very brave and honorable warriors who had proven to the great spirit they were worthy of such an honor. This white prisoner seemed to like them and to want to know them and their ways. Bree moved freely about the village watching the women at their chores and offering her help. In the time she had left among them she wanted to learn their ways, their language. She wanted to understand these people who worked so steadfastly to help themselves and who faced their hardships with such stoicism.

The women seemed to accept her offer of friendship. Even Toschee's shrill tongue was stilled.

When it was time to go to the fields, Bree took up a hoe and followed the women. Once there she tended the plants. Shyly, Milakee came to work beside her and the two girls laughed together softly. The sun was warm with promise on her head and shoulders and Bree felt strong under its light. As they worked Milakee began to teach Bree the Seminole language and that evening after supper Cooee came to sit at the chickee and continue the lesson. Bree knew he was there as much for Milakee as to help her.

Shocaw had not come near her since she'd awakened the night before. Bree felt hurt. She'd wanted him to see how she'd changed, that she was strong and flexible. She didn't want him to think of her as the weak, frightened girl he'd first brought to the village.

"Cooee," she asked now about something that had bothered ever since she'd come to the village. "What does Shocaw's *hoke-tee* mean?"

"It means you are Shocaw's woman," Cooee answered.

"But I'm not," Bree cried. Somehow she'd sensed the words had meant just that.

"It is best that others think you are," Cooee replied, and she could see the wisdom of his words. Although the villagers appeared to accept her, she could still see hatred in Lopochee's eyes each time he looked at her. His wife Toschee and Katcalani had remained aloof and cold to her overtures of friendship.

Although she'd seen little of Shocaw since the medicine man healed her, she knew her presence in his chickee still gained her his protection.

"Shocaw is very busy these days," she said now to Cooee.

"Yes," Cooee replied, and Bree railed inwardly at the Seminole's natural reticence.

"Is he angry with me?" she asked.

"He does not say," Cooee said, looking at her with rounded eyes. He was surprised at the thought. "He does not take time with anyone. He no longer sits around the campfire with the men. He stays alone. He has many things on his mind."

"I see," Bree said, and wondered if he ever thought of her.

"I will race you to fill the gourds and return to the village," Cooee said to Milakee, "and perhaps

you'll have time for a swim." Milakee smiled at
him sweetly, then leaped to her feet. Bree followed after them, feeling left out of their laughter and play.

The Indian women taught Bree many of their
skills, showing her how to weave the reeds and
grasses into sleeping mats. One day Bree went
with the women into the swamps to dig coontie
plants. She was as impressed by the women's
knowledge of the swamp as she had been by the
warriors. Carefully, as she'd been instructed, she
dug out the roots and placed them in a reed
basket.

Back in camp the women pounded the coohtie
root with rocks until it was pulverized. At first
Bree was clumsy in her attempts, but soon she
felt comfortable and worked quickly. They put
the pounded root to dry in the sun so it turned
fine and powdery. Then they sifted it through a
fine cheesecloth until it was as light and airy
and free of lumps as that used in the kitchens at
Greenwood. She would appreciate the breads and
pastries at home more, Bree vowed as she stood
at one end of the cloth and tossed the fine powder into the air. There was much laughter and
cheerful exchange of words which Bree didn't
understand, but she shared the mood of the
women.

She marveled at still another example of the
Seminole women's ability to find laughter and
joy in the midst of the danger and poverty they'd
endured for so many years. As her fear of the
Seminoles lessened and disappeared her understanding and admiration for them grew.

"Milakee, why do the women wear so many
beads?" Bree asked as they walked along. Most
of the women wore so many strands of the brightly
colored glass beads that their necks were covered
right up to their chins. Obviously they valued

their finery. Even Milakee wore two strands and seemed inordinately proud of them.

"When girl become *hoke-tee,* a woman"—Milakee smiled at finding the right word—"get one neck-lace beads every year. Many beads mean many years. Give much honor among our people."

"How old are you, Milakee?" Bree asked, and watched as the young girl signaled fourteen years with her fingers.

"How old Bree?" Milakee asked, and Bree showed her as she had been shown.

"Bree *hoke-tee,*" Milakee said. "Need more beads than Milakee." Bree nodded her head in agreement.

She was deeply touched when later in the evening Milakee brought her several strands of beads to wear around her neck.

Life was very hard for the people of Horse Creek Village and the young people assumed their duties at an early age. Yet they seemed happy for it. They were treated with love and respect and returned that respect to their elders. Even the Seminole boys were taken with the men when they went on their hunting trips, although they were left behind during the war parties. During those times the young boys carried their weapons, ever aware of their roles as protectors.

Bree had also noticed the boys were allowed to attend the black drink ceremonies with the men. She had often observed them proudly trailing after the men as they left the village for their secret meeting place. If a lot was demanded of the young people, they were rewarded with all the rights and privileges of the other men of the village.

In the evenings Bree perched on one end of the fire logs with the children while she listened to the songs and legends repeated to them and watched their mothers preparing food. It was her favorite time of the day. She tried to make herself useful in small ways and would hurry to the stream for water or play with a cranky child whose mother was busy. She loved the little Indian babies with their shiny button eyes and cheerful fat faces.

She had also become more familiar with the swamp sounds and knew how to get to the bathing pond without Milakee to guide her. She'd even made her way to the garden site, which was nearly two miles from the village. Her confidence in her ability to move about in the swamp grew daily.

One day as Bree was carrying the gourds to the stream for water, she made a wrong turn in the path and ended farther upstream than she'd intended, far away from the flowing stream where the sweet water could be found. Instead she came into a small secluded clearing where Cooee and Milakee stood staring into each other's eyes. So engrossed in each other were they, they didn't hear her approach. Cooee had lain aside his breechcloth and leggings and Milakee's colorful skirt and blouse were in a heap on shore. They had been swimming and now stood in water up to their brown thighs. Stunned and embarrassed, Bree stood where she was as Cooee reached out to gently touch Milakee's hair. His trailing fingers brushed across her rounded cheeks and downward to the firm, young breasts. Milakee's eyes never left his as her lips curved in a smile.

Bree drew in a breath and took a step backward, afraid of being caught spying on this intimate scene. They thought themselves alone. How on earth was she to get back without letting them know she'd seen them?

Even as these thoughts raced through her mind, a large warm hand curled about her wrist. With a start she swung around and confronted Shocaw.

For a moment his dark eyes filled with lights of amusement, looked deeply into hers, causing her to blush, then they raised to look beyond her to Cooee and Milakee. Quietly he drew her away, back down the path. Bree blushed to have him think she had been deliberately watching them.

"I—" Whatever she'd been about to say was cut off as Shocaw swept her against him and settled his mouth lightly over hers. Startled, Bree at first stood quietly in the circle of his arms. His lips were cool and firm against her own. His clean outdoor scent assailed her nostrils, the scent of the fragrant root with which he must have bathed recently and the lingering traces of leather and campfires. It was a rugged, masculine smell, which contrasted sharply with the sweet scents of the foppish men who'd always pursued her.

Those sensations flashed through her mind, chased by the thought that she shouldn't allow this. She brought her hands upward and settled them against the broad chest, intending to push him away, but the touch of his warm, bronzed skin beneath her fingertips and the quick hammering of his heart against her moist palm made her pause. Her own heart was pounding just as hard.

Shocaw drew back and looked deep into her eyes, their breaths mingling, then slowly, deliberately he lowered his head again. He was giving her time to resist if she wished, Bree sensed, but there was no will within her to push him away. Instead her arms slid up the smooth bulge of muscle and shoulder bone and around his neck as she raised her mouth to his.

Once again the firm lips touched hers, softly brushing against her full, soft mouth, which seemed to swell and tingle in anticipation of the contact. Her lashes lowered and her lips parted beneath the touch of Shocaw's tongue. Still he didn't claim what she'd surrendered so readily.

His lips continued to brush across hers, his moist
tongue touching then retreating until she felt a
trembling begin somewhere in some secret untouched part of her and spread outward to her
whole body. She felt the leap of nerve endings
and her breasts swelled fuller, straining to brush
against the bare chest of the tall Indian who held
her.

Shocaw, she realized dimly, must bend his head
down to fit his mouth to hers and her hands
reached upward and still could not meet around
his neck. Instead they moved restlessly, wantonly, back over his shoulder and chest muscles,
seeking to discover and memorize each dip and
valley, each curve and bulge of his sinewy body.

She longed to move downward to the hard ridges
of muscles across his lower chest and stomach
and to trace with her hand the curve of his
tapering waist, but that would have meant moving away from him and she had no will to do
that.

She stood like a captive bird while his tongue
and lips continued to tantalize her lips and cheeks.
A groan escaped her, and as if that were what he
was waiting for, Shocaw pulled her tighter into
his arms, his tongue plundering the sweet virginal recesses of her mouth. Now her breasts
were flattened against his hard chest, their hard
tips aching with sweet yearning at the contact.
The thin cotton blouse was nothing between their
two bodies. The heat of his body was searing
against hers.

His strong arms held her tightly and Bree was
forced to stand on tiptoe in an attempt to fit
herself to his tall stature. As if aware of her
discomfort, Shocaw shifted his hold on her, his
mouth never leaving hers, as his hands slid downward and gripped her buttocks gently, lifting her
upward against him. Now she could feel the bulge

of his aroused manhood against her own warm mound and felt a wild urge to part her legs and wrap them around him.

Shocaw lowered her back to the ground, letting her body slide slowly down his. His hard arousal raked across the sensitive mound of her own body, making her nearly cry out as if in pain, but she realized there had been no pain, only a terrible longing for more. As if he'd guessed her feelings, Shocaw pressed her down to the ground. His hands were quick and sure as they pushed aside the full skirts.

For a moment he hovered above her, then she felt his knee, hard and urgent, parting her soft thighs. She felt the brush of something hard and smooth and hot against her soft flesh. Her eyes opened wide in surprise, staring up at his intent face. She opened her mouth to protest, but it was too late. His eyes were dark with passion. With one mighty thrust he invaded her body.

Too late he learned the truth of her innocence. Too late he saw the pain on her face, heard her muffled cry, and he cursed himself even as his passion spilled forth into the silken warmth of her. He was helpless to withdraw. Groaning in regret, he buried his face in the golden tumble of hair in the warm hollow of her throat.

She lay quiet beneath him and he couldn't even feel her breath. He moved his lips along her cheekbones in a silent plea for forgiveness and his lips tasted the salt of her tears.

"I didn't know," he said softly. "I thought you were like the other white women I've known. Even the Seminole women go willingly with a man if she is unmarried." His large hand held her head as he gazed into her eyes.

"Have I hurt you?" he whispered, and mutely she shook her head. She felt too humiliated by what had happened to admit her pain. Disgust and shame raged with disappointment within her. There had been such desire pulsing through her, feelings she'd never known before, and they'd ended in pain and a curious feeling of emptiness. She wanted to run into the jungle and hide herself. All the wonder and peace of the past days seemed forever tarnished now.

Suddenly Bree felt angry and confused by what had happened. "Let me go, you filthy savage," she cried out, breaking out of his embrace and swinging an arm to catch him in a stinging slap across one lean brown cheek. "Don't ever touch me again," she cried. Her voice shook with denial and fear, fear of herself and her own responses to this Seminole. Shocaw's eyes became hard and cold as he released her arms.

Bree looked at him in confusion. Her angry, insulting words rang in her ear and part of her longed to call them back, while part of her was glad she'd said them, glad she'd made a stand against his assault on her senses. Now maybe he would leave her alone. She was going home soon, back to where men kissed a woman's hand and asked for no more. Flinging Shocaw one last look, she leaped to her feet and raced away down the path, the water gourds forgotten behind her.

When she reached the village, she went to Shocaw's chickee, hating that she had no other place to go, yet knowing this was where she was the safest. Besides, Shocaw seldom came here anymore. She huddled on the floor of the chickee and watched as the women moved about the fire.

Why had she responded to Shocaw as she had? she wondered wearily. She had been wanton, but she'd never known such feelings existed between a man and a woman. From all her knowledge, and it was admittedly limited and distorted by the girlhood discussions back at school, she had

thought the love between a man and a woman
was a comfortable, soothing emotion not unlike
what she felt toward her parents or her brother.
Growing up on a plantation, she'd learned early
what men and women did to make babies, but
she'd thought it was just something one did quietly and dutifully as one carried out other duties. She hadn't realized there were such feelings
involved, such a rush of emotions, savage and
untamable.

She thought again of the pressure of Shocaw's
body against hers and the sensuous, demanding
kiss that had left her heart pounding and her
body clamoring a new message to her brain.
Aghast, Bree pulled her legs tightly to her chest
and looked around furtively. Fervently she hoped
what had happened didn't show on her face.

When she was rescued, would her friends and
family know what had happened to her? Would
they turn their backs on her?

Suddenly the magnitude of what had happened
washed over her. She was no longer pure and
virginal. No man would want her now. She would
be scorned and whispered about behind her back.
She would no longer be received in certain homes.
She would become an outcast there just as she
was here. But it would be so much worse, for she
would be among her own people.

Well, no one would ever know. She would never
tell, she thought fiercely. She would pretend it
had never happened. She would never think of it
again. No, and she would never marry. She would
become an old maid and no one would ever learn
of her shame. Her secret would be kept safe
within her own memory. In abject misery Bree
cradled her head against her knees, not allowing
herself the comfort of tears.

In the distance she could see Shocaw returning to the village, carrying the water gourds with

him. He had taken time to fill them. What would she say to him, she wondered miserably the next time she saw him. She couldn't live here in his chickee with him now, yet no other chickee would take her in. She had been labeled Shocaw's *hoke-tee* and she must remain his prisoner until the time she was returned to her own people.

She must remember that. One day soon she would be returned to her own world. Then Shocaw and his power over her feelings would be forever behind her. She would be home at Greenwood with her mother and father. Her life would once again be as she had known it. These confusing emotions would be behind her. She prayed so, fervently she prayed so. She closed her eyes so she would no longer see the bronzed warrior.

Chapter 7

Bree did not go to the fire pit for food that night, electing instead to stay secluded in the chickee. Thankfully, Shocaw did not return to the chickee, but ate his food with a group of warriors who sat on their haunches in a circle away from everyone else. Tomorrow they would leave for another encounter with the white soldiers and they were deep in conversation.

Shocaw sat with the other braves, letting their talk swirl around him, his thoughts on the girl in his chickee. He hadn't meant to take her. He'd seen her on the path, the water gourds in her hands, and had known she was on her way to the stream. When she'd made the wrong turn, he'd followed her, afraid she might become lost. When he'd come upon her watching Cooee and Milakee, he'd taken her arm, meaning simply to lead her away quietly.

His kiss had been meant to silence her—or at least he tried to tell himself that. Inside he knew it wasn't true. He'd felt a hunger for her from the beginning, and when she'd turned to him with wide, startled eyes, her soft, pink lips parted in surprise, he seized the moment to do what he'd wanted to do all along.

The feel of her in his arms, the look of wonder in her eyes, and that small helpless groan of pleasure had made him forget restraint and give way to his passion. She'd felt his passion, had answered it briefly with her own, but he'd pressed her too soon. Women of the white men were not brought up as the Indian girls, with the freedom to express such feelings. She had been like a startled doe, quivering and uncertain on the edge of discovery, then she'd turned into a furious spitting tiger, striking out at what she hadn't understood. Shocaw cursed himself as he thought of her words. Had she really meant them?

Why did he bother? he asked himself angrily. He was going to return her to her people, who set great store by a woman's virtue. She'd been virginal when he'd taken her. She should have been returned to her people, her innocence intact. With an inner groan he set aside his uneaten food and turned his attention back to the talk of the other warriors. He must return the white prisoner soon, he decided.

Shocaw and his men left the village early the next morning, and from the excited murmurs of the women, she knew they had gone to fight against the soldiers. She tried to tell herself he was going out to kill her people, but it was hard to feel horror over that thought. The Seminoles were trying to survive in their homeland. It was the soldiers who were the aggressors as they hunted down the Indians, attacking their villages and killing their women and children. Her sympathies lay with the gallant people who struggled just to eat and stay alive in the swampland, asking little except that they be allowed to remain here in peace. Yet she didn't want to see her own people killed. Each day Bree's confusion grew.

Two days later, Shocaw and his men returned. There was no talk of fighting, but Shocaw in-

structed her in a cold, impersonal tone to ready
herself. She was being returned to her people.
Just like that. Bree could hardly believe her ears
as she stared at him. At last her trial was over.
She was going home. She was glad. Oh, she was
glad, she thought, as she flew around the chickee.
At last she admitted there was nothing for her to
get ready and she went to sit on the edge of the
platform and soak in the unbelievable, happy
fact that she was going home.

They left early in the morning of the following
day, before the sun had even tipped over the
black silhouette of the forest. Milakee was there
to bid farewell to her, and in spite of her joy at
returning home, Bree felt a twinge of sadness
that she would very likely never see Milakee
again. The two girls clung to each other briefly,
then broke apart, each giving the other a bright,
brave smile.

"*Mot-to*, thank you, Milakee," Bree cried.

"Thank you, Bree," Milakee repeated in her
gentle voice, the words heavily accented, yet how
proudly she said them to her new friend. Milakee
walked with them through the swamp to the
stream they would travel.

Bree's sadness over her parting with Milakee
was soon replaced by her happiness to be returning home. There was an eagerness in her eyes
and face and she smiled readily, even at Shocaw,
who was unable to keep his eyes from her face,
snared by the radiant beauty he saw there. How
happy she seemed to be going home. She looked
as if she felt no sadness at leaving the people of
Horse Creek Village. What had she once called
it—a godforsaken place. Tightening his lips,
Shocaw looked away from her and helped his
braves pull the dugouts from their hiding place.
It was best this way, he reminded himself.

This time Bree traveled in a far different style

from that in which she'd arrived. Dressed in the
sturdy cotton and calico of the Seminole women,
she was better protected against the insect stings
and the scratches of the sawgrass. Her legs and
feet were encased in moccasins of alligator and
deer hide to protect them from the rough coral
along the pathway. Her long golden hair had
been caught up in a knot much like that the
Seminole women wore, and she carried a small
gourd of water and a pouch of food fastened at
her waist.

They were to go by boat through the watery
swamplands, and Bree eagerly stepped into the
low wide canoe and sat on the flat bottom while
Shocaw took his place in the back and began to
pole away from shore. Cooee sat in the other end
of the canoe while other canoes followed.

"Aw-lip-ka-shaw," Milakee called to her from
shore, and Bree turned back to wave to her. In
such a short time Milakee had become a friend, a
sister to her.

"Aw-lip-ka-shaw," Bree called back, then
straightened as the canoe surged forward. A morning fog lay over the swamplands, and as she
looked ahead the stream disappeared into hazy
shadows of unknown terrain. A sudden chill swept
over Bree and for one moment she looked back
longingly at the shore.

Don't be afraid, she told herself. You are going
home. That's what you want. She thought of her
vision when her canoe had sat in the middle of
the stream and she had felt torn between two
shores, unable to push the canoe one way or the
other, until a current carried her along.

Above her, Shocaw pushed against the pole
and the canoe glided forward. I'm just being fan-
ciful, she thought, and resolved to think only
happy thoughts until she was back with her father and mother. Soon her nightmare would be

over; she was none the worse for it, thanks to Shocaw's mercy.

He was a strange man, she thought. He was obviously the leader of his people but he was nothing like the Indians she'd heard her father's friends speak of. The Seminoles were not so different, not so fierce and savage. She would tell her father that when she was home. Perhaps it would help if the soldiers and politicians knew that the Seminoles were concerned only with feeding their families and trying to live in peace. Knowing that, the two races should be able to end this terrible war and live together side by side. Perhaps with peace between the white man and the Indian some other young girl such as herself would not have to undergo the harrowing experience she'd known.

They traveled all day by boat, drifting through a world of beauty and danger. The sun burned away the mist and Bree's lips felt parched, yet she only took sips of water now and then. She'd learned the Indian's way of enduring the discomfort of heat. Shocaw seemed tireless in his poling of the broad dugout, taking only a moment now and then to rest. At midday they paused long enough to eat a cold meal of raw fish wrapped in palm leaves and dried jerky before resuming their journey.

At times they traveled through high, thick grass that closed about them like a wall and Bree wondered how Shocaw was able to keep his bearings. He seemed never to hesitate.

In the evening they paused in a clearing along the stream. Bree was glad to get out of the dugout and stretch her legs. They ate a cold supper, for Shocaw wanted no fires lit this close to the soldiers' encampment. They were getting close, Bree realized with a surge of joy. So close! By tomorrow she would be home. She would have some of Clemmy's ham sliced thick and fried until it curled around the edges. She wanted some fluffy biscuits and some of Mama's watermelon-rind preserves, her favorite, and pecan pie. She sat on a log fantasizing about her return to the plantation. She would take two baths every day and use a pound of Mama's French soap.

Shocaw came to stand before her, his black eyes somber and unreadable as he looked at her. There seemed to be an air of sadness about him, evident in the line of his shoulders and the planes of his face. All thought of food and luxuries offered by Greenwood fled from her mind as she studied him. She'd noted this sadness in Shocaw's eyes before and with a jolt wondered if it was because of her.

Shocaw reached out a hand, capturing a tendril of hair that had fallen from her knot. Gently he wound it around one finger, looking at its pale color against the tanned bronze of his skin. Bree held her breath. She could feel a trembling begin deep within and was confused by it. Shocaw's hand released her hair and moved to brush across the soft curve of her cheek and chin. His midnight gaze moved over her face like a caress.

Bree closed her eyes against the feelings that welled within her at his touch, remembering that day by the pond when his kiss had seemed to sear her very being. Suddenly she wanted him to touch her again, wanted to feel his lips on hers, his hand on her breast, and the thought made her eyes fly open and gaze directly into his.

His glance was magnetic, capturing her thoughts like scattered minnows in a pond. She saw his desire, naked and savage, undeniable, and some wild, untamed part of her longed to run to meet it with a desire of her own. Her breath was caught in her chest and she couldn't draw it out.

She was suspended in time and time whirled past them.

Kiss me, her eyes seemed to say, and her soft lips parted as if in anticipation. She wanted to feel the fire of his touch, his finely etched, sensitive mouth against her own. Her body longed to arch against the hard body bending over her. She wanted to throw off her clothes and lie on the soft ground before him, and at the same moment she felt that desire, she denied it. He was a savage. She couldn't feel this way about him. She was returning home. No decent well-brought-up young lady dared to feel such things for a man, much less a savage Indian.

Shocaw saw her emotions at war behind the stormy gray of her eyes, saw the desire, hot and intense as his own, and the denial and shock that followed. He saw the quick flush of shame at having felt desire for a half-breed Indian. He'd seen that look too many times in the eyes of the women of his youth and he'd taken great pleasure in erasing that look, changing it to one of supplication and acquiescence.

For a moment he thought of doing the same with her. He'd endured her taunts. It would be a sweet revenge to bend her will, to have her mewling and pleading for his touch before returning her to her people. She would carry forever the memory that she'd given herself to him willingly and she would hate him for it. Sighing, Shocaw drew back. Ever since that day by the pond he'd felt remorse that he'd taken her so thoughtlessly. It was best now if he returned her to her people and forgot her. Whirling, he walked away into the woods. He could hear her drawing in a quivering breath of air.

They arrived at their destination early the next morning. Once again a haze lay over the swamp, but Shocaw had gone unerringly to the spot. The

canoes were hidden deep among the mangroves
and two braves were left to guard them. The rest
of the party moved quietly down the path leading away from the stream. A taut wariness seemed
to possess the warriors. They traveled for nearly
an hour by foot and Bree was growing hot and
tired when Shocaw signaled the party to a halt.
With a few hand signs he sent half of his braves
off in one direction, and leaving Cooee behind
with Bree, he led the others in the opposite direction. Bree opened her mouth to ask what was
happening, but Cooee motioned her to silence.

As silently as they'd gone, the warriors returned
and with quick movements of their hands con-
versed with Shocaw. Tersely, he nodded his head
and signaled the party forward. Once again they
moved down the trail, their rifles ready, their
eyes alert as they constantly watched the undergrowth on either side of the path. At last they
came to a clearing.

The soldiers were already there. A folding table and camp stools had been set up and food
and bottles of whiskey set out. As Shocaw and
his party entered the clearing and paused near
its edge, a tall, thin man rose to greet them and
urge them forward. Bree recognized him from
the party the day she'd been kidnapped.

"Welcome to our good Seminole friends." The
officer came forward, his hand outstretched in
friendship. "I am Lieutenant Whitlock." His lips
were curved in a fixed smile, but his eyes were
guarded, moving restlessly from one face to another without meeting a single gaze directly. Bree
felt strangely unsettled by his nervousness.

"I am Shocaw Hadjo, nephew of Tollosee,"
Shocaw answered, and clasped Whitlock's elbow
in the traditional Seminole greeting.

"We are honored to have such a warrior chief
in our midst," the lieutenant said. His darting

glance had already caught sight of the slender
figure standing behind the warriors.

David Rikkar's words of outrage still rang in
his ears. They had not made enough progress in
rescuing the captain's daughter. At last he had
her. Returning Miss Rikkar to her father would
surely earn the wealthy plantation owner's gratitude.

"It is the Seminole who are honored," Shocaw
replied; his tones were clipped and pure with no
trace of the accent Cooee and the other Seminoles had.

"We have met many times in battle," he was
saying to the tall, young lieutenant. "You are a
brave and fierce warrior."

"I'm glad we meet in peace," the lieutenant
said, and again urged Shocaw forward. Still
Shocaw stayed where he was, his black eyes moving around the clearing, taking in the number of
soldiers. At the other end of the clearing sat an
old man, dressed in his ceremonial robes, and it
was obvious he was the Seminole chief who was
to be traded. His wife and children sat beside
him, their eyes downcast, their hands folded demurely in their laps.

"As you can see we have your chief," the lieutenant said, waving a hand toward the other end
of the clearing. "Would you like to speak to him?"

"I will greet him," Shocaw said, and followed
the lieutenant across the clearing. Bree started
to follow, but one of the soldiers gripped her
shoulder, holding her back. Shocaw's braves
passed around them and followed their leader,
fanning out in a protective flank. Bree was surprised at the small number of braves. She'd
thought they'd started out with a much larger
number.

When Shocaw and his small group of warriors
were halfway down the length of the clearing,

the lieutenant paused and stepped to one side, waving them on to speak to the captured chief in private. Idly Bree looked about her.

A muffled sound made her swing her gaze to one side and there she saw a soldier, branches and palm leaves tied about his shoulders and waist, shift position, his rifle raised to fire, his finger tightening on the trigger as he lined up the sights.

It was a trap! The lieutenant wasn't going to trade the chief for her, he was going to kill Shocaw and his men. All the times Shocaw had saved her life flashed through Bree's mind, and thinking of nothing else, she cried out.

"Shocaw!" Her cry echoed through the swamp and small clearing before the quiet was rent by the explosion of a rifle, then all was noise and motion. She saw Shocaw whirl and look back at her as one of his braves fell to the ground. Other shots rang out as Shocaw's men dropped to the ground and rolled to one side, seeking cover.

With a quick movement, Shocaw pulled the lieutenant in front of him, using him as a shield, his knife pressed against the lieutenant's exposed throat.

One of the soldiers, the one who had detained her when she would have followed Shocaw, gasped and crumpled to the ground, while behind her the sounds of shots being exchanged between Shocaw's men and the soldiers could be heard. Shocaw had left some of his men along the trail. He'd suspected a trap.

All around her men were shooting. Instinctively Bree dropped to her knees and looked around, not knowing where to go, which way was safest.

"Tell them to stop firing," Shocaw ordered the lieutenant as he pressed his knife point downward. Bree could see blood well around the point and run down the lieutenant's throat and onto

his shirt collar. His eyes rolled with terror and
she remembered all too well the helpless fear.
Still the lieutenant remained silent.

"Tell your men to cease firing," Shocaw ordered again, his face was fierce, his eyes implacable and cold.

"C-cease firing," the lieutenant called. The cry
echoed around the clearing and one by one
the soldiers stopped shooting. At last the clearing was silent, the soldiers and Indians standing
tense and expectant. Bree was reminded of a
scene from a play she had once seen, just as the
curtain went up. Any moment now the action
would begin, but for now all eyes turned to the
tall Indian whose strong, bronzed arms held the
lieutenant captive.

"*Ah-es-chay*," he ordered the old chief and his
family, nodding his head. At first the chief sat,
stunned and uncertain, his face reflecting myriad questions. He rose to his feet and his family
clustered around him.

"*Ah-es-chay*," Shocaw ordered again, and Bree
knew he was giving the old chief a chance to get
away first, while he held the lieutenant and his
soldiers at bay. For a moment more the chief
hesitated, his old face expressing a flare of hope,
then even to Bree's eyes, the hope changed to
resignation and he sat down again. His wives and
children sank back to the ground beside him.
There was no reason for him to return to the
forest. He was too old to fight anymore and there
was nothing in the swamps for him and his family
but starvation and death. He would go to the
new territory with his tribe and try to make a
new life.

He stared stoically ahead and Bree knew his
decision was final. Her eyes swung back to
Shocaw. How would he escape now? she wondered, and felt her heart squeeze in pain. She

didn't want to see him captured, not because of her. She wanted him to be free.

"Shocaw," she said, and the cry was wrung from her heart. His gaze swung back to her, then he was urging the lieutenant back across the clearing. The remaining braves stayed close beside him, their rifles cocked and ready, their dark eyes darting here and there at the soldiers who surrounded the clearing. The soldiers' rifles were ready to cut down the Indians the moment they knew it was safe for their lieutenant. At the moment it was a standoff, but one which Bree knew Shocaw must lose. He was outnumbered. Lieutenant Whitlock seemed to feel the same way, for he began to urge Shocaw to give up.

"You're never going to get away now, Shocaw. You might as well give up and not get any more of your men killed," he gasped as Shocaw half pushed him across the clearing. They came to a halt beside Bree. Shocaw's dark eyes bored into hers.

"*Aw-lock-chay!*" he ordered fiercely.

"No! No!" Bree cried. "You can't take me back." With a nod of his head, he indicated to one of his braves to bring her along and began to move back along the path. A shot rang out, a cry echoed through the swamp, and one of the braves fell to the ground. Bree screamed as he fell at her feet. Shocaw's blade sank deeper into the lieutenant's throat.

"Agh," the officer cried in pain. "No, cease firing," he ordered, and the clearing was silent once again. Silent shadows moved forward to gather up the fallen brave and carry him into the swamp. Numbly Bree moved along behind Shocaw, one of his warriors gripping her arm tightly. Their going was slow for the lieutenant hung like a dead weight on Shocaw's arm. The sounds of his whimpers carried back to Bree.

"Give up, Shocaw, otherwise you'll all be killed," he urged desperately. "At least, let me go. I won't let my men fire on you, I swear it. You can go free. We can forget all about this."

The man's voice babbled on. The soldiers were left in the clearing behind them, their rifles at the ready but useless since their commanding officer had called the cease-fire. Uneasily they looked at each other, uncertain what to do. As the group of Indians moved down the path and out of sight, they began to mill about. One soldier moved to the old chief and pointed his rifle at him in warning, but it was an unnecessary action. The Seminole had already made his position clear and made no move to escape.

When they had turned a bend in the path and could no longer be seen by the soldiers, Shocaw heaved the lieutenant away from him into some underbrush and, grabbing Bree's hand, signaled his men to race to the canoes. With Shocaw pulling her firmly along, Bree had no choice but to run as fast as she could. Her moccasined feet pounded on the spongy path as she ran, mindless of the brush and grass that tore at her clothing. Ahead of her Shocaw's men raced, their ranks thinning as some of them seemed to disappear into thin air. Behind her she could hear the lieutenant bellow to his men and heavy bodies crashing through the underbrush.

"Go get them. Kill them!" the lieutenant ordered, and she could hear the men giving chase like a pack of hounds after a fox. A hail of bullets pounded into the tree trunks around them. Had they no fear of killing her as well? she wondered, and renewed her efforts to keep up with Shocaw.

Ahead of them, Shocaw's men had disappeared, and as they rounded a bend in the path Shocaw wrapped an arm around her waist and leaped off the path sideways, his feet sinking into the mire. The braves who had been behind them ran on down the path. Shocaw placed her on her feet, pushing her toward a concealing thicket. They stood hidden, holding their breath as the soldiers ran past.

The thought crossed Bree's mind that she should call out. Shocaw had not covered her mouth and now she cast a quick glance at his face. His eyes were studying her. He knew what she was thinking, still he made no move to ensure her silence. He was letting her make her own decision. Bree stared into his eyes. If she called out, the soldiers would surely catch him, shoot him down in the mud like an animal. Her lips remained tightly clamped as she listened to the last soldier pass.

When they had gone, Shocaw signaled to her and they moved across the bog away from the path. Bree's skirts were wet and dragged in the mud with every step. She lost track of time or of how far they'd gone as they struggled through the swamp. At times they waded in water up to their thighs and Bree struggled to stay upright and keep moving forward. When she thought she could not pull herself out of the sinking mud for one more step, Shocaw's hand was there for her to cling to, his strength untiring.

At times they rested, half hidden in some rotting tree trunk or within the roots of a cluster of mangroves. No words were spoken. Shocaw was tense and watchful and Bree was too numb with disappointment. Had she only dreamed she'd be home by this time? The dream had seemed so real.

At last they returned to the spot where they'd hidden the canoes. Cautiously they approached, halting when a thin, melodic birdcall sounded on the air. Shocaw put his hand to his mouth and repeated the sound. From behind trees and bushes where they'd been hiding came his men. They were all there, save for the two who'd lost their lives in the clearing. Silently the braves pulled the dugouts from their hiding places. Shocaw helped Bree into one of them and she huddled down on the floor. She was becoming accustomed to this type of travel, she thought bitterly, and watched the shoreline as they left it behind.

So close! She'd come so close to being rescued. Why had the soldier tried to trap Shocaw? He had tried to act honorably, but they had met him with treachery. If not for the lieutenant's actions, she might be on her way to Greenwood this very moment instead of back to the Indian village. Bree lowered her head into her hands and felt like weeping, but no tears came. She was becoming too much of an Indian even to cry anymore, she thought bitterly.

They traveled late into the night before stopping to rest for a while. They took no time to build shelters but slept in the dugouts instead. Bree lay huddled against the side of the canoe shivering in the damp evening air. She felt feverish and hot, yet her body shivered uncontrollably.

She awoke once during the night to find Shocaw crouched over her, the moonlight reflecting the concern on his face. She must have cried out, she thought, and lay her head back. She half dozed, too cold and uncomfortable to rest well, moving about restlessly as she searched for a warm and soft spot to lay her head.

Sometime during the night she dreamed she was in her warm bed at Greenwood, her head finally resting on a soft pillow, another clasped to her chest for warmth. She awoke in the morning to find Shocaw lying beside her, her head pillowed on his shoulder, his arms wrapped around her for warmth. Silently she pushed against the warm wall of his chest and he opened his eyes and looked into hers for a long moment. Bree's breath caught in her chest as she returned his gaze.

There were so many questions to ask him, but now was not the time or place. Perhaps later when they were back at the village. As if he understood her thoughts, Shocaw rolled to his feet and gave a short sweet birdcall. In a matter of minutes the dugouts were under way again.

"She called a warning?" the general asked in disbelief, glaring across his desk at his junior officer.

"Yessir," Lieutenant Whitlock said, meeting his gaze steadfastly. His clothes were dirty and torn and there was a bandage at his neck.

"Are you sure? He may have sensed a trap."

"No sir. The Indian was walking into the trap as we'd planned when she called out. Several of my men heard it."

"Why would she do that?" the general asked no one in particular. David Rikkar shifted in his seat, his lips tightening in anger.

"She's gone Indian, sir," the lieutenant offered. "It happens to people when they get taken and held for a long period of time." He paused, casting a glance at the seated man. "She could be his woman."

"Be careful what you say, Lieutenant." Rikkar rose from his chair, his gray eyes flat and threatening.

"Sorry, sir," the lieutenant said. "It's just that we see this happen at times."

"My daughter is very tenderhearted. Perhaps this Indian was kind to her, saved her life, and she wanted to return his kindness. She surely wouldn't have wanted to see anyone killed in cold blood under a flag of truce."

The young officer's face paled at the criticism. "I was only following orders, sir," he said stiffly.

"Orders? My God, General." Rikkar turned to the commanding officer. "Haven't we had enough of this treachery? Are we to bear the dishonor of this war and its betrayals forever? It must stop."

"I've been ordered by Washington to end this war, Rikkar, any way I can," the general replied. Opening an inlaid wooden box, he took out a cigar and rolled it between his fingers. "You landowners are the ones who demand we get the Seminoles out of Florida. You can't have it both ways."

"What about my daughter's life?" Rikkar tried another tack. The things the general had said were all too true. "When you set this trap, did you give any thought to the safety of my daughter?"

"Of course, we did, sir," the lieutenant replied. "One of my men detained her at the end of the clearing. He had been assigned to protect her. When she cried out, he was shot and the Indians recaptured her."

"You were supposed to be rescuing her, not trying to capture a Seminole warrior against whom you all have a personal vendetta. For all we know she may have been killed."

"No sir, she wasn't. She ran with the Indians."

"Was she being forced to run?" the general asked.

"No, sir." The lieutenant glanced at Rikkar.

"Of course she was running." Rikkar cried, rounding on them. "What else could she do with her own soldiers shooting at her?"

"We weren't shooting at her, sir," the lieutenant said patiently.

"All right, you were shooting at the Seminoles. That's a mighty fine distinction when the bullets are whizzing past your head." Rikkar glared at him and this time the lieutenant dropped his gaze.

"I did what I thought best," he said.

"Now, now, Captain Rikkar, I can understand your concern—"

"Can you? Do you have a daughter, General? Has she been kidnapped by Indians? Was she shot at by your own soldiers?"

"See here, Captain Rikkar, I don't appreciate your tone."

"And I don't appreciate the way you've handled this, General. The Seminoles approached us with an offer to trade their prisoner, my daughter, in exchange for some tired old chief, who's too beaten down and weary to have much fight left in him, and you tried to set a trap. What chance is there of getting my daughter back now?"

"Begging your pardon, Captain, but there is a chance we'll find the village and rescue her."

"You'd better pray that you do, Lieutenant," Rikkar said hoarsely, "for if my daughter isn't returned to me alive and well, I'll hold you personally responsible." He said no more than that, but the lieutenant felt the same shiver of fear he'd known when the Seminole warrior held a knife at his throat. He had little doubt his life was meaningless if David Rikkar's daughter was not returned. He saluted and left the room. For the thousandth time he cursed the fate that had brought him to this hellhole.

Chapter 8

By late afternoon they were back at the village. The people came hurrying to greet them, murmuring in surprise when they saw the white captive was still among them. Katcalani's face was a study in fury.

Shocaw told of the betrayal and of the two men they'd lost and a moan of grief went up from the crowd. Some of the women turned angry, bitter eyes to Bree. Because of her, death had once again struck at their number. Menacingly, they moved toward her, but Shocaw's voice rang out. Bree could tell by the expressions on their faces that he was explaining how she'd called out and saved them all from capture or death. Their looks of anger changed, timid smiles replaced their scowls, and their bright eyes mirrored their acceptance of her. Only Katcalani's face continued to be hostile.

Food was prepared and the tired travelers repeated their story of the white man's duplicity and of the old chief Tallosee's decision not to return with his people to the swamps. Sorrow and a wary hopelessness settled upon their faces. Someday, would they too be faced with such a decision?

In spite of their joy over the warriors who'd
escaped the trap set by the soldiers, there was
much sorrow in the village for the two braves who
had been killed. As the night shadows fell, the
women moved about preparing their bodies for
burial. First, the dead men were clad in new
clothes, their faces painted according to their
status among the warriors. At sunrise they would
be buried.

Quietly Bree made her way back to the chickee.
So much had happened that day, but now in the
quietness and security of the village she could
begin to think of all that had transpired and to
mourn for her lost chance to return home to her
people. As much as she'd grown to care for the
people of Horse Creek Village, she wanted even
more to see her own family once more. She wanted
to go home.

She lay on her mat and thought about Greenwood, giving in to the anguish she'd felt ever
since they'd escaped Lieutenant Whitlock's am-
bush. She wanted to go home! Childlike, she
sobbed the words out loud.

Even in her grief she sensed that someone was
there at the edge of the shadows, listening, silently offering her his comfort and strength, and
she knew it was Shocaw. She turned away from
him and his unspoken offer, curling over as if to
hug her grief to herself. She was still too frightened
of her feelings for him, too confused by the emotions he aroused to trust what he offered.

Long after her sobs had quieted and her breathing drew deep and regular, Shocaw lingered,
watching the slender figure resting on its sleeping mat. At last, he turned away and went to his
makeshift lodgings.

Just before dawn the village people rose and
carried their dead deep into the swamp to their
secret burial place. Bree stayed behind in the

village, but she could hear their mournful death chants long after they were out of sight. They sounded lonely and sad.

Much subdued, the Seminoles returned to their village and set about their tasks. The men took up their weapons and went into the swamp to hunt for game. The women gathered their hoes and rakes and went to tend the fields. Bree followed after them. Silently she worked, her thoughts on Whitlock's betrayal. Once again she was Shocaw's prisoner, and she was more troubled than ever about her feelings for him. Her keen disappointment over not being traded back to her own people had lessened somewhat, replaced by a hopelessness about returning, a feeling that she would spend her remaining days here in this Indian village. Sleep was long in coming to her that night.

When she awoke the next morning, the village seemed strangely empty and she assumed the men had once again gone hunting in the swamp. She joined Milakee in tending to the hundreds of chores that seemed to fall to the Seminole women. Milakee seemed to bubble over with happiness, glad to have her friend back with her. Soon Bree could no longer resist the younger girl's infectious gaiety and joined in the laughter and snatches of talk as they worked.

In the afternoon as Bree worked in the small garden at the back of the chickee, laboring over the green plants as if she had no other care in the world except their growth, Shocaw came to her. His long muscular legs and feet, encased in soft deer and alligator hide, first caught her attention and she glanced up to see him smiling down on her. Caught off guard she could only stare at him.

"Come," he said, and held out a hand to help her rise, "it is time we talk." Together they strolled through the forest until Shocaw steered her to a quiet place by a stream. The sun shone through the leaves of the oak and quivering aspen to make a dappled pattern on the ground. Tropical orchids bloomed in trees nearby, the parasitic plants drawing life from the very trees that supported them. Spanish moss trailed from branches in an airy lacy pattern. Brightly colored birds filled the air with their sweet songs.

Bree and Shocaw settled themselves on the bank of the little pond and Bree thought of how beautiful she'd come to find the swamp. No wonder the Seminoles loved it here and didn't want to leave.

"What is it you wish to tell me?" she asked.

Shocaw studied her face for a moment, his eyes somber. "Once again your people have betrayed the flag of truce," he said. "This time my people will seek revenge." His features were grim and he no longer looked at her.

"Why do you tell me this?" she asked.

"Each day when we return, I see the question in your eyes, I sense the fear that we have fought and killed your people."

"It is true, I do feel those things," Bree admitted. "And yet I understand the Seminole's anger. I felt the same anger as we fled through the trees. I feel it when I look at your children and see the fear in their eyes."

He turned to gaze at her with eyes suddenly filled with hope. "You do not condemn me then for what I must do?" he asked. In sudden despair Bree turned away from him, hunching her shoulders in a defensive gesture. It wounded him to see her thus.

"I do not condemn you. I understand," she cried, "but I do not want to see my own people killed. How can I care for someone who may bring death and destruction to my family."

"Bree!" he cried, and reached out a hand to touch her shoulder. Something in the small, stiffly held body made him draw back. "I understand your pain," he said quietly. "I feel it too."

Suddenly she was reminded of the dead warriors they'd buried the day before and her anger melted. How could she possibly understand the dangers and choices Shocaw and his people faced every day and the measures they must take to protect themselves. How could she judge him by the standards of her own world when her own people acted without honor? She turned back to him and sought to speak of other things.

"How did you come to speak English so well?" she asked.

"I went to the white man's school as a youth," he replied.

"How did that come about?" Bree asked, thinking it a sign of goodwill between the Seminole and her people if they had accepted the Indian children into their schools.

"My father was a white man, an adventurer who came and took what he wanted from the Seminoles, then left without ever returning to find I existed. My mother was shunned by her people for her alliance with the white man. She had nowhere to go, so she went to live with a white man who was my father's best friend. He took care of her until I was born, then she returned to her people. At last they accepted her back, but her lot was hard. She died when I was ten and Billie came and adopted me. I lived with him until I was old enough to make the choice to return to my own people."

"He must have loved you very much to take you as his own child," Bree said, picturing an orphaned ten-year-old boy with dark rebellious eyes and a flashing smile.

"He did," Shocaw said softly, his thoughts

turned inward. "But I think he loved me because of my mother. He always hoped she'd return to him."

"Was she very beautiful?"

"Yes, she was," Shocaw said, and turned to look into Bree's eyes. "She had a gentle way about her."

"Why didn't you stay with the white man, why did you return to the Seminole?"

"Because I am Seminole. I belong with my own people. It is hard to live in exile from your own kind." His words were thoughtful and seemed to hold a special warning for Bree and for himself.

"Why did Lieutenant Whitlock try to trick you like that?" she asked.

"That is a question I wish to ask of you."

"But I wouldn't know the answer!" Bree cried.

"Neither do I. Many times the white men have tricked the Indians, capturing them when they go in to talk under a flag of truce or capturing their families to force the war chiefs to surrender. They have dealt with us dishonestly for many years. Their treaties are written on paper that flies before us like the leaves from the great oaks. We see them, then they are gone forever. The Seminoles no longer believe the white man's words."

Bree watched him, her eyes filled with sympathy. She longed to reach out and touch his shoulder to smooth the raven-black locks from his broad forehead. Shocaw glanced up and caught the look of compassion. Pride and anger flared in his eyes, then as he looked at the soft mouth and the face filled with tenderness and concern, the anger and pride died away to be replaced with something else.

Bree saw the light of desire growing in the dark velvet of his glance and shrank back. She wasn't ready yet to face her feelings for this man, but Shocaw had already reached out to capture her wrist with one large hand. He paused, measuring her retreat, then seeing the fire kindle in her expressive gray eyes, he swept her into his arms.

His strong arms lifted her toward him and she was sitting in his lap, his hard, sinewy thighs beneath the soft plumpness of her buttocks, the hard wall of his chest pressed against the yielding softness of her breasts. Her full lower lip was caught between small white teeth as she looked up at him through half-lowered lashes. Then as his hot breath struck her cheek, her eyes widened to stare into his, the message of passion unmistakable.

"Bree," he whispered, "my little bird, so wild and fierce." His lips closed on hers, hot and moist, his tongue lighting a trail of fire. She couldn't breathe and her heart hammered in her ears.

She pulled his head closer, parting her lips for his kiss. When at last he had gently tasted every wellspring of sweetness her mouth offered, he pulled back slightly and looked into her eyes. He saw the flare of passion and desire in the stormy depths and his lips lowered to trace the delicate softness of her closed eyelids before swooping once more to the soft fullness of her mouth.

His searing breath moved across her cheek, the tip of his tongue touching lightly at her sensitive earlobe and the hollow below sending a trembling through her limbs. One lean, brown hand traced the outline of her cheekbone, then the line of her jaw, the long graceful curve of her throat and collarbones, and downward to the soft mounds of her breasts. She could feel the heat of his palm through the thin cotton of her blouse as he cupped the full breasts and hardened nipples.

Her own hands moved frantically across the

broad shoulders, plucking resentfully at the calico shirt that covered the smooth, bronzed skin.

"Shocaw." His name cracked on the muggy air and Bree pulled away, dazed. Shocaw still held one hand at her waist as he looked back up the path. Katcalani stood there, her lovely face an angry caricature of itself. Her dark eyes spit fury as she looked at Bree.

"Ho, Katcalani," Shocaw greeted her. *"Nock-a-tee?"*

"Micanopy chi-yot-chee!" she said, and her voice was angry.

"Hi-e-pus-chay," Shocaw said reluctantly, and looked at Bree. "The Micanopy wants me, I must go," he said, lifting her from his lap. He bounded to his feet and stood before her, his dark eyes caressing her face.

"Do not run away from me, little bird. I will return quickly."

"No," Bree cried. Katcalani's presence had given her time to collect herself. "I won't be here."

"Why not?" Shocaw turned back to her, his perplexed gaze sweeping across her face. "There is this between us."

"There is nothing between us. I—I lost my head. I didn't mean to . . . go any further."

"Why?" Shocaw asked, and his dark eyes bored into hers again, demanding she give an explanation for what she could not explain, not even to herself. How could she tell him she had come to love him? She didn't want to love him. She stood mute before him.

"Why?" Shocaw demanded again. "Is it because I am an Indian? What did you call me before, a filthy savage? Is that why?"

"I—no—yes," she cried, looking up into his eyes. His anger hit her like a blow, crushing her breath from her, numbing any residue of passion she had left. What she read in his dark eyes was anger and hatred. Did he truly hate her, she wondered, and nearly cried out in pain at the thought. A moment before he'd held her and kissed her with more ardor than she'd ever known, now he looked at her with cold anger. Her knees trembled in the face of that anger and her own denied passions.

"Shocaw," once again Katcalani's voice reached between them, breaking the bridge of emotions that held their gazes locked. With a dismissive grunt Shocaw turned away and glided into the forest. Bree stood where she was, shaken by the depth of feelings she'd experienced in so short a span of time. At first she wasn't aware that Katcalani was still there observing her until the Indian girl moved closer to her.

"Shocaw mine, you not have," she said, and Bree looked at her, startled.

"I'm not trying to take Shocaw from you," Bree said. "I don't want him. I want only to go back to my own people." At her words, Katcalani's face grew slyly thoughtful.

"You want go back white man's village?" she asked.

"Yes, yes, I do," Bree cried. "I would be there now if I could."

Katcalani looked at her thoughtfully. "Tonight warriors take black drink. Tomorrow, fight soldiers. Tomorrow, Katcalani take you white village."

"You will?" Bree cried taking a step forward. "Do you mean it? Would you?"

"Katcalani not lie," the Indian woman said stoically. "No tell Shocaw anyone, they stop us."

"I won't," Bree agreed eagerly.

"Tomorrow, stay behind. No go to fields," Katcalani instructed.

"I'll pretend I'm ill," Bree cried.

"Wait. When women work, not see, Katcalani return. Take you to white soldiers."

"Thank you, Katcalani," Bree said. "I don't know how I can repay you."

"Shocaw belong Katcalani," the Indian woman said implacably. "You go away. No belong here."

"Yes, I'll go away," Bree said. It was what she wanted, wasn't it? This encounter with Shocaw only showed her more clearly how she needed to return to her own people where such passions were controlled and never felt. She would go with Katcalani back to her own people and leave behind all the confusing passions Shocaw aroused within her.

Katcalani had been right. That night the men were not in the village when the supper fires were lit. The women and children ate alone. The children were put to bed and the women gathered around the campfire to talk.

Without the presence of their husbands and brothers to inhibit their behavior, the women spoke freely of many matters of a personal nature and not a few men had been in for their share of comparison as the women's tongues clacked.

The Seminole women's attention turned to Milakee, who came into a share of teasing over her courtship with Cooee. Bree was startled when she realized the women knew of Milakee's affair with the young brave and did not disapprove.

"If not married, man and woman come together. It is good. If baby comes, woman keep. Take care." Bree looked at her in shock. How different were the Seminole customs.

"If married, man and woman come together, not husband, not wife. It is bad! *Hal-wuk!* Cut off nose!"

Bree shrank back in horror at Milakee's words. The Seminole laws were much stricter than those of the white man regarding adultery. How many husbands and wives adhered rigidly to their marriage vows in her own world? A sudden picture of some of the more elegantly dressed Southern aristocracy dancing about the room without any noses came to her and she giggled. Milakee giggled with her, not understanding the cause for merriment, but joining in nonetheless.

The soft murmur of the women wove around them, giving Bree a sense of belonging. She didn't really belong, she reminded herself, and after tomorrow she would never again sit around the campfire with these women who were not so unlike the women of her own people. The thought was sobering, and soon she found herself unable to enjoy the gentle evening. Excusing herself, she made her way back to her chickee and prepared herself for sleep. All around her she could hear the sounds of the swamp, sounds that had become familiar, if not comforting, to her.

The background noises were punctuated now and then by a high shrill war whoop.

"Yo-ho-ee-hee!" echoed through the night, drawn out and fierce. A shiver ran over Bree's shoulders and down her spine. Was this the right decision, she wondered. Should she try to escape tomorrow or should she wait until Shocaw made other arrangments for her release? Eventually he would, she was sure, and perhaps the next time the soldiers wouldn't try to trap him. She wasn't being treated badly. In fact, she'd come to enjoy her days here in the village.

Yet if she stayed, she knew the time would come when she could no longer pull back from the attraction she felt for the Seminole warrior. Even today, how close she'd been to giving herself to him again. To remember the feel of his hard body against hers brought a tingling ache to her own body. These feelings were too pagan for her well-brought-up notions. She wanted to go back home where she knew what to expect and where she was in control of her senses when a man kissed her. Wrapping her arms about herself, Bree huddled beneath the soft furs and breathed deeply, willing herself to sleep. Tomorrow she would begin her journey home and leave Shocaw and his fiery lovemaking behind forever.

"Bree!" A voice penetrated her dreams.

Bree raised her head and looked into Milakee's merry eyes.

"Ha-sha-i-sit!" the girl said, and pointed upward to the golden sunshine. *"Aw-lock-chay."*

"Munks-chay," Bree said, shaking her head negatively. Sitting up, she held her head in a pantomime of feeing bad. Instantly Milakee's face showed concern.

"Bree sick?" she asked sympathetically.

"Ho," Bree replied, and laid her head back on her rolled pad. She must make Milakee believe she was too sick to go with them into the fields. Milakee believed her and soon left to join the other women, casting glances back over her shoulders. Bree stayed where she was, her head down, her lashes lowered as if sleeping. Through slightly parted lids she observed Katcalani leaving with the other women. She too cast glances at the chickee where Bree lay. When the women had disappeared down the path, Bree sat up and threw aside the robes, uncertain now of what she should do. Should she follow after them and let Katcalani know she was ready to go? The question was answered for her when the Indian woman came hurrying back to the village square.

"Come, quick," she ordered, and barely gave Bree time to climb down from the chickee before she plunged into the swamp, going in the opposite direction the women had taken. Bree hurried after her, startled that Katcalani had taken no time to gather food and water for their journey. It had taken two days when she'd gone with Shocaw and his men, but Katcalani moved too quickly for Bree to ask.

In no time at all they were well away from the village and the dense semitropical growth closed about them. In the muggy heat Bree's blouse was soon soaked with perspiration and her hair clung to her cheeks. The sun rose high in the sky, burning down on them relentlessly. Bree often put up her left hand to shield her eyes from its glare. They had been walking for hours and she felt as if she couldn't take another step.

"Katcalani," she called breathlessly, but the Indian woman moved on doggedly. Did she never tire? Bree wondered.

"Katcalani, I am tired. I must rest for a moment," she cried, her voice startling a flock of birds.

They swirled in the air, calling out warnings to one another, finally flocking together to fly eastward into the sunlight.

Bree paused, shielding her eyes and looking after them. They had become mere silhouettes against the sky. A tremor of warning shot through her. The birds had flown into the sunshine, flying eastward, and all morning she had been shielding her eyes with her left hand. If they were going northward toward Fort Brooks, the sun would have been on her right.

Perhaps there was a reason. Perhaps it was easier to travel by land this way or maybe Katcalani was skirting some large marshy area and would swing back north soon. But her heart hammered in her chest. She knew it wasn't true. They'd traveled for too many hours in this direction. They were going south!

"Katcalani," she called, hurrying down the trail. The Indian girl had disappeared ahead of her. Bree hurried to catch up.

"Katcalani!" she called again, but there was no answer and no glimspe of a brightly colored skirt on the path ahead. Frantically, Bree ran on, calling the Indian woman's name, but her voice echoed emptily in the great swamp. Everything had grown silent and still, the animals startled into silence by her unexpected presence and the panic in her voice.

"Katcalani!" Bree screamed, and the scream turned to a sob. She couldn't have been left alone here in the swamp. Katcalani couldn't be so cruel. Bree stopped running and looked about her with wide, frightened eyes, her chest heaving as she drew in air. Katcalani's name died on her lips and in its place came another name.

"Shocaw," she whispered, and the sound was like a prayer. She looked around the vast deadly swamp, and all too clearly she could see her folly. She had trusted Katcalani, the one person she shouldn't have trusted. The Indian woman had seen Shocaw embrace Bree and had felt jealous and threatened by the white captive. She'd never intended to take Bree back to her own people. She'd meant only to lose her in this endless tract of swamp. Surely, Bree would die here.

"I won't die, I won't!" Bree cried. Springing to her feet once again, she began to run wildly through the jungle looking for some path or trail she could follow. "I'll find my way back," she said out loud, for the sound of her voice gave her some measure of courage. "I won't die!"

She ran on, heedless of the heat until her breath was coming in great heaves and the perspiration rolled off her brow and into her eyes. Too tired to go on, still she pushed herself onward until she tripped over a piece of coral and fell sprawling across the path.

Her cry of terror and surprise turned to sobs of despair and she lay where she was and wept. At last the sobs slowed and she drew in great gulps of air. She might have stayed where she was, indulging in more tears, but the familiar bay of an alligator split the afternoon stillness and she sprang to her feet, her legs trembling beneath her.

Her life was truly in danger, more than at any time since she'd been captured by the Seminoles, and if she were to survive, she must calm herself and use some common sense. She had little hope that any of the Indian women would come after her once they realized she was missing. Even Milakee would not come, though she might want to.

"Shocaw will come," she whispered, and knew with certainty deep inside her that it was so. He would track through the swamp and find her when he learned she was missing, but he and the other braves had left before dawn, and who knew how long they would be gone. Sometimes they did not return to the village for several days. She was on her own.

The thought brought a moment of panic, then she calmed herself and looked about. In her wild plunge she had lost all sense of direction. The sun sat straight up in the sky now and gave her little clue as to which way to go. A second bout of panic assailed her and was subdued when her frantic eyes noticed the moss growing along the ground and up one of the tree trunks. It grew on the north side of the trees Cooee had pointed out to her once. She and Katcalani had traveled southward all morning. She had only to reverse the direction and walk back to the village. She would be back before the evening meal, she told herself, and started out confidently. It would be satisfying to see Katcalani's face when she walked back into the village.

Keeping that thought uppermost in her mind,

she walked through the sunlit swamp. It wasn't
nearly as frightening to her as it once had been
and she reflected on how much she'd changed
since her capture. She was learning to be as
independent and self-reliant as the Seminoles
were.

The afternoon dragged on and Bree pushed
onward, determined not to give way to the panic
that waited just on the edge of her consciousness.
The thought of finding a tiny Indian village in so
vast a swamp seemed childishly optimistic to
her, especially when she remembered how well
it was camouflaged by the swamp growth. Still it
was the only hope she had to cling to. Stubbornly
she pushed on, skirting black watery bogs and
deceptively still ponds of water where alligators
waited, their crafty eyes looking at her lazily as
she hurried away from them. Great cypress trees
growing from the watery soil, their branches
draped with limp wisps of Spanish moss, often
blocked the path, the skeleton of the bony knees
of their roots interlacing in impenetrable barriers.
Time and again she had to backtrack around
some obstacle she couldn't remember passing when
Katcalani had led the way. Once she even discovered she'd simply traveled in a circle and
arrived back at the same point from which she'd
started. After that she tried to be more careful in
reading the signs that led her northward.

The sun began to move downward across the sky
and Bree knew her time was running out. As if
pulled by its own weight, its setting was quicker
than its rising that morning. Panic sat in Bree's
mouth like bitter bile.

As the sun disappeared behind the trees and
shadows deepened in the swamp forest, she grew
frantic and rushed on heedlessly, no longer paying
attention to the moss and other forest signs that
might have helped her. She hadn't eaten or drunk

all that day and she felt weakened, her mouth dry and cottony. Her stomach growled its needs to her.

When the sun had set and there was no light in the swamp, she couldn't tell where the dry hammocks ended and watery sawgrass began. She knew she was in danger of stumbling into poisonous snakes or alligators, but still she couldn't bring herself to stop until she tripped over a root and plunged full-length into a muddy pool.

Snorts and cries greeted her headlong sprawl, making her leap to her feet and back onto the last bit of dry land her feet had touched. Her screams turned to whimpers as she huddled on solid land once more. She couldn't go on like this. She must find a place to sleep. Spending the night in the swamp held a special kind of terror for her, but she had no choice. Feeling about with her hands, straining to see through the darkness, she found a relatively solid piece of land and settled at the foot of a tree, her feet tucked beneath her.

She was sure she would never sleep. Her eyes were wide with fright as she stared into the darkness, listening to the screams and cries of the teeming life of the swamp. Her muscles grew stiff as she sat on the hard ground. Forcing herself to relax, Bree leaned back against the tree and lay her head back.

Would she ever see Shocaw again, she wondered. What would he say when he returned and saw she was no longer there in his chickee? Would he care? She was startled that her thoughts had turned to him and not her parents as they once would have done. She hadn't been wrong to try to escape the dominating presence of the Indian chief. His mastery over her mind and emotions was too complete. Yet, she wondered, peering through the darkness, listening to the swamp's song of danger and death, was it better for her to die here in the swamp than to submit to Shocaw and the passion he aroused within her? Yes, she told herself while her mind whirred with the thought that her life was a terrible price to pay to resist that passion. Wearily she lay her head back and closed her eyes. Just for a moment, she thought, just for a moment.

She awoke with a start, wondering where she was. The early morning sunlight streamed through the trees to touch her face. Looking around, memory returned to her. Her eyes darted here and there. Some sound had awakened her. What was it? Again she peered around, checking for danger, and her gaze caught the glimpse of movement.

Again the scream of a bird rent the air and now she understood why. An alligator had left the water and was hauling his long, fat body up the steep embankment toward her, his short fat legs scrabbling for a hold in the slippery mud. His evil eyes were fixed on her in a hypnotic stare. Bree drew in her breath and scrambled to her feet, putting the tree between herself and the approaching lizard. Steadily he crawled toward her.

With a cry she turned and plunged through the undergrowth, unmindful of the pain as branches ripped her clothes, skin, and hair. She ran, her hair streaming behind her, climbing over the tangles of vine and cypress roots, her fear lending her strength to tear through their restraining barricades. As she ran, she cast frantic glances over her shoulder at her evil pursuer. At last, thwarted by the roots and underbrush, the alligator gave up the chase and went back to his pond, where morsels of food could be had with less effort. On open ground he could have caught her easily. Bree ran on, not trusting that she was really safe from him.

Chapter 9

Shocaw pushed on through the swamp, pausing now and then to look for footprints in the soft earth. He had left as soon as there was light enough to see, dread growing within him that he was already too late.

He had returned late last night, tired and discouraged. He and his warriors had joined Coacoochee, who was their most respected war chief. Once Coachoochee had fought at the side of the mighty Osceola and had often outfoxed the soldiers, leading his men to safety from under their very noses. This time they had attacked a supply train and captured badly needed ammunition and other supplies, but there had been little or no food. What good did it do? he reflected. They could fight on for a few more weeks, a few months, but every day their number dwindled as the beaten Indians made their way out of the swamps to the stockades at Fort Brooks. As they neared camp, his thoughts turned to Bree and he looked forward to seeing her, to sitting across from her in the chickee while they ate the food she'd brought from the sofkee kettle.

He had gone directly to his chickee, but Bree was not there. As he'd stood debating where to

look next, Milakee had come with lowered head
to tell him Bree was gone. She had forced
Katcalani to lead her into the swamp. Katcalani
had escaped and made her way back to the village. The women had gone to look for Bree, but
had not found her. She was still lost in the
swamp.

"We took the northern trail," Katcalani had
said when he questioned her, but later Milakee
had come to him and spoken in her shy, quiet
voice.

"When Katcalani returned to the camp, she
came from the south," Milakee had whispered,
her face filled with concern for her lost friend.

Now Shocaw moved on, widening the circle as
he searched for a sign that two women had passed
this way. At last he found their trail and it was
heading south. Katcalani's prints were first leading Bree away from the camp. His eyes narrowed
and only the tightening of his lips showed his
rage as he pressed on.

He traced them to the place where Bree had
paused to watch the flock of birds fly into the
sun. He saw where Katcalani left the trail, jumping wide into the underbrush so she left no trail
to be followed. Only another Seminole who was
familiar with the practice could have found her
footprints. He followed the print of Bree's moccasins as she ran along the trail, the deeper heel
print giving silent testimony to the panic she'd
felt.

Quickly he pushed on, his heart beating un-
evenly in his chest as he followed her erratic
trail. At one of the ponds where fat, lazy alligators nested about the shoreline, the trail disappeared and Shocaw searched carefully about the
bank, looking for some item of clothing, anything
that might have been left behind if the alligators
had taken her. Then he moved backward, searching

for more prints. His heartbeat evened out when he found one. She'd seen the danger and skirted it. Hope rose within him.

In the afternoon he found the place where she'd spent the night and felt a moment of anger at the alligator that rushed him. At another time he would have taken the giant lizard for its skin, but now he ignored it and walked on. Her prints had disappeared and his heart tried to deny what his mind told him must be so. Somewhere she'd met her fate.

Shocaw tracked backward, looking for any sign that Bree had left the path, but there were no small footprints. He tracked all the way back to the bank where the alligator had charged at him and stood looking at the ugly reptile, wondering if this was where Bree had ended her struggle. He raised his eyes to the sky. He wanted to cry out his grief to the wind and the trees.

An unexpected breeze rattled the branches and Shocaw glanced around, wondering where to go next. It was the movement of a tiny piece of bright cloth waving in the breeze that caught his eye. He plunged into the watery undergrowth. Catching the cloth to him, he looked about expectantly. It was from Bree's skirt. He remembered the color. She'd passsed this way, scared from the trail by the rush of the bull alligator. Hastily Shocaw moved on.

She had left the safest part of the trail and ventured into water that was thick with poisonous snakes and fish. If he were to rescue her in time, he must hurry. His muscular legs churned in the ankle-deep water, kicking a spray of crystal droplets ahead of each step.

He did not ask himself why he felt this fear for his captive's safety. He'd already worried it about in his mind for too many days. It was time to put aside the excuses and accept the truth. His race through the swamps was not to save a valuable white captive useful for bartering with the white soldiers. Although he would have tried to save anyone lost in the swamp, he wouldn't have felt this numbing sense of helplessness, this panic that threatened to invade his practical mind and strictly controlled emotions. It was the thought of Bree's flesh torn from her bones by the greedy teeth of the sly *al-la-pa-taw*, the alligator, that set his heart pounding and his feet churning relentlessly onward. Gladly he would give his life for hers. She had touched him as no other woman had. Shocaw, the mighty warrior, the brave war chief, had fallen before the gentleness and beauty of a mere woman.

When he first caught a glimspe of her, he felt confused, disbelieving. His blood sang in his ears. His muscles were tensed, ready to fight off any danger that threatened her, and there she sat on a stump, holding one foot over a knee, rocking back and forth, a tear staining one cheek. A sadly worn moccasin lay discarded on the ground beside her.

The late afternoon sun cast a glimmer of gold through her hair and around her figure. The trailing Spanish moss and the deep green forest were dramatic backdrops for the slight figure who perched like a brilliant, delicate butterfly. Birds and insects lent their music to the moment. So beautiful were the swamp and the figure of the girl that Shocaw stood for a moment, spellbound.

She looked so at home here, so unafraid, that he wondered if he'd panicked himself into believing she was in danger. Then he remembered the fat alligator that had driven her from the trail and the other dangers that lurked beneath the waters of the swamps, and the enchantment was broken.

"Bree," he called softly.

She looked up, startled, and saw him standing there. Her gray eyes grew wider as if in disbelief, which then changed to relief and joy. Heedless of her bare feet, she flew across the short expanse of water and flung herself against his chest.

"Shocaw, oh Shocaw," she cried, and her slender arms twined about his neck and shoulders. His own arms closed about her slim body, catching it to him, holding her tightly against his pounding heart.

"Shocaw, you came for me. I knew you would," she cried, half laughing, half crying as she rained kisses on his hard jaw and neck.

As the first surge of relief wore away, she drew her head back and looked deep into his eyes. Her words were between them. She'd known he would come for her. There'd been little doubt of that, just as there was little doubt of the other feelings that existed between them.

Shocaw felt it too. His breath was ragged as he held her against him, his shoulders curved as if he would wrap himself around her and thus protect her from any dangers she might face. She was alive! His heart seemed to beat out the joyous refrain and only then did he know how much he cared for her. He held her away from him and looked at her face, pale with exhaustion and fear. Sweeping her up in his arms, he waded through the shallow water back to the knoll where she'd been resting when he first found her, and there he set her gently back on the stump. Taking up his water skin, he held it out to her.

"Drink," he commanded gently, and her eyes met his gratefully, while her hands closed about the water pouch and raised it to her lips. "Slowly," he ordered when she would have drunk too quickly, and obediently she took small sips.

Shocaw opened his pouch and brought out coontie bread and venison for her, and while she ate, he knelt on the muddy ground and tied the moccasins in place about her slender calves.

Bree sat with her foot propped on his bent knee, looking at the raven-black hair and the strong planes of his face. How gently he tended to her, and yet how strong he was. Suddenly she was glad Katcalani hadn't taken her to the soldiers. She might never have seen Shocaw again! Her very soul seemed to cringe at the thought. Hungrily her eyes studied every line of his lean body. Shocaw looked up and caught her look.

"Bree!" he whispered, his dark gaze moving across her face, then he lifted her against his chest, so her lips were level with his. For a moment more she returned his gaze, her expression full of wonder at this discovery between them, then her lips were raised to his, opening beneath his questing tongue, returning as fervently as they received his message of love and commitment. There were no reservations. They might come later, but for now there was only Shocaw, only his tall, invincible body and his lips branding her as his own.

She gave no thought that she was his prisoner, that because of him she had been taken from her family and the life she'd known. In that moment she realized she'd never existed before this man touched her. She was his, more of a prisoner than he had ever thought to make her, because she gave herself willingly, wholeheartedly.

Her kiss told him everything, all her feelings, her pledge of commitment, even the lingering reservations that might arise in the future. She gave herself into his keeping and Shocaw accepted the gift as one to be treasured and handled lovingly. It was a gift he wished never to lose.

His arms, strong bands of sinew and muscle and bone, held her protectively, giving comfort, giving strength. His lips gave a promise, a pledge of love that would never fail her.

At last, both drew back, breathless. Their eyes shone with lights of joy and sudden shyness in the face of such overwhelming emotions. Their minds sought for more everyday things to lend a touch of reality to their dreams.

"What happened? How did you come to be here?" Shocaw asked. He wanted to hear her side of the story.

"Katcalani tricked me," Bree said. "She told me she would take me back to the fort. Instead she brought me out here and left me."

"She will be punished," Shocaw said, then paused, one question still nagging at him. "Why did you leave?" he asked, his dark eyes searching her face.

"I was frightened," Bree whispered.

"Of me?"

"Of myself."

"Are you frightened now, little bird?" he inquired softly.

"A little," she admitted, "but I won't run away again."

"You will never need to." Shocaw said. He lifted her small chin so their eyes met. "When you wish to go, I will take you to your people."

There was nothing for Bree to say. She had no desire to return to her people, not now. Perhaps someday she would return to see her mother and father once again, but her life was with Shocaw now.

"We must go," he said to her, for some instinct told him this was no longer a time for words. He must still go slowly until she'd gotten used to the commitment she'd made.

She'd pledged herself to him, thrown away her old ties, given a silent promise to become part of his world. She felt overwhelmed by her feelings and groped backward in her mind and feelings for that girl she'd been when she'd first galloped into the pine forest. But that girl was forever gone. Again she felt frightened.

Shocaw stood up and, taking her hand gently in his, pulled her to her feet. His grip was firm and reassuring. Glancing up, Bree saw the warmth and understanding in his dark eyes. He would not rush her, he would give her time to adjust, to be sure, but he would always be there when she wanted him. And she would always want him. Her heart surged with happiness and she smiled up at him, a smile filled with sunshine and a joy for living, a smile that took his breath away.

Like others before him, he was captivated, enchanted, and for a long moment he stood gazing into her eyes. His strong fingers stroked her trembling ones as he folded her hand against his chest. Beneath her palm she could feel the beat of his heart, strong and sure, and like everything else about him, it reassured and sustained her.

Her knees trembled with fatigue. She had spent the last two days and night fighting an overwhelming fear, and now that Shocaw was here that fear was gone. She wondered how he had such an effect on her. Gratefully she accepted it as part of her life now.

"We'd better go if we want to reach the village before nightfall," Shocaw said, gently stroking the soft skin of her arm. "Are you able to go on now?"

"With you here I am," she replied simply, and followed where he led her. They wound through the cypress trees, through ankle-deep water until they reached the high ground that sat a few inches above the marshy water.

The snake struck swiftly, sinking his fangs deeply into Shocaw's thigh. Bree saw it happening, saw the long glistening body strike then leap away, slithering into the underbrush, but Shocaw made no outcry. At first she thought she'd been mistaken, that her eyes had played tricks. Then, as if in slow motion, she saw Shocaw grip his leg and fall forward to the ground. Even as he fell, his hands were reaching for his pouch.

"Shocaw," she screamed, jerkily dropping to her knees beside him. It couldn't be, she thought. It couldn't be happening. She was having another nightmare, but the grimace on his normally calm face was all too real. At first she couldn't tell where the snake had bitten until she saw the puncture wounds through the light leather leggings just above the knee. Before she knew what was happening, Shocaw had his knife in his hand and was cutting away at the leggings, then with quick downward strokes had sliced across the wound.

"What are you doing?" Bree cried in consternation.

"I must suck the venom out before it kills me," Shocaw said, and bent his head.

Bree watched as he tried to reach the wound with his mouth. A shudder passed through her. Again and again Shocaw strained toward the puncture, and at last sat back and looked at her with hopeless eyes.

"Quickly, tell me what to do," she cried, looking into his eyes. There was no hesitation within her. She was Shocaw's *hoke-tee,* his woman. She must help him.

"You must draw out the venom," Shocaw said, "but don't swallow it or it will kill you. Spit it out each time. Can you do it?" His hand gripped her arm, his eyes held hers. She sensed he would rather die himself than risk her life.

"I can," she answered strongly, while inside she trembled with uncertainty. He must not die. Kneeling beside his thigh, she bent over and placed her lips on the hard muscular flesh near the wound, and as Shocaw guided her, she drew the venom from his body with her mouth. Her mind was filled with a jumble of half-formed prayers for his safety.

"That should be enough," Shocaw said finally when the wound bled freely and the blood ran bright red. Reaching inside his satchel, he took out a powder and had her sprinkle it into the wound.

"What is this?" she asked, doing as he'd instructed.

"It is a medicine from a special root here in the swamp. Don't worry, little bird, Seminoles rarely die from snake bite. We have magic medicines we use against it."

"Oh, Shocaw, I hope it works," Bree cried, longing to throw herself into his arms yet sensing she must show strength now. Instead she tied a piece of her calico skirt about the wound.

"Come help me to my feet," Shocaw said.

They made their way along the leaf carpeted path, Shocaw using her slight form as a support. She never winced at the weight of his body. She was too happy to have him there.

They stumbled into the village after dark, and if it had not been for Shocaw's mumbled directions, she would have walked right on past. A dog barked a warning and the villagers came running. Someone took the weight of Shocaw's body upon his own shoulders, then others came to lift him and carry him to his chickee.

The villagers gathered around Bree, asking questions, expressing their happiness that they were back safe. In the background Bree could see Katcalani skulking, her face closed and angry. There would be time enough later to deal with her. For now she must see to Shocaw.

"I'm all right," he murmured in protest as they settled him on his sleeping mat, but the medicine man was sent for.

After the medicine man had gone to the four corners of the chickee and called upon the forces of nature to heed his chants, he turned to the waiting villagers and spoke. Bree crouched at Shocaw's side, unsure if he was out of danger or not. He had fallen asleep and his chest fell slowly and evenly. That was surely a good sign.

Later, when Shocaw stirred and awakened, water and shells filled with boiled meat and vegetables thickened with corn mush were brought. Bree sat her own bowl on the floor while she bent to feed Shocaw. It was the first time she'd seen him so vulnerable and it made her feel protective and even more loving toward him. After she'd fed him and he had feebly pushed aside the spoon, she got more water and bathed his face. The medicine man looked on silently, and when she was finished, he grunted his approval. With a few quick words he directed some of the braves to come into the chickee and pick up Shocaw.

"Where are you taking him?" Bree asked in dismay, following after them.

"You stay," the medicine man said imperiously, and turned away.

"No. Bring him back," Bree cried, and ran to catch up with the men. "Where are you going with him? He's ill."

"Do not worry, Bree," Cooee said. "He is in good hands."

"But where are they taking him?"

"They are going to the sweat lodge. They will sweat the poison out of his system. It will make him well and strong again. You will see. Do not worry." Cooee touched her arm and turned to follow the other men. Milakee came to stand beside Bree, her hands gripping Bree's in friendship. She had been very worried over the fate of her friend.

"Come, sleep," she said to Bree, and together the two walked back to the chickee. Reassured by Cooee's words and his quick smile, Bree's worries over Shocaw abated somewhat and fatigue set in. Weariness and the aftermath of fear and worry had taken their toll and she was unable even to unfold her sleeping mat. Milakee seemed to understand and hurried to prepare a place for Bree, then she took down a mat for herself and the two girls settled themselves beneath the warm furs. Although she would have preferred to have Shocaw beside her, Milakee's presence was comforting to Bree.

"Milakee glad Bree back," the Indian girl said hesitantly, and Bree reached out to take her hand.

"I'm glad to be back," Bree said. "I feel as if I've come back home."

"Home," Milakee repeated, and smiled. The two lay side by side, communicating with each other in the few words of English and Seminole they shared and conveying more than many people do with a full command of language. The moon rose in the velvet night sky and the village stilled. Bree's taut muscles relaxed and at last she slept.

Bree awoke with a feeling of renewed vigor. She was safe back at the village. She and Milakee put away their sleeping mats and hurried to see about Shocaw's condition. However, the sweat lodge was closed to them and in her halting language Milakee informed Bree that no woman was allowed to enter. Bree thought of storming the male stronghold, then relinquished the impulse and returned to her chickee. There was nothing for her to do but wait. She must trust that Shocaw was in good hands. The people of the village held their war chief in high esteem and none of them seemed worried now as they went about their daily chores.

None of the women went to the fields that day. They stayed in camp, working on the deer hides and carefully drying the venison the men had brought in from their hunting. Calicoes had been obtained, probably from a raid, Bree surmised, and pushed the thought out of her mind. She watched as the women chattered excitedly while they worked on needed clothing. The two girls helped with the chores until there was nothing left to do, then turned toward the bathing pond.

"Bree hear Milakee's good news?" the Indian girl asked, her expression eager. "Milakee will marry Cooee."

"Oh, Milakee, I heard and I'm very happy for you," Bree said warmly, and was rewarded with a radiant smile. "Cooee is a brave warrior."

"Yes," Milakee agreed, and there was a hint of reticence in her smile. Although she was willing to share almost everything with her white friend, the feelings she had for Cooee were private and special.

"When will you marry?" Bree asked, wondering how the Seminoles went about such things.

"At the Green Corn Dance at the first moon," Milakee replied matter-of-factly. "Happy time for Seminole. Many weddings then, games, races. New year begin. All bad deeds forgiven. Good medicine for Seminole." Bree listened intently as Milakee described the most important ceremony of the Seminoles. Once again she was struck by

the similarities between their customs. Although
the Seminole's new year occurred in July, its purpose was not so different from the white man's
new year. Both were seen as a time of beginning
anew with all mistakes left behind in the past
and much hope for the year to come.

The two sat talking, half in the white man's
tongue and half in the Seminole language. Sometimes Bree stumbled over a word and Milakee
giggled merrily. Her laughter was infectious and
soon Bree joined her. It occurred to Bree that
like the Seminoles, she had begun to keep her
voice and laughter soft and low so it didn't carry
through the swamps as it once might have.

A shadow moved out of the trees, and startled,
the two girls ceased their laughter and looked
up. Shocaw stood before them, his eyes clear, his
brow free of the sweating fever he'd had the
night before. His broad chest was bare, as were
his legs. He wore only a breechcloth and a pair of
moccasins. A bandage was tied about his thigh.

"Shocaw," Bree cried delightedly, and would
have scrambled to her feet and run to him except
that she still had not donned her clothes from
the swim. Her discarded skirt and blouse lay
over a bush nearby. She sat with her legs folded
to one side, her long golden hair covering her
bare breasts. To rise would mean exposing more
of her nude body to his gaze.

Milakee seemed to feel no such reserve as she
quickly rose and pulled her skirt and blouse on.
She seemed not to notice Bree's frantic signal to
bring her clothes to her. With a quick, mischievous smile she bid them good-bye and hurried
toward the path.

"Milakee, wait," Bree called, feeling a moment
of panic, but the Indian maiden was gone. Bree's
glance flew to Shocaw's face, then lighted on her
folded hands in her lap.

"You are well?" he asked soflty, and Bree's panic gave way to remorse that she hadn't asked about his health.

"Yes, I am," she replied, then her gaze went to meet his. "Are you all right?"

"The Indian magic has done its work well." He smiled at her. "Because of you, I am alive."

"I was so frightened for you," she answered, and her voice was soft and warm with feeling. Shocaw looked into the glistening gray eyes that captivated him so.

"Then what you said in the swamps yesterday was true?" he asked gently.

"I don't remember what I said," she stammered, and looked down at her hands again. Shocaw watched her, his gaze fastening on the small, bare shoulder peeping through her hair.

"You said many things," he replied. "You said them with your eyes, with your kiss. Have you really forgotten them?" When she didn't answer, he went on in his soft, husky voice. "Perhaps you wish they hadn't been said."

"No, I don't wish that," she said breathlessly. Her gaze was direct now, her eyes wide, as she sought to reassure him and yet something held her back.

Sensing her timidity, he leaned backward and looked at the herons wading at the other end of the pool. "There are many beautiful and wild creatures here in the swamp," he observed, and Bree followed the direction of his gaze. Silently she watched the great blue herons as they moved about, majestic even in their feeding. At any unusual sound she knew the birds would quickly take to wing. Her heart fluttered in her chest.

Gently Shocaw took her hand raised it to his lips, planting a hot kiss in the soft, moist palm.

"You are very beautiful too, Bree, but you do

not belong in the swamp." There was a note of regret in his voice.

"I feel as if I do," she said softly. Silently Shocaw studied her. Was it too soon? he wondered. Once he'd moved too quickly and frightened her. He didn't want to do so again. Still her eyes held a message he couldn't ignore.

"My brave, proud Bree," he whispered. "So fragile and yet so strong. Like a flower in a storm. Like the great ibis, graceful and majestic."

"I am strong," Bree said. "Stronger than I thought I could be. I've discovered so many things about myself since I've been here." She looked at the man lounging beside her. His bare chest was broad and brown. She wanted to touch it with her fingertips, taste his skin with her tongue.

Fleetingly she thought of the reactions of her family and friends. What would they think if they could see her now? They would be appalled at her nudity and the intimacy between Shocaw and her. And yet it felt natural and right. It no longer mattered to her what others might think.

"I have changed," she said out loud.

"Neither am I the same," Shocaw answered. Their gazes met and held. His eyes were deep and hypnotic. Once again he clasped her hand and carried it to his lips.

"My little bird," he said softly, "let me help you discover more." His kiss on the leaping pulse at her wrist was hot. "Let us explore together." His tongue touched the sensitive skin between each of her fingers. Her hands trembled in his like wild birds that might fly away any moment.

Her sigh was his answer, yet some small core of resistance still remained within her. He sensed it and was determined to overcome it. There would be no shame for her this time. He would awaken her to the true nature of her passion.

Placing her arms about his neck, he buried his lips for a brief moment against the pulse of her inner elbow. He felt the quick surge of hot blood pulsating beneath the delicate skin. His arms pulled her to him while his mouth hungrily sought hers. His lean brown hand floated over the curve of her back and settled on the flare of her hips as he pulled her more securely against him. Bree felt her bare breasts crushed against the hard, smooth chest and her heart leaped.

His breathing was fast and uneven when he ended the kiss. His eyes were dark with desires she'd seen there before. Now his hands moved around the sides of her body and were resting on her quivering stomach. His gaze captured hers. Lost in the dark lights she found there, she made no murmur as he lightly stroked the sleek softness then skimmed up over the tiny waist and delicate rib cage that barely contained her rapidly beating heart.

His fingertips spread out over the fullness of her breasts and Bree closed her eyes against the flood of desire she felt, willing his long, sensitive fingers to touch those aching peaks, but his hands skimmed downward, swift and sure, setting up a clamor in her body while his lips settled lightly on each eyelid. He smiled as she held her face up to him. His mouth was gentle yet insistent on hers as he parted her lips to taste the sweetness beyond.

Slowly he awakened her, coaxing her to a new awareness of her womanliness, bringing her to a peak of pleasure she'd never known existed. Timid at first, she grew bolder as she touched the high cheekbones, the straight, dark slash of his eyebrows. Her fingers buried themselves in the raven-black locks, glorying in the feel of his vibrant hair between her sensitive fingers. Was there a part of her body that was not aware of his, she wondered, and her hands grew bolder in their exploration of his body.

She felt the slight roughness of his cheeks and chin, the powerful neck, the solid, hard muscles of his shoulders, the smooth, hairless chest with the hard ridges of muscles. She remembered the time she'd seen him with water glistening on his skin and the overpowering urge she'd had to touch his smooth skin with her tongue. She did so now, marveling at the clean, masculine taste of him. She heard his quick intake of breath and came to the satisfying realization that she held power over this bronze giant. Experimentally she moved her mouth across his chest to the dark aureole of his nipple. Tentatively, her small tongue flicked at the tip and she heard him groan deep in his chest.

Her own nipples tingled with desire and instinctively she did the things she wanted to do but hadn't been able to name, not even to herself.

Small white teeth settled gently on the tiny, hard bud and again Shocaw groaned deep in his chest. Both hands seized her arms, pulling her up and against him as his lips settled on hers once again. How well they fit together, she marveled, and yet how different they were. Her body was soft and pale against his harder, darker one. Her bones were finely wrought, his were larger. Her skin was like fine satin, his like smooth leather.

Her hands could not stay still. Having begun their exploration, she could not stop them as they lovingly touched this body that would lie beside her for the rest of her life.

Shocaw's lips glided over her skin, going to claim one rosy nipple with a swiftness that startled her, then pleasured her.

Her legs relaxed and fell apart naturally, wantonly, in their innocence. Her hand touched the hard shaft resting against her thigh. Surprised by the hot smoothness of it, she drew back, then touched again. Shocaw's hands moved over her in an increasing tempo that brought her to the edge of a high precipice.

Her body arched upward, her senses screaming for a release she wasn't sure existed, then Shocaw was there, his body stretched over hers. With mighty thrusts he carried her over the edge and into a world she'd never known before. A world of passion and ecstasy. Her cry of fulfillment echoed through the swamp long after her sweating, writhing body had gone still beside his.

She had indeed died, she realized, and now she was coming alive again. Alive to the noise and motion of the world around her. Alive to the incredible man beside her. His eyes were closed, his broad chest still heaved as he drew in great gulps of air. She lay watching him, marveling that the ferocious war chief who had captured her, now lay on the cool grass beside her, trembling and breathless as she herself was.

If she were his prisoner, then what was he, for surely he was captive to her as well. She smiled at the knowledge that this was so.

Shocaw, feeling her gaze upon him, turned to smile into her eyes and gather her into his arms. They lay side by side, her head on his shoulder, one small hand resting lightly over his pumping heart. One of his large muscular legs was thrown over her slimmer tapering ones, holding her in loving captivity. They rested, drinking in the sight and smell of each other, their mouths tasting and touching, the sound of their hearts beating in unison.

When they'd rested, they ran into the water, splashing and playing like children, their laughter quiet and intimate. The afternoon waned and they made love again in the water, glorying in the touch of beloved flesh made slippery and cool, while inside themselves there was so much fiery passion.

They dried each other and began dressing only to tear away the constricting, concealing clothes and take each other yet again on the patch of grass already crushed by their entwined bodies. Only when twilight fell and Bree shivered in the damp coolness of the evening air did Shocaw gather up her clothing and help her dress. Arm in arm they walked back to their chickee.

Chapter 10

"Bree ready?" Milakee called.

"I'm ready," Bree called back, and quickly finshed rolling the sleeping mats and put them away. Several weeks had passed since her ordeal in the swamp. There had been many changes in her status here in the village since then.

No longer did the others look at Shocaw and her with bright-eyed interest. They accepted her as Shocaw's *hoke-tee*. Bree smiled happily while she straightened the bedding. She'd never felt more complete in her life. She'd begun to think of the village as her home.

"I'm ready," she repeated to Milakee as she hurried down the steps of the chickee. For several weeks she had been working with Milakee, learning to tan the soft deer skin Shocaw had left on her doorstep. She smiled when she thought of her first gift from him.

At first she'd been startled, then apprehensive at the thought that she was expected to clean the skin herself. Then Cooee and Milakee told her of the custom of the Seminoles. The courting brave left a deer at the doorstep of the maiden he desired to show that he was a good provider. The maiden, she was told, must make a shirt to show

215

she accepted the warrior's courtship, so Bree
had labored long and willingly over the deer skin
until it was soft and pliable.

Milakee had been by her side all the way,
instructing and advising, a sad, longing light in
her eyes, until the day Cooee left a deer on her
doorstep and the happy, dark lights shown once
more in her eyes. Together the two girls worked
on their skins. The other women cast indulgent
smiles upon them, remembering the excitement
of their first courtships.

Only one woman seemed angry at the turn of
events. Katcalani skulked about the edge of the
women's activities and Bree noticed that few of
them paid her any attention. The Indian woman
had been severely chastised for her deception
and now awaited trial at the annual *Shot-cay-taw*,
the Green Corn Dance ceremonies, a religious
ceremony of great importance to the Seminole.

"Why must she stand trial?" Bree asked Milakee.
Now that she was safely back at the village and
under Shocaw's protection, she no longer felt
anger at the woman. She understood the reason
for her deed. But the other Seminoles were not
so forgiving.

"She do bad thing. She take you swamp and
leave, not help you. She lie everyone, even war
chief, Shocaw. Very bad." Milakee was still angry for the danger in which Katcalani had placed
Bree. Still, Bree felt sympathy for the outcast
woman. What would she have done, she wondered, if she saw someone else winning Shocaw's
love? The thought cast a black cloud across her
day.

"Bree sad?" Milakee said, noting her expression.

"No, not sad," Bree assured her, and smiled,
but the smile did not reach her eyes. Milakee
was quick to notice, but said nothing more. The

two girls worked together quietly. At last Bree glanced up with troubled eyes.

"Milakee, was Shocaw—I mean did he and Katcalani—" She paused, not sure of what she wanted to ask and if she had the right to ask it.

"Katcalani very beautiful," Milakee said. "Not Shocaw's *hoke-tee*. Only Bree." She flashed her beautiful smile and suddenly the day seemed brighter to Bree. Now her eyes sparkled with good humor as she returned Milakee's smile.

The deer hide was ready at last. Bree planned to make a shirt of it according to the old custom, but was persuaded by the women and Milakee to make leggings instead. The shirt would be made of calico, which would be much cooler.

"One time, warrior wear shirt of deer skin," one woman told her in her halting English, "north, not here in swamp. Too hot."

So Bree cut the soft deer skin into leggings and Milakee showed her how to sew them together with thin strips of leather and one of the precious needles left over from the more prosperous days when the Seminoles traded for such goods from Cuba. The women gathered in one chickee to do their sewing. The companionable silence was broken now and then with quiet conversation. Next to the time she spent alone with Shocaw, these were the moments that Bree loved best.

The nutlike smell of boiling sofkee filled the air, with the quiet murmur of the women's voices making a soft musical backdrop for the bright voices of the children as they sang folk songs about the horned owl, the raccoon, and the little red rabbit. The motion of the needle, in and out of the soft deer skin, set a pattern that soothed her in a special way.

Often the old women spoke of the time before the first Seminole war, which had occurred long before Bree was born. They reminisced about the time when their farms were prosperous and food was plentiful and fat cattle grazed in their pastures. There had been horses to ride and trade and the Indians had wanted for little.

Wide-eyed, the younger women listened and wondered. They had never known such riches. That had been long before the Seminoles had been pushed deep into the swamps. A constant struggle against poverty and starvation were all they'd known in their lives. Now even that life was being threatened by the white men who wished to send them to an alien country.

In the evening Bree put away her sewing and went to help the women with the cooking chores or tend to the fat babies while she waited for Shocaw's return. Like the other women she brought her dishes to the fire to fill them from the sofkee kettles, making sure choice pieces of meat and vegetables were added especially for Shocaw.

"Tell me about the *Shot-cay-taw*," she instructed as they ate their meal. Shocaw lay aside his bowl and spoke.

"It is sometimes called the Green Corn Dance ceremony because it is the time when we thank the Gods for our harvest," he answered. "It is the beginning of a new year for us. We put aside all our problems of the past year and atone for our crimes against others. It is a time when we renew ourselves."

"How can you thank your God when so many of your people suffer?" Bree asked. She'd come to care deeply for his people. Their pain and sorrow was hers.

"We have survived for another year," Shocaw replied. "We must have hope for the next year." His voice was sure and firm, and suddenly Bree felt ashamed for her lack of faith. Still, her mood was despondent. She put aside her own bowl, unable to eat now.

"The *Shot-cay-taw* is a time of joy for our people," he said, trying to dispel her gloom. "We meet with people from other tribes. There is much feasting and happiness among our people. There are many ceremonies and you may participate in them if you wish," he offered, taking her hand in his.

"Would I be able to join the races with Milakee?" she asked eagerly, then hesitated as she remembered Milakee had said it was a mating race. Shocaw grinned at her.

"If you wish," he replied. "I will race as well." His dark eyes held hers in an unspoken message of his intentions. If they raced Shocaw would catch her.

In the days that followed she thought of his unspoken pledge often as she worked on his shirt. Now more than ever, she wanted to have it completed before the *Shot-cay-taw*.

One evening she and Shocaw lay together after making love and stared at the velvet sky above them.

"The stars are very important to my people," Shocaw said, pulling her closer to his chest. Bree snuggled her head into the warm curve of his shoulder, drinking in the special smell that was all his.

"Look, look." He pointed suddenly at a line just below the edge of the chickee roof.

Bree traced the pattern his finger had indicated through the sky, but her eyes couldn't catch up with the falling comet.

"I didn't see it," she exclaimed like a disappointed child.

"Never mind," Shocaw said, tucking the blankets about her shoulder. Together they lay on their stomachs and peered up at the sky. "There is the *Ho-nit-claw*." He pointed at a bright star.

"*Ho-nit-claw*," Bree repeated. "We call it the North Star and the stars that are next to it are called the Big Dipper. See its outline?"

"No," Shocaw said, flashing her a bright teasing smile. "That is the outline of a Seminole boat, see?" His hands slashed through the air, outlining the boat, and suddenly Bree could see the shape he meant. She laughed with delight. "Oh, wait until I tell Jared," she cried, then fell silent as a wave of homesickness washed over her.

"Who is Jared?" Shocaw asked, his heart constricting with sudden fear. No man had yet claimed Bree, he knew, for he'd found she was a virgin when he took her by the pond, but maybe some man had laid claim to her heart and now she pined for him.

"Jared is my brother," Bree said, and the tightness eased in Shocaw's chest. "You would like him. He is very gentle and he is very sympathetic toward the Seminoles and their suffering."

"That is rare in a white man," Shocaw said, and the bitter edge of his voice was not lost on Bree. A feeling of hopelessness swept over her. The differences and hatred between Shocaw's people and her own never seemed greater.

"Jared would like you as well," she said, and in her soft tone he heard her wish that the two races would live in peace and harmony. My poor little bird, he thought, and caught her up in his arms, cradling her against his chest.

There is only pain and sorrow for us. This thing between us was not meant to be. In the future legends of the Seminole, there may be some mention of the beautiful, fair-haired maiden who came and stole the heart of a war chief, but like many of our legends grounded in reality, there will be no happy ending to our story.

Unaware of the thoughts racing through Shocaw's head, Bree snuggled closer to him, reveling in the warmth and comfort he gave just with his physical presence. She loved the feel of his arms holding her, closing out the rest of the world. There were only the two of them, drifting through the midnight sky in their chickee with the moon casting its magical sheen over everything and the stars lighting the sky above.

"Tell me," she sighed contentedly. "Why is there a Seminole boat in the sky?" She'd already discovered there was a practical reason for every symbol, every custom, and tradition in the Seminole's life.

"Once a Seminole went on a journey and lost his way and found himself in the sky," Shocaw said softly. "Only his boat remains to remind other Seminoles of him."

"Perhaps that is why the Seminole is so careful to hide his canoe and remember where he left it," Bree murmured, remembering how the warriors had kept track of their dugouts.

"Perhaps," Shocaw agreed.

"Look, there is the Milky Way. I suppose the Seminoles have a story for that as well?" she asked in mock exasperation, her slim hands on either side of Shocaw's face as she looked into his eyes.

"As a matter of fact, we do," Shocaw said, and felt an urge to laugh. How quickly this lovely golden-haired girl gave him back a moment of joy. "Once upon a time," he began, and felt her settle herself more comfortably against him, almost childlike in her anticipation of the story she was about to hear, "the Breath Maker set out on a journey. He took seven warriors with him. They walked a long way, all the way to the end

of Florida where the great ocean begins. Breath
Maker taught the men how to fish. He showed
them the coontie plant and taught them how to
use it for food. Then he blew his breath into the
sky and made the Milky Way. If the Indian is a
good person, the Milky Way will shine brightly
and light the way to his home with the Breath
Maker."

"How beautiful," Bree murmured. "Our worlds
are not so different. Our God is the same. We
have a story of God giving bread to his chosen
people while they wandered in the desert. Our
God is the same."

"Yes, our God is the same," Shocaw replied
sadly, and for a moment Bree felt him pulling
away from her. "But the white man does not
obey his God as the Seminole does."

"Some of them do," Bree said. "You mustn't
judge all my people by a few bad ones. Some of
them are kind and caring just as some of yours
are."

"There are not a few bad ones among your
people," Shocaw corrected her. "There are many
white men here in Florida and they seek to destroy my people. It is hard for me to believe in
the kindness and caring of the white man when
he shows me only his hate. Every day I see more
of my people dying." Shocaw's voice had grown
bitter.

"Still you must not hate us, or me. You would
not wish me to judge all Seminoles by Lopochee
or Katcalani, would you?" she asked.

"No, I wouldn't," Shocaw answered, and
wrapped his arms about her once more. "Our
worlds are different, little bird," he said softly,
and she noted the deep sadness within him. It
struck a chord of dread deep inside her. She had
been living in a dreamworld the last few weeks,
trying to pretend the rest of the world as it was

didn't exist. She'd tried to pretend she was only a maiden from a different tribe, and although their customs were different from those of her people, the differences could be overcome.

He'd made her face the reality of her situation. She belonged to a different world from Shocaw, and those two worlds were at war with each other. It seemed impossible to end the fighting between them, and even if it could be ended, the memories and hatred would go on for many years. Although many of the women had accepted her presence, there were others who did not and never would. To them she would always be an outcast, a hated white man's woman. Convulsively, Bree's arms went about Shocaw's neck as she buried her head against his strong shoulder.

"Hold me," she whispered, and they lay for a long moment, two beings who had, with their love, forged a new world between them and now felt the foundations of that world being threatened by the demands of the old.

"Kiss me, Shocaw," Bree whispered, raising her tear-streaked face to his. "Make love to me. Let's make the night last forever." Understanding her needs, he moved his body over her, his long legs capturing hers, his arms shutting out the night, halting the coming dawn with all its threats. His mouth on hers opened the door to their special world, bright with passion and love. Feverishly Shocaw's kisses covered her face and he tasted the salt of her tears.

There was no future for them, he knew. One day their separate worlds would reclaim them and there would be nothing left for them together, but for now they had the star-studded night.

In the days that followed, Bree woke feeling depressed. It seemed to weigh her down, tying her to the earth when her spirit struggled to soar. She tried to hide her feelings from Shocaw, and as he and his men went out more and more often to fight the increasingly savage soldiers, he had little time to notice her sad preoccupation.

One evening as the women sat around the fire pit working, now and then casting anxious glances over their shoulders, watching for the warriors who were due to return that night, they heard a noise, the sound of many people moving on the outskirts of the village. Instantly everyone froze, their faces startled and fearful, their eyes darting about the lighted square. Had soldiers found the village? Where were the lookouts who were always kept posted? While they sat with held breaths, the rustling increased, then the bushes parted and Shocaw and his warriors entered the village.

Bree sprang to her feet with a glad cry. Around her the women let out a collective sigh of relief. But the warriors were not alone. Behind them straggled women and children, their faces streaked with dirt and blood, their bodies slumped with fatigue. Their brightly colored clothes were muddy and ragged.

Mutely the group stood in the center of the village square while Shocaw told of the tragedy that had befallen them. Their village had been attacked by soldiers. Shocaw and his men had arrived in time to help the warriors fight off the first attack, but they were outnumbered. They had fought until the women and children escaped, then they'd retreated into the swamps themselves. Crouching behind trees, they'd watched as the white men destroyed the precious food stores and set fire to the chickees.

There was much murmuring among the people of Horse Creek Village as they listened to the tale. It could just as easily have been their own village. The women hurried to give aid to the wounded and to prepare some of their small store of food for the refugees. Room would be made for the newcomers and somehow the store of food would be stretched to feed everyone. All knew within their hearts that the winter months would be lean. There would be hungry stomachs unless the Great Provider brought about a miracle.

Stoically the women set about feeding the children and settling them into chickees for the night. The villagers would share their chickees until new ones could be built. Bree moved about among the wounded and weary, offering water and trying to tend to their wounds, but when they saw her pale skin and the long golden braid falling across her shoulder, they drew back, hissing in anger at her. Sadly, Bree relinquished the gourd and turned back to her own chickee.

From a distance she watched as the medicine man chanted his prayers over the wounded. At last fed and reassured of some safety, the travelers settled wearily by the fire, perching here and there on the logs and in the warm sand between.

The storyteller came forth into the light. He stood with great dignity; his face, seamed by time, was proud and noble, for the storyteller was an important person in the Seminole village. He carried forth the legends of the people, legends and stories that taught valuable lessons about their ancestors and their Gods. His tales were of nature and its great mysteries.

Expectantly the people waited, the silence broken only by the crack of the coals in the fire pit or the cry of a panther deep in the swamp. Swallowing her hurt pride, Bree left the chickee and went to stand beside Shocaw, moving close enough for her arm to brush against his in a gentle reminder to herself that he was home and safe for yet another night. Standing beside Shocaw, she could face all her adversaries in his world and hers, she vowed, and turned her attention to the storyteller.

"Long ago, an Indian boy, Nanabozho, lived with his grandmother, Nokomis," the storyteller began, and the children who had not been put to sleep in the chickees stirred and looked at one another. They liked stories about children even better than stories about animals. "He was the son of the West Wind and could do many wonderful things. As a hungry baby he once turned himself into a rabbit so he could eat grass." The children stirred again. The story would be about animals as well. Their bright eyes moved back to the storyteller as he told them of how the clever Indian boy stole the fire from a magician who had gone to the underworld and brought back a fiery torch.

As the Indian boy raced through the forest with the flaming brand, the trees and grass caught fire and glowed with beautiful, fiery colors. The Indian boy gave the fire to his old grandmother so she could cook her meat and eat it and live. He gave his fire to the other Indians as well, who learned how to warm themselves with it and to cook their food.

Nanabozho was so proud of himself he made the woods blaze each year with flaming colors, so he might be remembered for what he had done.

It was a beautiful story and the people felt encouraged by it. They looked at each other and smiled. Somehow they had survived this misfortune as they had so many others and in the fall they would be here to see the woods turn to reds and golds in honor of Nanabozho.

Slowly the people drifted off to their chickees to rest. It had been an exhausting, frightening day for them, but they had survived and now it was time to rest and go on with their lives. Bree and Shocaw walked back to their own chickee.

He was more silent then usual and Bree felt her heart pounding in dread.

He did not speak of what was troubling him until they were beneath their warm furs and blankets, their arms wrapped around each other. Although he held her close, Shocaw made no move toward more than that. Again Bree felt a chill of foreboding. Was he growing tired of her or was there some bad news that weighed on his mind?

"Tomorrow, Coacoochee will come to the village. My men and I will join him to fight against the soldiers," he said slowly.

"I have heard of this Coacoochee before," Bree said in a small voice. "Is he a great warrior?"

"Yes, Bree, he is," Shocaw said against her temple. "The number of our warriors is dwindling. Soon there will not be enough of us to fight."

"What will you do?" Bree whispered fearfully.

"Go on fighting; although we will die, we will go on fighting."

"Don't say that," Bree cried, shocked and frightened by his words. Her arms flew around his neck to pull him close. "I don't want you to die, Shocaw, not you."

"I have no choice," he said sadly.

"Yes, you have, give up." She felt him pull away from her in the darkness, and hurried on. "Give up and go to the Arkansas Territory. I'll go with you. You and your people will be safe there."

"Do you know what you ask of me?" Shocaw demanded.

"Yes, I ask that you live," Bree pleaded.

"Would it be living to beg your government for food to stay alive?" Shocaw asked, and she felt the anger growing inside him.

"Yes" she cried. "Yes it would. I would beg too, if it meant your life."

"I cannot," Shocaw said finally. "I will never leave Florida. It is my home."

"Shocaw, please consider it," Bree pressed.

"I have considered it," Shocaw said hoarsely. "Ever since that afternoon by the pond, I have thought of it, but it can never be. Not for us. I will return you to your people."

"No," Bree cried, and pressed herself to him in a defiant, yet heartrending gesture of love and fidelity.

"One day, it must be," Shocaw sighed. "We cannot change the way things are."

"I will stay with you always," Bree cried, holding on to him more tightly.

"One day you will change your mind," Shocaw said with such certainty that it broke her heart. "When you are ready to return to your people, you must tell me. I will return you."

"Have we any time left?" she cried.

"Very little," Shocaw answered hoarsely, then pulled her against his chest, burying his face in her fragrant golden hair. His fingers stroked the bright strands. How he loved the silken feel of it, the satin of her skin, the perfume of her body, the nectar of her mouth. Gently he made love to her, touching her body as if memorizing every curve and dip of it. There was a sweet poignancy to his touch that wrenched her heart. I will never leave you, she vowed silently. I will never leave you. She lay exhausted by his lovemaking, the tears of desolation running down her cheeks.

The next morning the women hurried to feed their families and the newcomers and to do their chores. The sand in the village square was freshly swept with tied bundles of reeds from the swamp. Extra food was prepared. Coacoochee and his men would be hungry after their journey through the swamp.

Rabbits and chunks of venison were put to

roast on sticks over the fire pit and turtles were cooked in their own shells. The sofkee kettles were filled and set to simmer.

Children ran about excitedly, watching for the great warrior. They had all heard of his bravery and wiliness with the white soldiers and of his great escape from the fortress where he'd been imprisoned with Osceola. Like a wily cat, Coacoochee had slipped through the bars of the cell and led his men away from the fortress to safety. He had earned the name of Wildcat that the white men had given him.

Excitement was at a pitch when Coacoochee and his men finally entered the village. Bree was surprised to see him walking just like the other warriors. She'd half expected him to be carried in on a dais as the Micanopy once might have been. There was little doubt, though, as to who was chief. Although shorter than many of his warriors, Coacoochee's dignity, his graceful agile body, and his noble carriage set him apart from his men.

He was dressed in an ermine-lined robe of the English nobility and a turban like that belonging to another age and country. Bree was puzzled by his attire until she listened to him explaining to the amused villagers how he had attacked a band of traveling actors and captured several trunks of costumes. Now Coacoochee and his men sported their fine clothing proudly.

On any other group of men the costumes might have looked ridiculous, reducing the Indian chief to the level of a buffoon, but so great was his natural dignity that Bree found herself admiring his flair and his humor. Many stories ran around the village of Coacoochee's exploits, of how time and again he had eluded the pursuing soldiers and turned back to taunt them for their failure to capture him.

Coacoochee's visit to the village raised the drooping morale of his people. Amid so much tragedy, the villagers laughed, enjoying the exploits of one of their mightiest warriors. Tomorrow they would face the coming winter and the shortage of food, the constant struggle against starvation and attack, but for today they would enjoy a moment of hope.

Bree's heart was torn by the Seminole's ability to laugh in the face of such overwhelming adversities. For herself, she felt like flinging herself on the ground and giving way to the tears that pushed against her eyelids. Shocaw would be leaving with Coacoochee and would not be back until the *Shot-cay-taw,* the Green Corn Dance, if then.

With dry eyes the women watched as their men left the village and followed Coacoochee. There had been talk of attacking one of the forts and raiding their storehouses for food and ammunition. The supplies were much needed to carry the Indians through the winter. As much as they hated to see their men leave, the women fervently hoped they would be successful.

Too many times they'd seen the pinched, hungry faces of their children, had felt the clutch of hunger within their own bellies. Like the other women, Bree stood at one side, quietly watching as the warriors prepared to leave. Milakee stood beside her, her own eyes bright with unshed tears, for Cooee was also going with the great chief Coacoochee.

Gathering their rifles and extra moccasins, their pouches filled with more ammunition and their knives, the warriors lined up, their faces filled with pride and purpose, their gazes darting now and then toward their loved ones. For some of the less fortunate it would be their last glimpses of a beloved's face. The raid would be dangerous and many of them would meet their death at the fort.

Shocaw's dark gaze captured Bree's across the space and she could feel his love and farewell as warm and comforting as if he were holding her, then he looked away and signaled to his men to follow him as they moved toward the path and quickly disappeared in the swampy jungle.

"Shocaw," Bree cried silently, the tears she'd held back were rolling down her cheeks.

"Women wait," Milakee said sadly, looking longingly in the direction the men had taken. "Harder to wait. Come." She led the way back to the chickee, where they set to work on the shirts and leggings.

"Time go fast, we work," she told Bree, and Bree nodded in silent acquiescence. The time would not go fast. It would be a torturous lifetime before Shocaw was back and somehow she must endure. She would stay busy. It would stop her from worrying and from thinking. She'd sensed the other women's wishes for their men to succeed, and for a moment, thinking of the children and the extra mouths they must feed in the months ahead, she'd prayed for their success until she'd realized she was praying for the defeat of her own people. Now she tried to sort out her confusion and make some sense of the conflicts that raged within her. She hardly felt the prick of the needle on her fingers or saw the drops of blood because of the tears in her eyes.

The days dragged as Bree had known they would. During the day she went to work in the fields, tending the gardens with care and skill. Soon the corn would be ripe enough to pick, as would many of the other vegetables. Their silken tassels had dried and lay like ugly insects on the fat ears of corn. The pumpkin vines, which had been patiently staked up the sides of trees to save precious growing space, were heavy with green pumpkins. Soon the pumpkins would begin to turn in the hot sun, ripening to a bright orange. Then they too would be picked and dried.

Sweet potatoes grew plump beneath the ground, waiting to be dug up and roasted. Conch peas had been gathered and dried and stored in gourds in the special storage chickee. It was the only chickee in the village that sported sides from floor to ceiling and a door, which was carefully guarded. With extra mouths to feed, food was an ever-present source of worry.

In the evening Bree and Milakee would wander down to the playing field and watch the young boys left to guard the village as they played a game of stickball. Most of them wore only breechcloths and tails made of white horsehair and quills braided together. Their slim bodies, not yet broadened with the musculature of a mature male, were quicksilver fast, moving tirelessly from one end of the field to the other.

Although they'd been taught from birth not to compete with each other, the game proceeded at a lively pace as each boy strove to hit the ball with his playing stick of hickory wood. At each end of the field was a goal post made of netting of finely laced leather thongs.

"At Green Corn ceremonies, man use much magic," Milakee told Bree. "Put medicine bowl with turtle hide at each end." She pointed at the goal posts at each end of the playing field. "Make ball come net," she said with a wide smile. It was clear she considered the antics of the men to be almost childlike at times.

Her laughter was contagious and suddenly both girls were holding each other's shoulders and laughing. Now and then one of the players would cast the amused girls a glance before hurrying down the field to block the ball from the net. Not wanting to offend the young boys, who were earnest in their attempts to appear manly, the two girls wandered down to the pond and sat on the grass, staring disconsolately at the still water. Each of them remembered the touch of her lover's lips against her own, the feel of his body, and each longed for her man to return.

Bree lay back and stared up into the trees where the sunlight streamed through the silvery wispy strands of Spanish moss.

"How beautiful," she murmured. "It looks so fragile."

"Once upon a time, Seminole girl agree to marry chief of Creeks. Creeks and Seminoles fight for many years. Many braves killed. Seminole girl marry Creek chief, no more war," Milakee said. "Peace, friendship between two nations. Creeks proud men, Seminoles proud too. Seminoles not like Creeks. They fight, many killed. Creek chief killed.

"Bride grieve and mourn." Milakee's shoulders drooped in an imitation of the grief the Seminole maiden felt. "Cut hair and hang in trees." Her dark eyes raised to the tall trees beneath which they sat. "Seminole bride kill self." Milakee plunged an imaginary knife into her heart. "Hair turn silver, spread from tree to tree."

Bree listened, enchanted as much by Milakee's acting out of the story as by the tragic tale itself. Would that happen to Shocaw and her? she wondered. Would the people of the two nations fight until Shocaw was dead? Would she be left to cut her hair and drape it in the trees while she mourned his death and finally went off to take her own life?

"Only story," Milakee said softly, touching her arm, and for the first time Bree was aware of the tears wetting her cheeks.

"I know," she said, sitting up and wiping at

her cheeks while she attempted to smile. "It's just such a sad story."

"Sad," Milakee agreed.

"Let's go back to the village. I want to work on Shocaw's shirt before it grows dark," Bree said, and scrambled to her feet. Milakee followed her back to the chickees, her face troubled. It was the first time a Seminole story had not made Bree laugh.

Milakee was sorry she'd made her friend sad, but then her thoughts turned to Cooee and she picked up her needlework and went to work, her bowed head hiding the gentle smile as she thought of the young warrior.

Cooee was head of his household. He was a friend of the war chief Shocaw and one day would be a war chief himself, such was his bravery. He was a noble warrior, one of whom a maiden could be proud. He would always protect her and provide for her. Besides—and the thought brought a bright flush to Milakee's cheeks—she liked the way Cooee touched her, the way he looked deep into her eyes. His body was very strong and tireless and gave her much pleasure. Milakee knew Cooee planned to race for her at the Green Corn Dance ceremonies and she planned to run slowly enough so he could catch her. She smiled again.

The Green Corn Dance drew near and still the men were not back. The women pressed on with their preparations, only the shadows in their dark eyes reflecting their concern for their men.

For days the medicine man had been directing the women, and as Bree watched and listened she determined that the *Shot-cay-taw* was a great holiday for the Seminole, not unlike New Year's Day. The chickees were all cleaned, the old roofs taken down and burned while new roofs of palmetto fronds were laid. New clothes, tools, and weapons were made in honor of the coming event. Milakee explained to Bree that the old things would be burned. Bree began to understand why the Seminole were as healthy and free of diseases as they were.

A sense of excitement pervaded the air as the day drew nearer and the women became nervous, watching openly now for the return of the warriors.

A low cry went up when they were sighted along the trail the day before the ceremonies were to begin. Anxiously the women watched as the warriors straggled into the village. It seemed to Bree that far fewer warriors returned than marched off behind Coacoochee.

She stood among the other women, craning to catch a glimpse of Shocaw's tall figure, but he was not at the front of his men. Nor was there any sign of a tall figure painted with the vermilion markings of the war chief anywhere among the weary, discouraged warriors.

Looking at their bodies and faces still smeared with paint, Bree remembered the day she had been captured. She had found them fierce and frightening then. Now, only a few men, such as Lopochee and some of his close friends terrorized her. Beneath the masks of war paint, she saw the fear and anger, the pain and weariness of men who were fighting a losing battle and knew it. Silently she watched as the men entered the village square and quietly acknowledged their loved ones. Only when she'd caught a glimpse of Cooee did she go forward.

"Cooee, where is Shocaw?" she cried, gripping his arm, and her voice was little more than a whisper.

"He will come," Cooee said, but he avoided her eyes. "He stayed behind on the trail to see if the soldiers were still following us."

"'You left him?" Bree cried, her eyes disbelieving as she looked at him.

"He ordered me away, Bree. I must obey him."

"Cooee," Milakee cried, and ran forward to throw her arms around him, heedless of the smear of paint on her cheek as it touched his. Her laughing eyes were filled with relief as she hugged him again then drew away. Her gaze fell on Bree's stricken face and her own laughter died.

"Where is Shocaw?" she asked, but Bree turned away without answering. Numbly she made her way back to the chickee she'd shared with Shocaw. It couldn't be so, it couldn't be, she thought, and went inside the home she'd so carefully cleaned for him. Milakee and she had gathered the fresh palmetto leaves that lay across the roof slats. Lovingly she'd woven new bed mats of swamp grass to replace the old, dreaming of the ecstasy she would find on them with Shocaw. Numbly she looked about the chickee, then with a single groan sank to her knees, huddling against the cypress post much as she'd done when she'd first been captured. Her eyes were wide and wild with grief as she looked around her. Outside in the village square were laughter and motion as the returning warriors were fed and pumped for tales of their adventures, but here in the chickee, all was quiet and still; not even a heartbeat could be heard.

Bree pulled her knees tightly to her chest and bowed her head upon them. Within her a dreaded certainty had grown. Shocaw was dead or else he would be here.

Chapter 11

How long she sat there, frozen into an aching ball while in the village square people laughed and talked and embraced, she never knew. Now and then there was the sound of keening as other women discovered the fate of their men. Slowly the sounds faded as the warriors, their hunger alleviated, went to their chickees to collapse and renew themselves in slumber. Some women sat beside their men, rocking themselves as they chanted a hymn of thankfulness, while other women sat in lonely sorrow and discarded their beads and rent their clothes and lowered their long black tresses over their faces in grief. They would not wear their beads again or rearrange their hair until their year of mourning was up.

The village grew quiet. The moon rose, washing its golden light across the deserted square and still Bree sat as she was. In the swamp she'd heard the hoot of an owl and the baying of an alligator, but it made little impression on her.

"Bree?" The name was spoken softly and at first she thought she'd only imagined it. It was Shocaw's voice. Were the Indians' claims of mysticism and spirits true? She raised her head and looked about. Shocaw stood before her. Slowly she got to her feet, her gaze riveted to his face. Was he really here? Was he alive or was it his spirit returning to her? She knew of only one way to find out. Fearlessly she dashed forward and threw herself into his arms.

He was alive and real. His body was solid, not ethereal. She held him, crying against his chest, letting her fears dissolve with the tears she shed. He held her close to him, drinking in the scent of her hair and sweet body, feeling the fineness of her bones and the softness of her flesh. His head dropped back and he stared at the sky while the muscles of his throat worked convulsively.

Their time together was so short, and he had no way to prepare her for it, for he could not prepare himself. Defeat was bitter in his mouth. Too many men had been lost in this battle. One day he would not return to her. His escape had been narrow tonight as he'd led the soldiers away from his retreating men and the paths to his village. Each time the soldiers came nearer to their home. One day they would find them. The soldiers were slowly chipping away the Seminole's resistance. Soon it would be over.

He held her to his heart, this woman of his enemies, and felt a sad rage at all he and his people had lost and all they must yet lose. When he turned his face from the sky and buried it in her pale hair, he felt the wetness of his tears on his cheeks.

Shocaw was back. Bree's heart sang. She'd spent the night in his arms and now she rose with more energy than she'd felt in many a morning. Her stomach, which had rebelled time and again lately against the limited fare, felt strong and she smiled happily as she slipped from the warmth of Shocaw's side and quickly dressed. She hurried down the steps and headed to the fire pit to get some food for Shocaw. He'd not eaten when he returned the night before and she knew he would awaken with the appetite of a bear and a temper to match. The thought of the night before brought a smile to her lips. It had been more wonderful than any they'd shared, poignant with a special tenderness and gratitude that they had not been lost to one another.

She had gone to the pool with Shocaw while he bathed away the paint of war and death. She'd offered herself shamelessly on the moonlit banks where they'd first made love. His touch held so much tender caring, she wanted to cry out with the fullness in her heart. Shocaw loved her as deeply as she loved him. Somehow they would find a way to be together forever. She was confident of it.

Now she knelt and placed food from the sofkee kettle into a shell bowl. As she rose quickly to her feet, a wave of dizziness swept over her, making her sway for a moment while the square spun around her.

"Bree ill?" Milakee was there beside her, taking the bowl from her nerveless fingers and leading her to a seat at one end of the fire log.

"I must have stood up too quickly," Bree muttered, and clutched at her stomach. The fluttery nausea was there again. She hadn't eaten since breakfast the day before, and with all the worry about Shocaw it was little wonder she felt weak and trembling and her stomach fluttered uncontrollably.

"I'll be all right," she said, smiling at Milakee, then stared into Milakee's bright, knowing eyes. What on earth was wrong with her? Bree wondered. "I'll feel better after I've eaten," she said, and rose slowly from the log.

"Let me get you another bowl," Milakee said, and hurried to dish up another bowl of the hot

corn mush. She handed both bowls to Bree and
stood looking after her friend as she turned back
to the chickee. Did she know yet? Milakee wondered, then smiled. She would say nothing. It
was between Bree and Shocaw. Happily she
turned back to the sofkee kettle to get food for
Cooee. Her smile reflected her own happy memories of the night before.

The Green Corn Dance celebration was upon
them. That evening the men dismantled the old
fire pit with its radial pattern of eight logs. In
the center of the town they placed four large logs
specially cut and stripped for this day. The logs
were placed so they formed a cross with the
outer ends pointing to the four directions of the
earth. All the fires in the village were put out,
the ashes scattered and the fireplaces sprinkled
with clean white sand. On the morrow each household would be given the start for a new fire.

When the last preparation was completed, the
villagers went back to the chickees to wait the
coming of dawn, for then the five days of ceremonies would officially begin. Each Seminole
thought of the meaning of the ceremonies and of
his own participation in them. They would be
cleansed and purified and begin a new year,
perhaps a year that would be better than the year
they'd just endured.

For Milakee, sleeping alone in her chickee, it
would be her wedding ceremony. She would become Cooee's wife at last. For Katcalani, it would
be a day of trial and possible punishment as she
went before the council and pleaded for clem-
ency. The warriors thought of the strength and
renewed bravery they would receive during the
ceremonies and the medicine man thought of the
great Ishtohollo and of how he would be pleased
by the villagers' diligence and prayers.

All the villagers were awake before the sun

streaked the far horizon. The firemaker faced the rising sun and struck a piece of flint, letting a spark fall upon the bundle of dried grass. A thin column of smoke rose and the dry grass burst into flames. Tenderly the firemaker nursed it and placed it in the center of the new logs, carefully feeding it kindling. At last the new fire was made and from it would come all other fires with which the villagers would warm themselves and prepare their food.

Happily they danced around the fire, singing ceremonial songs. Many of them wore rattles made of coconut shells with pebbles inside. They stamped their feet to keep time with the chanting. Bree stood beside Shocaw in the soft morning light, watching the villagers, and knew from the seriousness of their expressions that this was a deeply religious part of the ceremonies. As the dancing and chanting ended, each woman stepped forward to be given an ember from the new fire.

Quickly they moved back to their homes where they relit their fires. Bree went forward and received her ember on a piece of bark and carried it back to the fireplace before Shocaw's chickee. Her heart swelled with pride as she enacted the ritual of relighting the fire. Shocaw's eyes shone with a special light as he watched.

Now the council meetings were held and all Seminoles who had broken their tribal laws were to be judged. One by one villagers came with their prolems and the wise men of the council listened. Divorces were granted, disputes considered, and judgments passed.

Katcalani was among those who went before the council. Her crime was for stealing property and lying about it. Katcalani made her appeal very well, standing before the assembled men with modestly lowered eyes and bowed head. Her hair was worn loose and fell about her shoulders in a silken black curtain. Her beauty would be an asset for her and she was subtle in her use of it. Meekly, she raised her dark eyes to meet the gaze of the judges while she spoke in a soft voice.

She told of how Bree wrested her knife from her and forced her to act as a guide to lead her to the soldiers at the fort. Bree gasped as Katcalani told her version of what had happened. Only Katcalani's quick thinking had made her lead the prisoner away from the soldiers' camp rather than toward it, she maintained.She told of how she led the prisoner deep into the swamp, where she was at last able to escape and make her way back to the camp. She had nearly been killed by the slashing knife of the prisoner, but she'd managed to get away.

She hadn't meant to lie to Shocaw about where he might find the prisoner, she said humbly. She had just been so frightened she hadn't remembered which direction she'd taken, only that it had been away from the fort. She herself had become lost on her way back and circled far beyond the village, and had returned from the north. It had only been natural for her to believe she had started out in that direction.

The council was lenient with her and only a minor punishment was given. Many of the council were untouched by Bree's position as Shocaw's *hoke-tee*, feeling he should not take a white woman for himself. There were Seminole women who were far less trouble.

Meekly Katcalani listened to her punishment, expressed her thanks to the council, and turned away, allowing her dark hair to fall forward and shield her victorious smile. Only when she passed Bree did she raise her head again, her dark eyes glittering triumphantly.

Bree shivered and felt a moment of fear pass

through her. Katcalani was a dangerous enemy, she realized, and the promise of reprisal was all too clear in her hate-filled eyes. Bree darted a glance beyond the Indian woman to seek Shocaw's reassurance, but he had already turned away and was speaking heatedly with a member of the council.

With one last scathing glance Katcalani moved away and sought out Toschee among the waiting women. Together the two women began to talk, throwing malevolent glances at Bree, who tried to pretend she didn't notice, suppressing another shiver.

"Don't let her bother you," Milakee came to her side. "Katcalani jealous Shocaw choose you, not her. She not act like good Seminole."

"I can understand her anger," Bree said. "I would feel that way too if Shocaw did not return my love."

"Come, we go," Milakee said. "Council finished for today." They moved down to the other end of the square where a half log had been raised on stumps a few feet off the ground. Men and women were already lining up on either side of the log, their faces bright with anticipation. To one side a line of young Seminole boys waited, trying not to show their nervousness. They wore only breech cloths and moccasins.

The medicine man stepped forward and, waving his feathered stick, began his chants. He called upon the spirits of Ishtohollo, the Mighty Goodness, the Breath Maker who brought all good things to man. His voice rose as he entreated the evil side of the two-sided God, Yohewah to turn his face from them. He reminded the Gods of the diligence of the boys as they prepared to become warriors and asked for bravery as they submitted themselves to the *In-sha-pit*.

He spoke of the Seminole's ability to endure

pain stoically and ended by reaching into the
fire and pulling out a live coal with his bare
hand. He placed it upon his wrist and waited as
the glowing coal cooled and turned black. His
face gave no indication of the pain he must have
felt.

When the coal was black, he calmly placed it
back on the fire and brought out a second live
coal and again placed it on his wrist. Murmurs of
approval ran about the onlookers. The faces of the
young boys seemed to grow paler.

Having demonstrated his own fortitude, the
medicine man placed the coal back on the fire
and motioned to the first boy. Without hesitation
the boy stepped forward, his face deliberately
blank, although his dark eyes showed his dread.
With an imperious slash of his arm the medicine
man motioned the boy toward the elevated log.

At first, the boy's dread gave way to relief at
not having to endure the hot coals on his own
flesh, but as he leaped up on the end of the log,
fear showed itself again in his eyes. For a moment he paused, took a couple of deep breaths,
while the villagers watched avidly, then the boy
stepped forward.

Bree could see the people at the log had knives
in their hands, and as the young boy stepped
forward their knives flashed, slashing out with
precision and control. At first there were only
long, fine cuts, little more than scratches on the
boy's legs, but as he took another step forward
and another, the knives flashed faster, leaving
deeper cuts.

In horror Bree watched, swallowing against
the bile in her throat, her eyes moving in disbelief from the medicine man and the waiting boys
to the youth on the log. Why were the Seminoles
engaging in such cruel behavior against their own
children? she wondered in dismay.

The boy reached the end of the log and jumped to the ground, while behind him the villagers gave a low cheer of approval. He had passed the challenge of the *In-sha-pit*. Heedless of the blood pouring down his legs, he stood proudly facing his people. Another boy mounted the log and the Indians readied their knives.

Bree could bear no more. Wildly she fled through the onlookers to her chickee. Her roiling stomach pressed upward and she hurried to the edge of the tiny garden she tended so carefully and knelt in the sand. When her stomach was emptied of the light breakfast she'd eaten, she held a cold, trembling hand to her forehead and made her way to the chickee.

At last the rites were finished. Bree heard the medicine man pronounce the boys warriors, ready for the battle of life as the Great Spirit decreed. The villagers walked back to the center of the square, their voices low as they discussed the valor each boy had shown. Not one had failed the test.

The square emptied as people went to their chickees to rest awhile. Soon it would be time for those who had violated the Seminole laws to undergo their penance. Cooee had already explained it to Bree. The men seeking penance would be placed in a sweat tent where the great stones would be heated. They would be given the black drink and cold water would be poured over the hot stones, making steam rise. If the men were able to endure the combination of the purging drink and the sweat lodge stoically enough, their transgressions would be forgiven and they would be allowed to join the feasts, which would occur later. It required great control over one's body. More barbarism, Bree thought, shuddering.

"Why did they cut those boys today?" she asked Shocaw when he returned to the chickee.

"Men must be brave and strong," he answered. "They must learn not only to endure pain, but to bear it with honor."

"But they're only children," she protested.

"They are men now. There is no greater honor for a Seminole man than to bear pain. He is able to endure what other men cannot. It is why we have lasted so long against the armies of white soldiers."

"Can't you teach them in some other way?" she muttered softly.

Shocaw laughed. "It is not so bad for them, Bree. They will bear the scars of this day proudly. Even now they strut among the *hoke-tee-chees*, showing off their marks of manhood." He paused and looked at Bree's troubled face. He wanted her to understand everything about his people. "It is a harsh world in which a man must walk," he said. "He must be made strong and brave, able to endure, or he will fail himself and his people. He must learn this lesson well and prove to others that he has learned it. He did not approach this moment alone. He has prepared for it all his life and there are many who have helped him prepare."

Bree sat staring at him. "Did you have to go through these things?"

"Yes," Shocaw replied. "I was younger than some of these boys, for my white father wished me to go to the white man's towns and live with him. My mother's brother decreed I should be initiated into the rites of warriors. I went to the white man's world as a man and not as a child."

Wordlessly, Bree looked into his face, seeing in her mind's eye the young boy Shocaw, his gangly body still that of a child but his purpose as clear as that of any man as he ran along the log of the *In-sha-pit* and accepted the burning coal on his wrist. Some part of her wanted to go to him and clasp him to her, to take away the memory of the pain he must have endured, but he had no need of such comfort.

He was a man nearly invincible in his pride and belief in himself and his ability to survive. With sudden clarity she saw that he was such a man because of the conditioning he'd received as a boy.

"I understand," Bree said softly, meeting Shocaw's gaze apologetically.

"That is good." Shocaw moved to take her into his arms and look down into the clear, gray eyes that touched him in such a special way. "Our ways are strange to you now; perhaps someday they will not seem so different from what is expected of your young men," he said softly.

"It is different," she replied, thinking that a youth's passage into manhood was usually marked by his first drink and a visit to one of the fancy houses in the seamier section of town. She didn't tell Shocaw that.

"There is hope within my breast that someday the rest of your people will come to understand the Seminole ways. Then we can begin to live in peace."

"I want that too, Shocaw," Bree whispered, and laid her head against his chest. She could feel the slow, constant thud of his heart beneath her cheek and wondered what her life would be if she could not be here with Shocaw like this.

"I must go now. Will you be all right alone?"

"I am not alone." Bree smiled at him reassuringly. "I have Milakee."

"Good. Will you partake of the black drink with the other women?"

"Yes, I will." Her small hands curled around his. "I wish to purify myself and prepare myself for the new year."

"I am pleased you take to our ways so readily,"

Shocaw said. Quickly he kissed Bree and left the
chickee while she stood staring after him. He
was pleased she accepted his ways and she tried
very hard, but sometimes she longed for the gen-
tler world she'd known at Greenwood. Shocaw
would never go to the plantation and live with
her there. He was half white and yet her people
would never accept him as one of them, not as
most of the Seminoles had accepted her.

At the thought of the villagers Bree smiled
happily. She felt as if she truly belonged here
with them for as long as she wanted to stay.
Throwing a light blanket about her shoulders,
for she suddenly felt a chill in the hot afternoon
heat, she hurried away to find Milakee. The black
drink ceremony would be next. The Seminole
believed the drink purged one's body of evil spirits that dwelled within, of bad deeds and thoughts.
She would drink to cleanse herself as the other
Seminoles did. She wanted to drink with Milakee,
for to do so signaled a pledge of friendship that
could never be broken.

After the purging rites there would be a feast
and dancing. Bree determined she would join in
the festivities as wholeheartedly as if she were a
Seminole herself.

On the second day of the ceremonies, the rites
of purification continued as people scratched
themselves with sharp needles or slivers until
blood was drawn, then the feather dance was
held. The dancing was accompanied by low musical chanting and the soft whir of pebbles inside
shell casings.

The following day, there was still another dance,
or was it a ball game? Bree was never sure, for
the men and women danced about a festival pole,
entwined with palmetto leaves and flowers, tossing a ball for the men to catch. The dance started
at sunset and lasted throughout the night. Sing-

ing, the women moved in time to the music as they threw the ball at the pole in the center. Using small bags fastened around bent bowlike sticks, the men tried to catch the ball. The dance game went on until the sun rose over the treetops in the east.

Bree and Milakee were eager to play in a game that allowed women to participate. Too often such activities were denied the women. Their young bodies moved swiftly and gracefully about the pole, their faces flushed and happy as they played across from Cooee and Shocaw. Laughter rang out often as the game progressed.

When they were so tired they could not go on, Shocaw and Bree made their way back to the chickee and fell on their mats for a few hours of sleep and rose again to participate in the next set of ceremonies.

There was another event of vast importance and one to which Milakee had loked forward from the beginning of the *Shot-cay-taw*. It was a race in which a brave must catch a girl before he may court her. Cooee and she had missed the race during the ceremonies the year before and Milakee wished to participate in it this year. Although she and Cooee would be married before the *Shot-cay-taw* ended, Milakee didn't want to miss any part of her courtship. One day she would tell her grandchildren how swiftly she had run and how easily her strong young suitor had caught her.

"Shocaw and Bree race too," Milakee suggested, and Bree declined laughingly until she saw the light in Shocaw's eyes. It lit a fire deep inside her and suddenly her laughter was gone and she breathlessly agreed to enter the race. All the young unmarried maidens and braves would be running. The girls need not be caught if they did not wish the courtship of a particular brave. Usu-

ally, though, the maidens allowed themselves to
be caught.

"I shall have to look over the other braves and
see which one I wish to have catch me," Bree
announced airily, and scrambled away, giggling
as Shocaw reached for her. He caught her up
against him and they wrestled off the mats and
onto the wooden floor, her laughter nearly drowned
by his whoops.

For a moment Cooee and Milakee watched
them, then with special smiles for each other
melted into the night shadows. At last Shocaw
elicited a promise from Bree that she wouldn't
be too fleet of foot and rewarded her with a kiss
that grew in warmth. Bree wound her fingers in
the coarse raven locks, urging Shocaw's mouth
down to hers with increasing fervor until they
were both breathless and trembling.

His hands brushed against her body, touching
lightly before moving on to touch again. Their
message of urgency was all too clear. The tips of
her young breasts yearned upward to him, aching to be touched and kissed.

Bree let her hands move over the broad shoulders that were so familiar and loved by her, then
slid down the broad tapering back to the narrow
hips and the hollows that dipped inward before
the buttocks flared. Shocaw groaned as he remembered they had company. He cast a quick
look about his chickee and gave a sigh of relief
upon seeing it empty. Cooee was not only a good
warrior but a tactful friend as well.

Shocaw's lips dipped once more to Bree's, tasting the moist sweetness. His large hands moved
over her body, smoothing and touching every curve
which he knew by heart. What beauty and passion she'd brought to him, he thought, wrapping
his arms tightly about her and rolling onto his back.

Now she sat above him, straddling his slim

hips. He could feel the heat of her body against his manhood and it surged to readiness against her. Bree's smiling eyes grew wide with surprise, then turned teasing and seductive as she traced a pattern up his bare chest and along the thick column of his neck. Shocaw swallowed and Bree laughed softly.

It still amazed her that this big, ferocious warrior could become as helpless as she in the face of the passion they shared. Her laughter rang out again, low and intimately seductive as her fingers trailed back down his ribs to pause tauntingly at his navel then downward to the sash holding his breechcloth in place. Slowly she loosened the sash and drew the cloth away, exposing his body completely to her gaze.

How she loved to look at him, at the long limbs of his body, the broad shoulders and narrow hips, the curve of his calf. Even the arches of his feet were objects of wonder. Her fingers trailed back up his hard thighs to the hard shaft that sprang up so arrogantly. Her wandering fingers stopped just short of touching as her eyes sought Shocaw's dark gaze. Then she was moving with feverish haste, all thought of teasing him gone as she divested herself of the full calico skirt and cape blouse.

When her clothes were gone, she lowered herself to him, straddling him once again, her hips settling over him slowly, while his body arched upward to meet her. Deep within she felt him touch her very core and her body responded to that touch. Arching backward, she rode with the night wind, oblivious to all else save the tumultuous roar that filled her head and carried her to the peak where an explosion of feelings washed over her, making her finally curve forward and cling to Shocaw's body, the only thing solid enough to keep her from drowning in her surging emotions.

At last, with a shudder, she lay forward on his chest, her breasts against his chest, her face buried in the curve of his shoulder as she waited for her breathing to slow. She could feel the pulse leaping in Shocaw's neck and placed her lips against it, waiting until it slowly returned to normal. They lay in each other's arms, not moving, lest the passionate connection be broken.

The chill night air finally drove them to move and Shocaw got up to spread the blankets over them. He settled himself and pulled Bree against him, savoring this moment between them as much as he did the moments that had gone before. Bree lay beside him quietly, her body relaxed and warm, her wide, gray eyes studying the stars above them.

"The *Shot-cay-taw* is very beautiful," she said softly. "I think I liked the feather dance best. It was so graceful."

"I will like the race tomorrow," Shocaw teased her. Bree's eyes returned his laughter, then grew serious. "The *Shot-cay-taw* is a time for your people to thank God for his help over the past year," she said quietly. "Isn't it hard for them to give thanks for a year when so many of the Seminoles have died?"

"Many of them lived and are still in their homeland," Shocaw said softly. He couldn't tell her how difficult he'd found it to give thanks for the past year.

"They find hope where there is none," Bree said sadly, and felt Shocaw's arms tighten around her.

"As long as there is one Seminole in Florida, the Seminole nation is alive and with life there is always hope," Shocaw said. "There are Seminoles who will never leave Florida." Although his voice remained soft, there was an edge of hard determination to it. Bree knew he would be

one of the Seminoles who remained in Florida
no matter what the cost to him. And there were
others like him. The harder the white man tried
to push the Seminoles from their homeland, the
harder they would resist until there was no man
left alive among them.

Yet Bree knew there were some Seminoles who
had given up, overwhelmed by the superior numbers and weapons of the soldiers, defeated as
much by the starvation and diseases they'd endured as by the soldiers. More and more chiefs
were laying down their arms and taking their
people in.

Some of them had been taken by treachery,
their children kidnapped and held for ransom until the chiefs brought the rest of their tribes to
Fort Brook. Other chiefs, who were willing to
parley under the white flag of truce, were given
too much liquor, then surrounded and taken prisoner. It seemed the white man's treachery was
boundless.

Bree felt ashamed of her people as she thought
of the atrocities they'd committed against the Indians. Where was their sense of honor? How
could they justify what they did? She lay beside
Shocaw and thought of all he'd said and slowly
came to understand the reason for his underly-
ing sadness. The Seminole were diminished with
each battle they fought. Back in their villages,
the people grew weak from lack of enough food.
Hadn't she seen evidence of this herself?

The summer, she perceived, was a gentle time for
the Seminole and it was hard enough to endure.
Even with the gardens and the game the hunters
brought in, the fare was limited, without variety.
When the warriors were gone several days at a
time and the village must depend upon those too
young or too old to fight, the fare had become even
more limited and the portions strictly rationed.

On those days Bree had seen the pinched looks on the faces of the children. Her own stomach had rebelled against the diet. What would the winters be like? What would happen if the soldiers came and destroyed Horse Creek Village and all the crops they'd worked over so diligently. She remembered the people who'd come from the Bear Village; she'd seen the fear in their faces, the despair and hopelessness, and yet they'd escaped. They'd been fortunate, or had they?

Bree shivered in Shocaw's arms and felt them tighten around her protectively. She understood the sadness she'd felt in Shocaw and the desperate look on the faces of the other chiefs. They feared for the future of the Seminoles here in Florida. Now that future touched her, for she could never return to her own world and be happy. Yet to remain here forever was impossible. The end for the Seminole's life here in the swamps was looming nearer.

What was the Arkansas Territory like? Bree wondered idly. Vast tracts of desert, the men in her father's study had said. Could she live there after the wild greenness of Florida? She'd just returned from exile; could she impose another exile on herself from the land she loved? Beside her, Shocaw had fallen asleep, his chest rising and falling rhythmically, but Bree was unable to find comfort in such short oblivion. For the first time she found no comfort in the presence of the Seminole warrior and his protecting arms.

Chapter 12

A level course had been laid out for the race and everyone gathered about it with great expectation. Courtships had flourished throughout the three days of the festival. It was not impossible that some of the participants in the morning's events would participate in the evening ceremony of weddings.

This was a happy occasion, a welcome relief from the more demanding ceremonies of purification. Many a dark eye flashed to meet the dancing lights of others as the racers lined up at the end of the racing course. The young, unmarried women stood, arrogant and proud, waiting for the race to begin. No maiden had to accept the attentions of a brave unless she wanted to— all went to the race as equals. The brave who wished her must catch her to win the right to court her. If she didn't want to be caught and was fast enough, she could outrun him and retain her freedom to be courted by others. However, most of the girls had their eye on a particular brave and determined to allow themselves to be caught.

Bree stood in line, looking back over her shoulder at Shocaw. In the golden morning sunshine, amid the merriment of his people, Shocaw had

put aside the weight of his office as war chief.
His dark eyes were bright with mischievous lights
as he looked at Bree.

Bree felt her pulse pound in her ears as she
looked at him. He was so tall and strong. His
shoulders were thrown back with confidence and
pride, his head held high with a natural dignity
that had never been surpassed by any man she'd
known, not even her father. Bree could see many
similarities between the two men.

Her father was the master of his world, moving easily and with authority through it while
lesser men looked up to him. Such was the case
with Shocaw. Yet both men were sensitive and
knew when to lay aside their cloaks of power and
respond to their needs as human beings, the need
to enjoy, simply and fully, life and the love of
others.

Bree smiled, unaware of the contentment and
love reflected in that smile. Her smile faded when
she glanced up to see Katcalani standing in the
line as well, her dark eyes gazing contemptu-
ously at Bree. Who would be racing for the Indian woman? Bree wondered. Looking back at
the men, she saw that several braves were already vying for her attention. Katcalani was a
beautiful woman. There was little wonder several warriors were racing for her.

Bree turned her attention back to Milakee, who
stood beside her. The little Indian maiden was
radiant this morning. Today she would become
Cooee's bride. The waiting was over for her. Her
dark eyes gazed at Cooee, who waited next to
Shocaw. They exchanged a fleeting smile, then
the old chief raised his white feathered stick and
everyone fell silent, their breath held as they
waited for the feather to dip downward.

The chief's eyes moved about his waiting people as he stood relishing this moment, prolonging

this short time of communion and happiness among them. An impatient twitch of a leg muscle, a narrowing of the riveted eyes, made him relent and the stick slashed downward in a quick motion. The racers were off.

At first timidity made Bree go more slowly than the others. Milakee ran ahead of her, as did several of the more fleet-footed maidens. Behind them the crowd of onlookers cheered as the old chief signaled the men to begin. She could hear the pounding of their feet on the hard-packed ground.

Katcalani shot past and veered slightly toward Bree as she eluded the grasp of one of the faster braves. Bree felt a sudden twinge of sympathy. The brave had been one of the most persistent of Katcalani's suitors and must surely have believed she welcomed his courtship. The fickle Indian maiden ran on, staying only a few feet in front and to the side of Bree.

Now Bree could hear the heavy breathing of the men behind them and realized if she didn't make more of an effort she would be too easy a conquest for Shocaw. Ahead of her Milakee was running as hard as she could, her brown legs churning across the ground. Although nearly every person in the village and not a few of the newcomers were aware of the little maiden's love for the young brave, she would not make his victory too easy for him.

Bree made more of an effort herself and soon drew abreast of Katcalani. Behind her she heard the pounding footsteps of Shocaw and knew he had kept up with her effortlessly. He was, she realized, being careful not to catch her too soon and she wondered if it was for the benefit of the spectators, who cheered everyone on, or for the benefit of her pride. Whatever his reason, she loved him for it. Her long, slim legs pressed onward over the level ground, running easily and smoothly, the calico skirts clutched above her knees.

Shocaw was close now, she could feel him behind her, while up ahead, Cooee reached forward and swept Milakee into his arms. From the corner of her eye she could see yet another brave reach forward to take hold of Katcalani. Suddenly the Indian woman veered toward Bree yet again. Bree veered away herself, and as she did so, she saw Shocaw's arms flash out for her. Katcalani was there between them, an elbow gouging a way for herself, pushing Bree away, then the Indian woman was in Shocaw's arms.

Bree stopped running and stood in the middle of the racecourse while the last of the runners hurried past her to reach the finish line. All around the racecourse people cheered and clapped couples on the shoulders while brave and maiden looked at each other with bright bold lights in their dark eyes. Bree stood where she was, her chest heaving as she watched Katcalani turn in Shocaw's arms and wrap her own arms around his neck. Astonishment was plain on Shocaw's face and his hands sat lightly, tentatively on Katcalani's waist. His dark eyes flew to Bree's face and Katcalani turned her own gaze to the girl. The triumphant look on her face spoke all too clearly. She hadn't been avoiding an unwanted suitor; she'd deliberately thrown herself into Shocaw's arms. To the onlookers it must have looked as if he had chosen Katcalani over Bree.

All around them the villgers milled, talking to the other racers, but none approached Shocaw and Katcalani. Their bright, curious eyes flashed time and again to the trio, speculating about what was being said. Suddenly Bree was unable to bear the humiliation. Whirling, she ran through the small groups of people back to the chickee, where she huddled on the floor in abject misery. Anger ran like silver-hot lightning through her and she longed to go to Katcalani and scratch her face and eyes. The thought shook her. She had deemed the action barbaric when the Seminole women did it.

Shocaw would be here shortly, she thought, and he would wipe away the awful feelings of anger and jealousy. Bree raised her head and stared with unseeing eyes back toward the racecourse. Jealous? Of course she was. She couldn't deny it. Shocaw was hers and Katcalani had deliberately thrown herself between them.

Bree put her forehead on her knees again, her fingers curving unconsciously into claws. Shocaw would be here soon and he would explain away her anger and doubts, smooth away her jealousy, although he might tease her for it. She would wait for him; he would be here soon.

But Shocaw didn't return to the chickee as she'd expected. Bree waited for most of the morning. In the distance she could see the villagers moving on to yet another activity while other women tended the pots of simmering food.

By early afternoon, Shocaw had still not returned, and Bree had begun to worry. There was a disturbance at one end of the square, but she chose not to go and investigate. She would wait for Shocaw awhile longer.

She was just about to swallow her pride and look for him when Cooee and Milakee hurried across the square toward her.

"Congratulations," Bree said, forcing a smile to her lips. The young couple looked at each other, their smiles radiant. Their eyes grew somber again as they turned back to Bree.

"I was just about to go look for Shocaw," Bree said to fill the awkward gap.

"He will be here soon," Cooee said. "Milakee and I will wait with you."

"That's kind of you." Bree reentered the chickee and graciously motioned them to sit beside her. She had no desire to return to the ceremonies and meet the speculative gazes around her. Although Cooee and Milakee had been too far ahead of them to see what had happened, they didn't ask her to explain now. "What is happening now?" she asked, suddenly feeling like an outsider with the people she'd come to love as her own family.

"The villagers are planning a day for coontie gathering and a ceremony for syrup boiling later when the maple gives up its sap," Cooee said.

"Men talk hunt, hunt, hunt," Milakee interjected, her dark eyes flashing. Still they didn't quite meet Bree's gaze. Uneasily Bree shifted.

"When will the weddings take place?" Bree asked, and was surprised at the flush that stole up Milakee's dark cheeks. The little maiden bowed her head and concentrated fiercely on the pattern of her wide calico skirt.

"At sunset the groom goes to the home of his bride," Cooee answered, "but first there will be ceremonies and prayers in the square."

"Are there many who will marry tonight?" Bree asked softly. Her thoughts were troubled, for it had occurred to her that she might never be able to participate in such a ceremony herself, not even back with her own people. No man would want her now, for the Southern gentlemen, indeed all men, seemed to set such store by a woman's virginity. How willingly she'd given away her innocence, still, no matter what the future held for her, she had no regrets. Her thoughts were interrupted by a commotion in the square and the outcry of one of the women.

"What is it?" Milakee and Bree asked together

as they all sprang to their feet to peer through the afternoon shadows.

"Stay here," Cooee instructed. "I will go see what is wrong." Quickly he crossed the square and disappeared among the milling people. Bree and Milakee waited with anxiety for what seemed like an endless time. There was a roar of disapproval, and anger and war cries from several of the warriors. The old chief mounted the platform and held up his hands to get his people's attention. The medicine man stood beside him, his face scowling and angry as he glared at the crowd. Behind them stood Shocaw and the rest of the men of the council.

At last the crowd quieted and the old chief spoke. When he was finished, the medicine man stepped forward, followed by Shocaw. Bree and Milakee strained to hear what was being said but could not make out the words. Bree had just about decided to disregard Cooee's instructions and move closer, when she saw him leave the throng and hurry back to them.

"What is wrong?" she cried when he was close enough to hear her.

"A warrior from the Otter Village has come to warn us that the soldiers attacked the village yesterday during the ceremonies of the *Shot-cay-taw*," he said. "Many people were killed, the village burned, and the prisoners taken back to Fort Brooks. They will be shipped to the Arkansas Territory. The village of the Otter is no more."

"No," Milakee cried, horrified. She had played with children from that village. The people of Horse Creek had gone to the village of the Otter to visit and make maple syrup only the year before.

"How horrible," Bree gasped.

"The warriors of our village are very angry. They wish to take up arms and go to punish the soldiers for what they have done, but the Otter warrior told them it is too late. The village and the people who once lived there are gone. Our chief and medicine man say we must stay and finish the prayers and ceremonies or Ishtohollo will be angry. Shocaw says the soldiers are expecting us to attack now out of anger. It is best we wait until the soldiers grow careless again.''

"How far away is the Otter Village from Horse Creek?" Bree asked, and saw the fear reflected in Milakee's eyes.

"It is only a few hours' march from here," Cooee said softly. "Do not be afraid, Bree, the soldiers are on their way back to their fort."

"But they'll come again," Bree said. "They've found one village, they'll come to look for more."

"I know," he admitted. "Shocaw has posted heavy guards and lookouts around the village. We are better hidden than the Otter Village was. We will be safe."

The three of them sat, thinking of the news and what it would mean to their own village. So lost in thought was she that Bree was not at first aware of the irate villagers who walked past the chickee casting angry looks at her. Not until she heard Toschee's voice did she look up and see the knot of women gathered outside.

"We will kill the whites as they kill the Seminole," one called, and the other women nodded their heads in agreement. Bree was not surprised to see that Katcalani was among the women.

"Kill the white woman," the Indian woman called, and Toschee took up her cry.

"Go to the back of the chickee," Cooee said, and Bree and Milakee moved back into the shadows, crouching low on the floor of the house.

"Toschee, Katcalani" Shocaw called. "Go back to your cooking pots," he commanded. "Make no more trouble at my chickee."

"She is the enemy. She must die," Toschee said hotly, but her defiance was short-lived in the face of Shocaw's anger. For a moment she glared at him, then meekly lowered her head and led the women away. Toschee was too used to obeying her cruel, overbearing husband to defy Shocaw. Katcalani was another matter entirely. She stood glaring at Shocaw before turning and arrogantly stalking away.

"Shocaw," Bree called when the women had dispersed, but he moved away across the square toward the council platform. Hadn't he heard her, Bree wondered, staring after him, or had he deliberately ignored her call?

Now that the women were gone, Bree and Milakee moved back to sit at the front of the chickee. Cooee crouched beside them, his eyes moving about the square restlessly, his hand resting near his knife handle.

"You must not feel bad about the behavior of our people toward you. They are angry about the soldiers attacking the village, but their anger will cool enough for them to see you are not to blame for what happened," Cooee said to her.

"I'm afraid they'll never accept me now," Bree whispered, near tears. "My skin is white, they can't see beyond that."

"Bree Shocaw's woman," Milakee said softly. "Seminole people not forget that. Bree do Shocaw honor, Katcalani bring dishonor to him."

"Dishonor?" Bree asked. "How does Katcalani's behavior dishonor Shocaw?"

Milakee looked away, her eyes going to Cooee for help. It was obvious she was holding something back.

"What is she talking about?" Bree demanded of Cooee.

"It is for Shocaw to tell you," the young brave said, looking away himself.

"He won't even come near me. What is it, Cooee? You must tell me." Bree's gray eyes were beseeching as she looked first at him then back at Milakee. "Milakee?" she asked softly. "You are my friend, you must tell me."

Milakee raised her face to Bree's and her eyes were full of pain and sympathy for her friend. "Shocaw marry Katcalani," she said hesitantly. Stunned, Bree stared at her for a long moment, uncertain she'd heard right, then she gave way to the roaring that filled her head.

She fainted, swooning across the rough boards of the floor. Milakee and Cooee leaped to help her. Milakee bathed Bree's face, crooning as her eyes opened. Slowly they focused on the dark face bending over her.

"Milakee, no," she whispered brokenly, grasping Milakee's hands in her own. Milakee kneaded the icy hands between her own, trying to work some warmth back into them.

"Shocaw say no, he no marry Katcalani, but she go to council. Tell how he make promise. He put deer on step of chickee. She make shirt, he take. He catch her in race."

"He didn't, Milakee. Cooee, he didn't mean to." Bree sat up and stared at each of them hopefully. "She threw herself into his arms."

"That what Shocaw say," Milakee said. "Council say Shocaw war chief, need Seminole wife, not woman of enemy."

"What did Shocaw say to the council?" Bree asked quietly, all hope draining from her heart.

"He agreed to marry Katcalani and send you to your people," Cooee said reluctantly, his head bowed.

"No!" Bree's cry echoed on the afternoon air. Quickly she looked around to see if anyone had heard her. Shocaw stood in the entrance to the chickee, his dark eyes moving over her face, the anguish clear on his own. Then, as if a shutter fell, the black eyes grew flat, without expression, so like the look he'd worn when he first brought her to the village.

"Shocaw," she whispered, and leaped to her feet. Quickly Cooee and Milakee rose and left the chickee. The silence stretched between Shocaw and Bree long after they were alone. Bree took a small hesitant step toward him, shaking her head in disbelief, a smile trembling on her lips.

"Cooee and Milakee told me—they said—" Her pitiful attempt at a smile faded. "It isn't true, is it?" she pleaded. Slowly Shocaw shook his head in acknowledgment. "Why?" Bree cried. "Why are you doing this? You don't love her, you love me."

"Bree." He sprang forward to take her into his arms. He held her against his pounding heart, his lips pressed against her temples. "Bree," he said again, and the pain grated in his voice. "It can't be helped."

"Why not?" Bree cried. "She lied and tricked everyone. How can they believe her against you? You are their war chief."

"That is true and as their leader, I must—" Shocaw faltered. "I must take a wife of my own people," he said finally. "Especially now. There are so few of us left."

"But Katcalani tricked you, she lied to the council."

"It doesn't matter, Bree," he explained as he would to a child.

"It does matter." Bree broke away from him. "You wouldn't have caught her in the race, you wouldn't marry if she weren't forcing you to." At the look on his face, she stopped. "You wouldn't, would you?" she whispered.

"I don't know, Bree." He buried his head in

his hands in anguish, turning his back to her. Bree looked at the noble head, bowed now, the broad shoulders hunched in pain. She felt he was facing a more painful decision than he'd ever faced before. She longed to rush to him and force him away from his decision, yet she stood rooted helplessly to the spot.

Slowly, Shocaw turned to face her. His eyes were haunted. "Bree," he began. "We've been living in a dreamworld, a world I had no right to bring you to. I should have returned you to your people long ago, but I could not. I couldn't bear to lose you, to lose the feelings we've shared."

"But now they mean nothing to you and willingly you give me away, back to my people."

"It is best for you."

"Is it?" Bree's gaze moved over his face. "Katcalani is very beautiful; perhaps you have grown tired of me and are glad of this decision from the council."

"You know the truth of that," Shocaw said flatly, and Bree lowered her angry, accusing gaze. In her heart she knew the truth. He wasn't tired of her.

"If you don't desire her, why do you marry her?" she asked, wanting to be reassured. "Is the council forcing you to marry Katcalani?"

"They can't. It is not the way of my people."

"Are they theatening me, my life? Is that why you do it, to save me?" Bree asked with sudden hope. She would brave any danger as long as she had Shocaw at her side.

"No," he said quietly, and they stood staring at each other. Shocaw began to speak, and with each word, Bree wanted to cry out a denial of all he said, for she knew it was a reasoning against which she couldn't win. Shocaw's love for his people had driven him to make his decision and that love was stronger than the love he bore for her.

"I want you to understand, Bree," he said, "so when you return to your own people, you can make them understand. The number of the Seminoles in Florida grows smaller each day. Our future is dim here, still we have no choice. We must fight to the last breath. We must watch as our children die. Soon we will all die. The white man will win."

"No," Bree moaned, tears streaming down her face.

"In this final hour the Seminoles must stay together," Shocaw said. "We must remain united with one another or our end will come even sooner. I do not wish you to die, I do not wish my own people to die."

"I will stay here and die with the Seminoles," Bree cried.

"No, Bree, your place is with your own people. Go to them and tell them of the things you've learned of the Seminoles, tell them so they will understand us and our need to remain here in our home. We will never leave here. Make them understand that."

"How can I tell them, make them understand, when I don't understand myself," she cried wildly, the tears rolling down her cheeks.

"You do understand. You cannot deny what your heart knows. I have seen it grow in your eyes these past few weeks."

"No," Bree whispered, denying his words, denying the pictures he'd painted. Was it only last night she'd known there was no future for them? Was it only last night she'd lain in his arms knowing there was little time left.

The anger and denial died from her eyes and she stood gazing at Shocaw, her reluctant acceptance of his words growing. At last she lowered her lashes and looked helplessly at the floor, her shoulders and back curving inward as she sank to her knees on the floor. Tears rained down her face as she wept silently as the Seminole women wept.

Helplessly, Shocaw watched her grief, unable to change it. It was done. Crossing the short space between them, he laid a hand on her bright head for a moment.

"Aw-lip-ka-shay." He whispered the farewell and his anguish was deep and unending. He would never be free of it again. Swiftly he left the chickee and now the hoarse sobs she'd held back escaped her throat and followed him as he crossed the square toward the council platform. His people moved about the square, their faces pinched and worried looking, the merriment and joy of the *Shot-cay-taw* forgotten in the face of the latest tragedy.

There was one more day of ceremonies left, but already the terror of war and death had touched them. Uneasily their gazes darted to the paths and dark swamp beyond their village. Death came on silent, unexpected feet, and if the God Ishotollo had brought good things to the Seminole people, he had most certainly brought evil as well.

Bree lay in her chickee long after the sun had set and fires were lit against the evening chill. In the square young couples were feted in a time-honored way among all people whatever their race. As the sun dipped lower in the sky, Bree sat up to watch the celebration, her eyes automatically seeking Shocaw out in the line of men. He stood in back of the other men, his face turned away from the festivities.

Katcalani was in the forefront of the young women who were to be married. Her face bore a triumphant smile. Not able to watch more, Bree turned away, burying her head on her knee in heartbreaking misery. Her lonely reverie was interrupted by a gentle touch on her head, much as Shocaw had touched her earlier, and for a brief moment hope flared then died as she raised her head.

"Milakee, what are you doing here?" Bree asked in a voice husky with repressed tears. "It's your wedding night, you're missing the ceremonies."

"We wait." Milakee smiled, gesturing to Cooee, who stood behind her. Quickly he knelt beside Bree.

"Are you all right?" he asked with concern.

"Oh, Cooee." The tears filled her eyes again and she turned away. Even now she couldn't master the Indians' stoic acceptance of things. She cried too easily. Soon she would be back with her own people, who accepted crying, and she would cry all night and all day, she thought bleakly. Now she swallowed away the sobs and shakily turned back to her two friends. "Why are you waiting?" she asked.

"We'll marry tomorrow," Cooee replied. "It is the last day of the ceremony and will have greater significance with the spirits. They will not have so many couples to guard."

"Milakee not marry same night Katcalani marry," Milakee said implacably, her fine eyebrows drawn down in a fierce scowl, and Bree knew that was the real reason for their delay. At first she felt like laughing at the Indian girl's fiesty attitude, then the significance of what she'd said came to her. Milakee had given up her own wedding plans because of Bree's pain over Shocaw.

"Oh, Milakee, Cooee," Bree said, gripping each of their hands. "We'll wait together."

"Together," Milakee said, and settled herself beside Bree. It was obvious she and Cooee had no intention of leaving her alone throughout the night. Cooee got down the sleeping mats and furs and they wrapped themselves in them and sat talking, studiously avoiding any mention of the revelry behind them in the village square.

They talked of the stars and old legends were repeated. Milakee and Cooee told her of their childhood growing up in the village, and as they talked, Bree watched Cooee. He had not a drop of Indian blood in his veins, yet he was accepted as Seminole. Why couldn't she have been accepted as completely as Cooee? She would gladly have lived with the Seminoles as Shocaw's wife. She should have told him that, made it clear she would share his fate with him and his people, but then he'd known and refused. He would return her to her people and it was too late for words or pledges.

Even now the villagers were escorting the men, Shocaw among them, to the homes of their brides. The torches moved from one chickee to another of the young women who were receiving their husbands. Tears stung the back of Bree's eyes as she thought of the night they would spend together. The image of Shocaw holding Katcalani in his arms, her long brown limbs wrapped around his, brought her more pain than she'd thought imaginable and with a gasp she lay back against the post and held her forehead.

"Bree not cry," Milakee said soothingly. "Shocaw love Bree." The memory of Shocaw's words here in the chickee only a few short hours before came to her and she was comforted. He did love her, but he was a chief and the fate of his people must be considered more than his personal needs.

Still, she could have been his wife, could have loved him and helped him, working in the fields to grow their food by day and stitching his clothes in the evening. The memory of the shirt and leggings she'd yet to give him came to her. She would leave them in the chickee when she left the village and he would find them and know how she'd loved him, how she'd tried to become a Seminole for him.

The village quieted and the long night stretched ahead of them. Bree could see that Cooee and Milakee were weary but were determined to stay awake and keep her company, so she pretended a fatigue she did not feel and lay down. Her tearful, unseeing eyes stared into the darkness. Without Shocaw she could see that her future would be as dark and bleak as the night.

Chapter 13

She was awakened at the first light of dawn by the nausea that had plagued her mornings. She hadn't eaten the evening before, yet now she was driven from her bed by the need to empty her stomach. Even the black drink hadn't purged her system as relentlessly as this.

She lay against the ladder, unable to move, and lay her weak and trembling head against the wood. Weakly she wiped at the beads of sweat that covered her brow and cheeks. Was she coming down with the dreaded swamp fever? If so, she had little hope for her life. She'd heard of too many who'd died of the ravaging disease.

"Bree?" Shocaw said. Slowly, Bree forced her eyelids open to look at him, at the face she loved so much, at the thick dark hair. Even now her fingers trembled with longing to sweep through the dark locks. The black eyes that could unlock her passions with just a glance were fixed on her now with concern.

"Don't come near me, Shocaw," she gasped. "I think I have the fever. You'll get it too," she warned, but he made no move away from her. Gently he wiped her mouth and gathered her up in his arms and carried her back into the chickee.

He placed her back on her sleeping mat, the one she'd shared so many times with him, and pulled the blankets around her. His hands were gentle as he touched her cheek briefly and moved away. She heard him move down the ladder and wanted to call him back, but she was too tired. Wearily she closed her eyes and slept.

When she awoke, Shocaw was there with something for her nausea. Supporting her head, he held a cup of liquid to her lips and urged her to drink. Bree did as he said and drew back, coughing and sputtering. The liquid blazed a fiery trail down her throat to her stomach and almost immediately she began to feel some relief as it warmed her stomach. It was miraculous, she thought. She hadn't contracted a fever; that was obvious. Perhaps her stomach was just unsettled by the kinds of food she'd eaten here in the camp.

Patiently Shocaw waited as she lay back on the mat and rested. Soon she felt the dreaded lethargy that had held her prisoner the last few days leave her. With renewed vigor she sat up. Her glance encountered Shocaw's thoughtful gaze.

"Take this and eat," he said, handing her a flat cake made of coontie flour.

"My stomach feels better now. Food might bother it again."

"You will need to keep bland things on your stomach for a while," Shocaw said. "Eat it." Bree took the cake and nibbled on it. An awkwardness seemed to settle between the two of them. What was he doing here? she wondered. Why wasn't he at Katcalani's chickee? He was her husband now.

As if reading her thoughts, Shocaw spoke. "Katcalani is my wife, my first wife. She will always carry that honor." Bree glanced down at her hands, twisting them in her lap. His words were so final, so without any hope for her. Then he spoke again.

"She will always carry that honor until she no longer wants it." Katcalani will never change her mind, Bree thought dismally. Shocaw paused, looking at her bowed head. "I ask you to be my second wife," he said, and waited for her answer, his eyes shuttered and unreadable.

"Your second wife," she repeated scathingly. "I would never marry you when you are already married. I won't be second." She wanted to wound him as he had wounded her when he walked away from the chickee to marry Katcalani, yet some part of her, a part she'd never known existed, made her calm her anger and speak to him quietly. "Yesterday you spoke of returning me to my people," she reminded him dully.

"Do you prefer to go to them?" Shocaw asked, and waited for her answer, his dark eyes still and quiet as they watched her. Bree's gaze roamed over his strong noble face and fled back to her lap. Did she prefer to return to her people? Yes, some part of her cried out, while another part cried out just as strongly her need to stay near Shocaw.

She remembered her vision of the dugout that floated between two shores while she stood undecided, feeling the call from both and unable to make a decision. Now she was confronted with the reality of that dream and felt the same agony.

Patiently Shocaw waited. Nothing save the twitch of a jaw muscle gave any indication of the tension he was under. She must come to this decision alone. At last she spoke, slowly and with the same dignity with which he'd addressed her.

"I cannot become a second wife to you. You come from your bride's mat to speak to me of marriage. I have accepted many of the Seminole's ways, but this one I cannot accept. I wish to have you for my husband, but I won't share you with another woman. There is nothing left for me here. I will return to my own people."

"Could you share me with a mother or a sister?" Shocaw asked.

"Katcalani is not your mother or your sister. She shares your sleeping mat," Bree said, her voice breaking.

Still, she fought for control and was unaware of the heartrending dignity in her eyes as she forced herself to meet his gaze. The anguish she felt had darkened the soft gray of her eyes, turning it to the dark storm clouds of the *ha-notch-e-fo-law,* the whirlwind storms that blew across the swamps at times.

"Katcalani will never share my sleeping mat. She will be like a mother or a sister. She will never bear my children," Shocaw said, and Bree's face lit with a moment of hope before it settled back into lines of despair.

"She is your wife," she said dully.

"She is my first wife, the wife of a Seminole war chief." He paused. "I wish you to be my second wife, to share my chickee and bear my children."

"What of those things you wished me to tell my people about the Seminoles?" she asked.

"We will find another way," Shocaw replied. The tightness in Bree's chest eased somewhat as she considered all he'd said. Could she stay and live with him under these conditions? "You have a choice. If you refuse, I will take you to your people."

The words penetrated Bree's wall of uncertainty and rejection. The choice was very clear to her. "I choose to stay here and be your second wife," she said softly, and could no longer bear sitting apart from him. Rising to her knees, she reached for him, but he brushed her arms aside and rose to his feet. His dark eyes looked into her startled, hurt ones and seemed to beg that she understand.

"I will tell the council," he said quietly. "We will be married tonight. Until then we will not meet again today. Milakee will stay by you until then." Shocaw nodded his head in Milakee's direction. The Indian girl had awakened and was sitting quietly. Now she nodded her head in agreement. Cooee threw aside his blankets and rose to his feet. Together the two men left the chickee. Bree stared after them, her face reflecting the bewilderment she still felt over Shocaw's rejection.

Milakee came to sit beside her. "Shocaw married," she explained. "Seminole laws very strict." Suddenly Bree understood. She'd once seen an Indian woman from another village whose nose had been cut off because she'd been adulterous. Shocaw had been protecting both of them from such accusations.

"Wait here all day. Go marriage ceremonies tonight. Milakee glad she waited," the Indian girl said, and suddenly the two girls were in each other's arms, laughing and talking at the same time.

They spent the morning in the chickee away from the other villagers, for Shocaw had left strict orders. He feared for Bree's safety among the visitors who didn't know her as their own villagers did. Although he hadn't expressed his concern over Katcalani's reactions to events, Milakee had guessed he feared her wrath as well. Katcalani had proven herself to be unscrupulous in getting what she wanted. Many men had wanted her and she'd played the field, but now that it was obvious that Shocaw desired someone else, Katcalani wanted him for herself.

In the afternoon the two girls went down to the bathing pond, where they washed their hair

and spread it out to dry as they sat and watched
the birds wading in the shallow water at the
other end of the pond. It was a peaceful time,
which seemed to quiet the tumult in Bree's heart
and brought some natural color back to her cheeks.

When they returned to the chickee, Cooee came
to tell them the council had accepted Shocaw's
request to take a second wife so soon after the
first. Excitement grew between the two girls as
the afternoon passed and they readied themselves
for the ceremony, putting on their new blouses
and skirts. Bree took out the leggings and shirt
she'd made from their hiding place and gave
them to Cooee to take to Shocaw. If they were
not to see each other until the ceremony, she
would have no chance to present them to him
herself.

When all was ready, the two girls sat waiting,
the anxiety and anticipation building in each of
them. Milakee thought of all the years she'd loved
Cooee and dreamed of being his wife and Bree
thought of her parents, wishing they could be
here for this ceremony. How different it would
be from a wedding held at Greenwood.

She could imagine her mother's excitement as
she planned the event. There would have been
so many elaborate arrangements, it would have
taken weeks, perhaps months to prepare them.
The large rooms would have been thoroughly
cleaned and decorated with fresh palmetto fronds
and flowers from her mother's garden. The cooks
would have been busy for weeks, baking and
preparing food for all the guests who would have
come. And there would have been many guests
just as there had been here for the *Shot-cay-taw.*

The spare rooms would have been filled to
overflowing and the neighboring plantations called
upon to put up extra guests. There would have

been an orchestra of musicians. The tables would have groaned under the weight of the food served.

Her father would have walked her down the aisle and claimed the first dance for himself before handing her over to her groom. Here, Bree's pretty pictures ground to a halt as she imagined her groom. He would have been the son of one of the planters, no doubt, sleek and spoiled and already going soft from the indolent life he led. She couldn't imagine Shocaw there in satin breeches and a frock coat.

Without Shocaw the beautiful wedding seemed meaningless. Willingly she'd give up the trappings of such a wedding if she could have Shocaw as her husband.

"It is time to go," Milakee said beside her, and Bree turned a dazzling smile on her. She is happy in spite of being only a second wife, Milakee thought, and felt happy for her friend. Though she would be only the second wife, she would be the best loved, Milakee was sure of that. She'd seen Katcalani's unhappy face that day and guessed what had happened between her and Shocaw. Now with Shocaw taking Bree as his second wife so soon, Katcalani's pride was assaulted yet again.

Milakee put aside her thoughts. She'd postponed her wedding for her friend, and spent all day watching over her, but now it was her wedding night and she would think of nothing else except her handsome husband.

Bree squeezed her friend's hand, silently thanking her for all her kindnesses, then the two girls stepped forward as the villagers began the beautiful wedding chants and prayers. The brides looked from beneath lowered eyelashes at their solemn grooms and smiled in a knowing womanly fashion. Both men were handsomely attired in the wedding shirts and leggings Bree and Milakee had made for them.

The villagers moved about the circle in step with the rhythm of their chants, their faces reflecting the beauty and solemnity of this ceremony. Bree moved with them, her eyes searching out Shocaw across the flickering light of the fire. His eyes had already found her and now held her gaze in a dark promise of love that took her breath away.

The anguish she'd felt the night before was behind her; ahead lay a life as Shocaw's wife. On this night she perceived the hollowed dugout had been poled to one shore. She had chosen and the people who waited on the other shore must disappear from her life. They would never forget her, but their pain would diminish as the years went by. Perhaps one day, when the war was finished, she could send them word of her safety or even return for a visit.

Shocaw stepped forward and took her hand in his, its cool strength reassuring her that he would always be at her side, guarding her, protecting her, and loving her. Freely, Bree gave her hand and moved beside him in rhythm with the chanting. Their eyes met and held.

At the appropriate time, with much chatter and merriment, the women escorted the girls to their chickees and scurried away to stand at a proper distance. As Milakee was left at her chickee, she turned to cast a last look at Bree over her shoulder. Her face was lit with a radiant smile.

When the brides were back in their chickee and just as the sun was setting in the west, the men escorted the grooms to their chickees and withdrew a discreet distance as each groom slowly climbed the steps to his bride. Now the villagers returned to their dancing and chanting, their sounds filling the night air with a special music that lent encouragement to the hearts of the timid bride and groom and highlighted the mood of those more bold. Eager lips met, hands reached out to touch and convey love on the chosen mate as each newly wed couple celebrated their union.

In their chickee Shocaw and Bree looked at each other. They'd been apart for only one night, but it seemed far longer.

The days since their last night together had been filled with such extremes of feelings, sorrow, anger, pain, and at last hope and love again. It seemed an eternity since last they'd stood here in their chickee free to give themselves to each other. Breathlessly they stood apart, their eyes devouring each other. Remembering his rejection earlier in the day, Bree felt timid and unsure until Shocaw's long arms swept forward and pulled her against him.

"Bree," he said, and his hot, quick breath fanned across her cheek, building a fire within her.

"Oh, Shocaw," she cried, wrapping her arms around his waist, splaying her hands across his back, feeling the width and breadth of him. Only the thin shirt she'd so carefully made for him kept her hand from his smooth skin. She could feel the warmth of his body beneath her palms and fingertips. Her hands moved across his back, seeking each remembered and favored hollow and curve, while a humming began somewhere deep along her nerve endings.

Shocaw's hands swept over her impatiently, possessively, yet tenderly, as if making sure that every part of her was still there warm and eager for his touch. His mouth met hers, his lips capturing, dominating, hungry for her after almost losing her. His tongue blazed a fiery trail down her cheek and throat. Impatiently he pushed aside the blouse, wanting to taste her skin.

Together they fell to their knees on the sleeping mats, their hands and mouths caressing, touching. Her blouse was lifted over her head and flung away. As the full skirts were unfastened and pushed down over her hips, the moonlight made a silvery outline over her skin, turning it to warm, living marble.

Shocaw was caught by her beauty and sat back on his heels to watch her for a moment. Her slim young body rising from the graceful folds of her skirts was like a statue sculpted by a master. As reverently as one of the finest art connoisseurs of Europe, this native of a savage new land worshiped at her feet, marveling at the perfection of form and line of her body as he lay her back against the mat. His dark fingers moved over her pale beauty, cupping the perfect breasts in his hands, feeling the warmth of her nipples burn into his palm, then bending to catch each tender dark bud between his teeth and suckle it.

The beautiful woman beneath him gasped and plunged her fingers into his dark locks, her body arching upward in an invitation he knew too well. Slowly, he moved down her body, his lips touching every rib with a soft feathery kiss, his touch flicking at the shadowed recess of her navel, his hands splaying gently over the slight swell of her abdomen.

He lay his cheek against the silken skin, his ears listening for any sound of movement, although it would be many months before such life would be there. He would wait patiently. He smiled to himself and raised himself to kiss her eager mouth once more. His long fingers stroked her, holding her against his chest while he stroked her back, the long column of her throat, the warm fleshy mound of her buttocks, and back to the stomach that quivered beneath his touch.

Helplessly Bree lay beneath him as he caressed her body, bringing her to life once more. Her own hands traveled over the smooth muscles of his shoulders and back and down to the throbbing arousal that pushed so impudently, impatiently, against her belly. How she loved him, this man who bore such responsibility for his people, this man who had been willing to give her up if it meant the end of the war and peace for his people. But in the end, he hadn't been able to give her up and she could forgive him for all the other. He loved her and she returned that love as completely, as wholeheartedly, as she always had.

Impatiently her hands moved on him, urging him to her, and with a groan he moved across her, his member going unerringly to the place it liked best. Her body was like a flower opening to him, needing him as a flower needs the sun and rain. His body plunged against hers, bringing new heights of pleasure before it withdrew only to plunge downward again and again. Her long slender legs wrapped around him to still the plunging body and hold it in a final consummation of passion.

They lay side by side, chests heaving, and Bree thought of how Shocaw had touched her. There had been impatient hunger, yes, but there had been a tenderness, a reverence in his touch that moved her. He truly loved her. That was why he had changed his mind and taken her as his wife. He'd had to choose between what he thought was best for his people and his need for her. He had chosen her. She had won. He'd loved her too much to send her away. Now she had to show him that she could be a Seminole too.

"I love you, Shocaw," she whispered.

"I love you, Bree," he whispered back, his arms tightening about her to pull her closer.

"We will have many years, happy years together," she said, and lay dreaming as most brides do of their future years together. "The war will end," she continued, "and we will be able to live in peace and raise a family."

"It will have to end soon then," Shocaw said, his hand going again to her stomach, moving across the satiny planes. "My son will not wait."

"What do you mean?" Bree asked, startled into stillness, her large, gray eyes peering through the darkness at Shocaw.

At her tone he raised his head and looked down at her. "I am speaking of the son you carry in your womb," he said, and felt her pull away from him. "What's wrong, Bree, you will not be unhappy that it is not a girl, will you?" He found the thought hard to take. Anyone would be proud of a son, he thought. Oh, someday he wanted a girl to tease him and comfort him when he sat in his chickee at night, a little girl who looked like her mother, but first he wanted a son. In the moonlight he could see Bree's shock and growing alarm.

"What is wrong?" he asked gently.

"Why do you think I carry your son?" she asked, and her voice was strangely without emotion.

"Even a man knows these things," he said, and wished he'd said nothing. Obviously, she'd wanted to surprise him and he'd spoiled that. "When I saw your illness this morning, I knew."

"Morning sickness," Bree said softly, her voice floating out of the darkness toward him. He sought to pull her back into his arms but she pushed away. She lay stiff and silent beside him, her mind raging.

A baby, she was going to have a baby, suddenly it all fell into place. Milakee's sly, knowing looks, the mornings when she couldn't look at food, the lethargy that swept over her at odd moments so she was forced to go back to her chickee and sleep. Shocaw had seen her this morning as she lay against the ladder, ill and unable to move, and he had known what was wrong. Was that why he'd asked her to be his second wife?

"You knew about the baby before you asked me to marry you?" she said now in a low, dull voice.

"Yes, Bree, what difference does it make?"

"If you hadn't found out I was pregnant, would you have changed your mind about sending me back to my people?"

Shocaw was silent beside her, his mind following her woman's thinking and understanding the doubts she felt. Yet he could not lie to her. "No, I would not have asked you to stay," he said quietly. "You would be safer with your own people, you might be able to intercede for us with the general. My people need that help, but I have a wish to see my son."

"Your son, not me, but your son," Bree said, her voice rising. She rose from the sleeping mat and stood looking down at him, trembling in the damp night air.

"Bree, why are you angry?" Shocaw asked, rising to stand beside her. He couldn't understand her behavior. "I love you. You need never doubt that."

"You say you love me, but you were willing to send me back to my people while you married another woman until you realized I carried your child."

"That is true, Bree. I have been selfish and I take a chance with your life in keeping you here, but I couldn't bear to lose you and my son. I—"

"No more! I don't want to hear any more," Bree cried.

"You have to listen, you have to try and understand."

"Why, Shocaw? Always it is I, a white woman, who must understand you, the Seminole. It is I

who must make allowances, who must change
and accept your ways. I have done that. I've even
become a second wife, a position that will only
bring me shame among my own people and one
that carries little status among your people. But
I did it because I thought you loved me as much
as I love you. But it is the baby I carry which you
love more."

"That's not true," Shocaw cried, and moved to
take her in his arms. Women who carried an
extra life within them sometimes had strange
moods. He must be patient with her. He must be
gentle and show her his love.

"No," Bree cried out, eluding his reaching
hands. Her cry echoed around the sleeping village. "I want you to leave me now," she said
quietly and implacably. Looking at her, Shocaw
knew it was useless to argue. Picking up his
clothes, he left the chickee and made his way to
the banked fire in the village square.

Her words hounded him and as he sank onto a
log to stare into the winking coals he had to
acknowledge the truth of what she'd said. He'd
been willing to sacrifice what they had between
them for the good of his people. He'd even accepted a wife he could never love, a wife who'd
won him by trickery and lies because he'd wanted
to show his people he was a true Seminole in spite
of his white blood and the white woman he loved.

She had a right to her anger, he acknowledged,
although she was wrong when she said he hadn't
loved her. He *had*, all too well, and it had been a
fear of the power of the love between them that
had made him act hastily. He could not undo all
the things that had happened, couldn't call back
the hastily spoken words that caused so much
misunderstanding, but he would prove to her
that he loved her, truly loved her, and not just
for his seed which she carried within her.

She was his woman, Shocaw's *hoke-tee*, and she carried his son. He wouldn't give either of them up easily. Shocaw stretched himself on the sand between the logs, far enough away so he wouldn't be burned, but close enough to be warmed by the heat.

As the stars winked above him he lay dreaming of his beautiful son and of all the things he would teach him, of the pride they would share in each other. In all the dreams was the presence of his beautiful second wife, whom he loved more than he could ever tell her.

Bree lay huddled on her sleeping mat, cold without Shocaw's warm body beside her. The loneliness seemed to seep into her very soul. He hadn't really loved her, she told herself, or he wouldn't have left the chickee, even if she had ordered him to. He would have stayed and made her believe in him. She wanted to believe, she needed to, for she'd taken steps away from her own people toward his and needed the reassurance of his love more now than ever before.

Where was he now? she wondered. Thrown out of the chickee of one wife, had he gone to the other? He had said he would never share Katcalani's sleeping mat, but had he changed his mind? Bree raised her head and looked about the square. It was empty. She wasn't able to see him nestled between the fire logs. She lay back beneath the warm blankets.

Her hands settled on her stomach. It was so flat, she thought, Shocaw must be wrong. Yet she knew from the morning nausea that it was true. She was going to have a baby, a baby! The wonder of it struck at her and she lay thinking of the life growing within her. Would he look like Shocaw? Of course he would. He would have the same black eyes and black locks falling across his forehead.

He would be chubby when he was little, like Chofee, whom Sofangee carried on her hips. His eyes would shine with a merry light when she made him laugh and she would make him laugh often. She would tend to him herself, even taking him to the field with her, and she would make him rattles of shells and pebbles.

Suddenly she thought of the big, comfortable nursery back at Greenwood where she and Jared had grown up. It still held all the toys they'd played with. There had been a painted riding horse and a wooden train and many, many picture books. There were ponies to ride and fat geese to chase and plenty of food to eat all the time. A cold shiver washed over Bree.

For Shocaw, the coming of the baby had meant a change of mind. He wanted her here in the village with him, yet for Bree it meant a change of mind as well. The health of her baby depended upon her. She must return to her own people, where there would be doctors to care for them and proper food so her child would grow strong and healthy. The people of Horse Creek had survived for the summer and there was enough food, but what about the future? What would happen in the long, hard winter months ahead when the weather grew cool and the soldiers took advantage of it to move after the Indians more diligently?

Bree rolled about on her sleeping mat, unable to sleep. The night seemed as long and dismal as her thoughts. How could she leave Shocaw, she wondered, and yet how could she not? Her baby depended on her.

As the morning sunlight streaked the horizon Bree rose from her sleeping mat and made her way through the village and down to the bathing hole. Fog lay around the trees, lending an ethereal beauty to the ghostly swags of Spanish moss. She

sat on the banks watching the sun burn away the
mists, thinking of the Seminole maiden who had
draped her hair in the trees. The legend seemed
symbolic of the Seminole's approach to life, accepting the inevitability of death and separation
stoically, softening the pain with a tale of beauty
and noble courage. If only she would accept what
must be with the same courage as the Seminole.

Unimpeded by man's problems, the sun rose in
the sky, changing the swampy landscape. Bree's
heart was weighed down by sadness. She'd come
to feel at home here in the swamp. She'd learned
to rely on her instincts and the things she'd
learned from the Seminoles about survival here.
She understood the swamp's dangers beneath
its beauty and still was able to find pleasure in
the treasures it unfolded for the eyes of those
who wished to see.

The sun rose above the treetops and shone
down on the little pool. The echo of laughter
she'd shared here with Milakee and Cooee and
the love she'd discovered here in Shocaw's arms
seemed to fill the air about her. She sat now with
her legs tucked beneath her, her tearstained face
turned to the sun, and it was thus that Shocaw
came upon her. He paused for a moment, enjoying the wash of golden sunlight as it spilled over
her hair and skin.

Wearily she lowered her head and studied the
sun-spangled water. Shocaw could see in the slope
of her shoulders, the curve of her bowed head,
the decision she'd made. Some part of him longed
to rush forward and touch her, hold her, pull her
back to him, but something told him it was too
late. He was losing her. She was slipping away
from him as surely as the fog was leaving the
forests, burned away by the relentless rays of
ha-shay. A sad enchantment lay over the pool and
the girl beside it. Reluctantly, he walked for-

ward into it, dreading the words he sensed would come.

"Bree." He said her name softly and it floated on the soft morning air toward her, making her turn to look over her shoulder at him. The wide gray eyes stared at him unblinkingly, their expression full of all the feelings, all the sadness and love within her.

Getting to her feet, she turned to face him. "Ho, Shocaw," she said softly. Her glance moved over his face and shoulders as if she would memorize the look of him at this moment, then fled back to meet his gaze. She waited for him to speak first, knowing the things she had to say would bring an end to everything between them.

"We go to join Coacoochee's warriors," he said. "We are leaving soon. We must talk and clear up this misunderstanding between us."

"Yes," Bree agreed, her gaze sweeping over him again.

"I love you, Bree," Shocaw said simply.

"And I love you, Shocaw." So many words to be said, but these were the most important and would make the others easier to bear.

"I'm sorry if I've hurt you, I didn't mean to." His voice was warm and deep, full of love, and she believed him.

"I know," she replied, "but you were right. My place is with my own people."

"You said you chose to stay here and be my wife. If you are doing this in anger—"

"I'm not," she assured him. "I forgive you for your slight, I truly do, but I want to go home to my own people."

"But you're my wife now. You carry my son."

"He's my son too," Bree said, and marveled that neither of them had considered that the baby might be a girl. "He's my son too," she repeated, "and for that reason I'm going home, if you will take me. I want my son to be where it's safe, where there is plenty of food, where he will never be hungry or ill, where death won't come to claim him in the middle of the night."

"Death brought by your own people," he said angrily.

"With my people that death will never touch him," Bree returned calmly. Her decision was made, there was no turning back from it now.

"I don't want to lose either of you," Shocaw said hoarsely, his eyes black with despair.

"We have no choice. You told me once I had a choice, but I see there is none, not for our son. Let me return to my people, Shocaw, there is nothing left for me here. You will have another child with Katcalani, a true Seminole. I free you from your vow not to give her your children."

"Bree." Shocaw moved forward as if to take her into his arms, but she backed away, holding out a hand to ward him off.

"I have made my decision, Shocaw," she whispered. "I ask you to honor it."

"Think about it for a while longer, Bree, think about it until I come back. Then if you feel the same way, I will return you to your people." Bree hesitated and he pressed on. "Promise me you'll do nothing until I return," he asked, and seeing the pain in his eyes, she could do nothing else.

"I promise," she whispered.

"Will you kiss me good-bye?" For a long moment she looked deeply into the eyes she loved so much and with a sob flung herself into his arms. Her decision was made, but she would never stop loving this tall, gentle warrior. He held her fiercely, wrapping his arms about her tightly, holding her against his breast, his face buried in her long golden hair. He breathed in the scents of her, impressing upon his senses the feel and warmth of her small, slim body.

"Bree, Bree," he cried hoarsely as his lips claimed hers in a passionate kiss. She returned his kiss with the same wild abandonment, ignoring the tears that coursed down her cheek.

"Shocaw!" Cooee called his name softly and slowly Shocaw released her, raining a last few kisses on her dampened cheeks and lips.

"I must go," he said, and Bree nodded her head in understanding.

"Remember your promise to me," he said, backing away.

"I'll remember; I'll wait," she said, and watched as she gave one final glance over his shoulder and disappeared into the forest.

"Shocaw," Bree cried, running forward a few steps, but he didn't answer and she stopped, wiping at her cheeks. She would not go back to the village to watch the warriors leave. She'd had enough of good-byes for one day.

"Shocaw," she whispered longingly as she sank to the ground, her cheek pressed against the cool grass where once Shocaw and she had made love to each other on a happier day that seemed so long ago. One part of her life had ended here forever on this grassy bank and a new one had begun. Now that life must be put behind her and she must think of the future of their baby, Shocaw's and hers.

But oh, the pain of letting go of what she'd learned to love so well. Sometimes there are hurts that go too deep for tears to help, so Bree lay silent and still while the golden light of the *ha-shay* shone around her, its rays unable to light the darkness that had seeped into her soul.

Chapter 14

The warriors didn't return within a few days as expected. No longer did the women go off to the fields to harvest and tend their crops. The soldiers had penetrated the swamps too deeply. The smoke of their campfires was too near.

A tenseness, out of character with the normal serenity, had invaded the village and its inhabitants. Campfires no longer brightened the village square at night. Only the main fire was lit and then only until the food was cooked, then it was banked down and the kettles placed between the logs to be kept hot.

Not all the men had accompanied the war party. Sentries had been left behind and they were posted outside the village. Many of them slept at their posts and entered the village only for food and to visit briefly with their families. Their faces were tense and wary as they sat beside the nearly dead fire.

Voices were more subdued than normal. Although the heavy brush of the swamp blanketed sound so it didn't carry, the villagers took no chances of discovery. As the days passed, Bree began to notice the small children and babies had disappeared from the village and she asked Milakee about them.

"Mothers hide babies in swamp," Milakee replied. "Dig hole, hide baby. Soldier come, baby not killed." Bree was horror stricken to think of the panic the mothers and their babies must feel. More than ever she knew she must keep to her decision and return to her own people. She couldn't bear the thought that her own child might die in the swamp. The days dragged by.

Nearly two weeks had passed since the *Shot-caytaw*. It seemed like a dream. Had they ever really been that gay and happy, Bree wondered, and doubted if they'd ever feel that way again. The time since then had been filled with worry.

One morning Bree awakened to the sound of small birds chirping in the trees and lay listening to their innocent song. All too soon she must rise and then the fear and anxiety of the villagers would close around her again. For now she was content to lie in bed and listen to the birds' song.

The awful nausea had left her at last, but she tired easily still. Milakee said that too would pass. When she returned to Greenwood, she would sleep late every day until this terrible weariness had left her, she vowed.

Her reverie was interrupted by something, she couldn't have said what, perhaps some change in the very air. The birds were no longer singing, the swamps seemed ominously silent. Throwing aside her blankets, Bree sat up and looked about the square. The women stood still, frozen in place, their faces raised as if they were sniffing the wind, only their eyes moving, darting here and there.

There was a snap of a branch in the underbrush, a sense of a body moving slowly through the trees. Was a large animal lumbering too near the village? she wondered. If so, the guards would surely spot it and scare it away. There were few bears left in the swamps, but now and then a stray one found his way too close to a village and was as frightened by the encounter as the villagers themselves.

Another rustling sounded in the brush, followed by a snapping and a sudden shout cut off in midair by the loud report of a rifle. Suddenly the village square erupted into a mass of confusion and fear. Soldiers rushed into the clearing, firing their rifles at any Indian, woman, or child who came into their sights. Women screamed and tried to run away but they were quickly cut off. Other women ran to shield their children. The soldiers had come too early in the day and the women had not yet taken their babies into the swamps to hide them. Now they clutched their babies to their chests, running about wildly, looking for a place to hide them from the soldiers and the death they brought.

Bree lay in her chickee, pressed flat against the floor, her slight body hidden by the pile of furs and blankets, watching in horror as she saw soldiers fire again and again at defenseless women and old men too feeble to escape. Quickly the villagers were rounded up and herded together in the center of the square. Still Bree had not been discovered. As the soldiers brought in the stragglers, she crawled to the back edge of the chickee. Perhaps she could make it to the swamp and hide there? she thought wildly. She crouched behind one of the thick cypress posts and peered from beneath the chickee at the scene in the square.

The villagers were subdued now. No one was struggling or trying to run away. They stood docilely, a voice raised now and then in anguish over a loved one whose life had ended with a soldier's bullet. Among the groans and cries a low sad death chant rose among the huddled Seminoles. The soldiers stood in a circle around

them, their rifles cocked and ready, their eyes
alert and edgy. Some of the villagers simply stared
at their captors in stoic acceptance.

A word went around the soldiers and they
came to attention, glancing over their shoulders
as their leader came into view. He was a tall,
slender man who moved with confidence and
purpose. His shoulders were thrown back, his
head high as he surveyed the pitiful group of
captives. There seemed to be no sympathy in his
brusque attitude as he spoke to his men. Something about the man seemed familiar, but Bree
couldn't make out who he was until he took off
his hat. His pale blond hair shone in the sunlight.

"Lieutenant Whitlock," one of the men called,
and Bree drew in her breath with a gasp. This
was the same man who had set a trap for Shocaw
and his men. He had been ruthless in his attempt to catch Shocaw, uncaring of the innocent
people he might have killed. The people of Horse
Creek could expect little mercy from him.

"We got the chief," the man called, and pushed
Micco Onnitchee forward, sending him sprawling onto the ground. "Get up, you redskinned
heathen," the soldier cried, and aimed a kick at
the old man's middle. Bree clamped a hand over
her mouth to keep from crying out. There had
been no call for such cruelty; the man was feeble
and harmless.

"So this is Onnitchee," the lieutenant said.
His eyes raked over the frail figure as the chief
struggled to his feet. "You're too old to lead your
warriors into battle," the lieutenant said. "Where's
your war chief, this Shocaw we hear so much
about?" The chief didn't answer, staring straight
ahead. "Where is he?" the lieutenant shouted,
barely containing his anger. His hand lashed out
and struck the old man, the heavy ring on his
hand tearing the fragile skin. The chief bent be-

neath the blow but straightened himself and stared into the distance, his head held proudly.

"Scotty," the lieutenant called.

"Yes, sir, Lieutenant." A short red-haired man stepped forward.

"Ask him about his warriors and this Shocaw Hadjo," the officer commanded, and the man stepped forward. He spoke Seminole well, better than she did, Bree realized. Still the old chief would not answer. Again the lieutenant struck him and again was met with silence. Frustrated, the lieutenant walked up and down the square, eyeing the women.

"Harrison," he called.

"Sir." Another man stepped forward.

"How long has it been since your men have been into town and had a woman?"

"A long time, sir," the man said, grinning.

"There are some young ones in there. Might not be too bad. Tell your men to have a go at them."

"Yes, sir." The man saluted and turned to his men.

"Just make sure you keep your guards up. We don't want any smart-assed warriors jumping us when we're not ready for them," the lieutenant called after him.

"Yes, sir," Harrison replied. Turning back to the chief, the lieutenant put a cigar into his mouth and struck a match.

"Do you see what is happening to your people, Chief?" he asked. "Worse things are going to happen if you don't tell me where I can find Shocaw Hadjo." The old chief did not move an eyelash. All around him the soldiers were grabbing hold of the younger women, who cried out and struggled against them, still the chief stood unmoving and unspeaking.

"Ah, I'm beginning to think he's dead," the lieutenant said in disgust.

"Yes, sir," Scotty replied. "I believe he might be. The Seminoles cremate their dead, don't they, sir?" Scotty said, and grinned at the old man.

"You're right, Sergeant, they do." The lieutenant looked at the chief speculatively.

"Reckon we ought to just go ahead and cremate him where he's standing?" the sergeant suggested, leering at the old man.

"Might be a good idea," the lieutenant said, watching the old chief's face for a flicker of acknowledgment. Still the chief stood still, his face without expression. At a signal from the lieutenant, the sergeant stepped forward and, lighting a match, held it to the ends of the old chief's turban.

At first the material just smoldered, the smoke rising to the Seminole's nostrils; still he made no movement, not even to extinguish the fire. The smoldering line of fire caught hold and began to burn across the material, gathering momentum as it licked upward greedily.

Surely the old chief felt the fire now and would put it out, Bree thought, biting against a knuckle to keep from crying out. But he did nothing. Standing as straight and tall as his frail old figure would let him, he stared ahead impassively. Now the flames licked upward and engulfed the whole headpiece.

Suddenly an old woman, the chief's wife, leaped forward and knocked the burning turban from his head. The soldier called Scotty raised the butt of his rifle and brought it down over her head so she lay in a heap at her husband's feet. Again the soldier swung with his rifle and Bree could hear the crunch of bone breaking. The old woman would never serve her husband again.

The horror of what she was seeing made her want to back away, but her gaze was caught now by the soldiers who had thrown several of the

women on the ground and were taking turns
raping them. The women made little outcry, struggling silently with their attackers. Their resistance was quickly crushed with the swing of a
fist or a kick to their ribs, so at last they lay still
and unresisting. She saw Katcalani as she was
flung to the ground.

Where was Milakee? Bree wondered, searching frantically among the women. She caught a
glimpse of the young Seminole maiden at the
back of the square struggling against a soldier.
He held her arms behind her back and attempted
to throw her to the ground. Milakee fought with
all the strength in the slim, young body, and
when the soldier had her down, she lashed out
with her nails, then rolled away from him. Springing to her feet, she looked about wildly, then
darted toward the edge of the square, her bare
feet kicking up sand as she ran. Another soldier,
laughing at her plight, caught her in his arms
and held her fast, while she beat at him with her
small fists, butting at his chin with her head, to
no avail. Easily the man held her.

"Milakee," Bree cried out from her hiding place,
half rising to her feet to go to her friend's aid,
but even as she rose, Milakee lashed out with
one foot, landing a well-aimed kick in her captor's groin. With a howl the man let go and
Milakee leaped clear and ran for the cover of the
swamp. A bullet whizzed by her.

"Run, Milakee, run," Bree cried, leaping to her
feet. Her heart was beating in her throat so she
could hardly breath as she stood praying that
Milakee would make it. She was so close, only a
few more steps. If she could just make it to the
trees, she would be able to hide. The soldiers
would never be able to find a small woman-child
who knew the swamps and its ways as well as
Milakee did.

There were only a few steps to go. Bree stood where she was, tears stinging her eyes, the anxiety waning a little as she saw that her friend was going to make it. The lumbering soldiers could never catch her now. Milakee ran with the fleetness and lightness of a deer. Agilely she leaped over a branch and then over a log. A shot rang out, catching her in midair as she sprinted over a log.

"No," Bree cried as Milakee fell like a wounded bird. For a moment she lay still, then the small body moved and she was up and running again. Bree's chest was tight with lack of air as she watched her friend's last desperate struggle for freedom. She'd left her hiding place by the chickee and now she began to run across the square.

"Milakee," she cried out, her heart pounding in her chest. The Indian girl ran on toward the swamp. Once again shots rang out. Milakee's body jerked, her arms flung upward as she ran on a few more steps then crumpled to the ground.

"No, Milakee." Bree's scream could be heard around the square as she ran toward the inert figure of her friend.

"There's another one," a man shouted, and a shot whizzed past her head. Bree's pace didn't falter as she ran on. She had to get to Milakee. She had to help her. Her heart hammered painfully in her chest as she frantically pushed away the fear that she was too late. Another shot kicked up the dirt at her feet and still she ran on.

"Jesus, don't shoot, that's a white woman," another man cried, and she could hear them pounding behind her. But she was at Milakee's body now, her wide eyes taking in the bright blood soaking the back of the blouse and one shiny strand of hair that had fallen free.

"Oh, Milakee, Milakee," she cried. Frantically she gripped the Indian girl's shoulders and turned her over. The front of the blouse was covered with round spots of spreading blood. Some of the bullets had passed right through her slight body. A tiny trickle of blood trailed from Milakee's lips.

"Milakee," Bree cried, shaking her as if to awaken her, but the girl made no move. Her limbs were limp in abject surrender to death, her dark lashes lay still against her cheeks. Bree would never see the gentle laughter and caring in those dark eyes again, would never see the face light with a smile of joy.

"No, please, God," Bree cried, gathering the girl's slight form in her arms and rocking her in an age-old attempt at comfort. "Milakee," she moaned, her tears soaking the dead girl's face. Behind her the soldiers came to a stop and took in the scene.

"Look at that hair, she's white all right," one of them said.

Lost in her grief, Bree ignored them. A sad, mournful chant of the Seminoles came to her lips and she sang it, her voice low and grieving as she formed the words. She'd heard them so often in the weeks she'd been in the camp and always thought them beautiful. She had never known the pain behind them. Not until now. Now she sang the words, tears streaming down her cheeks, her face raised to the rising sun. She sang for all the things that were forever gone.

Never again would she see her friend's smile or hear her happy laughter, never hear her call her name. Gone were the happy hours by the pools and all the sharing of dreams and hopes and knowledge and understanding. Milakee had been little more than a child, yet she'd already come to womanhood. She'd had strength and gladly given it to those she loved, just as she'd given her love, freely and unstintingly. Her life

with Cooee had just begun and now it was ended
and all of them who had known Milakee would
remember her and grieve for their loss.

"Jesus, look at her. She's mourning over that
dead Injun, just like she was family or somethin',"
a man said in disgust, and turned away.

"Lieutenant, you'd better come over here," one
of the men called to his superior officer.

Lieutenant Whitlock walked over to the group
of men gathered about. "What is it, Sergeant?"
he asked, and paused in shock, looking at the
beautiful girl holding the dead Indian in her
arms. Her golden hair was spread out over her
shoulders and down her back, reaching almost to
her waist. Her face, its cheekbones made more
prominent by the diet she'd subsisted upon while
in the Indian camp, was tanned a golden honey
color.

Christ, she was beautiful, the lieutenant thought,
watching her. It was the same woman Shocaw
Hadjo had tried to trade for the old chief back in
the spring, he was sure of it. He remembered
how she'd called out a warning to the warrior
and how she'd run with the Indians when they'd
escaped. Now he watched her as she sat rocking
the dead Indian girl against her breast, her voice
rich and low as she sang the Seminole death
chant.

"Look at her, actin' like a heathen Indian," one
man said, and the lieutenant waved him to silence. They waited until she'd completed her
chant. Her eyes were closed and he wasn't sure
if she knew they were there. When she had finished, she sat in silence, her face raised to the
sky. The sounds of women screaming and men
shouting could be heard from the square, but the
lieutenant and his sergeant stayed where they
were.

She was a white woman and they couldn't

rush her. She'd had too much of a shock already today. Obviously this dead Indian girl meant something to her, had probably been kind to her. It would take her awhile to realize she was no longer a prisoner of the Indians. Time passed and the sun rose and finally the lieutenant stepped forward and touched Bree on the shoulder.

"Are you all right?" he asked gently, and Bree opened her eyes and looked at him in puzzlement. His voice was kind, yet he was the same man who had set the old chief's turban on fire, he was the man who'd ordered the men to attack the women. He wasn't kind. He was evil. She closed her eyes again and gripped Milakee's body to her more closely.

"I'm Lieutenant Whitlock," the officer tried again.

The long lashes fluttered upward and once again the gray eyes, dark with pain and grief regarded him. "I know," she whispered, and he saw the fright in her eyes.

"You don't need to be afraid anymore," he said softly, touching her shoulder once more. "We've got you now, you're safe."

"No, no," she cried, burying her face against the dead girl's shoulder.

"We'll have you back with your people in no time," the lieutenant said, and slowly she raised her head to look at him. Tears matted the long lashes, but the look in the wide eyes had changed, carrying a spark of hope within them now.

"My people?" she asked.

"Yes, back to Greenwood. You are Captain Rikkar's daughter, aren't you?" he asked. For a moment her gaze moved over the trees and grass and the body she held in her arms, then returned to his.

"Yes," she said haltingly, as if awakening from a long sleep. "I'm Brittany Rikkar. Captain

Rikkar's my father. He—" Whatever she'd been about to say was interrupted by a woman's scream in the square. Startled, Bree listened as a man's rough shout could be heard and then more screams.

Wiping the tears from her cheeks, she gently placed Milakee back on the ground and straightened her head. Tenderly she folded the little brown hands over the dead girl's chest and straightened her skirt and blouse. When the Indian girl had been prepared properly, Bree rose to her feet and faced the men.

The lieutenant felt a ripple of shock as he met her gaze. Now the eyes, flat and unfocused only minutes before, were steely with determination and purpose.

"Lieutenant Whitlock." She drew her slender frame straight and met his eyes unflinchingly. "Your men are acting like barbarians. Make them stop," she commanded.

"Shee-it!" one of the men said, and turned away. She was an Indian lover, that was for sure, he thought. They'd done all this fighting and searching for someone who loved these filthy Seminoles more than she did her own kind.

"Harrison," the lieutenant called to his man. "Call the men to order."

"To order? But you said—"

"You heard me, Harrison. I want the men back in formation in three minutes."

"Yes, sir." Harrison saluted and cast a quick glance at the woman who had knelt once more by the side of the dead Indian. Jesus, Harrison thought, she was a white woman and she was bound to have seen the way they'd treated the Indians so far. No wonder the lieutenant wanted the men back in order. He hurried away.

The lieutenant moved back to Bree. His face was grim as he looked at the dead girl. "The man who did this will be reprimanded," he said.

"And what of you, Lieutenant Whitlock? Will you be reprimanded for giving your men the order?"

"I never ordered them to shoot this woman," the lieutenant declared.

"Did you order them to shoot the other women and children who've died today?" Bree snapped. Once again tears spilled over and ran down her cheeks, but she disregarded them as she sought to still the trembling in her body. She had never felt such rage.

"Madame, I asked you to calm yourself. You're distraught."

"Yes, Lieutenant, I am distraught. I've seen an innocent young girl shot down in cold blood simply because she wouldn't submit herself to your men's bestial demands."

"Miss Rikkar—"

"No, don't touch me," Bree cried.

"I was merely offering aid to you," the lieutenant said quietly. "You have been through a terrible ordeal. You're bound to be upset. I wish only to help you—"

"If you wish to help, Lieutenant, you'll see that my—my friend is taken back to her village."

"Of course." The lieutenant turned to call an order to his men. "Scotty, have two men take this body back to the square."

"Yes, sir," the redheaded man said, saluting. "Harrison, two men for burial detail, on the double." Two soldiers left the group guarding the women and walked out of the village toward Bree and the lieutenant. Bree was glad to see they were not the same men who'd fired the shots that had killed Milakee. Their young faces displayed some anxiety and shame for what had occurred. At the Scotsman's orders they picked up Milakee's slight body, one at each end, and carried her back to the village square. Bree followed along behind, anguish washing over her again. This was the last time Milakee would travel these paths back to her village. Her struggle for life here in the swamps was finished.

The men took Milakee back to her chickee, the home she'd shared with Cooee on their wedding night. There would be no more nights for Cooee and Milakee, Bree thought, and stood weeping. The two young men gently placed the body on the edge of the platform and hurried back to their duties.

At last her weeping ended and Bree turned to look with tear-swollen eyes around the square. Milakee was forever lost to her now, but she might be able to stop some of the other atrocities against the people of the village. Slowly she moved across the square, her shocked gaze taking in the carnage and destruction.

Bodies lay everywhere, draped in macabre poses of flight and terror. There lay the old chief's wife, her head bashed in by a rifle butt for the help she gave her husband. Toschee, that disageeable woman who had made her life miserable when she first came to the village, lay still and quiet, her raucous voice forever quieted. There were other bodies of women who had laughingly instructed her in the art of sewing or in the tanning of hides, women she'd come to know and care about. Now she was left to grieve for them.

Bree halted near the fire pit, blinking her eyes to clear her vision as she caught a glimpse of the bright skirts and blouse of a familiar figure. Sofangee, the young girl who'd tended the small children, lay cradled between the fire logs, her white blouse stained with her blood.

"Oh, no," Bree cried, raising her face to the sky as sobs shook her body. Why should this be? she asked herself, and wondered at the two-faced God who had allowed death to come to the inno-

cent on a bright, promising morning. At last her
weeping subsided enough that she was able to
look again at Sofangee's slight body. The young
girl still clasped Chofee to her breast. The chubby
Indian baby who'd always laughed so readily
and had been a favorite of everyone in the village
lay as if sleeping. There was no mark on him
that Bree could see. Hopefully she crawled over
the log and pulled the baby from the dead girl's
arms and hope died. The bullet had passed
through Sofangee's slight body and buried itself
in the baby's. Gently, Bree put him back in
Sofangee's arms, then turned away, her hands
gripping her own stomach in an instinctively
protective gesture.

Her stomach roiled and she lurched across the
log and gave way to the flood of bile that rose in
her throat and stained the clean white sand. She
should get up and move away from the cooking
fire, she thought dimly. The others would be
angry with her for this desecration of the new
fire pit, but her legs were too weak to move. She
lay where she was, her brow wet with sweat, her
body trembling with chills.

The lieutenant came to help her, called by one
of his men who was afraid to approach her, afraid
of the fever she might carry. The lieutenant knelt
beside her, seeing the trembling, sweating weak-
ness and the girl and baby behind her. She'd had
too many shocks for one day, he thought, and
moved forward to help her to her feet.

When she was once more standing, Bree shook
away his helpful hand and turned on him with
her ravished face and accusing eyes. "These were
children, Lieutenant," she whispered, then her
voice grew in intensity until she was nearly shouting. "Do you make war on the women and children of the Seminole nation?"

"No, ma'am, we don't," he replied. "But when

we go into a village, we don't know where the
warriors are. We have to fire quick and sometimes innocent people get killed. It happens with
our own people, Miss Rikkar, only then the heathens mean to kill them. I'd save my tears, if I
were you, for those who deserve them."

"An innocent baby is certainly worthy of anyone's tears," Bree said scathingly, her gray eyes
flashing across his face, "no matter what his
heritage."

"Maybe," the lieutenant said, "and maybe not."
Whirling about, he walked away from her.

"I shall report every atrocity I've seen here
today, Lieutenant," she cried after him, and was
surprised when he turned to look at her again,
his face calm.

"You can if you want to, ma'am," he said. "I'll
be putting everything into my report anyway."
Again he turned and walked away and Bree was
shocked at his lack of concern. Obviously he had
little fear of reprisals for his orders this day.
Stunned by all she'd witnessed, Bree looked about
her.

The women were huddled on the ground in
the center of the square, silently helping each
other with wounds or reassuring their children.
Some of them cast looks of hatred at Bree as she
stood free and unharmed before them. She wanted
to cry out that she hadn't done this thing to
them, that she'd tried to help, but she knew they
wouldn't understand or believe her.

The old chief had been persuaded to sit on a
log while his second wife hastened to tend his
burns. His face still stared into the distance of
another world where soldiers and death did not
mar the bright beauty of the morning.

While she stood undecided about what to do,
shots rang out. She looked around to see the
soldiers taking pot shots at the pumpkins grow-

ing up the trees. When a shot was accurate, the pumpkins exploded, raining pulp and seeds all around.

"Lieutenant," she cried, running to pull at his arm. "Tell the soldiers to stop. They're destroying food, badly needed food. Without it the Indians will starve."

"That's the idea," the lieutenant replied calmly, his blue eyes cool as they met hers.

"You can't mean that," Bree cried. "That means women and children will starve to death."

The lieutenant took a deep breath. His voice was deliberately patient, as if he were speaking to a not very bright child. "I do mean that, Miss Rikkar," he said. "If the Seminoles have no food, they become hungry. When they are hungry, they can't fight. They come out of these godforsaken swamps and give up, then my men and I don't have to come in here and get them. That's how it's supposed to work."

"But—but they're dying of starvation and still they won't give in to you. They never will," she cried, but the lieutenant was already moving on. He had more unpleasant tasks to do before they could be quit of this village and he wanted to complete them as quickly as possible. Brittany Rikkar had reminded him all too well of how barbarous they'd become in this war. He longed now for an orderly drawing room somewhere, a glass of wine and civilized conversation with pretty ladies wearing satins and perfumes, a place where the Seminoles were just an idle topic of conversation and not a hideous reality.

"Lieutenant," Bree called after him one last time, and stopped where she was in the hot sandy square. Perhaps she herself could stop the soldiers from destroying all the food. She would get one of their rifles and threaten to shoot them if they didn't stop. Wildly she looked around, but her attention was caught by a loud wailing among the women. Bree looked at them, but they had fallen silent again, their eyes black and empty as they watched something at the other end of the square. Bree turned to see what had disturbed them and a scream caught in her throat. The braves that had been left behind by Shocaw to guard the camp dangled from the ends of hastily tied nooses slung over tree branches.

"No," Bree screamed, and raced across the square toward the soldiers. "Stop! Let them down," she cried, shoving at one of the soldiers.

"Here now, we've got our orders," one soldier cried out, and pushed her away, his grip on the rope tightening.

"Stop, you must stop." Bree ran to another soldier, pulling at his arm.

"You're crazy, lady," he cried, and gave her a hard shove that sent her sprawling backward across the ground. She rolled over and over, coming to a stop some feet away from the warriors hanging from the branches. Involuntarily her gaze moved upward over the writhing, jerking bodies to the faces made grotesque in the act of dying. She scooted backward over the ground, trying to get away from the horror of the bodies moving in this, their final dance. Bile rose in her throat, darkness came up to claim her, and gratefully she gave in to it, closing her eyes against the nightmare that would haunt her for the rest of her life.

Chapter 15

Bree opened her eyes and looked around. She was lying on a makeshift stretcher. A hefty-looking soldier at either end stood ready to lift the stretcher on command.

It was a scene from hell itself, with the bodies of the dead Indians hanging from trees and the burning village. Beyond the nightmare of the village, the tranquil beauty of the swamp seemed untouched by the death and destruction that had claimed the morning.

The roofs of the chickees were ablaze, the acrid, thick smoke of the fresh thatch rising high in the air. The palmettos, still fresh and green from the *Shot-cay-taw*, smoldered instead of leaping into flames, but the thin rafters holding the thatch were dry and burned like kindling. Soon the roofs plunged downward to the wooden platforms and the structures were blazing.

Tears rolled down Bree's cheeks as she watched Shocaw's chickee burn. There were so many memories there. Milakee's chickee was burning as well, the fire sweeping from the roof, down the poles to the floor, and Bree thought of Milakee lying there. At least she would be cremated; her body would not be left for the wild creatures of the swamp to mangle. Her spirit could walk untroubled into the other world.

The kitchen chickee where the women had prepared their meals, their happy voices calling to one another, caught fire. Its roof burned quickly and caved in, leaving smoldering, blackened cypress poles reaching upward in grotesque supplication to Yohewah, the one who had brought such evil to the village.

With a roaring explosion the storage chickee caught fire. Bree watched helplessly as the roof caved in over the dried corn, peas, and sweet potatoes the women had so carefully preserved for their winter food. Had the soldiers found the main garden as well? Bree wondered. She understood now why the main garden was so far from the village.

Weakly she lay back on the blanket, her eyes staring at the bland, innocent sky. She willed herself to shut out the unbearable horror of the present and concentrate instead on the happiness she'd known, the times of discovery and joy, of love and, yes, of sorrow, but never the depth of sorrow she'd known this day. She remembered all the things that had happened to her here in Horse Creek Village and of how they had all led to her becoming Shocaw's wife.

"I won't go home," she whispered fiercely. "I'll stay here with Shocaw. I'll tell him I understand about his love for his people, his need to protect them. I won't mind being second wife and I'll bear him many sons. I won't be afraid anymore, for I have seen the worst that can happen."

The sound of women weeping drew her attention and once again she raised her head. The women were being herded onto the path, their clinging, frightened children roughly separated from them and shoved farther along the path. The mothers would not be allowed to travel with their children; that way they would be less tempted to free themselves and slip away into the woods. The women were bound together with a looping chain of rope that allowed them to walk freely, yet kept them from escaping. The wounded were tied in as well. They were expected to walk back to Fort Brook.

Lieutenant Whitlock came to stand over her and Bree lay back on the blanket, turning her head away from him. Squatting down, he looked at her for a long moment, taking in her delicate beauty.

"I know this is difficult for you," he said kindly. "You've seen things most white women never even hear about, but soon you'll be home and you'll forget this horror."

The picture was burned into her mind. She would never forget. She thought of Shocaw and the other warriors when they returned and found the village burned, the crops destroyed, and their loved ones dead or captured. What anguish they would feel.

Suddenly she remembered the promise she'd made to Shocaw and tried to rise from the pallet. "I can't go yet," she cried wildly. "I have to wait for Shocaw. I promised him I wouldn't go."

"Shocaw?" The Lieutenant's voice was sharp with interest. "Shocaw Hadjo?" Bree looked up at him with wondering eyes. He knew Shocaw. "Where is he?" the lieutenant demanded, gripping her shoulder. His blue eyes were cold and intense as they stared into hers. "Is he coming back here?" Something in his tone warned Bree. She lay back on the blanket, forcing her stunned mind to think coherently.

Of course they wanted Shocaw. Lieutenant Whitlock had tried to trap him once before. But even more than that, she remembered the conversation in her father's study that afternoon so long ago. Now it returned to her with startling clarity and she remembered Ulcie Thompson and Lieutenant Whitlock discussing the important chiefs. Shocaw Hadjo had been one of the names they'd mentioned.

"I—I want to go home," she cried, making her voice deliberately vague. "I promised Papa I wouldn't leave the house, wouldn't ride—my horse." Turning her head, she looked at the lieutenant and the man who stood behind him with blank eyes. "Papa? Jared?" She smiled with sudden recognition. "You've found me!" she cried joyously.

"She's out of her head, Lieutenant," the man said.

"It's been too much for her." The lieutenant rose to his feet and looked around at the burned village. He felt a deep satisfaction. They'd destroyed a major stronghold of the Seminoles. There was one less place for the Indians to hide here in this swamp. If only they'd gotten the leader as well, the war chief Shocaw Hadjo. The old chief they had was merely a figurehead. It was the younger one, the one who dealt swiftly and fatally with the soldiers, that they wanted. If they could bring him in, it would help break the resistance of the other war chiefs and the rest of the Indians. He cast a speculative look at the girl on the pallet. Maybe this was his way of getting Shocaw Hadjo, he thought. Maybe he had only to be patient and wait. Whatever her story, she was clearly in no condition to be questioned today.

"Get the men together, Scotty," he ordered. "Let's get out of this hellhole."

"Yes, sir!" the Scotsman said with alacrity. For a moment there he'd been afraid the lieutenant might want to stay and try to capture this Shocaw Hadjo. For a man whose ancestors had come from the stark open moors of Scotland, the

dense, vine-matted trees growing from the water
and the rank ground underneath his feet were
menacing. He imagined an Indian lurking behind every clump of mangroves. He longed to return to Fort Brook where a man could at least
walk the shoreline and breathe freely without fear
of a heathen Seminole lifting his scalp.

They slogged through the swamps, not picking
the best land routes as the Seminoles would have
done, but pushing on blindly through water and
mud, losing their way and backtracking, yet somehow miraculously moving ever closer to the fort.

At first, Bree paid little attention to what went
on around her. Lost in grief over Milakee's death
and the horror of the Seminole warriors' deaths,
she sought to keep her mind numb, to shut out
the pain she felt. Then one of the marching
women fell to her knees, her body bent in pain.
A soldier jerked on the rope and pulled her aright.
The woman staggered forward for a few steps
then collapsed facedown in the mud.

"Cut her loose," one of the officers instructed,
and a young soldier stepped forward to free the
woman's hands from the rope. The woman lay
unmoving. "Get moving," the soldiers instructed
the marchers, and slowly the line started up
again. The fallen woman was left lying in the
muddy path.

"Wait," Bree called. "Put me down."

"Sorry, miss—" one of her carriers said.

"Do as I tell you. Put me down," she com-
manded with such authority that they obeyed.
"I'm feeling better now," she explained to them.
"Put that poor woman on the stretcher instead."
Without responding, the two men shuffled their
feet and looked at one another.

"Well?" Bree said when they made no move.

"I, uh, I don't think the lieutenant's going to
like this," one of the soldiers said. "Besides,

these women don't seem too friendly to you right now. If I was you, I'd climb right back on this here stretcher and let us carry you."

"But you aren't me. I feel much better and there's no need for me to ride when there are others who are injured."

"What's the delay back here, soldier?" the lieutenant asked, slogging up to them.

"Well, sir, we was just—"

"I'm afraid it's my fault, Lieutenant," Bree said, stepping forward. "I've given my pallet to this woman who is very ill. I will walk."

"I see you're much better now," the lieutenant said, and Bree glanced away from his gaze. He knew she'd been faking earlier, but it was too late now.

"If you'll just have your men put this woman on the stretcher, I will gladly walk," Bree said.

Frowning, the lieutenant looked at the fallen woman, then with the toe of his boot flipped her over. Kneeling, he raised one eyelid as he examined her.

"This woman is dead," he said, indicating her wound. "She has no further need for a stretcher." Bree bit back a gasp, her eyes taking in the woman's face. She remembered her. She was the mother of the baby Chofee. Bree bit back an outcry and turned to the lieutenant.

"Then if you will give my stretcher to one of the other women who is too ill or wounded to walk . . ." she said.

The lieutenant turned to look at the women huddled together. Some of them supported the weight of others, as they waited for the march to begin again. "I can't spare the men to carry the wounded," he said, and waved to the men who held the stretcher.

"You were able to spare men to carry me on a stretcher," she cried.

"You're a white woman and I thought you quite ill," the lieutenant said.

"Some of these other women are badly wounded. If you force them to march all the way to Fort Brook, they'll surely die," Bree protested. "Surely you—"

"Miss Rikkar." The lieutenant fixed her with a steely gaze. "I have soldiers who are wounded and they are walking. I won't have my soldiers carrying stretchers when they are needed to guard the detail against attack from the men of these women. Furthermore"—he raised his voice as Bree tried to speak—"I want no more delays. Is that understood?" He waited for her answer.

Stubbornly, Bree refused to be intimidated. "You'd make better time if you carried some of the women who are badly wounded."

"If they can't keep up, they will be left behind," the lieutenant said.

"How can you be so inhumane?"

"I have my detail of men to see to as well as these women and children. We are low on supplies of all sorts. If we tarry too long, the Seminoles will track us down, Miss Rikkar. You worry about getting back home to your daddy's plantation and I'll worry about the best way to move these Indians to the fort. Sergeant Harrison," he bellowed along the line.

"Yes, sir!" The man came running back to his officer.

"Miss Rikkar has recovered enough to walk. Take her to the front of the line and keep her there." The lieutenant turned back to her. "Since you've recovered so well, Miss Rikkar, I will look forward to asking you some questions tonight, especially about this renegade, Shocaw Hadjo."

"Come with me, miss," Harrison said. Shoulders slumped in defeat, Bree followed him. She wanted to hate the lieutenant for his callous treatment of his prisoners, but there'd been a ring of truth to his words. Even more there'd been a look in his eyes of self-disgust and regret. He was as much as prisoner of the horrible war as the Seminoles were.

As she marched along, Bree watched the other soldiers. Some of them were young men barely older than she was and their faces reflected the fatigue and depression they felt as they battled daily against the heat, insects, and dysentery that weakened them. If their behavior toward the Indian women had been brutal, so too had the war brutalized them.

They pushed on through the swampland that repelled and frightened them, fighting an enemy who had ceased to be clearly an enemy as they saw how poorly the Indians lived and how little a threat they really were to the white men. Who would want to live in these swamps anyway? they wondered. Surely not they. Give them some scrubland somewhere where they could raise a few head of cattle, plant a garden, and have a passel of kids and they'd be happy enough. Let the Indians have this devilish swamp.

Bree tried to sort out her feelings. She'd lived with the Indians for months and had come to accept them as they were, understanding their pride and traditions. She was horrified by the killing of the gentle people she'd lived with for so many months, people who'd come to accept her finally as Shocaw's *hoke-tee,* yet she understood the feelings of the young men who plodded beside her. She felt their fear, understood it, and longed to reassure them.

What was wrong with her? she wondered. After seeing the carnage and brutality of the soldiers in the village, how could she care about their feelings now? Yet they were her people as Shocaw and the Seminoles were not. Shocaw had kidnapped her, the women had beaten and terrorized her, and yet she'd been able to forgive them and live in peace and friendship with them. Could she deny her own people the same forgiveness and understanding? Each day she'd watched Shocaw and his men go out to burn and pillage the land of her people, and although she'd never asked him, she'd known soldiers had been killed. Even now, if Shocaw and his warriors came upon them, he would deal swiftly and fatally with the soldiers.

The war must end, she thought dully. Somehow she must do as Shocaw had asked her. She must try to make the white man understand, so there could be real peace talks with the Seminoles and treaties that would be honored by both sides, not these empty words and broken promises that brought shame to everyone.

Her head hurt as she thought of all these things, and the sun beat down on her. Fear for Shocaw and his men, that they might have already been tracked down and captured, tore at her heart. The lieutenant's words weighed on her mind. He wanted to question her about Shocaw but she would tell him nothing. Nothing! Still she knew the interview would be an unpleasant one.

The interview never took place that evening or the one that followed. Chills overtook Bree, making her clutch her arms about herself to still the shaking of her body and clamp her teeth together tightly lest her chattering teeth bite down on her tongue. The stretcher was brought up and once again she was settled onto it, and this time she did not protest.

The long afternoon passed and at last the lieutenant called a halt. They made camp on a hummock that rose out of the swamp water, affording them some dryness for the night. Fires were made and the meager supply of food prepared. Bree could eat nothing. She huddled beneath her thin blanket, her body racked with chills. She remembered how Shocaw had prepared a shelter for her that first night she spent in the swamp. She'd been dry and warm on her mat of Spanish moss.

It was little wonder the soldiers hated the swamp so much, she thought. They'd not learned how to use it and all it gave to make themselves at home here. They were aliens and would forever remain so. She pulled the thin blanket beneath her chin and tried to be grateful for its warmth. Some soldier was probably going without a cover tonight because of her. She thought of the Indian women who'd not been allowed to gather their blankets and cooking pots before being forced onto the trail. She longed to give her blanket to one of the children, but knew the soldiers would not allow it. She drifted in and out of a feverish sleep.

The next morning Bree was worse. All day the soldiers carried her stretcher while she shivered and rolled about so restlessly in her feverish state, they feared she would fall out of it. By night, the lieutenant was faced with the possibility of losing his charge before he'd even gotten her back to the fort. The thought was not comforting. He remembered Captain Rikkar's threat when he'd failed to return his daughter the last time. He forced liquids down her throat and hoped for the best. If she lived through the night, she might make it to the fort.

She lived in a dreamworld, a world that she could control, leaving out the unhappiness and horror and embracing only the happy moments. In a shadowy dreamworld she was vaguely aware of men moving through swamps and of herself being carried on the makeshift stretcher. There was a rocking of boats moving through endless

water and men in blue coats who came to talk to
her and went away shaking their heads.

She could close them away from her so they
didn't bring her pain and death and horror. Instead she lived in a world of tropical birds and
flowers and silver-hued ponds where she swam
and laughed. There was someone in the dream
with her and he made her feel happy and secure.
It was a good place to be, this dreamworld, so she
stayed there, presenting to the world a bemused,
dreamy smile on her otherwise blank face. The
men with their rough voices and persistent questions didn't penetrate her protective bubble.

Dimly she perceived she was in a room with a
soft bed beneath her. The bed was too soft, but
she didn't move from it. She lay where she was,
her body fighting when her mind no longer tried
to. A door opened, footsteps approached her bed,
and a well-remembered voice spoke softly.

"Bree, Bree," her father said, and she opened
her eyes.

"Papa," she cried, and his arms were around
her.

"Bree, we'd given you up for dead," David
Rikkar said, and sat on the edge of the bed to
rock her in his arms. Bree gave way to the tears
she'd held inside for too long, ever since that day
she'd seen the soldiers hang the warriors at Horse
Creek Village. Now all the memories came rushing back to her, crowding in upon her, until she
felt overwhelmed by them all. She couldn't speak,
and after trying, she simply lay her head against
her father's chest and cried, her sobs a sad la-
ment for the deaths of those she'd grown to love.

David Rikkar was a wise man and sat holding
his daughter, rocking her, smoothing her hair
back from her face, knowing, as she did not, that
the healing was beginning with those tears. When
at last she lay too exhausted to move, he tucked

her back under the covers as he had when she was a child.

"Tomorrow we'll go home," he told her. "Mama is waiting for you."

"Mama? And May?" Bree asked childlike.

"Yes, May too," her father said, heartened by the smile she managed. "My dear, sweet child, I'm so glad we found you," he whispered fervently as he brought her small hand to his lips.

Could a man love one child more than the other when he loved them both so intensely? he wondered, watching her as her lids lowered and she slept. This fairy child had touched him in a special way because she was so like her mother. He touched a long golden strand of hair. What horrors had she been through? What had she seen that had nearly driven her out of her mind? He had tried to help the Seminoles, but now he would become their fiercest enemy for what they'd done to his daughter. He sat for a long time beside her bed, watching over her, reluctant to let her go even for a few hours. At last he rose and went to find the commanding officer. That night he sat at the commander's table listening to Lieutenant Whitlock's report on how he'd found the kidnapped girl.

"I appreciate what you did for my daughter, Lieutenant Whitlock," Rikkar said. "She seems to be recovering from the horrible ordeal she's endured, although it will take some time before she's completely recovered."

"Yes, it will take time, sir," the lieutenant agreed. "When a person's been kidnapped like that, they get scared. They forget who to trust and who's their enemy. They form attachments to anyone who's kind to them."

"What are you talking about?" Rikkar asked, looking at the young officer. He was obviously an intelligent young man and had been well spoken of by his superior officer.

"When we found your daughter, sir, she was crying over one of the Indian women who'd been killed in the shooting. She sang some Indian chants over her and seemed quite disturbed over her death."

"Bree is a gentle, loving girl," Rikkar replied. "She would be disturbed by the death of someone she'd grown close to."

"There's more, sir," the officer said. "As you know, it's been our practice to hang those renegade warriors who've given us the most trouble."

"Yes, so I've been told," Rikkar said, and it was clear he didn't agree with the practice.

"Your daughter witnessed—the hangings," the lieutenant said.

"Good God, man," Rikkar exclaimed. "Surely, you took some steps to protect her from that."

"Yes, sir, I thought I had, but in the confusion, she eluded the guard and went to the hanging site." He paused and the room was silent as the men sat thinking of the horror their patient had witnessed. Rikkar's hands doubled into fists on the table.

"There's more, sir," the lieutenant continued, and Rikkar's head came up, his gray eyes dark and steely. For a moment under that stare, the lieutenant hesitated, then shrugged aside his doubt. He wanted Shocaw Hadjo, no matter what the cost. "Your daughter seems to have aligned herself with this war chief, this Shocaw Hadjo. When she was delirious, she mentioned his name often. I'd like to question her later when she's up to it."

"If my daughter is willing to talk to you about this Indian, I will notify you," Rikkar said, and his voice was flat and final.

"Thank you, sir," Lieutenant Whitlock said.

Bree awoke the next morning remembering the warmth of her father's hand gripping hers and his promise that she would be returning home that day. Just the thought of returning to Greenwood lent her strength. She put aside the covers and got out of bed. The room tilted dangerously, then settled back into place. Bree looked about her in wonder. She'd been too sick to notice the room before, but now she took in each detail of it from the bright pieced coverlet on the bed to the wildflowers in the vase on the bureau. Above the bureau was a mirror. Quickly she crossed to it and looked at herself.

Surprise at what she saw made her gasp and step backward. She'd changed so she hardly looked like herself. Her face was thinner and her fine bones stood out in arresting planes. Her long blond hair was the same, lying about her shoulders in thick masses. The biggest difference was her eyes. They stared directly into the mirror. There was no fluttering of the eyelashes, no coy glances, none of the artifices she'd practiced so religiously at the girl's school. Instead her clear gray eyes held a stoic dignity she'd often seen in the Seminole's expressions.

She was brown! One small hand glided upward to touch her cheeks and brow. Mama would be so angry with her, she thought. She hadn't taken any care to protect her complexion from the sun's rays. Instead she and Milakee had deliberately lazed in the sun after a bath, allowing it to dry their skin. She was, she knew, nearly as dark beneath her clothes as on her face and arms. Mama would certainly be disapproving.

Suddenly the ludicrousness of such a thought after all she'd endured touched her and she sat on the side of the bed laughing until the laughter turned to hiccups and then to sobs.

She was home and the horrible part of it was,

she wasn't sure she wanted to be. She wasn't
sure if she belonged here or back in the swamps
waiting for Shocaw and his men. Who was she?
Surely not the Brittany Rikkar she'd been so
many months before when she'd first returned
from France, not the pampered and spoiled rich
planter's daughter. She was a different Bree, who
had learned to survive in the swamps, how to
cook over an open campfire and tan a deer hide.
Where did she fit in now, here in the rich, indolent life of the Florida planter, and what of her
baby?

A knock at the door interrupted her anguished
thoughts and she scrambled to get dressed. "I'll
be right there," she called.

"Take your time, Bree," Rikkar said. "Do you
need some help?"

"No, I can manage." Although a clean dress,
borrowed from one of the wives at the fort, had
been laid across the bed, Bree couldn't bear the
thought of wearing it. Perhaps it belonged to the
wife of the man who had murdered Milakee, she
thought, and hastened to put on the skirt and
blouse of the Seminole.

Her father was waiting in the general's sitting
room when she entered, standing before the fireplace, his hand resting on the mantel. He swung
around when she entered and stood staring at
her.

"Papa?" she said softly, and suddenly he was
across the room, taking her into his arms, holding her against his chest. Her cheek brushed
against the soft wool of his coat, and she breathed
in the dear familiar fragrance of spice and tobacco, smells she'd always associated with her
childhood.

Rikkar just held his daughter for a few minutes, his heart giving thanks that she was back,
unshed tears brightening his eyes. Finally with a

shaky breath he drew away. "Thank God they found you," he said fervently, rocking her in his arms again. "We've been frantic ever since you were taken. Are you able to travel? Your mother is out of her mind waiting to see if you're all right."

"Yes, oh, yes, take me home, Papa," she cried, and all the pain she felt was in those words, tearing at Rikkar's heart. Gathering her up in his arms, he cradled her against his chest as he had when she was a little girl. Gently he settled her against the leather-cushioned seat of his buggy.

Bree smiled as he took up the reins and guided the team of horses back toward Greenwood. Soon she would be home again. As they moved down the dirt road, she looked about her. The green lushness of spring had given way to the dusty heat of summer.

"What day is it?" she asked suddenly.

"July twenty-third," Rikkar answered. Bree leaned back against the seat again. She'd been with the Seminoles for nearly four months. So short a time and yet it had been a lifetime. Time enough for her to grow to love Shocaw and conceive his child. At least she carried Shocaw's baby. If she never saw him again, she would always have a part of him with her. But how would her parents and the rest of their friends accept her now?

Tears of grief for the loss of the Seminoles she loved and anxiety for her future at Greenwood welled in her eyes. Her father's strong arm gripped her shoulders, pulling her closer. He would help her through the weeks and months ahead. Gratefully she leaned against him for the support she knew she needed so badly.

Chapter 16

The carriage swept down the drive beneath the canopy of green branches and came to a stop before the portico with its stately columns. The house rose from the rich Florida soil in regal splendor, its white walls reflecting the bright sunshine. Even as her father opened the door of the carriage and stepped down, Bree caught a glimpse of servants rushing about, calling excitedly.

"She here, Miss Lainie, she home." Then Lainie was rushing down the steps. Rikkar took Bree's hand as she alighted from the carriage and was caught in her mother's embrace.

"Brittany, thank God, thank God, you're alive," her mother said, sobbing, and drew back to look at her daughter. Lainie had never thought they'd have her back. It was a miracle. Lainie's hands moved over her daughter's hair and face, her shoulders and hands, and back to her face, as if to reassure herself that her child was safe and whole. Tears trembled in her sooty lashes, but she raised her chin and forbade herself that luxury. She would go to her room later and cry alone and say her prayers to the Almighty for His mercy in returning their daughter.

Her practiced eye noted the pallor beneath the abominable tan and the fatigue in her gray eyes. Her sensitive fingertips felt the sight tremor in the slender shoulders that said all too well that Bree was on the point of collapse.

"There's a hot bath waiting in your room," Lainie said, and urged Bree forward. Slowly Bree climbed the steps, her eyes looking at the columns, the graceful arch of the great wooden doors, the large sunny entrance hall, and the sweeping stairway that led up to her room and the warm, scented water that awaited her. Around her the servants chattered or watched with beaming faces as she looked around.

"I'd forgotten how beautiful it is," she said, looking at the chandeliers hanging on golden chains from the ceilings. She already missed the trees with the sunlight streaming through the silvery green leaves.

"Ah, it's good to have my baby home." May was there, looking older than she had the last time Bree had seen her, clasping Bree in her thin old arms. "I knowed you'd be home. I knowed it," the old servant cried. She stepped back and looked at Bree. "Yo' got skinny. We got to fatten yo' up again."

"Oh, May, I missed all of you so much," Bree whispered, and couldn't stop the tears that gathered in her eyes. "I really am glad to be home again." Everyone beamed at her. Slowly, greeting each one of the house servants with a special smile and a personal word or two, she moved toward the stairs and paused, clinging to the banister. She'd never make it to the top, she thought. Suddenly her father was there, swooping her into his arms and hurrying up the stairs with her.

"Ruby, come help your mistress," Rikkar called as he led the way to the room that had been

Bree's from the day she emphatically stated she was too big for the nursery anymore.

Lainie followed them and watched as her daughter was settled on the bed, moving forward quickly, protectively, when she saw the tears slide from beneath Bree's eyelashes. "My poor baby," she cried, cradling her daughter's head in her arms. "Your nightmare's over, darling. You're home safe again. We'll never let anything happen to you again."

"Mama," Bree began, then pulled away from her mother, turning her face away at the hurt look she saw on Lainie's face. She was tired and anxious about what her mother would say when she knew about the baby. She couldn't face telling her now, not at this moment. She wanted only to sleep.

"Let her rest, she's tired," Rikkar said gently, and put an arm around his wife's shoulders. With a nod to Ruby, indicating she was to stay and help her mistress, he led Lainie from her room.

"I don't understand," Bree heard her mother say as they closed the door behind her.

Poor Mama, Bree thought. What a shock everything was going to be. There was so much to do, so much to work through, both in her own mind and in dealing with others. First she wanted only to sink into the tub of fragrant water and bathe her weary body, then she wanted to return to this soft downy bed and sleep forever.

She smiled to herself as she stood, letting Ruby disrobe her. How easy it was to fall back into old habits, she thought, but she was so terribly tired. When the Seminole skirt and blouse were off, Ruby held them out away from her, a look of distaste on her face.

"I goin' burn dese fo' yo'," she announced, laying them on the floor by the door.

"No!" Bree sat upright in the tub. "No, don't

do that. I'd like them washed and brought back to me."

"Yo' not goin' wear them?" Ruby asked with round, disbelieving eyes.

Bree smiled. Once she would have reacted in the same way. "No, I just want to keep them. I want to remember," she said softly to herself. Casting a last disbelieving look over her shoulder, Ruby left the room, carrying the clothes with her, and Bree lay back in the tub, shutting out all thoughts, all feelings, concentrating only on the lilac-scented water that soothed her aching body.

The days passed in a haze for Bree and soon they became weeks. At first she was content just to take each day as it came, giving little or no thought to the future, content to eat her meals in her room, to bathe in fragrant, warm water, and return to her bed where she seemed never to get enough sleep.

At first Lainie accepted her daughter's need for rest and privacy and the chance to recover from her frightful experience, but when time passed and there seemed no sign that Bree meant to leave her room and return to a normal, active life, Lainie began to urge her.

"Come down and have supper with us. We've invited the Coopers. Mavis has been so concerned about you," Lainie would say, and Bree would simply shake her head and beg fatigue.

"Darling, our friends want to see you, to know you're all right. Please put on that pretty sprigged muslin dress and come down to the garden for tea this afternoon." But Bree pleaded a headache.

At times Bree tried to tell her mother about the Seminoles and her life with them, but Lainie would shush her with well-meaning sounds of comfort. "Don't speak of it now," she would say, bustling about Bree's room, arranging fresh flowers or straightening her covers. "You're home now. You can forget about those savages. They'll never hurt you again." Bree would fall silent, stricken by guilt and uncertainty. Feeling as she did, how could her mother ever accept her baby?

Yet Bree felt a need to tell someone. To speak of the baby would make it seem more real. She needed to talk to someone about her feelings for Shocaw, but who would understand? Her sense of isolation was complete. She withdrew further.

"I don't know why she's doing this," Lainie confided to May one afternoon as she tended her roses. Her lovely complexion was shielded from the sun by a large, straw hat tied on with a yellow ribbon.

"Yo' leave that little girl 'lone. She got lots to think 'bout," May advised.

"I know she has, May. I'm just afraid this will become a way of life for her," Lainie said, her lovely face marred by the lines of worry that had begun to form on her brow.

"She be all right after she have that baby," May said.

Lainie's face was filled with stunned surprise, then swift denial. "God in heaven, no!" she cried. Why hadn't she thought of that? Swiftly she got to her feet, her glance moving to the second-story windows. Bree stood looking down at her mother and the rose garden. She was still in her gown, the white ruffled and beribboned collar buttoned high up on her throat. Her long golden hair was brushed smooth, held back from her face with a single band of ribbon as it tumbled about her shoulders and back. She looked like a little girl standing there and Lainie's heart went out to her.

What she must have endured in the Indians' camp, Lainie thought, and her heart beat with renewed anger and hatred for the Seminoles. First

they had taken her brother when he was but a
baby and now they'd defiled her daughter, her
precious daughter. Well, it wouldn't happen.
There would be no heathen offspring born in
this house. There were ways, ways she'd almost
tried once, and she would help her daughter.
Throwing down her gloves and trowel, she turned
to her old maid.

"May, go to the slave quarters," she ordered,
and May looked at her in surprise.

"Here, Bree, drink this," Lainie said, and held
out a cup of dark swirling liquid. It reminded
Bree of the black drink she'd seen the Seminoles
drink as they cleansed themselves for the Green
Corn Dance.

"What is it?" she asked, raising her gaze to her
mother's distraught face.

"It doesn't matter, darling," Lainie said tersely,
urging the cup to her lips.

"What is it, Mama?" Bree demanded, grasping
her hands and holding the cup away. She'd never
realized her frail little mother could be so strong.

"It will take the baby away from you," Lainie
said, her dark eyes anxious and determined at
the same time.

"Mama—"

"Shh, shh, don't talk, Bree. I understand. Oh,
what you must have gone through, my poor baby.
Just drink this and it will all be behind you."
With trembling hands Lainie carried the cup to
Bree's lips once more. Tears sparkled in her dark
lashes.

Bree was stunned. "How did you know about
the baby?" she asked.

"May told me. Oh, Bree, you should have told
me yourself. You shouldn't have been afraid. No
wonder you didn't want to leave your room. But

there are things we can do. You aren't to blame
for this and I'm going to help you."

"Do you mean this will kill my baby," Bree
asked, unable to believe her mother meant this.
Her hands clutched convulsively at her stomach.

"Yes, darling, you don't have to have this baby.
Just drink this. It will all be over in a little
while."

"No, Mama." Bree shoved the cup away. Some
of it spilled on the white coverlet, leaving a stain
of deep blackish red. In horror Bree looked at it.
It lay like a bloodstain between her mother and
herself. "I can't kill my baby," she cried, and her
gray eyes were wide in her thin face. "You can't
make me."

"Bree, please, you don't know what you're doing.
You can't carry a savage's baby. Take this. No
one need to ever know."

"I would know, Mama, I would know. I can't
kill my baby." Bree's voice rose hysterically. She'd
thought her mother meant to help.

"Think of what everyone will say. They'll think
you gave yourself to a filthy Indian. No white
man will ever touch you again. Think of your life
here at Greenwood. You can't stay shut up here
in your room."

"I know, Mama, I know," Bree cried, tears
streaming down her cheeks.

"You could marry any one of the sons of our
friends, young men who will one day inherit
their fathers' plantations. You could live a life of
leisure and refinement. All of that, all of it will
be lost if they find out you're pregnant with
some Indian's baby."

"I don't care, Mama. I don't want to marry any
of them, ever," Bree cried.

"The Seminoles are like animals, Bree. You
can't have a baby by one of them."

"Stop it, Mama, stop it. They aren't like that.

They're like you and me, like Papa and Jared and all our friends—" Her words were cut off by the slash of her mother's hand across her cheek.

"Don't say that," Lainie raged. "They're not like us. They kill and destroy. They killed Metoo, who was like a sister to me, and they took my brother away. Who knows what hellhole in that swamp he died in. They're murderers of women and innocent babies."

"Our soldiers have done the same and much worse. I've seen them. I watched as they raped young girls and shot fleeing women in the back. They killed my dearest friend, who had helped me and protected me. Ask Papa about our noble soldiers."

"It's not the same, Bree," Lainie cried.

"Why? Because the Seminoles are only Indians. If you only came to know them, Mama, as I have, you would see they don't want to fight. They're forced into it because the white man wants the Seminole to leave Florida. Each day they watch their children's hungry faces, they bury their dead, and they pray to their God that he will deliver them. Mama, if we were starving and being forced off our land, wouldn't you want to fight too?"

"Don't." Lainie clasped her hands over her ears so she wouldn't hear Bree's words. When Bree fell silent, Lainie took her hands away and turned to stare into Bree's eyes. A look of steely determination crossed her lovely features as she walked to the table and stared into the bowl. "Why won't you take this and end all the sorrow? We've lived with too much over the past few months, Bree. You can't expect us to accept this thing."

Once again Bree felt guilty. "I'm sorry, Mama," she said, and the tears poured down her cheeks and fell off her jaw to the crisp white gown with its dainty lace. "I don't want to make you and Papa unhappy and I don't want to bring shame to you. I'll go away to have my baby."

"But why?" Lainie's voice dropped to a whisper. "Why, when this would be so much easier? Do it, Bree honey, do it for Mama." Lainie held out the bowl and Bree could only shake her head from side to side as she fought back the sobs. So she would have to leave Greenwood as well. Now where would she go?

"Why?" Lainie asked again, her eyes pleading.

"I loved Shocaw, Mama. We were married. I want to have his baby."

The words were like painful blows raining on Lainie, so she closed her eyes against them, denying their sound and meaning. "You'll get over him. You'll forget him. It was a nightmare that's over now, Bree." Lainie's eyes opened and her voice rose from a whisper with a force that couldn't be denied. "Take this and be done with it forever," she commanded.

For a moment, Bree wavered. It would be easier if there were no baby. She wouldn't have to leave Greenwood. She could stay here forever. No one could ask her questions for which she had no answers. For a moment she wavered.

"Take it, baby, drink it." Lainie held the bowl out to her once more and Bree reached out to take it. She sat staring down at the swirling liquid. In just a moment it would be over, forever behind her, and she could go with her life. Slowly Bree raised the bowl to her lips. Lights danced in the black liquid and she remembered the light shining in Shocaw's black eyes as he stretched beside her in their glade.

"No," she cried, and threw the bowl across the room. It crashed against the wall, cracking into several pieces, spewing the deadly contents onto the dainty wallpaper and across the carpet. Slowly it seeped into the rug. Her cry echoed around the room and she fell sideways across the bed, the sobs pushing upward out of her chest and throat, filling the room with their hoarse sounds.

"Bree," Lainie cried, taking a hesitant step toward the bed.

"Leave my baby alone. She ain't goin' do it," May commanded, and was there pulling Bree into her arms. "She want this baby," May said over Bree's head as she rocked her gently. "It be a sin to make her kill it. Yo' 'most make this mistake once befo'," the old Negress scolded her mistress. "Dis girl want her baby. Yo' leave her be. I tell Rikkar on yo'. I nevah go 'gainst yo', but I do dis time. This chile wan' her baby, she goin' have it. Yo' don' wan' her here, I take her 'way sumplace. I take care o' her. Don' yo' worry, Bree honey. Ole May's heah. She goin' take good care o' yo'."

Lainie stared at her daughter and May for a long moment, then with a swish of her skirts turned and walked out of the room, closing the door behind her quietly. After that she stayed away from Bree's room, unable to accept her daughter's feelings. Neither woman knew how to mend the rift between them.

Rikkar came often to sit beside Bree's bed and hold her hand. As if the incident with her mother had broken down previously erected barriers, Bree began to tell him of her captivity. At first she spoke hesitantly, and he read the fear in her eyes, the fear that she would be blamed for all that had happened to her

He felt pain and denial as she spoke of Shocaw and her love for him, then grateful acceptance came. He could accept anything as long as Bree, his little girl, was alive and back with him. Gripping her hand in silent support, he listened as she told of the soldiers' attack on the village. He

read the guilt in her eyes that she was alive
when so many of them had died.

He saw how often the small brown hand curved
protectively around her stomach and his heart
sank within him. His little girl had grown to
womanhood. Lost in the swamps among the savages, she had managed to survive, yet the old
Bree was forever gone to them. So be it, he vowed.
He would take her back on any terms. He would
protect and cherish her.

Gently he dried her tears and stroked her hair
until she slept. Maybe now that she'd talked, for-
getting could begin. He fervently prayed it would
be so.

One morning as Bree knelt over her chamber
pot, her body jerking in spasms of sickness, her
mother entered the room. Bree turned helpless
eyes toward her, unable to rise.

Lainie stood looking at her daughter, seeing
the dark circles under her eyes, the hollows of
her cheeks, and the almost emaciated body beneath the voluminous nightgown. Bree's strength
was nearly depleted, Lainie saw. She'd under-
gone too much in the past few months. Pity and
love for her daughter made her dash across the
room and kneel beside the sick girl.

"May, come quick," Lainie called, and gathered Bree in her arms. Gently she rocked her,
holding her until the last spasm had passed. Getting a cool, damp cloth, she bathed Bree's face,
then helped her to her bed.

"Where's Ruby?" Lainie demanded when May
appeared. "Bree should never be left alone like
this."

"It's all right, Mama," Bree protested. "Ruby
is running an errand for me. Besides, I'm not
helpless. I'm a grown woman."

Her words tugged at Lainie. "Yes, you are,"
she said softly, pushing back the silken locks of

hair, "but you'll always be my little girl, no matter what happens to you." Her eyes begged for forgiveness.

"Oh, Mama," Bree cried, and her arms went about Lainie. The two women sat holding each other, tears mingling in mutual forgiveness. May stood in the doorway shaking her head at the two headstrong women who'd been her charges nearly all their lives.

Now Lainie listened to Bree as she spoke of the Seminole. Her prejudice against them could never be overcome, nor could she help wishing Bree were not pregnant with Shocaw's baby, but she felt grateful for the tall warrior who'd saved her daughter's life more than once and had even urged her to go home with her own people.

"Mama, what did May mean when she said you'd nearly made the same mistake yourself?" Bree asked one day as they sat on the veranda. May's words had haunted her ever since that day in her bedroom. She was startled now to see a flush creep up her mother's pale cheeks.

Lainie looked away evasively, then as if coming to a decision, she raised her chin and turned to look at her daughter. "When I was carrying Jared, your father and I—weren't close as we are now. I felt a terrible anger for something he'd done and I wanted to hurt him as I'd been hurt. I—I knew how much he'd wanted a child, so I went to the old slave woman down near the swamp. She gave me a brew—the same that I gave to you. But, like you, I couldn't do it. I couldn't take my baby's life." Lainie gripped her daughter's hand and looked earnestly into her eyes.

"Please believe me, Bree, at that moment as I contemplated what I was about to do, I realized how much I loved your father and how much I wanted our child too. I—I was so grateful when he was born and then soon after there was you, my little princess, so beautiful and sweet." Lainie's hand stroked back a fine strand of golden hair from Bree's cheek.

"That day in your bedroom, when you threw the cup, I was so ashamed, ashamed that I'd nearly forced you into that mistake, but I didn't know how to tell you. I'm sorry, Bree. Can you ever forgive me?" Her dark eyes were wide and anxious as she waited for Bree's answer.

"I already have," Bree said, and put her strong young arms around her mother. She had never felt closer to her, as she thought of all they'd shared. For the first time she saw her mother as less than the perfect human being she'd always seemed. Lainie Rikkar made mistakes and suffered for them just like everyone else. Bree hugged her tightly.

Bree began to attend teas and suppers again and at each one she was asked about her experiences with the Seminoles. Carefully she answered the questions, striving to help others understand the Seminoles better.

One night, she and her parents were invited to the home of Aaron Spencer, an influential man, who had worked hard to bring the war with the Seminoles to an end. When they arrived, Bree was surprised to see several officers from the fort were present, among them Lieutenant Whitlock. Some part of her rebelled at the thought of supping with the man who had brought death and destruction to Horse Creek Village. She would, she decided, avoid him as much as possible. But that was not to be. Lieutenant Whitlock was seated on her left at dinner and good manners dictated she at least remain civil.

"Miss Rikkar," he said, bowing over her hand. "You're breathtakingly lovely. You seem to have recovered from your ordeal."

"Thank you, Lieutenant," she said curtly, and turned to her dinner partner on the right, but he continued to speak to her.

"I've gone to Greenwood several times to inquire after you but your mother said you were ill."

"For a time, I was," Bree returned, "but I've recovered. Now if you'll excuse me." She turned away.

"Certainly," he said. "First, I wish to ask you when I might call upon you. I'd like to talk to you."

"I'm sorry, Lieutenant Whitlock, I'm rather busy."

"I have some news of the Seminoles." His voice was low and urgent, the words meant only for her ears.

Bree turned back to face him. "What is it?" she asked quickly, her heart hammering so loudly in her chest she was sure he must hear it.

"Seminole warriors attacked the fort the other night and helped some of the Indians from Horse Creek Village to escape."

"I can't say I'm sorry to hear that, Lieutenant," Bree replied evenly, and made to turn away.

"I see life among the savages didn't change your bleeding-heart sympathies, Miss Rikkar." Whitlock sneered.

Bree's gaze was bright with surprise as it met his. "No, Lieutenant, it didn't," she replied firmly. "If anything, it's only strengthened my convictions of the injustices done to the people of the Seminole nation."

"That's a pity." Whitlock was undaunted by her response. "Nevertheless, I must ask for your cooperation."

"Why certainly, Lieutenant. I hadn't realized I was being uncooperative."

He ignored her sarcastic tone. "We think their

leader is Shocaw Hadjo." With satisfaction he noted the flush on her cheeks and the rapid movement of her bodice as she caught her breath. Her eyelashes lowered so he couldn't see the sudden light in her eyes. Shocaw was still alive then! Her heart sang within her. "What do you know of Shocaw Hadjo?" Whitlock insisted. She had been more than just a prisoner to the war chief, he was sure of it. With any kind of luck he could use her to get Shocaw.

"I can tell you nothing about him, Lieutenant," Bree repied, shrugging her shoulders slightly.

"I think you can." Whitlock was not to be denied. "You were there in his village for nearly four months."

"Yes, I was," Bree agreed, "but I didn't get to know all the Indians who came and went. Besides, you know how it is, Lieutenant, one Indian looks very much like another." It was a commonly held notion among people who didn't like the Indians and the lieutenant had made his feelings all too clear. He dispatched his duties against the Seminoles with a little too much zeal to Bree's liking. Thinking she had finished with him once and for all, she turned toward her other dinner companion.

"Tell me about your time at Horse Creek Village." Whitlock again claimed her attention.

"I have no wish to discuss my captivity with the Indians," she replied.

"But I understand you've spoken often on just that subject," he pressed.

"I speak only of the customs of the people, not of my own personal experiences."

"Personal experiences?" he asked, his pale eyes studying her, his voice filled with innuendos that made her squirm. She had resolved to leave the table in order to be free of this odious man when he spoke again.

"Some of the Indians spoke of a white woman who was Shocaw's *hoke-tee*. Was that you, Miss Rikkar?" Whitlock asked, and his voice was deceptively soft. Now the flush of her cheeks receded. Her face went pale, her eyes wide and defenseless as she cast a quick glance about the table. No one had overheard their conversation. Her pleading glance turned back to him. She looked ready to faint. Quickly he reached for her glass and held it to her lips.

"Sip this," he said.

"Thank you," she whispered gratefully. A little color was coming back into her face. "Please, I beg you, Lieutenant, do not speak of this further tonight." Her voice was low and intense.

His thin, bloodless lips curved in an indulgent smile. "You may depend on my discretion, Miss Rikkar," he said. "However, I must insist that you speak with me privately on this matter."

"Yes, all right," Bree agreed woodenly. "Come for tea day after tomorrow."

"I'll be there." His hand pressed hers boldly.

"Lainie, I do believe our Lieutenant Whitlock is making a conquest of your daughter," Denise Payne said coquettishly. Robert Whitlock raised his eyes and looked at the older woman. Displeasure was clear in the vivid depths of her eyes and for the first time he cursed himself for his dalliance with her. Denise Payne had been a convenient way to while away some lonely nights, but he hoped she wouldn't become a nuisance now. She was a lovely woman but she had a viper's tongue.

"Bree, darling, tell us some more about your experiences with the savages. You haven't spoken about them at all this evening."

"I've told you everything," Bree said quietly. "I'm afraid I'll begin to bore you."

"Nonsense," said Mavis Cooper, an old friend

of her mother's. Few people are captured by those savages and live to tell about it." Those words were all Bree needed.

"Actually, the Seminoles are not savages," she said. "They are very civilized." She went on to tell the group about the Seminoles and their customs. Soon everyone was listening and asking questions about the ceremonies and laws. Once she'd gotten over her nervousness, Bree talked easily on the subject.

"You should take your daughter with you when you go to Washington next week, Rikkar," Ben Marlow said. He was one of her father's neighbors and a known liberal about Indian rights. "She seems to know a lot about the Seminoles. Maybe she could give them some pointers on how to handle these last rebels so we can end this war once and for all."

"Would the things I have to say help the Seminoles?" she asked eagerly. What an opportunity this would be. She'd been able to talk to only a few people here in Tampa at dinner parties and teas, but in Washington she might be able to get some help for the Seminoles and help end the war. This was what Shocaw had wanted her to try.

"I'm sure it would help. It certainly wouldn't hurt," Ben Marlow urged.

"I'm not sure my daughter is well enough to travel," David Rikkar said, offering her an out if she wanted it.

"No, Papa. I am well enough," she answered. "I want to go to Washington and do whatever I can."

"Then I guess it's settled," Rikkar said, and the look in his eyes was one of approval and pride in his daughter.

Bree glanced out the window at the swiftly moving landscape. It was her first time on a train and the experience was still novel to her. Though other ladies, heavily swaddled against the cinders and smoke that blew back on the passengers, complained often of their discomfort, Bree seemed not to notice.

Seated across from her were Lieutenant Whitlock and her father. At first Bree had been unhappy upon learning that he would accompany her father and her to Washington. Then she'd realized he was her only link to Shocaw. For that reason alone she was wiling to tolerate his company. She thought back to the day he'd come to tea at Greenwood.

Lainie had held it on the wide, low veranda at the back of the house, where comfortable wicker chairs and cool drinks made the hot summer afternoon bearable. How boldly the lieutenant's eyes had moved over the house and gardens, even over Bree herself, as if he were assessing the value of each of them. His pale gaze had pinned Bree with a stabbing directness.

"Are you Shocaw's *hoke-tee,* his woman?" he'd asked when they were alone for a moment, and she'd been compelled to answer.

"I was," she'd said simply, and waited for the derisive curl of his lips, the sneering speculation in his blue eyes. For a moment it had been there and then was gone, his expression carefully guarded.

"It's probably why you survived your ordeal," he'd said. When she'd made no answer, he continued. "You survived and now you are back among your own kind, Miss Rikkar. Don't let misplaced sympathy confuse your loyalties. Tell me what you know. Help me find Shocaw Hadjo."

"I know nothing, Lieutenant," she'd replied. "Even if you threaten to expose me to the community, it will do you no good. Shocaw never confided in me. I can't help you."

He'd gone away then and for a while she'd waited, expecting to be exposed, but Whitlock had kept her secret.

Washington took her breath away. She loved strolling along the Potomac or along the wide tree-lined boulevards. Driving around the city, she could hardly believe it had been attacked and some of it burned by the British just thirty years before. Quickly the city had rebuilt itself, repairing the damaged buildings and putting up new. Bree and her father went to see the White House, the south portico of which had just been added ten years before. They toured the museums and drove out to see Mount Vernon, the first president's home and burial site. They attended the play at the new National Theater and much, much more, but they did not see the secretary of war.

Day after day they waited for an appointment. Despite her father's status in the navy, they were kept cooling their heels in the anteroom. David Rikkar's temper grew and Bree became discouraged. Determinedly, her father made the rounds of the senators and congressmen, making his point time and again, but to little avail.

Lieutenant Whitlock was busy too. They seldom saw him. One day as they waited in the anteroom, hoping the secretary would make time to see them, the lieutenant came from the inner offices. His face flushed guiltily when he saw them sitting there.

"Did you get to see the secretary?" Bree asked.

"Yes, I had to make my report for General Armistead," he admitted reluctantly.

"Did you tell him this war must be stopped?" Bree asked eagerly. "Did you tell him of the plight of the Seminoles?"

"Uh, I mentioned it," he said, and looked away. Bree was sure he'd said nothing.

After that it was harder than ever to get in to see the secretary. His assistant told them coldly that there was little hope of a meeting. They might as well return home. Bree wondered if Lieutenant Whitlock had said something to damage their cause. Rikkar was sure he had.

One evening Bree and her father attended a dinner in the home of a sympathetic supporter, Senator William Humphrey. Listening to the distinguished guests, Bree was surprised to find they felt as she and her father did. It was time to end this costly war.

Bree spoke to the wives of the senator's guests and was delighted at the display of interest in the Seminole culture. The snobbery and prejudice present in the drawing rooms of the Florida planters was not in evidence here. Furthermore, everyone had already heard of Osceola and had seen the portrait of him by George Catlin. Their admiration of the courageous chief who'd fought so bravely and died so tragically was freely expressed.

At first Bree felt heartened by their reception. But what good was it to tell the wives of important men? She needed to tell her story to the secretary of war. Only he could stop the war and offer a future to Shocaw and his people. She felt more despondent than ever. They had only one more day in Washington and then they would return to Greenwood with nothing accomplished.

As they were gathering their wraps, preparing to leave, a tall, distinguished man approached them. His deepset blue eyes and wide brow lent a melancholy air to his aristocratic features. Bree liked him at once.

"Captain Rikkar," he said, bowing slightly, "and the lovely Miss Rikkar. I am Jonathan Taylor, the publisher of the *Washington Herald.*"

"Mr. Taylor." Her father shook hands with him. "This is an honor."

"Miss Rikkar, I have been mesmerized all evening by your tales of the Seminoles. I could hardly restrain myself from joining the ladies in the parlor after dinner, for I wished to hear more of your experiences among the Indians. I wonder if you'd be so kind as to call upon me at the paper tomorrow."

"Why, I'm not sure," Bree answered. "We have only one day left in Washington and we'd hoped to make one last bid to see the secretary of war."

"Try to come for tea at three. I'm sure I can offer you some help with your cause," he said. His fine eyes were direct and compelling. There was about him the air of a man who embraced causes wholeheartedly. Something about him drew Bree's trust. She cast a quick glance at her father.

"In that case, Mr. Taylor. We'd be delighted to come."

"Good. It's been a pleasure to meet you, Miss Rikkar. Captain." With a last brisk handshake he turned back toward his hostess's drawing room.

"Do you know who that man was?" David Rikkar asked later when they were in the carriage on their way back to the hotel. "Jonathan Taylor and his paper are one of the most influential voices in Washington."

"I wonder what he has in mind." Bree said.

"He seemed quite taken by your stories of the Seminoles. His interest can only help."

Their reception at the office of the secretary of war was considerably cooler the next morning. They were informed that the secretary was out of town and would not return for several days. Their last hope of doing anything for the Seminoles seemed to fade. That afternoon they went to their appointment with the publisher.

Jonathan Taylor was a dynamic man with impeccable manners. He showed them about his offices, explaining what it took to get a paper out each week. He moved easily from the print shop to the room where the great rollers whirled and spun, putting out copy after copy of his paper.

It was obvious he had a great love for his paper. They poked into every nook and cranny and were given such detailed accounts of how it all ran that Bree was sure she could have put out a newspaper herself. Yet the intense enthusiasm and excitement of its owner kept them from being bored.

At last he led them back to his office, where they settled into deep easy chairs. The decor of the room was decidedly masculine and several awards hung on the walls. A small portrait of a woman and child was displayed prominently. Obviously it was Jonathan Taylor's family.

Tea was served, and during the lively conversation that ensued, Bree began to wonder if the intent of his invitation had been simply social after all. Then the newspaperman put down his cup and fixed his gaze on her and she knew it was not. This was a man with a purpose and right now that purpose included her. She set her own cup down and waited expectantly.

"Miss Rikkar," he said. "I wonder if you realize what a wonderful opportunity you've been given?" He didn't wait for her answer. "You've lived among the Seminoles, seen them at first hand, gotten to know them, the way they think and act in a way few people have experienced."

"Yes, I know," she replied, and waited. Obviously he had more to say.

"There are hundreds—no, thousands of people out there who want to know the very things you've learned, and they have no way of getting that information themselves. Not unless you or someone else like you who's survived capture by the Indians tells us their story. Have you ever thought about writing down your story, Miss Rikkar?"

"No, I hadn't," Bree said, surprised and then pleased at this new possibility. "Would it help?"

"Would it help?" he repeated. Getting to his feet, he gazed down at her, yet she didn't feel intimidated by him, only caught up in his flow of energy and ideas. "Yes, Miss Rikkar. It could most definitely help your cause.

"There's been a public outcry against this war for some time now. So far it has cost our government millions of dollars and hundreds of lives. We can't afford those kinds of losses. The cost of the war is up to nearly a hundred thousand dollars a month. Some believe it's one of the major reasons our country is heading into an economic recession. Few see this as a noble war, especially since the capture and death of that brave Seminole chief Osceloa."

"So we've read," her father said, "but there are other issues than those of money."

"You're right. There are the moral issues involved." The thin man got impatiently to his feet and began to pace about his office. "The things we've done to the Indians will be a blight on the honor of this country for some time to come," he said. "We haven't done it just to the Seminoles. There are the Cherokees and Creeks and several other tribes. But it is the Seminoles who have resisted and it is the Seminoles who've been caught up in a bigger issue than Indian removal. That issue is slavery."

"I agree," David Rikkar said quietly.

"We the American people are being manipulated into fighting a war in defense of the Southern plantations' slaves. The Seminoles are paying a dear price for that war. I think it's time the people of this country understand what is really

happening down there. I want them to see that
we have become the tyrants in this issue. Sixty
years ago we fought the English and threw them
out of this country. We said this land is ours and
we have the right to govern ourselves."

"And yet we've been unwilling to give those
same rights to others," Bree said thoughtfully.
At last, there was someone who saw the real
issues involved and was unafraid to give full
voice to his opinion.

"And that's what I want the people to see."
Jonathan Taylor's fist pounded down on the corner of his desk, his eyes glowing. "We want the
people to see that the Seminoles are a patriotic
group of people fighting for their homeland just
as we once did. I want you to write a series of
articles for me, Miss Rikkar, and tell me about
these people, help me to know and understand
them. Show me and the rest of my readers that
these are not ignorant savages. They are a brave
people. Will you do that, Miss Rikkar?"

"You want me to write for the *Washington Herald?*" Bree asked. "I don't know what to say. I'm
not sure I could do it."

"Of course, you can," Jonathan Taylor said.
"Just write your stories the way you've told them
in the parlors and drawing rooms of Washington
and Florida. They'll receive a wider audience
than you ever dreamed of."

"All right, Mr. Taylor. I'll do it," Bree replied
firmly, and her eyes were unswerving as they met
the challenging gaze of the fiery journalist.

Later, when they were outside and the cold
wind blew against her hot cheeks, Bree thought
back over the meeting. If Jonathan Taylor wrote
anywhere near the way he talked, he could sway
people to do something about the war. She was
grateful for his support.

Suddenly, she wished Shocaw was here so she

could tell him. She wanted to see the lights dancing in his eyes and see hope return to his face. She longed for him as a woman, wanting to touch his strong body and feel his arms around her. She could feel a surge of grief well up inside her and swallowed against it, turning her face to look out the carriage window so her father wouldn't see her distress.

Suddenly, beneath her heart she felt a flutter, a movement of life, of a baby conceived out of her love for Shocaw. Again it moved, a small fierce promise of things that would never be forgotten. Her gloved hand pressed against the spot where her baby lay and she was comforted by this evidence of his presence. Shocaw was with her now. He would always be with her. Tomorrow she and her father would return to Greenwood and she would write the articles for Jonathan Taylor and his paper. Maybe somewhere Shocaw would know that she was thinking of him. Maybe he would know the great love she still bore for him.

Chapter 17

When Bree and her father were settled back at Greenwood, she wrote her first piece about the Seminoles' dress and customs and sent it off to Taylor. On an impulse she drew sketches of some of the women in their long skirts and of the men, tall and proud with their beaten silver gorgets and plumed turbans. Somehow writing and sketching the people she'd lived with during her captivity made her feel closer to them.

Every week thereafter she sent an article discussing various aspects of the Indians' life and religion. She wrote about the trails blazed through the jungle and the pumpkin vines growing up the trees to save growing room. She wrote of the legends and the Seminoles' belief in their Christian faith. She told of the Seminole woman's work and of her craft, with the intricate designs she pieced together. She told of tanning a deer hide. She wrote about their dying and their sorrows and of the poverty and starvation.

Jonathan Taylor printed her pieces as she'd written them. She had written of a subject she knew and loved and it showed. People read her writings and talked about them to friends. Other newspapers picked up the printing rights and her articles even ran in some of the London papers.

In her quiet existence at Greenwood, Bree was unaware of the furor she and her writings were causing. She concentrated on her work and watched happily as her once-slender figure thickened at the waist and her flat stomach curved beneath her full skirts. Robert Whitlock came to call often now and Bree almost looked forward to his visits, so hungry was she for company. Hardly any of her friends came to see her. She and the lieutenant sat in the garden, soaking up the few hours of winter sunshine and spoke of many things, seldom of Shocaw and the Seminoles. It seemed to her at times that the officer was deliberately withholding information she desperately needed to know. At other times it seemed he baited her to see what her reaction toward the Seminoles would be.

One day as Whitlock rose to take his leave, he leaned forward and with a hand beneath each elbow lifted her to her feet. Before she knew what he was about, his mouth descended on hers in a long, fervent kiss. Bree didn't struggle but neither did she respond. She stood quietly and when the kiss had ended spoke gently to the officer.

"Please don't, Robert," she said.

"I'm sorry, Bree," he said, using her first name for the first time. "It's just that I've wanted to do that for a long time."

"I'm sorry if you've entertained notions about me that can never be," she replied firmly.

"Can't they?" he asked, grasping her hand. "Do you know what my notions are? I wish to marry you."

Bree gasped in disblief. "I don't love you, Robert. I—couldn't."

"Many marriages are made without love," he replied. "Don't say no until you've considered my offer."

"Why would you want to marry me, knowing I don't love you?" she asked, perplexed.

"You are very beautiful, Bree." He paused, his blue eyes smiling and sure. "And so is Greenwood."

"Ah, yes, Greenwood," Bree said. At least he hadn't lied, although his proposal was an insult. "Have you forgotten my brother Jared? He will inherit Greenwood."

"True," Robert Whitlock answered blandly. "But I understand your family owns another plantation northeast of here near St. Augustine. Just think, Bree, with me as your husband, people need never know who the real father of your baby is. We can go to your familiy's other plantation and begin anew. I'm sure your father would be happy to offer it as part of your dowry, in order to see you safely married."

"Have you spoken to my father about this?" she asked.

"Not yet. I wanted to see how you felt about it," he answered. The truth was that he sensed Captain Rikkar's dislike of him and hoped Bree would be grateful enough at his proposal to help persuade her father. Now he stepped closer and took her hand. "I hope you'll consider my proposal," he said. "It could be a solution for you and your baby."

"I'm sorry, Lieutenant Whitlock." Bree drew herself up stiffly. "I would be giving you false hope if I told you I would consider it. I am already married to Shocaw Hadjo."

His face drained of color and he dropped her hand. At the same time there was a speculative gleam in his eyes as he considered her news. "I see," he said slowly. "In that case, Miss Rikkar, I bid you good day." Whirling, he left the veranda, making his way back through the house and to the stables.

Bree stayed behind, thinking of all Robert Whitlock had said. One hand went to touch her lips, which still tingled from his kiss, and suddenly she was remembering the first kiss Shocaw had given her by the pool that day she'd seen Milakee and Cooee together. How his kiss had enflamed her.

She could never love another man, she thought, pacing about the garden. She was still Shocaw's woman as surely as if he'd put a brand on her. She would never marry, never give herself to another man. Slowly, she paced, all her thoughts about Shocaw. So real were her memories, it seemed as if Shocaw were very near. All she had to do was call out for him and he would come.

Sadly she looked around. She was here at Greenwood and Shocaw was out there somewhere in the swamps fighting for his people. Their paths would likely never cross again and she must accept that. Sighing, she gathered up her needlework and went inside.

So the weeks and months passed. She had no idea of the temper of things until she went for a rare carriage ride with her mother one early spring afternoon. As their carriage rolled down the muddy streets of Tampa, Bree began to notice old friends who no longer waved at her mother, people who turned their heads away when they passed, pretending not to see them. Deliberately they would turn to chat with someone else, casting knowing looks back over their shoulders.

Lainie appeared not to notice, but Bree knew she was stung by the reactions of people with whom she'd lived and worked for so many years. Mama had long been a social leader in this thriving new town. Now, because of Brce, she was being treated as an outcast. They made a stop at a dry-goods store for Bree to buy more thread for her needlework. Even there she could feel the disapproving eyes of the other patrons. Quickly she made her purchase and turned back to her mother.

"I'm finished, Mama," she said quietly.

"Just a moment, Bree. I wish to look at some of these silks," Lainie said. She had no intention of being intimidated by these women. As if unaware of the whispers about her, she made a thorough inspection of a pile of brightly colored materials.

"Lainie Rikkar, imagine seeing you here." Denise Payne's voice was deliberately high and carried around the store. Several women cast a quick glance from beneath the brims of their bonnets.

"Good afternoon, Denise," Lainie said calmly. "I see Mr. Brady has some new silks. Bree needs some new gowns."

"Yes, I can see she does." Denise's glance flew to Bree's waist.

Was it so evident already? Bree wondered, and couldn't suppress the flush to her cheeks. She had thought her wide skirts and shawl had made her condition less noticeable.

"Bree, darling, what color would you like?" Lainie asked, ignoring Denise's barbed words.

"I'm not sure," Bree said, moving closer to the counter where her mother stood. She was painfully aware of the other women watching them. Even the shopkeeper, as if sensing some drama, paused in his measurement and looked up expectantly. "I don't know what color would be best for me," Bree said.

"Try scarlet, darling. It would look marvelous on you," Denise said. A woman snickered in the back of the shop. Lainie's cheeks burned with angry spots and her dark eyes spit fire.

"I really don't want any new dresses right now, Mama," Bree said quickly, stepping forward. "I'm most anxious to get back home. I have some letters to write."

"Go home and write some more about those heathens you lived with," some woman called.

"Shh, Maudie," her friend admonished.

"If she likes the heathens so much, she ought to go back out there in the swamps and live with them," the woman replied, and Bree whirled to face them, eyes blazing.

"Perhaps I would," she said quietly, "if they were allowed to live in peace in the swamps as they wish. But the white men, your husbands, have decided not only to take the good Indian land, but the swamps as well. As for the Seminoles, God knows they showed more Christian kindness than many of you ever have."

"Don't go getting on your high horse, missy." A woman stepped forward. "I've known you and your family since you was a baby and I can tell you, Bree, you're wrong."

"Am I?" Bree countered.

"Those varmints have murdered and burned good white folks for years."

"And what do you think the good white folks are doing back to them?" Bree cried. "Don't you think we're to blame for any of this? The Indians are slowly starving to death, even the children, while you women are more concerned with keeping your little world intact." Bree paused and drew a breath, refusing to allow the tears that had filled her eyes to spill over. She'd not cry in front of these women. Proudly she held her head high, her eyes filled with anger as she looked at her accusers.

"While you're buying silks and ribbons, some

Indian woman is out there trying to grow food on land where little can be grown. While your children are in safe, secure nurseries with their mammies to watch over them, Seminole babies are hidden in holes dug out of the dirt and mud in the swamps so they won't cry out and bring discovery and death down on their villages. While you—" Her voice broke on a cry and her mother was there, an arm about her waist, leading Bree back toward the door. Lainie paused before leaving the shop and looked back at the women, her glance scathing. Her dark eyes settled on the aging, spiteful face of the woman still standing near the silks.

"Denise Payne," she said, and her voice rang out clear. "Don't you ever speak to my daughter in such a manner again. If ever a woman here should wear scarlet, it's you. We've all known for years who comforts the homesick young soldiers here at this fort and your ministrations go far beyond the call of duty." Bree heard Denise's gasp and saw the mottled red staining the woman's angry face, but now her mother was guiding her out of the store, across the wooden sidewalk and into the carriage. Tom whipped up the horses and the carriage rumbled out of the town toward Greenwood.

"Mama, I'm sorry for the shame I've brought on you," Bree whispered tearfully.

"Don't you be sorry, Bree," Lainie said fiercely. "I don't understand your need to defend the Seminoles the way you do, after what they've done to you and our friends, but no one is going to hurt my daughter like those women back there tried to do."

Bree looked at her tiny, dainty mother. "Mama." She laughed, then put her hands over her lips and tried to speak again, but the laughter came spilling out.

"What is it, Bree? Why do you laugh?" Lainie demanded.

"You stood up to Denise so fiercely, she—did you see her face?" Lainie stared at her for a moment, then slowly her anger melted away and her laughter mingled with her daughter's. They put their cheeks together for a moment, remembering the way they'd faced down the disapproving women and let laughter heal some of the hurt they each felt over the occurrence.

In the weeks that followed Bree stayed home more and more often, content to sit quietly in the sun-drenched morning parlor, stitching baby clothes. Her stomach was rounding now and even her wide skirts could no longer hide her condition. It no longer mattered to her. She felt a contentment invade her very soul, making everything else seem unimportant. She still missed Shocaw horribly, but as his baby grew within her the longing was made more bearable.

Her articles had reached many people by this time and she began to get letters from people who wanted to know more about the Seminoles. Lainie began to help her with answering the letters. Sometimes there were letters that said foul things, but these vicious attacks didn't bother Bree as much as they once might have. Patiently she answered them as well, explaining that if people got to know the Seminole customs, they would understand and not think them so immoral.

She'd nearly finished with her articles. There were only two more planned. Soon she would have told her readers everything, everything except that she was the second wife of Shocaw Hadjo. She kept that information back, hugging it to herself fearfully. It was best if she kept as low a profile as possible while she waited for the birth of her child. Certainly she had no intention of going back into town—that is, until the day the message arrived at the plantation for her father.

"They brought Coacoochee and most of his men in," her father said, reading the message, and suddenly Bree's fragile world was turned upside down.

"Does he say if—if Shocaw Hadjo was captured also," she asked, walking toward him, her hand resting protectively on her protruding stomach.

"He doesn't say. It could be they don't know. They can't always identify some of the chiefs, especially if they've never been captured before. No one would know what he looks like."

"That's true," Bree said thoughtfully. "Shocaw never really dressed differently from his warriors, only his war paint is different."

"His war paint?" Lainie asked with a small shudder.

"Yes, Mama. The war chief wears vermilion. If he wasn't wearing any, they wouldn't be able to identify who he is." She paused, looking at the message her father still had. Quickly she made up her mind. "Papa, I want to go see Coacoochee."

"Bree, you can't mean that," Lainie cried.

"I do, Mama. I couldn't bear not knowing if Shocaw has been captured."

"And if he's there, what good will it do you or him? You can't help him. Why go at all?" Bree took a deep breath. Her mother had come a long way in accepting her concern and work for the Seminoles, but her own prejudice still had not been overcome and likely never would. "If he's there, Mama, and is being shipped to the Arkansas Territory ..." She paused, knowing what she was about to say would only hurt her mother, but it must be said. "If he's being shipped out there, I'm going with him," she finished quietly. Her mother gasped in outrage and disbelief. Her

father stared into her eyes steadily, reading her
purpose there and closing his eyes against the
sudden thought that they might yet lose her to
the Seminoles.

"Papa," Bree said softly, her eyes on his face.
Rikkar opened his eyes and looked at her. "Will
you go with me to the fort?" she asked.

"I forbid you to go. Bree, I forbid it," Lainie
cried out, rushing to stand before her daughter.
Bree looked at her with tears in her eyes.

"Lainie, you don't mean that," her father said.

"Yes, Rikkar, I do," Lainie said implacably. "If
Bree leaves this house to go to this—this Indian,
then she needn't come back here." Lainie stared
at her daughter and Bree felt her heart break
within her. How close she and her mother had
grown over the past few months. She'd cherished that closeness, depended on it for the
months ahead, but she had to go.

"I'm sorry, Mama, I must go," she said quietly,
and left the room, hurrying away to put on stur-
dier boots and a warm cape against the chill
winter wind that blew off the gulf.

Her father had the carriage brought around by
the time she came back downstairs and her mother
was no place in sight. Bree suspected she'd retired to the small morning room, which was her
favorite room, and thought of going to her to try
and placate her, but sensed it would be useless.
Her mother's hatred for the Seminole was too
deeply rooted in her own terrible experiences.

Bree buttoned the cape about her shoulders
and quietly closed the great door behind her. Her
father was quiet on the drive to Tampa, obviously distressed over Mama's outburst and his
own fears for Bree. The horses were the fastest
Greenwood owned and very soon they were on
the outskirts of the raw pioneer town and turned
toward the gates to the fort.

Through a haze Bree realized her father's presence once more opened doors for her that would not be opened for ordinary civilians.

"Bree," Lieutenant Robert Whitlock said, taking her hands. His glance included her father as well. Since that day he'd kissed her in the garden, his visits had grown infrequent over the past few weeks. "I'm sorry you've come right now. The officers are about to meet with Coacoochee."

"I'll wait," Bree said anxiously.

"It's important to her," Rikkar said. "General Armistead has given his permission."

"Yes, I have his communiqué," the young officer answered. "Why don't you wait in here where it's warm? It's the general's quarters, but he won't mind. There's a fire going."

"Did you say the general is about to meet with Coacoochee?" Bree asked.

"That's right. He's being brought to the parade ground now," Robert said, and it was obvious he was anxious to be away himself.

"Robert," Bree said. "Might I attend the meeting as well?" She couldn't bear to wait in here when Shocaw might be only a few feet away. Besides, he might be with Coacoochee and she would have missed a chance to see him.

"Yes, well, I'll see to a chair for you," Robert said, and guided them out the door into the middle of the square. A table had been set up before the general's headquarters and officers were gathered in a formal line behind it. Other soldiers flanked either side of the square, leaving a large center arena.

Robert placed a chair discreetly to one side for Bree and gratefully she sank into it. David Rikkar stood behind her. There was a hushed tension in the air as everyone waited. The sun shone down on them, warming the square with its light. A soft breeze stirred the leaves of the palm trees towering over the fort walls.

At the other end of the square a gate opened and a small group of Indians appeared, guarded on either side by more soldiers. The anticipation was so great among the officers that the quiet appearance of the chief and his warriors seemed almost anticlimactic.

Coacoochee was dressed in the same theatrical costume he'd worn the first time Bree saw him at Horse Creek Village. She heard a ripple of derisive laughter from the line of soldiers. A stern look from their officer quelled it.

The war chief came closer, walking with such dignity that the soliders were abashed by their earlier reaction. This was Coacoochee, the greatest war chief of the Seminoles after Osceola. He had been a formidable opponent for all these years and at last they had captured him. Their respect for him was immense.

Haughtily the slender figure made his way toward the waiting officers, and the onlookers felt their awe grow. They'd expected a giant of a man, yet this Indian was smaller than most of them. What a fierce, wily fighter he'd been. Proudly his warriors followed behind him, their noble faces stoic and impassive, their proud heads unbowed.

Bree's eyes searched the faces of the Indian warriors who stood behind their leader, searching for the one familiar face, the tall figure of Shocaw. He wasn't there, he wasn't there! Was he dead then, she wondered, and knew she couldn't accept that thought. Coacoochee's voice rang out strong and clear around the square and Bree turned her attention back to him.

"We greet you, Coacoochee." General Armistead stepped forward. Stiff, formal greetings were returned. Calmly the Indians listened to

the general as he spoke, then Coacoochee stepped
forward. An expectant hush fell over the assembly.

"The whites have dealt unjustly by me," he
said, and every man present was drawn by his
magnetism and eloquence. "I came to them, they
deceived me. The land I was upon I love; my
body is made of its sand; the Great Spirit gave
me legs to walk over it, hands to aid myself, eyes
to see its ponds, rivers, forests, and game, then a
head with which I think." Coacoochee paused
and raised his eyes to the bright winter sunshine.

"The sun, which is warm, as bright as my
feelings are now," he continued, raising his hands
expressively, "shines to warm us and bring forth
our crops and the moon brings back the spirit of
our warriors, our father, wives, and children."
Bree drew in her breath at his words. Her heart
ached for the great chief and his defeat.

"The white man comes," Coacoochee said.
"He grows pale and sick, why cannot we live
here in peace? I have said I am the enemy to the
white man. I could live in peace with him, but
he first steals our cattle and horses, cheats us,
and takes our lands. The white men are as thick
as the leaves in the hammocks; they come upon
us thicker every year." His voice grew louder as
he spoke and his eyes flashed with pride. "They
may shoot us, drive our women and children
night and day; they may chain our hands and
feet, but the red man's heart will be always free."

Tears were streaming down Bree's cheeks and
she found that sometime during Coacoochee's
speech she had risen to her feet. The square was
silent when he stopped speaking and it was plain
that not an officer or man present would ever forget
the words the great chief had said here this day.

Now Coacoochee and his warriors were being
led off. They would be put directly on one of the
ships in the bay, for the general was taking no

chance that Coacoochee might escape—as he had done once so long ago at the beginning of the war. Slowly the soldiers dispersed and Robert came to lead Bree and her father to the stockade. His hand clasped Bree's elbow firmly and she was grateful for his support.

The stockade was not as appalling as Bree had feared. Although the space was small for the number of Indians awaiting deportation, some effort had been made to see to their comfort. Hesitantly, Bree walked inside the stockade. Robert and her father followed close behind. Indians lounged on the dirt floor of the enclosure and women cooked over an open fireplace much like the ones in their villages. Children played a game of stickball in one corner. Some old men sat in a corner, staring numbly into the distance. In a thatched lean-to several Indians lay on pallets of woven straw. It was obvious they were ill with a fever.

"You can't go any farther, Bree, it isn't safe," her father admonished.

"I must search for Shocaw," she said.

"Think of your baby." His words slowed her steps and she stopped, trying to look deeper into the stockade without walking farther in, when a voice called her name. Bree turned around and confronted cold, angry eyes.

"Cooee, Cooee!" she cried, and ran to him.

"Why are you here?" he demanded when Bree would have thrown her arms about him. His rigid body made her pause and look at him in surprise.

This was not the young brave who had brought her food and acted as her interpreter. There were no lights of friendship in his eyes now. Gone was the trusting young boy and in his place stood an angry man filled with a savage anger.

"Oh, Cooee." Bree repeated his name softly, tears springing to her eyes at the thought of all he'd been through to turn him into one of the embittered, hate-filled warriors.

"I'm so sorry," she said, taking a step forward.

"For what?" Cooee asked, his eyes cold.

"For your being here, for Milakee. I was there, I held her, but she was already dead. The bullets—" The tears were running down her cheeks freely and it was hard to talk past the lump in her throat. "I'm so sorry," she whispered again.

"Is that why you walk with her murderer?" Cooee demanded.

Bree glanced back at Robert Whitlock. "He isn't—he didn't kill her, Cooee,' she cried, then paused. Robert had not pulled the trigger, but he had ordered his men into the camp and he had allowed them freedom to commit such cruel and deadly acts against the defenseless Indians.

Once again an image of Milakee fighting off one of the soldiers then breaking away toward the trees came to her. It was true. She'd been unarmed and they'd shot her in the back. Her shoulders drooped in defeat. There were too many sides to these issues. She was tired of trying to sort them out, of trying to see both sides and act fairly toward everyone. She wanted the freedom to hate and to act out in anger against those who'd brought her pain, but it would accomplish nothing. In his pain, Cooee wouldn't understand.

"Is Shocaw here?" she asked dully, her head lowered, her words barely audible.

"No." The word was short, emphatic.

"Is he dead?" She couldn't breathe while she waited for the answer. Cooee said nothing. Fear hammered in Bree's chest. Her head snapped up, her tear-filled eyes met his.

"Is he dead?" she cried, and her words rang out on the quiet air like a bell, sharp and piercing. Cooee saw her pain and his hatred thawed a little.

"No," he said quietly, and watched the relief wash over her face. Unconsciously her hands moved to the swell of her belly in a protective gesture. Slowly she raised her eyes back to his.

"Where is he?" she asked. "Is he well? Where is he, Cooee?"

"Why do you ask? Do you want to tell your soldier lover?"

"My soldier lo—" Bree halted, her gray eyes searching Cooee's face, unable to believe the accusation he'd hurled at her.

"Do you hate me so much? Do you really believe that the child I carry could be anyone else's but Shocaw's?" she asked, and it was his turn to look away. Slowly, Bree walked forward and touched his arm, a soft womanly touch, such as Milakee might have given him. Still he said nothing to her and at last she moved away from him, walking slowly toward the gate where two men in uniform waited for her.

The blond-haired man stepped forward to support her with his arm, but she recoiled from him, her great eyes studying his face before turning away. The older man reached out to take her arm and her figure seemed to crumple. He pulled her against his chest, one large hand smoothing the coil of pale hair, and Cooee perceived that she was crying. She had suffered too, he realized. Suddenly he was running across the ground toward her.

"Bree," he called. Whitlock whirled, his pistol out of its holster, its barrel leveled at Cooee's chest.

"Robert, no," Bree cried.

"Whitlock!" Rikkar's voice cut across the air, electric with danger and threat. The two men, the young Indian brave and the young officer, stared at each other. Cooee saw the hate and anger in the officer's eyes and knew the man wanted to kill him. Why? he wondered, and looked at Bree, her gray eyes wide and frightened, and Cooee understood.

When they'd entered the stockade, Bree had accepted the officer's hand at her elbow; there had been trust and acceptance in her attitude toward him. After she'd spoken to Cooee, she turned away from him. The man blamed him for it and was angry. He was in love with Bree! Cooee understood something else. Bree had not accepted the lieutenant as her lover, as Katcalani had reported. Had Katcalani lied when she said Bree had helped the soldiers destroy the village? Suddenly he was sure of it.

"Robert, he wouldn't harm me," Bree was saying, and the standoff between the two men was broken. Whitlock put his gun back in his holster and, casting one last angry look at Bree, stalked to the gate.

"I wanted to tell you, I don't hate you, Bree. It is only—" He paused.

"I understand," Bree said, and crossed to him, her hand going once again to his arm. "I understand," she repeated softly, and Cooee knew she did. "I've lost someone too."

She went up on tiptoe and put her arms about his shoulders, and with a strangled sob, Cooee caught her to him. They stood together, bound by their mutual losses, fearing the best of their life was behind them and their bright futures forever dimmed by their sorrow. At last Cooee released her again and stepped back. When she went away, he would never see her again and she would take a part of Milakee with her. He wanted her to take something of him as well; that way he could always think of their spirits as being somehow still intertwined in the heart of this, their beloved friend.

Slowly his hands went to the medallion he

wore about his neck. It had been his birth plate;
he had worn it when he'd come to the Seminoles
and it had been a part of him for all the years
since. He took the chain from around his neck
and lowered it over her head. It lay against the
rich wool of her cape, its pattern gleaming against
the dark cloth.

"I give this to the baby you carry, Shocaw's
son," he said. "It is for the baby Milakee and I
never had. It will guard him for all the days of
his life."

"I will cherish it always and see that my son
wears it with pride and honor," Bree said softly.
There was nothing left to do, no good-byes left to
say. Cooee looked at her for a moment more, then
turned and walked slowly away, his proud head
bent. Bree watched until he had disappeared
into one of the shelters.

"Come, Bree, you've done all you can," her
father said softly, and took her arm.

"Oh, Papa," Bree cried, her head going to his
chest. Slowly he led her out of the stockade. Bree
thought of all the laughter she and Cooee had
shared with each other and the people they'd
loved. Now it was gone, forever stilled. Stilled
by the bullets that had pierced a girl's slender
body, stilled by the ship that would carry Cooee
away to a distant land and by the soldiers who
still hunted a brave and desperate war chief
through the swamps. There were no more tears,
just as there was no more laughter. She was too
numb to cry. She sat silent and pale in the corner of the carriage as Tom drove them home.

Chapter 18

When the carriage drew up before the main house, Rikkar helped his daughter down, growing even more worried and fearful of the rigidity he felt in her thickening body. She'd borne too much, he thought helplessly, and half carried her up the steps. He took her to the small parlor and placed her before the fire while he hastened to get brandy for her. She was too still, too closed in upon herself, her eyes too blank. As he was forcing brandy through her stiff lips, Lainie came into the room.

"My God, what happened!" she cried, seeing Bree's face. Her earlier anger was gone.

"She's had too many shocks," Rikkar said. "Help me with her cape." Together they took off her cape, forced more brandy down her lips, and rubbed her hands, hoping their ministrations would somehow revive her.

"Bree, darling it's all right," Lainie crooned, holding her in her arms and rocking her as she had when she was a little girl. "We're here and we'll help you. You're not alone." She remembered the harsh words she'd uttered to her daughter earlier and longed to be able to recall them. Now she sought to soothe away the hurt that gripped her child in its numbing claws.

"Mama," Bree whispered. She stirred in her mother's arms and drew back to gaze into her eyes. "Oh, Mama," she said brokenly. "If you had only been there today, if you had heard Coacoochee speak, you would understand."

"Shh, daring. I'm trying to understand," Lainie said.

"If you'd been there, you would have felt the suffering of the Seminole people." Bree's eyes lit up as another thought came to her. "Shocaw wasn't there. He's still free. At least for a while longer and I'm glad. Hearing Coacoochee speak, I realized anew how the Seminoles feel about their home." Her trembling hands fumbled with the chain and medallion about her neck, and as if surprised at its presence, she looked down at it, her elation fading. "They captured Cooee though," she said. "Cooee was a young boy, only a little older than I am." The words stumbled over each other.

Good, Lainie thought. Let her talk it out.

"He used to laugh a lot and he was so kind to me when I was captured by Shocaw and his men. Cooee was in love with Milakee and they were married, but the soldiers killed her. They shot her in the back, not once but several times because she was trying to run away from them."

Lainie felt shock ripple through her. She'd never thought of women being shot in the back.

"Cooee had nothing left, only this." Bree opened her hand a little and looked down at the medallion. "Only this," she repeated. "He gave it to me for my baby. It was all he had left to give and he gave it—" She swallowed the sob back. Her hand trembled on the chain of the medallion and Lainie looked at the silver ornament. Her eyes widened in disbelief. She remembered that medallion so well. She'd seen her father wear it often and she had placed it about her brother's neck herself.

"Rikkar," she cried, grasping the medallion to look at it more closely, knowing in her heart that it was the one she'd placed around her brother's neck so many years ago, the one that bore the coat of arms for the Gautier family.

"What is it, Lainie?" Rikkar was beside her.

"This medallion—" Lainie whispered. "It belonged to my father. I gave it to Jean Pierre because he liked to look at it." Her eyes were wide with disbelief and dawning hope.

"Don't get your hopes up, Lainie. It doesn't necessarily mean your brother is still alive."

"Tell me about this Cooee," Lainie demanded of Bree. "Tell me everything, don't leave out anything. How old is he? What does he look like? Tell me everything."

Bree began to describe Cooee and the story of his capture by the Seminoles. Again and again her mother stopped her to ask her questions.

"It could be him," Lainie said softly. "It could be. I must go and see."

"Not today, Lainie. Bree's had too much for one day."

"She must, she must," Lainie said intensely. "Darling, I hate to ask it of you, but are you well enough to go back to the fort with me?"

"Yes, of course, Mama," Bree agreed, although fatigue made her shoulders slump.

Much to Rikkar's disapproval—for now he feared not only for Bree's state but Lainie's as well—they readied themselves. The carriage was brought around and both women climbed into it, sitting on one seat where they held each other in a nameless mixture of emotions. Rikkar sat on the other side, his eyes sharp and concerned.

The general was astounded when he heard the story, Robert Whitlock disbelieving. A man was sent to fetch Cooee while Lainie and Bree repeated their stories, then the door opened and the tall

Indian brave entered the room. His hands had
been tied behind him. A raw scrape along one
cheek bore evidence of the cuffing he'd received
since Bree had been there. How and why had it
happened? she wondered, her questioning gaze
going to Robert Whitlock. Puzzled, she turned
back to Cooee. The tall youth's eyes met hers in
surprise, then turned to the tall blond officer,
and hate blazed in their dark depths. Had Robert gone back and fought with Cooee after she'd
left? Bree wondered, and felt anger rise in her at
the unfairness of such an attack.

When Cooee had first entered the room, Lainie
had given a half-smothered gasp and leaped to
her feet. Now, she slowly circled the shackled
Indian before turning her gaze back to his face. A
trembling hand was pressed to her lips and tears
filled her eyes, but she didn't cry.

Slowly she turned away and took the few steps
necessary to reach the general's desk. There she
clung to the corner of the desk for support, her
head bowed, her shoulders hunched as if to ward
off pain or joy too intense to bear. She closed her
eyes and the tears rolled down her cheeks. But
her mouth bore a smile, tremulous and joyful.
Bree and her father looked at Lainie in alarm.

Rikkar took a quick step forward. "Lainie?" he
said in a low voice, seeking reassurance she was
all right.

Lainie opened her eyes and they were bright
with some profound gladness. "He's my brother,"
she whispered, then repeated the words in a
louder voice.

"Mrs. Rikkar, this is highly irregular," the general said.

"It's unbelievable," Whitlock spoke up. "This
man is an Indian."

"No, he's not," Bree said. "I knew when I first
met him that he was not a full-blooded Indian,

and as I came to know the Indian language, I was told the story of Cooee and how he came to them as a baby. He was kidnapped from one of the plantations and adopted by a warrior who admired his bravery."

"Yes, he was brave, even that night with all the death and noise around him. The Indian had just killed Metoo,"—Lainie paused for a moment—"and he was going to kill Jean Pierre but he didn't cry out, not once. He was so brave, so the Indian took him with him instead."

Behind them Cooee listened to what was said, his expression as confused as the general's, while his mind raced back over all those years of growing up in a Seminole village. He'd always known that he was white and that Nan-ces-o-wee had adopted him. Sometimes he'd wondered about his own people, but had worked harder than most boys to immerse himself into his Indian heritage. Could it be true? Were these his people? If so, where was his father? Was the tall, dark-haired man his father? No, he was Bree's father and the woman claimed he was her brother. Cooee stood with his weight balanced on the balls of his feet, tense and poised as if for flight, although flight was impossible with his shackles. He listened while the woman explained about the medallion he had worn.

"I hardly know what to say," the general said when Lainie had finished her tale.

"There is nothing to say. You must release him to me at once," Lainie said, pulling her slight frame as tall and straight as she could. Her brown eyes snapped with determination.

"But, madam, you can't be sure."

"The general's right. You can't come in here and make a highly emotional decision on so little evidence," Robert said.

"I have all the evidence I need. He is my brother. I have no doubts."

"Is there anyone else who could verify your identification?" Whitlock asked.

"I can, General." Rikkar stepped forward. "From the moment I saw him this afternoon, I was struck by a feeling I'd seen the boy before, that he resembled someone I knew. When he walked into the office just now, I knew. Jean Gautier was a friend of mine. I knew him for many years. There is no doubt in my mind that this boy is his son."

Everyone sat quietly for a moment, taking in all that had been said. Finally the general rose to his feet and made harumphing noises. "Wars sometime bring about highly unusual circumstances. This seems to be one of them, sir," he began. "However, there are certain considerations."

"None of consequence," Lainie said. "He is my brother. I want him released."

"It isn't that easy. For years he has fought against our soldiers, killing and robbing."

"He was acting as a Seminole because that's the way he was brought up," Lainie cried. "We can't blame him for everything that has happened to him."

"No, no, we can't," the general said. "However, we can't ignore what he has become. He is an Indian, a dangerous renegade. What would he do to innocent people if I turned him loose? No, no, I'm afraid I can't release him. He'll be shipped out to the Arkansas Territory with the rest of them."

"You can't mean that," Lainie cried.

"I do," the general replied. "I have to think of the well-being of the other people who live here."

"What if I take responsibility for him," Rikkar said. "I'll watch over him, see no harm comes to anyone because of him."

"I'm afraid—no, no, it's out of the question. Lieutenant remove the prisoner."

Lieutenant Whitlock opened the door and motioned to the soldiers.

"Come on," one of the soldiers said, and roughly pushed Cooee toward the door. Bree flew to the window in time to see them emerge from the building. Viciously the soldiers shoved Cooee forward. With his feet shackled and his arms tied behind him, Cooee had no way of regaining his balance and went sprawling into the dust. One of the soldiers shouted something at him, then kicked with his heavy boot at the downed man's side. Other soldiers loitering about the square laughed derisively. No one helped him as he struggled back to his feet. Lainie had joined Bree at the window, while Rikkar and the general argued over the case. Now Lainie cried out at the treatment of the man who was her brother.

"Why has he been bound like that?" Bree demanded, turning an accusing gaze on Whitlock.

"After you left the last time, Miss Rikkar, this redskin, Cooee, tried to escape. Fortunately I was there and helped prevent it. I had him put in chains and placed in the jail until he can be shipped out."

"I don't believe you," Bree spat out. "Cooee was never a vicious person and he wasn't trying to escape when I was there."

"Perhaps it was something you said to him," Whitlock said softly, his blue eyes cold and unfriendly. Bree looked away. Why had she ever thought he was a friend to her and therefore to the Seminole? The memory of their trip to Washington came to her and she wondered if he had really spoken for the Seminole when he saw the secretary of war. A cold certainty that he had not washed over her.

Lainie had continued to stare out the window

and now she turned back to the general. "Sir, what are those men doing over there?" she asked. The general moved to look out the window.

"Those men right there." Lainie pointed. "The ones who're removing people from the stockade and chaining them into the wagons."

"Those are slave hunters claiming their merchandise," the general explained. "As you no doubt know, madam, the Seminole gave haven to any slave who ran away. These men are reclaiming their property."

"But haven't these slaves fought with the Indians?" Lainie asked.

The general harumphed, rocked on his heels, and gave a curt shake of his head to indicate they had.

"Are they not considered dangerous renegades then?" she persisted.

"They are first of all someone's property and a claim has been made to recover that property."

"And you allow them to be returned to their owners rather than ship them to the Arkansas Territory with the Indians."

"Ah, yes," the general said. "I'm afraid we have to. There would be too big an outcry by outraged slave owners."

"General," Lainie said, straightening her shoulders, and Bree remembered the things Mavis Cooper had said about her mother. Lainie might look little and helpless, but she could be tough when she had to. Even the general seemed to sense a need for wariness as he stood before the petite figure.

"I am not here to claim my brother, after all," Lainie said, a glint of triumph in her eyes. "I am here to claim my slave, Jean Pierre, also known as Cooee."

"Come now, Mrs. Rikkar, this is an elaborate ruse," the general protested.

"I assure you, general, it is not a ruse." Rikkar stepped forward.

"But you said he was your brother," he protested, looking at Lainie.

"And so he is that, sir," Lainie said, "but he is also a slave. It is a condition we must accept here in the South. Jean Pierre was born to the mulatto slave woman, Elizabeth, who was my father's housekeeper. According to the law, as long as there is any drop of Negro blood in him, he is considered a Negro and is a slave. I claim my property, sir. I wish to take him with me immediately."

Bree's heart swelled with pride as she saw her mother in action. Now she understood what Mavis had meant when she'd said Mama was strong. The towering, hulking general was visibly backing down. He was about to give in, but then Whitlock stepped forward.

"Do you have papers proving your ownership of this slave?" the lieutenant asked, and Bree's heart sank. But Lainie was not to be so quickly outdone.

"Yes, sir, I do," she answered calmly. "I have his birth papers."

"May I see them." Whitlock held out his hand for the papers.

"I haven't got them with me, but I can get them," she answered.

"Then you may not take him," Whitlock replied in a crisp tones.

"We will get the papers and return," Lainie said.

"Why don't you do that. If all is in order you may take him with you tomorrow."

"All right, sir," Lainie agreed, and gathered up her reticule and prepared to leave. Bree stood where she was, watching Robert Whitlock, uneasy about the flash of light in his eyes. What had it been, triumph? Her father was shaking hands with the general and guiding her mother to the door. He looked back over his shoulder to see if Bree was joining them when something in her stance arrested his attention

"What is it, Bree?" he asked.

"I don't know, Papa," she replied. "I—I don't like leaving Cooee here. I have the strangest feeling we'll never see him again."

"It's only until morning, Bree," her father replied.

"I know, but I feel a premonition," Bree said helplessly. "Couldn't you get the papers now?"

"It's nearly dark and I think you and your mama have been through enough for one day," he answered. His gaze moved from Bree's troubled face to the dusty square outside and on beyond to the ships in the bay. They were the ships that were used to take the Seminoles to New Orleans. Rikkar glanced back down at his daughter's face then turned back to the general, who had already reseated himself at his desk.

"General," Rikkar said, walking back to the desk. "My family feels very strongly that this matter should be taken care of quickly. We wish to see the prisoner, Cooee, again, so we may be absolutely sure."

"That's impossible," Whitlock said, stepping forward.

"Why?" Rikkar snapped.

"He's already been returned to the jail," Whitlock said.

"Has he," Rikkar challenged, "or has he been rowed out to those ships at anchor in the bay?"

"Lieutenant Whitlock, is this true?"

"Sir, he was a difficult prisoner. We feared he might escape and thought it best to put him aboard ship ahead of time as we did Coacoochee."

"I think it best he be brought back until this

matter is settled with his family," the general said.

"Yes, sir." Whitlock saluted and left the room.

The general turned back to Rikkar and his family. "I regret this misunderstanding," he said, and Bree felt he meant it.

"Sir, if you could loan me one of your fastest horses, I'll ride back to Greenwood tonight to get the proper papers."

"Not only will I be happy to do that, sir," the general said, "but I will provide you with an escort. It will be dark before you return, and ladies, if you'd care to wait in my parlor, I'll have some tea and brandy brought to you."

"Thank you, sir, you're very kind," Lainie said with all the charm with which she'd once won over Commander Payne when she'd first come to the bay area.

So it was that Bree and Lainie waited in the warm comfort of the general's study, too tense to enjoy the tea he'd provided, while Rikkar galloped back to Greenwood for Jean Pierre's birth papers.

It was very late when the four of them were able to board the carriage and begin the ride back to Greenwood. An escort of soldiers had been provided by the general, who had recovered from being bested by the beautiful Mrs. Rikkar and was fast falling captive to her beauty and charm.

Very little was said by anyone as they rode along, the three of them trying not to be too obvious as they peered through the gloom at the stiff, angry figure of Cooee. He had balked at the thought of going with them, preferring instead to go with his Seminole brothers to the Oklahoma wasteland. He had remained silent all the way home, but as they turned off the main road down the long lane toward Greenwood, he spoke.

"I won't stay," he said. "I will return to the swamp and the Seminole."

"No, you won't," Rikkar said.

"I can't bear to lose you again," Lainie said softly, and her pain touched the confused young man.

"You can't go back, Cooee," Bree said softly, her hand reaching out to touch his arm.

They were his family, Cooee thought, his real family. A family he had never known existed, a family who loved him and had grieved over his loss. Because of them he would stay here in Florida instead of being shipped to the deserts of Oklahoma. Things were forever changed for him, he realized. A new life was beginning. The loss of the old one was a pain deep within him.

"I will stay for a while," he said at last. Lainie laughed with relief and Bree smiled at him.

"It was a day's work well done," Rikkar said as the carriage rolled to a stop before the plantation. They were home at last.

So a different life began for all of them. Bree and Cooee had always been close and their bonds were strengthened in the weeks that followed. Lainie was radiant as she fussed over her newfound brother. From the expression on Cooee's face, Bree could often guess what he was feeling. She remembered how difficult it had been for her to sleep in a bed after the hard sleeping mats of the Seminole. At times the bleakness on Cooee's face wrung her heart.

Often in those first weeks he stood at the edge of the fields looking toward the forests and swamps that had been his home. The voices of his loved ones called to him, the memory of his life with them pulled at him until he longed to tear away the white man's dress and plunge back into the swamps in search of all he'd lost. But they were gone, forever gone from him. The chickees of the village of Chillocotee were burned, its people shipped west. Only a few still roamed the swampland, dodging the soldiers and struggling to stay alive.

The memory of Milakee was always with him, and when he could bear it no more, he raised his face to the sky in a wild cry of anguish. It was then that Bree would come and take his hand and gently draw him back to the house. Because of Bree he stayed. She'd known and loved Milakee too. That thought gave him some comfort. So the two clung together, bound through their sharing of a common experience and by their losses.

The baby within Bree's womb grew quickly now and Bree grew rounder and more cumbersome. Cooee teased her unmercifully, finding some comfort in seeing her thus. Milakee might have looked that way if she'd carried his child. Sometimes Bree thought he was almost like the old playful Cooee, but then she would see the new hardness in his eyes and knew that Cooee, endearingly boyish and open, was gone. Cooee was a man now, a man torn between two worlds.

In spite of his sorrow and confusion, Cooee—or Jean as Lainie insisted upon calling him—was curious about every new thing he saw in the white man's world. Rikkar traveled with him to Belle Fleur, the Gautier plantation along the St. John River, once owned by Lainie's father. Lainie had kept the plantation, hoping against hope that Jean would return one day. Her eyes glistened with pride and happiness when she told him the plantation was his.

Cooee was amazed that he owned so much property. Among the Seminoles no man owned property except the chickee in which he slept and the weapons with which he fought and hunted. The land belonged to the tribe. He thought of giving the plantation land to his Seminole people, but knew the white man's laws would never permit it. Besides, who was left in Florida to claim it? Those warriors left behind were fighting for their survival in the swamps. They'd been driven southward against the sea. After his first visit to Belle Fleur, he never spoke of it again.

The matter of what to do with Belle Fleur was taken out of their hands one day when Rikkar received a letter and called all of them together.

"This letter is from Miles Wentworth, your father's old neighbor," Rikkar said to his wife.

"What is that scoundrel up to now?" she asked with alarm.

"He's still after Belle Fleur, I'm afraid. He's heard about Jean Pierre and points out that a slave is not allowed to own property. He's drawing up a petition to put the plantation on the auction block. Of course, we know who plans to buy it."

"That's outrageous," Lainie cried. "Obviously he's forgotten about me. If that old law still holds, then I'm my father's legal heir and as such I don't intend to see Belle Fleur sold. It's Cooee's land and I'll hold on to it for him."

"We'll go to St. Augustine and attend to this," Rikkar agreed, "but it brings another matter to mind. The question of Cooee. Feeling runs high against him around here. His mother was a mulatto and he was raised and fought with the Seminoles. It's hard for folks to forget that."

"Then I will leave. I will return to my people and go to the Arkansas Territory with them."

"No, Cooee—Jean," Lainie cried.

"What good would that do you, Cooee?" Rikkar asked. "If you went out there, you'd have a good chance of dying from the fevers and other illnesses that are killing people off. Even soldiers aren't immune to it."

"Then I will go back into the swamps and join Shocaw Hadjo and Billy Bolecks," Cooee cried.

"And I will go with you," Bree cried, her heart contracting painfully at the mention of Shocaw's name.

"Bree!" her mother admonished.

"You canot go in your condition, Bree. You would roll into a swamp and the greedy *al-la-pa-taw* would eat you," Cooee teased.

"There is something else for you to consider," Rikkar said. "You could go to school, get an education. Your people are going to need you in a different way in the future. They will need someone who knows how to fight for their rights. If you go to law school, you'll learn how to do that. You can help protect your people so something like this will never happen to them again."

Cooee listened to Rikkar's words thoughtfully.

"He could join Jared," Lainie said.

Cooee remained undecided, although he asked many questions about the school Jared attended. He hated the thought of leaving Florida when his friends still fought on in the swamps. Then, Lieutenant Whitlock came to call one day and changed everything for them all.

He asked to see Bree and stood in the entrance, his hat in his hands, his bearing stiff and official. His face registered his shock when Bree entered the hall and he saw how far along in her pregnancy she was. Her beauty seemed luminous to him, although he still detected that sadness about the eyes. She still grieved for the Indian, he thought, and straightened his shoulders.

"Lieutenant Whitlock," she said. Her manner and words were gracious yet reserved. The friendship between them seemed to have vanished since that day in the stockade.

"Miss Rikkar," Whitlock said, and bowed slightly from the waist.

"What can I do for you, Lieutenant Whitlock?" she asked, and he was keenly aware of her failure to invite him into one of the parlors or out into the garden for tea.

"I came today to inform you, Miss Rikkar, that we've captured a large group of Indians. We believe we have all but a handful of them."

"A group of Seminoles?" Bree said breathlessly. "And you want me to come and identify Shocaw Hadjo?" she said flatly.

"No, Miss Rikkar, that won't be necessary," he replied, and the corners of his mouth curved upward slightly; his blue gaze held hers. "We hanged Shocaw Hadjo yesterday."

The words pounded into her brain. The memory of the warriors she'd seen hanging from the tree branches in the villages so many months before flashed before her. She could see their bulging, beseeching eyes, hear their strangled cries, feel their bodies kick and jerk. Not Shocaw, she thought, not Shocaw. It couldn't have happened to him. A pain ripped through her body and her hands went to the roundness of her belly as she slumped over, her knees barely able to support her.

"Bree!" Cooee cried, and was beside her, lifting her in his strong young arms. Gratefully, she slumped against him. "Lainie, May, come quickly," he called.

"What in heaven's name is going on here?" Rikkar cried, running to Bree. His arms went out to take her from Cooee.

"Shocaw's dead, he's dead," Bree cried softly.

"How do you know?" His eyes moved to Whitlock. "Good God, man, you didn't tell her in this condition?"

"She asked me once to let her know if I heard

anything. I thought she would want to know we hanged him yesterday."

"You animal," Lainie cried, putting her arms about Bree as if to protect her from the words. With a cry Cooee leaped forward at the soldier's throat. His hands closed about his windpipe and tightened. It had happened so quickly, Whitlock had no time to draw the pistol he'd made sure was loaded before coming.

Strengthened by fury and hatred for this man who had brought death to the people he loved, Cooee bore him to the floor. The muscles in his arms bulged as he pushed downward against his enemy's windpipe. The blue eyes bulged, the pale face turned red then blue as Whitlock struggled to breathe.

"Cooee, stop," Rikkar cried, and laid Bree on the stairs. She gripped the railings, peering through the carved posts while she too called to the young man.

"Jean Pierre," Lainie screamed. "Let him go. Don't kill him." Her words had little effect. Rikkar launched himself at the young man and knocked him off the officer, pinning his struggling body down.

"Listen to me, Cooee," he said. "If you kill him, he will win. You'll be hanged too. He came here wanting to make you attack him, so he can arrest you and punish you. Don't do it, Cooee, don't do it." The young man ceased struggling, lying stiff beneath him. Rikkar could still see the anger and hatred in his eyes. Bree's cry drew their attention.

"It's the baby trying to come," May cried, and Lainie hurried to lift her daughter's shoulders.

"Rikkar," she cried.

"Help me, Cooee," Rikkar commanded, and Cooee knew he was only diverting him from the blond man who still lay on the floor, gasping in

air, but his concern was for Bree now. Togethe:
they gathered her up and started up the stairs
Rikkar paused for a moment and looked back
down at the lieutenant.

"Get out of here, Whitlock," he said, "and
don't ever come back here again. If you do, I'l
give you a beating myself." The officer gathered
up his hat and gloves and, casting one last bale
ful glance up the stairs, left, slamming the grea
door behind him.

That finished it with Rikkars, he thought grimly
and, remembering Bree's beauty and warmth
felt a moment of regret. Put her out of your mind
he told himself. She's little better than an Indian
squaw. What had the Indians called her. Shocaw'
hoke-tee. Driving his heels deep into hi
horse's belly, he galloped down the drive. Th
Rikkars had not heard the last of him yet, h
thought. There was one more little detail and h
needed Bree for that.

It was a difficult birth for Bree. As the long
nightmarish hours slipped away, she was lost i
a maze of images, images of Shocaw's smile as h
bent over her. The smile turned to a grimace a
the rope tightened around his neck. She saw hi
body swinging in the air, the beloved limbs jerk
ing in their macabre dance of death, and a woman
screamed over and over. She felt pain tearing
through her, and sometimes it mattered not at all
She uttered no sound until the dreams came
again, taunting her. She fought against the pain
fought against the images, and each time sh
lost. Her mother's worried face and May's chant
ing voice wove in and out of her dreams.

There was her father, speaking to her in a sof
tone, smoothing her hair back from her face as h
had when she was a child, shivering and fright
ened by a nightmare. A stranger's face appeared
and she heard someone call him doctor, but then

ne disappeared and she was left with her devil's
mages again of Milakee running from the sol-
liers' bullets and Shocaw with his turban afire.
Soldiers with blond hair and cool, blue eyes bent
over her. She felt their hands on her, tearing at
ner so she felt the pain deep within herself.

"Doctah, yo' can't force her. Yo' goin' kill dat
chile," May said.

"I'm trying to turn the baby," a voice said, and
Bree thought of little Chofee on Sofangee's hip
as they lay dead in the sand.

"The baby's dead, he's dead," she cried, lash-
ing out.

"Hush, don' yo' say dat," May cried. "I goin'
he'p yo' wid yo' baby, Bree honey. Yo' be strong
fo' ole May."

"Wait for me until I come back," Shocaw said
to her.

"I will, I will," Bree called out.

"That's my good girl," May said, but Bree didn't
hear her. Now the pain seemed to grow in intensity, ripping her apart. She screamed and screamed
again and then it was gone and she drifted downward into sunshine streaming through Spanish
moss. She was in a boat drifting between two
riverbanks. On one side May and Mama and Papa
called to her. She felt them touch her, trying to
pull her back, but it was too late. She saw Shocaw
waiting for her on the other bank and she pushed
the boat toward him.

"Wait for me, Shocaw," she called as the boat
drifted slowly through the river mists, then it
bumped gently against the rocks and she bounded
out onto the grassy bank.

"Shocaw, I'm here, I'm here," she called to
him, but no one answered. She looked around,
but no one was there. She stood on the riverbank
alone.

"Shocaw," she screamed but there was no

answer. Weeping, she cut away her long hair and hung it in the branches before sliding back into the darkness that awaited her.

When she awoke, sunlight streamed through the curtains at her windows. She felt tired, drained, and empty; her head pressed into the pillow. She sensed someone was in the room with her, but she had no strength to turn her head and see who it was. She felt a warmth at her side and heard nuzzling, mewing sounds followed by a thin, reedy cry. She looked down at the bundle lying in the crook of her arm.

"Bree, you're awake." Her mother started to her feet and stood over Bree's bed. Her face was ravished with fatigue.

"My baby," Bree said with wonder as she looked down at the squirming bundle.

"You had a son, Bree," Lainie said, "a beautiful little boy."

Joyfully, Bree reached out a weak hand to push away the covers and get her first glimspe of her son.

He was beautiful! So beautiful! Tears sprang to her eyes and her lips curved in a tender smile as she looked at the tiny face. The small rounded crown of his head was covered with black hair. His eyes were tightly closed but one tiny, perfectly formed fist wobbled near his mouth. Blindly he turned toward his fist and opened his mouth.

"He's hungry," Lainie whispered. "Do you feel up to feeding him or do you want me to get one of the slave women."

"No, he's my son, I'll do it," Bree said, and was unaware of the strength she seemed to gain from looking at her son. She guided his eager mouth to her swollen nipple and watched as he greedily began to suckle; her loving gaze moved over his face again.

"Do you know yet what you'll name him?"

Lainie asked, watching the mother love growing on her daughter's face. She'd known that feeling. It was a special time for all women.

"No, I don't know yet what I'll call him," Bree answered softly. "It must be a very special name, for his father was a great war chief of the Seminole." Pain washed across her face as she thought of Shocaw. Would she ever be able to erase the nightmare images of his death from her mind?

"I understand," Lainie said. Bree's eyes flew to meet Lainie's. Had her mother finally accepted her love for the Seminole? It no longer mattered, she thought. Shocaw was dead, forever lost to her. She held her son to her breast and wept quietly for all she'd lost. Lainie said nothing, letting her daughter express the pain she felt. Once she'd nearly lost the man she loved and she remembered the pain of that moment. How much worse was it for Bree? Helplessly she waited, her hand tightly holding her daughter's.

At last, when Bree had cried herself out, she looked down at her son. He had fallen asleep, his lips still clamped around his mother's nipple as if he had laid claim to her life. She was not alone, Bree realized. She would never be alone again. A part of Shocaw would always be with her. She raised her eyes to Lainie's and with relief her mother noted the new resolve in the gray eyes.

"Shocaw will never be dead to me. I have his son," she said simply, and Lainie smiled with relief. Perhaps now a new life would begin for Bree, she thought, and smiled down at her beautiful grandson.

It was Cooee who resolved the problem of a name for the new baby. He came to Bree's room a few days after the birth.

"Cooee, you're all dressed up," Bree exclaimed,

looking at the suit that covered his broadening shoulders.

"I'm going away, Bree," he said.

"No, you can't," she cried.

"Your father feels it is best. Whitlock's hate for me grows every day. Your father feels it would be best if I go north. I will attend school there and study law. Perhaps your father is right and someday I can help my people in a better way than I have in the past." Bree noted that he still called the Seminoles his people, but she said nothing. He couldn't be expected to put aside his feelings for them. She couldn't either.

"I shall miss you," she said softly, and was rewarded by one of the smiles that came rarely to him these days.

"I shall miss you," he answered. "Being with you has reminded me of Milakee. But now I must put that behind me as well, just as you must do with Shocaw."

"Yes," Bree agreed, "but it is not easy."

"No, it is not." Cooee moved to the cradle and looked down on her little son.

"He will never know the ways of the Seminoles," he said sadly. "He will never see the beauty of the swamps as we did or learn to hunt and test himself as a man."

"He will never be in the cutting ceremony of the *Shot-cay-taw*," Bree said, and wondered if she was really saddened at that loss.

"It is not so bad, Bree. You don't feel the pain because you are becoming a man."

"I suppose not." Bree chuckled. Once again Cooee's smile came, then disappeared.

"Now I shall be Cooee no longer. I will be Jean Gautier. It is a good name. I will try to carry it with pride."

"I'm sure you will do it honor," Bree whispered.

"I shall miss being Cooee." He looked back at the sleeping baby.

"May I use the name?" she asked hesitantly. Cooee looked back at her questioningly. "I wish to name my baby Cooee," she said softly, and was rewarded with a huge grin. He was closer to the old Cooee than she'd seen him in a long time.

"I will see he does honor to the name," she said, and waited for him to speak.

"So it shall be," he said lightly, touching the little hand of his namesake. The baby jerked, then settled into sleep again. There was a brightness in Cooee's eyes when he turned back to Bree. "As his uncle on his mother's side, I hold a place of importance in the life and training of this little one. I will teach him all the Seminole ways."

"That will please me greatly," Bree said.

For a moment more, Cooee hesitated. So many times he'd meant to tell her of Katcalani and of the lies she'd told, claiming that Bree had helped Whitlock and his men destroy the village and taking him as a lover before they'd even left the swamp. He'd thought to tell her of Shocaw's anguish and of his growing anger at Bree for her betrayal. His anger had reflected itself in the savagery with which he had dealt with the whites after Katcalani's accusations.

But Shocaw was dead. It no longer mattered. To speak of it now would only bring Bree pain. She'd endured too much already. It was best she go on believing Shocaw had continued to love her as she had him.

"Good-bye, Bree," Cooee said, and she understood the reason behind his sadness.

"Good-bye, Cooee," she whispered. Then he was gone from the room and she heard his boots on the stairs. She lay back against the pillows, listening to the voices drifting up from the drive, the rattle of carriage wheels on the shell drive, and Lainie's tearful voice calling a last good-bye.

So many partings, Bree thought, so many people coming into and leaving her life. She struggled from her bed and made her way to her son's cradle. She needed to look at him again, needed to know there was new life in the midst of so much death and parting.

He slept peacefully, his tiny face already plumping out from the milk he suckled so greedily from his mother's breast. Even now in his dreams his lips moved against his clenched fist, making Bree chuckle. He was alive and he was hers, Shocaw's gift to her. Without him, life was meaningless.

Now she straightened herself with pride and resolution. She was Shocaw's *hoke-tee*. She had borne his son and together they would keep alive the Seminole customs and legends. She would write about them, tell people of their bravery and courage. Like Cooee, she would do everything she could to help the remaining Seminoles to rebuild their lives. Coacoochee's words came back to her, and crossing to her desk, she pulled out a clean sheet of paper.

Casting one last look over her shoulder at her sleeping son, she dipped the pen in the ink. Soon Cooee would be awake and demanding to eat again, but for now she had time, time to begin again. She began to write.

Chapter 19

"I got a long letter from Jared," Lainie said. "Jean is doing well in his studies, but Jared says he doesn't seem very happy."

They were sitting in the shade of the huge oak tree, their needlework on their laps, Cooee's crib nearby. They had come here seeking an escape from the summer heat. The air was so hot and moist it was hard to draw a breath and damp spots stained the light cotton dresses they wore. Lainie wore a broad-brimmed straw hat against any sun rays that might penetrate the leaves, but Bree's hat, as usual, lay on the grass beside her chair. Mama never said anything these days about such things.

"It must be very hard for Cooee, I mean Jean," Bree said, and sucked away the bright bubble of blood from a needle prick. She still wasn't handy with a needle.

"Are you all right?" Lainie asked, folding the letter and putting it into her sewing basket.

"Um, I'm afraid I'm handier with a pen than I am with a needle," Bree murmured.

"I agree. That last article was really excellent," Lainie said. "Coacoochee's words were so moving. I never realized the Seminoles were so eloquent."

"They are a very intelligent race, Mama," Bree said, picking up her needlework again.

"What do you intend to write about next?"

"I'm not sure." Bree paused in her work and looked at her son playing happily in his crib. His chubby hands batted at the playthings tied above his head and he chuckled and babbled incessantly

He was a large baby for three months and growing more quickly every day. His black eyes, so like his father's, were filled with merriment except when it was time to eat and then he threw a tantrum that sent them all running. Bree chuckled in her throat. She was so proud of him. He won over everyone who met him. Her father was completely smitten with him, as was Lainie and all the servants, yet when he was tired and cranky, Bree was the one he wanted.

He would lie in her lap as he nursed, his chubby hand going up to touch her nose and face, his dark eyes taking in every detail of her appearance. Bree sensed the love growing within him for her and it helped her through the lonely sorrow-filled hours when she grieved for Shocaw.

"My, Bree, if he keeps growing, we'll have to have Jake make him a new crib," Lainie said, glancing at her grandson with an indulgent smile.

"His father was very tall, so Cooee will be too," Bree said with assurance, and thought of Shocaw as she'd first met him, when he'd carried her for hours through the swamps. How gentle he'd always been toward her, never treating her badly. Her thoughts went to the day he rescued her from Lopochee, claiming her as his slave. He'd sliced her arm, barely penetrating the skin to bring blood as he demonstrated to the village that he was the master. How she'd rebelled against

him, yet even then she'd understood he was forced
to make such a show of mastery.

Her mother spoke again and she put the thoughts
away. It was becoming less painful to remember
every day. Now she hugged her memories to her
like precious gems.

The afternoon passed tranquilly and shadows
lay long over the grass. Cooee had long since
tired himself and fallen asleep, his mouth moving in practice for his next eating time. Bree let
her needlework fall to her lap and lie forgotten
while she leaned back against the cushions and
yawned freely. She would close her eyes just for a
moment, she thought, and did so. The drone of a
bee in some nearby flower bed soothed her. The
warm air pressed down on her closed lids.

Her mother's gasp made her open her eyes and
look about. At first she saw nothing save the
sparkling, dappled sunlight, then she glanced at
her mother's face and saw shock and terror.

Turning her head, Bree was stunned. Indians
stood about the garden, stiff and silent sentinels,
their eyes alert, wary, yet cold and intent as they
looked at Bree and her mother.

"Don't be alarmed, Mama," Bree said, rising
from her seat. "They're probably looking for food."
They looked like they needed it, she thought.
They were little more than skin and bones and
their clothes were in rags. She took a slow step
forward, her hands held out, palms up to show
she carried no weapon.

"I'll get food for you, sofkee," she said, and
was about to call to May or Tom when the house
servants came out into the yard. Their faces were
full of fear. More Indians ushered them into a
small group near the rose beds. With a few words
they turned and went back into the house; Bree
could see them running about the yard, going to

the sheds and smokehouses. They emerged with
large hams and sides of pork while others carried
away bags of corn and flour.

"Oh Bree," Lainie cried, moving to stand beside her daughter, her arm going protectively
about her shoulders.

"It's all right, Mama. It's just that they are
starving and want some food. We can spare it."

"If only they won't hurt anyone."

"They won't," Bree said. "I'll tell them I'm
Shocaw Hadjo's *hoke-tee* and this is his son."

"Bree, must you?" Lainie breathed.

"Only if I have to," Bree said, and comforted
her mother as best she could. When the Indians
had taken as much food as they could carry
through the swamps, they seemed to melt away,
save for a few guarding the servants and Bree
and her mother. Surely they would go without
killing or burning as they did before, Lainie
prayed.

The Indians stiffened as another Indian came
into view, walking from around the side of the
house. The low sun was behind him, so Bree
and Lainie could only make out his shape. Bree
shielded her eyes from the glare of the sun, studying the shape. There was something about it that
tugged at her heart. Was this warrior one of
those who had fought with Shocaw, she wondered. He seemed somehow familiar.

He paused beside his men, keeping the sun
behind him as he studied the two women and the
small crib beyond. Bree could feel his hard gaze
sweep over her face and down her figure and her
heart hammered loudly in her chest. Before he
took that final step closer, she knew, and her
mind went numb with shock. The tall Indian
stepped forward and to the side and now his face
was revealed to her.

"Shocaw," she whispered, her eyes wide with disbelief.

He was thin, much thinner, and his face was haggard. Within the dark depths of his eyes blazed lights of anger and hatred such as she'd never seen there before. Once again his gaze raked over her, taking in the thin cotton dress, the ribbons and lace on it and the discarded needlework lying on the ground near her chair. His gaze moved on to the small crib, which he stared at hungrily.

"Shocaw," Bree whispered, moving toward him. "I thought you were dead. Whitlock said he'd hanged you."

Shocaw said nothing, his eyes still on the crib.

"Come, come and see your son," Bree said joyously, leading the way. "He is very large for his age. You'll be proud of him." Shocaw followed her to the crib and looked down at the sleeping child. "I named him Cooee," Bree said.

"Cooee," Shocaw repeated, and almost as if he'd heard his name, the baby opened his eyes and smiled up at his father. Immediately he began to wave his arms to be picked up and Shocaw's large hands went out to lift the small, fat body. There was no awkwardness in the way he handled his son and Cooee seemed to know instinctively that he could trust this large man. He cooed and gurgled enchantingly for his father.

Bree stood watching them for a moment, her face glowing with love and happiness, then, unable to contain herself, she moved forward and touched Shocaw's arm lovingly. "Oh, Shocaw, I can't believe you're alive," she whispered. "They said you were dead, that you'd been hanged. Whitlock came and told us."

"Did that bother you, Bree?" Shocaw asked, turning his dark gaze back to her face.

Bree took a step backward, dismayed at the

hatred she found there in his eyes and all of it aimed at her. "Why do you ask me such questions? I wanted to die myself."

"Why? Did it bother you because your new lover had killed your husand?"

Bree's eyes searched his face, trying to understand the reason for the hatred behind his words. "He was never my lover," she said. "For a while I thought he was a friend, not only to me, but to the Seminoles, but his true nature showed through. Shocaw, you must believe me," she said as his skepticism showed on his face.

"I saw you together here in this garden," he said. "You allowed him to kiss you."

Bree looked at him in amazement, remembering that time so many months before. The kiss had been meaningless, but afterward she had stayed in the garden feeling as if Shocaw were near to her.

"You were here?" she asked. "Why didn't you let me know? Why didn't you show yourself to me?"

"And have you turn your lover to kill me as well?" Shocaw asked.

"Shocaw, you're wrong, so wrong," Bree cried, taking a step forward, but he put a large hand against her shoulder and held her away from him. He held Cooee high against his shoulder.

"Katcalani saw you together and warned me. I came to get you, for I knew it was not true. When I arrived, I saw that the things she'd said were true."

"No, they weren't true. You must listen to me," Bree cried. "Katcalani has lied to you, as she has many times before."

"My own eyes do not lie," Shocaw said, and turned away. "We will go now." He still held Cooee in his arms. Fear swept across Bree's heart.

"I can't stop you if you wish to go, I can't make you believe differently of me, but you must give Cooee back to me," she said, striving to keep her voice steady.

"Cooee is my son. I'm taking him with me," Shocaw answered.

"No, you can't," Bree cried, staring with stunned eyes at him. She heard her mother cry out a denial. When Shocaw made no answer, except to wave his men away, Bree leaped forward, one hand clutching at his arm. "Then you must take me as well."

"Bree, no," Lainie cried out.

"Cooee is little. He will need me. I'm his mother."

"Cooee will have a mother. I will give him to my first wife," Shocaw said. "You are here with your people where you belong. I don't want you." He turned away.

"Shocaw, no." Bree raced after him, pulling at his arms, attempting to pull Cooee from his grasp. The baby began to cry. Shocaw's strong hands pushed her away, but she ran back at him, fighting and clawing at him, trying to reach Cooee, to no avail. Shocaw was bigger and stronger. The squalling baby was handed to another warrior, who took him and ran off into the fields, heading for the pine forest and the swamp beyond.

"No," Bree screamed, and attempted to run after him, but Shocaw's arms closed around her like steel bands. She struggled against his hold, kicking and scratching. The pins holding her hair in place loosened and her long golden tresses tumbled about her shoulders and back. Suddenly, Shocaw's hands were lifting her up against him and his face was buried in the silken strands.

"Bree." His voice was an anguished cry that stilled her struggles. Quietly she lay against him, feeling his pounding heart against her own, then he lifted his head and once again his eyes were cold and unreadable. He lowered her so her feet touched the ground and pulled away from her.

"Shocaw, please, please," she whispered pleadingly, but he whirled and was gone, loping around the stables and through the fields and into the forest beyond.

Bree stood where she was, staring after him, her chest rising and falling as she struggled to breathe. Behind her the servants were quietly crying and her mother was reprimanding them, sending them on errands, ordering them to action so they wouldn't spook themselves even more and end up fleeing the plantation.

"Bree," Lainie cried, coming to stand by her daughter. "He took Cooee. What can we do?"

"I don't know, Mama," Bree said. Perhaps Shocaw would relent and return the baby, but in her heart she knew he wouldn't."

"I've sent Tom to the fort to get your father and the soldiers."

"They'll never get back in time to catch them," Bree cried, walking back to the tiny crib that had held her son such a short time before. She clutched his blanket to her, breathing in his baby smell, trying to quiet her racing mind. Suddenly she whirled and raced across the garden and up the stairs to her room.

"Bree, where are you going?" Lainie ran after her daughter. "Bree." There was fear in her voice, but Bree couldn't help that now.

By the time Lainie reached her bedroom, Bree had already thrown off the dainty cotton dress and petticoats and was pulling out the Seminole skirt and blouse she'd worn when she first returned home.

"Bree, what are you doing?" Lainie cried again.

"I'm going after them, Mama," she said, hurrying into the Seminole garments.

"Are you mad? You can't follow them through that swamp."

"Maybe I can, Mama. I lived with the Seminoles for many months. I learned about the swamp." She was gathering up a cloth bag and stuffing things into it: Cooee's favorite toy, some tiny shirts, paper and pen for herself.

"Wait for your father, Bree. I beg you," Lainie cried.

"I can't wait," Bree said, gathering her things up. "If I go now, I can follow their trail more easily."

"It will be dark soon."

"It can't be helped. I must go now. I have to get Cooee back."

"Bree, if you go, I may never see you again."

"If I don't go, I may never see my son again. I must go, Mama," Bree said, and brushed past her mother's beseeching hands. Her own heart was beating wildly in panic.

"At least let Calusa go with you; he can help you track them and protect you during the night."

"I thought he went with Papa."

"Not this time, his wife was ill. I'll send for him." She turned away.

"Mama, I'm sorry—" Bree said suddenly, moved by her mother's stricken face.

"I understand," Lainie said, her face reflecting her pain and fear. "You must go to Cooee. I'll pray for your safety." She hastened out of the room. Bree took another hurried look around. I might never return here, she thought fleetingly, and spent no more time thinking of it. The things she loved and wanted were out there somewhere in the swamp and she must find them. She must.

Calusa was there on the veranda by the time

she came down and Bree paused only long enough
to hug and kiss her mother and May and then
she was off, plunging across the stable yard and
into the fields as Shocaw had done.

At first she led, given speed and strength by
the burning fear inside her that she might not
find them. Calusa followed closely behind her,
saying nothing, allowing her to run and use up
the terror-inspired energy. Finally she began to
slow and he stopped her with a hand on her
shoulder.

"It is best we go at a reasonable pace," he said,
and she nodded her head in agreement. After
that Calusa led the way, pausing now and then
to be sure they were on the right track. Once
when he noticed a deep moccasin print, he looked
thoughtful, but pushed on, saying nothing. The
Seminoles were making it too easy, he thought.
They hadn't eluded the soldiers for seven years
by leaving such a careless trail. Still, he pushed
on and Bree followed, going beyond the point of
exhaustion, driven onward by a mother's need to
see her child again. Shocaw had taken her son
from her and she would die trying to get him
back.

They pressed on until the swamp was too dark
for them to follow the trail. They bedded down
on a dry slope of land and were up at the break
of dawn pushing forward again. During her
months of confinement, Bree had once again
grown soft, but she forced her aching muscles to
keep moving.

At the end of the second day they still had not
come upon Shocaw and his men. Dimly Bree
acknowledged that they could travel on forever
and be always just out of reach of the warriors.
They spent a second night in the swamp.

In her eagerness Bree hadn't thought to bring

food, but Calusa carried a little in his pouch. They ate it cold and washed it down with sips of water. Bree forced herself to lie down and rest, knowing she would need to husband her strength if she were going to find Shocaw and Cooee. The next day they trudged on and now even Bree could see the trail being left for them.

Hope sprang up in her breast. Was Shocaw leaving it for her deliberately so she would follow? Late in the afternoon an arrow, swift and silent, whined through the air and embedded itself deep in Calusa's shoulder. Bree screamed and ran to the fallen Indian.

"Calusa, are you all right?" she cried. Horror welled within her. Had Shocaw lured her here to kill her? She knew the Seminoles dealt harshly with adultery. Perhaps in his anger and mistaken belief about her, he meant to kill her.

With Calusa instructing her, Bree managed to break the shaft of the arrow and push it the rest of the way through. She'd seldom seen the Seminoles use arrows. They'd always used rifles. Was their ammunition gone, making the rifles useless? Had they been forced to return to their bows and arrows? A hundred questions spun through her mind as she bandaged Calusa's shoulder.

"What do we do now?" she asked him.

"We wait," he replied, and she knew it was time for the confrontation with Shocaw. Near dusk, the Seminoles came out of the trees and along the path. Shocaw led the way, his eyes alert and ready as they moved about the swamp.

"We are alone. We brought no one else with us," Bree said.

"Why are you here?" Shocaw demanded.

"I came for my son," Bree answered.

"He is my son too," Shocaw said.

"That is true," Bree replied, "but if you take my son, then you must take me."

"I don't want you for my wife anymore," Shocaw replied, and Bree kept her expression blank, not letting him see how much the words hurt her. "I divorce you."

"All right," Bree said, taking a breath and keeping her gaze level with his. "In that case, you must return Cooee to me. It is the law of your people that the children and all other things go with the wife when there is a divorce. I accept that you don't want me for your wife. Return Cooee to me."

Shocaw's eyes bored deep into hers, their black depths hypnotic and compelling. Had there been a glimmer there for a moment, she thought, returning his gaze. His face was impassive.

"If you remain my wife, you must go with me into the swamps to live."

"I will do so," Bree agreed.

"We follow Billy Bolecks south into the mighty sea of grass near the oceans," he replied. "It will not be easy."

"I will go," Bree answered simply.

"So be it," Shocaw said, and signaled to his warriors to retreat. They melted into the shadows. One man stayed behind. Shocaw spoke to him rapidly, then turned to Bree. "My warrior will stay with your man until the morning light, so he does not follow us," he explained.

"I don't want him hurt more," Bree said.

"You have my word." His eyes were dark and deep and she knew she could trust him.

Quickly she knelt beside Calusa. "Tell Mama, I shall be safe. She mustn't worry about me," she said to the old Indian.

"I will tell her. Go with God," Calusa said as Bree turned back to follow Shocaw. He gazed after her for a long time after the figures had disappeared into the swamp, then he curled into a ball and prepared to sleep. Tomorrow he must return to Greenwood and tell his old friends that once again they'd lost their daughter to the Seminoles.

In his preoccupation he paid no attention to the snap of a branch nearby. The Seminole warrior spun and looked for the danger, but it was too late. Two shadows leaped from the trees and bore him down, their knives aiming unerringly for his heart. He died without a sound as did the wounded Indian Calusa. The shadows moved off through the woods.

The moon had moved well above the treetops by the time they'd reached the camp. As they entered the clearing with the central cooking fire and the hasty shelters built around the outside, the women and children stopped their work and turned to look at the newcomers. There was hostility in their glance when they saw the white woman. None of their faces were familiar to Bree.

"Why is she here?" one of the women cried. "Kill her!" She rushed toward Bree with a knife. Bree jumped back, but Shocaw's strong arm was already there, his hand gripping the woman's wrist.

"This is Shocaw's woman," he said. "She goes with us. She is not to be harmed." His glance moved about the clearing, meeting each pair of eyes, impressing upon them that they must obey. When it was clear that all had understood him, Shocaw relaxed his stance and walked toward the fire. Bree followed him and stood looking about eagerly. Where was Cooee?

"Katcalani," Shocaw called, and the Indian woman stepped out of the shadows. She was carrying Cooee and her fingers still pinched his nose to stop him from crying.

Angrily, Bree stepped forward, meaning to take Cooee from her, but Shocaw stopped her.

"Release him," he said to Katcalani, who removed her hand. Cooee had never been treated in such a manner before and proclaimed his anger loud and long, kicking so hard that Katacalani was forced to use both hands to hold him.

"Give him to me," Bree cried, but still Shocaw held up a restraining hand. "He is hungry," Bree said. "He wants me to feed him."

"You may hold him and nurse him, then you must give him back to Katcalani," Shocaw said, and when Bree would have sputtered a protest, he continued. "That is the way it will be while we travel."

He was afraid she might take Cooee and flee into the swamp, Bree thought, and wouldn't she, if given the chance? Even now, in the face of Shocaw's hatred of her and her anger for him, she didn't know how she would react if she were given the choice.

"Give me my baby and I will feed him," she replied. Her arms ached to hold her son again. Shocaw motioned to Katcalani to hand him over. Bree held him to her neck, cooing to him soothingly, letting him smell her familiar odor and be comforted by it, and when he had quieted a little, she settled herself on a stump well away from the fire and nursed him. Across the dark shadows of the camp she could sense Shocaw's gaze on her. Looking up, she caught his glance, unguarded and vulnerable as he watched the sight he'd dreamed of too many times during the past months. When he realized she was aware of his gaze, he turned away and joined the men and women who were busily sorting the supplies they'd brought from Greenwood. Quickly they divided the food into smaller portions and wrapped it in leaves, then they packed it into large bas-

kets of reeds and grasses. They would be leaving
at dawn for their new home deep in the Ever-
glade swamps to the south.

When Cooee was finally asleep, Bree laid him
on some blankets and settled herself on the ground
beside him, her eyes watching him as he slept.
How she'd feared she would never see him again.
She traced a finger over the delicate rounded
cheek of her sleeping baby, then closed her eyes
and quickly fell asleep herself.

The sound of a bird trilling in a treetop awakened her. The sky was black above them, for the
moon had disappeared but the sun had not yet
pierced the dark veil of night. Bree lay listening,
feeling uneasy. The bird trilled again and she
felt a sense of foreboding, remembering how such
a bird had sung the morning the soldiers attacked
the village.

Beside her, Shocaw sprang soundlessly to his
feet, his rifle in his hand. She could see his dark
silhouette against the sky. Quickly he moved
above the fire pit and other silhouettes joined
him. Terror mounted inside Bree. What was happening? She sat up, pulling a sleeping Cooee
against her chest. The clearing erupted in a frenzy
of sound and rifle flashes.

It can't be, she thought. No one would be attacking the village in the darkness. What were
Shocaw and his men shooting at? She heard the
cries of women and children about her and it
brought back memories of another village and
the cries of terror as its people died.

Something swiped past her and Bree drew in
her breath sharply. Instinctively she rolled away
as the clumsy figure paused and turned back
toward her. A pistol flashed and bullets thudded
into the ground where she and Cooee had been
lying. Crouching, Bree ran away from the clearing where all the noise was, bumping into trees,

crashing through brush in her terror. She could feel Cooee awaken and draw in a startled breath. He was about to cry out and she prayed he wouldn't, not until she was far enough away from the clearing so his cry wouldn't bring discovery and death down on them.

Cooee cried, impatient with being jostled so early in the morning, and Bree pinched her fingers over his nostrils as she'd seen Katcalani do, praying he'd understand her hardness someday. She sensed there were other figures moving through the swamp beside her, other women and their children fleeing the death in the clearing.

The warriors fought valiantly to hold off the soldiers while the women and children escaped into the swamps, quickly finding places to hide. Bree cuddled Cooee to her, trying to reassure him, trying to quiet him while she dodged through the trees. The pale gray fingers of dawn were stretching across the horizon, and she could see the darker shapes of trees and avoid them. Fearfully she plunged on, her breath coming in rasps, her chest tight and constricting from fear and fatigue.

The muscles of her calves ached. She scrambled over fallen tree trunks, fell sprawling over their lengths, and scrambled up to press on. Once she sprawled over a limb, landing on her hands and knees in the water. The jar of the fall loosened her hold on Cooee and he rolled from her arms. For a wild, frantic moment, as she groped blindly for him, she thought she'd lost him, then she heard him hiccup and let out a lusty cry. Quickly she had him in her arms, pressing his sweet face into the curve of her hot neck. He was hungry and there was little chance that he would remain quiet until he'd been fed.

Her pulse fluttered frantically and she knew

she could not go on. All around her the swamp
was still and silent. The other women had gone
on or had hidden. Bree knew that was what she
must do. Even now the shots in the clearing had
halted, and as the soft morning light waxed
stronger, orders were shouted to the soldiers.
Their voices rang out on the hot, muggy air normally filled with the shrill call of tropical birds.
Now the soldiers would track the Indians through
the swamp until they became discouraged and
gave up. Bree gave no thought to them as rescuers. She'd set her course with Shocaw and his
people once more. The soldiers were the harbin-
gers of death, flashing in the soft darkness.

She must hide from them. Frantically she looked
around until she found a tree on a rise of ground;
the water had washed away the dirt beneath its
roots, leaving a hollowed-out area. It was muddy
and damp, but she would be out of the snake-
infested waters and the clumps of fern would
hide her from the eyes of all but the most diligent searcher.

She lay down inside the hollow facing outward
and settled Cooee in her arms, his mouth pressed
against her breast. Warmed by his mother's body
and nourished by her milk, he soon stopped crying
and fell asleep. Let him sleep a long time, Bree
prayed fearfully and lay back, tense and stiff,
listening as the soldiers came closer. She could
hear them splashing noisily through the water,
careless of being heard as they called back and
forth. One splashed by her hiding place, so close
that she could make out the lacings on his boots
and the blue worsted of his pants. He went on by
and still she lay tense and watchful. Finally the
soldiers returned, their guns lowered, their steps
slowed with fatigue. The exhilaration of the battle had worn off and now they wanted only to

rest and return to the fort. They straggled back
to the Indian camp. Bree stayed where she was.

The sun burned hot in the swamp now. Cooee
awakened and nursed, and, frustrated with his
mother, who didn't want to play with him, finally
went back to sleep. Thirst began to nag at Bree,
but she didn't want to risk leaving her hiding
place. The time dragged by and the day passed.

As darkness began to fall, Bree crept out of her
hollow and looked around. She could see the
glow of a campfire back at the camp and knew
the soldiers were staying there for the night.
Cautiously she looked around and saw no sign of
any of the other Seminoles. Had they run away,
pushing southward toward the big swamp, or
were they like her, hidden in some trees and
bushes, even in the water itself? She couldn't
travel in the night with a small baby, so she
crawled back into the hollow and curled herself
around Cooee to keep him warm. She would rest
and tomorrow she would look for Shocaw and
the others.

She awoke cold and stiff and forced her muscles to move. Cooee lay beside her, strangely
silent. Worry raced along her nerve endings as
she moved aside his blanket and checked on him.
He was awake, his black eyes wide and expressive of the pain and fear he'd begun to feel. He
was not supposed to cry out; he understood that
now and lay waiting for what would happen next.
Bree put her face next to his and cooed softly
into his ear. She could feel the hot flush of his
cheeks and brow.

"Oh, God, don't let him be ill," she prayed,
and felt beneath the blanket. The rest of his
body was cold, even his chest and stomach. Bree
began to rub his tiny hands and arms and then
his legs and back, trying to rub warmth back into
his small body.

She must get him dry and warm, she thought frantically and, wrapping him back in the damp blanket, crawled out of the hiding place. She was covered with mud, but it didn't matter now. Her only thought was for Cooee. Fearfully she looked around. The swamps were silent, moisture dripping from the branches, for it had rained the night before. Had the soldiers left yet? she wondered, and began to move cautiously back toward the camp, pausing often to look around. Once she thought she caught a fleeting glimpse of a shadowy figure, but made no effort to call out.

At last she reached the hummock where they'd been camped and moved slowly and cautiously toward the clearing. There was a barely audible sound of voices, so she stopped behind a bush, unsure of whether to run away again or enter the clearing. Carefully she moved forward and peered through some branches. Shocaw and some of his warriors stood to one side of the camp talking.

Gratefully, Bree walked into the clearing. The sound of her approach made the warriors whirl around, their rifles and bows raised. One man gripped a deadly-looking knife in his hand. Their faces had gone fierce and menacing.

"White woman come back," Katcalani spat out, stepping forward aggressively. "You bring soldiers back with you again?" she demanded.

"I didn't bring the soldiers the first time," Bree flared.

Shocaw had taken a step forward and now, upon hearing Katcalani's words, he stopped.

"Cooee's sick," Bree said, looking first at Shocaw and then at his son.

Swiftly he crossed to them, taking the baby in his arms. His eyes were dark with concern. "Katcalani, get him dry and warm again," he ordered, handing Cooee to the Indian woman.

"I can do it," Bree said, reaching for her son.

"No!" Shocaw's tone was harshly commanding, not to be disobeyed. Katcalani smirked with triumph. "Katcalani will tend to my son."

"But he's my son too," Bree cried.

"You will go back to soldiers with him," Katcalani said as she moved away and knelt on some blankets and began to peel away Cooee's wet covers.

"I didn't run away before when I had the chance," Bree pointed out.

"Shocaw know soldiers come, he warn us. We run away." Katcalani paused in her ministrations to Cooee and looked up at Bree with venom in her eyes. "Maybe you bring soldiers back so they kill us next time."

"Why would I do that?" Bree cried, outraged at the accusation.

"You led soldiers to us once," Katcalani said, and her voice was low and sure.

"They must have followed me. I didn't know they were there," Bree said defensively. "You must believe me."

"We not believe you," Katcalani cried, and looking around the small circle of desperate faces, Bree could see the anger and fear. They wanted someone to be the scapegoat for their misfortunes and she was one of the hated whites who had destroyed the Seminole nation. Katcalani fanned their anger and hatred with her words. "You bring evil soldiers to our village."

"I didn't," Bree cried.

"You tell them, kill our people and burn our chickees."

"I didn't!" Bree cried again.

"You talked to soldiers. Tell them evil things to do. They not hurt you. Hurt Seminoles."

"You must believe me," Bree cried, and fell silent, looking once more around the circle of hostile faces. She had spoken to the soldiers when they came to the village, and to those who did not speak or understand the white man's tongue, it might have seemed she betrayed them. They couldn't know she had pleaded for their lives. But Katcalani had known. "Katcalani lies," Bree cried out.

"People know Katcalani not lie. They see how soldiers treat you. You their friend."

"No, I am one of the Seminole people too."

"At fort, you go free," Katcalani pressed on, venting all the hatred she felt for Bree. The white one had lost favor with her people. She no longer had to hide her feelings. "Seminoles put in pens like animals," she went on. "Watch while Shocaw's woman ride away with the white men."

Bree could not deny Katcalani's words. She was condemned by the events.

"At night, some of the people escape over the walls. Must leave behind old ones and children. Come back to swamp and tell Shocaw how you betray him. Now you die."

"But I didn't." Bree swung around, looking for Shocaw. Fairly or unfairly she stood accused by the Seminoles. She knew she might die this night. The Seminole punishment was swift and sure. Her glance flew to Shocaw's face and she saw the same condemnation there.

She wanted to turn and flee into the swamp again, but Katcalani had Cooee and she couldn't leave without him. Besides, the Seminoles were much better travelers through the swamp than she would ever be. They would catch her very quickly. If she ran, it would be an admission of guilt. Her only chance was to stand her ground and make them believe her.

"Shocaw," she said, straightening her shoulders. "I had no way to signal the soldiers to Horse Creek Village and I wouldn't jeopardize

Cooee's life by leading the soldiers to you now. I love him too much for that." She paused. She wanted to say she loved Shocaw too much for that as well, but she felt sure he would reject her words. Another thought came to her. "Besides, Calusa and I would not have been able to follow you so easily if you hadn't left such an obvious trail for us. You wanted us to follow you. Perhaps your trail led them to you."

"One of my braves followed you and erased the signs I left," he said.

"Didn't he see the soldiers following behind?" she asked.

"No."

She could see in his eyes that he was considering all these things. The hardness in his eyes and face softened a bit as he looked at her. He believed her, Bree was sure, but the rest of the Seminoles were being goaded on by Katcalani. Shocaw turned to them, a single word silencing Katcalani, but before he could speak, one of his men entered the clearing and went to him. They spoke in rapid, low tones. Shocaw's glance moved to Bree's face as he listened, then he nodded in understanding and the man stepped to one side. Shocaw approached Bree, his eyes flat and resigned as they met hers.

"The soldiers killed your guide," he said.

"Calusa? No!" Bree cried, and turned away to hide her grief for a moment. Calusa had been part of her childhood, hers and Jared's as they grew up. Now, because of her, he was dead. How her father would grieve for his lifelong friend.

Shocaw turned to the other villagers and began to speak. His words were too quick for Bree to catch more than a few. He was talking about her. At first the others shook their heads, their eyes filling with hostility as they flashed toward Bree, but as Shocaw talked, their denials ceased. They listened and finally one man stepped forward.

"We wish to hear what the white woman says," he said, and the other Seminoles nodded their heads in agreement. Stepping forward into the clearing, Bree raised her chin and looked around at her accusers. Then she began to speak.

"I have brought you no harm," she said, looking at the circle of faces. "I was taken from my people and my land by your warriors. I embraced the Seminole ways. When the white soldiers came to Horse Creek Village, I tried to stop the hangings, but I failed. I was returned to my people, but I did not forget the Seminoles and their plight. I went to Washington to talk to the *Ya-ti-ka-chic-o* to ask that the Seminole be allowed to remain in Florida. He wouldn't listen.

"I wrote stories of the Seminoles and their customs so my people would learn about the Indians and begin to understand. I gave Shocaw a fine son and named him after a great warrior. When my son was taken from me, like the Seminole women, I went into the swamps to find him.

"The white soldier tricked me as he has tricked your chiefs. Am I to die for the white man's treachery? I have returned to the Seminole people. I wish to live side by side with you, to share your sorrow and your happiness. I wish to work beside you and feel the same hunger you feel. I wish to drink the black drink with you and be friends."

When she'd finished speaking, she looked around the clearing again and knew she could do no more. Shocaw's eyes glittered with strange warm lights. He believed her!

Shocaw stepped forward and spoke again, asking for a decision from each Seminole present. Was she to live with them in peace or was she to be put to death? Bree waited as each person uttered his or her verdict. She was to live among the Seminole. Only Katcalani called out the verdict of death, her face twisted in rage.

"Bree speaks as a Seminole," Shocaw said. "She will join the Seminole and live as one." He stood before her, his black eyes capturing her gaze. "You are no longer Bree," he said. "You are Hilolo, you are Shocaw's woman, his second wife."

"So be it," Bree said quietly, bowing her head slightly to indicate her obedience to the Seminole laws.

Now the people began to search for their weapons and supplies. Some of the dugouts had been dragged into the clearing and fires built in them to render them useless. The thick cypress had been too wet and had burned too slowly for all of them to be badly damaged. The men chose the best ones and put them back into the water.

The women tried to rescue what blankets and unbroken pottery they could find. Much of the food they had carried from Greenwood had been eaten or destroyed. The flour sacks had been cut open, their contents scattered about over the trees and bushes and in the stream. The meats had been hacked and cut up and covered with soldiers' excrement.

Patiently the women searched for any food that might have escaped the soldiers' destruction and found little. Bree looked at their pinched, hungry faces and knew her own must look the same way. She had not eaten for nearly two days.

"Shocaw," she said, going to him, "we could send someone back to my father's plantation. I know he would give us food for the trip." Shocaw's eyes burned into hers.

"You have accepted the Seminole lot," he reminded her, and looking into his eyes, she understood at last the magnitude of her choice.

Greenwood and all its wealth of food and goods was forever gone. She would miss them, but she didn't regret her choice.

"How will we survive?" she asked calmly.

"We will eat the coontie root as we have in the past and we will hunt game. We will survive until crops are grown again," he answered simply, and looking at his face, Bree knew it was true. She had loved Shocaw for his courage and dignity and she recognized that she must have that same courage herself.

"Yes, Shocaw, we will survive," she said, and was startled and pleased when he touched her hand briefly. The look in his eyes was tender for a moment.

"Are you sure you wish to go with us?" he asked, and his gaze was penetrating. "It will be very different from the life you leave behind. We will be hungry many times. There will be no servants, no fine clothes."

Bree listened to his words, amazed that he thought those things were more important to her than her feelings for him and Cooee.

"Do you still wish to follow me?" he asked.

"Shocaw, have you ever heard the story of Ruth?"

"I do not remember the Spanish missionaries telling us the story," he answered, and for a moment she felt doubt. Was she being headstrong and foolish? The Seminole culture was so alien to her, how could she understand it and accept it as her own? Could she survive the isolation in which she would always live with the Seminoles. Their hatred for the white people was so intense, could she ever overcome it and live in peace and acceptance among them? Was her love for Shocaw enough to overcome all the obstacles she would face? Did he love her enough to be patient when

she couldn't change? Shocaw watched the doubts
flitting across her face and understood her agitation.

"Tell me of Ruth," he said gently, and Bree
raised her head to look into his eyes, at the dark
lights she loved so much.

"Ruth said, 'Whither thou goest, I will go, thy
people will be my people, thy God my God,' and
she followed Naomi to a land that was strange to
her—" Bree stopped speaking. What good was all
this? she wondered.

"And Ruth found love and peace in the new
land," Shocaw said gently.

Bree's eyes flashed up to his. Would she find
love and peace in the new land she and Shocaw
and his people would journey to?

"'We have a legend. It is not so different from
the story of Ruth," he said. His words, she knew,
were not only of the legend. He was trying to tell
her their worlds were not so far apart. Her life
with the Seminoles would be different from the
pampered rich one she would have led at Greenwood or some other great plantation, but this life
with Shocaw and his people would offer much of
the same joy and contentment. Hadn't she written about that for weeks in the Washington paper? How could she have come so close to forget-
ting?

"Do you wish to return to your own people,
Bree?" Shocaw asked.

"No, I will follow you," she answered, and this
time her tone was sure and strong.

"If you wish to go home, I will return Cooee to
you," Shocaw said softly, his dark eyes flashing
over her face. Her gaze remained steady on his.

"I will follow you," she repeated.

"So be it," Shocaw said, and she knew her
decision was made. There was no turning back
now.

Shocaw went back to his men, directing them

to pack their meager supplies into the damaged, but still floatable dugouts. Quickly the camp was cleared and the Seminoles got into the dugouts. As they drifted away from shore and the men took up the long poles, Bree looked back. The banks where they'd camped were fast disappearing and she knew she would never return here. Making her face as calm and serene as the other Seminoles, she turned and faced forward toward her new homeland.

Chapter 20

They traveled for days down the Withlacoochee River until it turned eastward, then they traveled through shallow streams and tributaries. Sometimes they were forced to portage the heavy dugouts and their few supplies overland for miles until they reached another stream. Finally they reached Lake Kissimmee, where they camped and fished for much needed food. Their meager supply had long since been depleted and they had been living on roots and an occasional rabbit or bird.

From there they traveled down the Kissimmee River, moving southward toward the big waters of Okeechobee. The men were tense and ever ready with their weapons as they traveled down this river. Fort Pierce was not that far away to the east. They dared not shoot game lest their shots be heard, so they subsisted on roots and raw fish. Just northeast of Lake Okeechobee a major defeat of the Seminoles had occurred two years after the war began, and the men who'd fought there were even more jumpy as they neared the big lake.

Shocaw gave them no time to camp and rest themselves on the shores of these waters. Quickly they turned westward, hugging the shores of the lake until they reached the mouth of the Caloosahatchee River. There at last they were able to rest and wait for Billy Bolecks and his people to join them. Fort Meyers was dead west of them at the other end of the great river, where it flowed into the gulf, but Shocaw and his warriors determined it was too far away for a detachment of soldiers to surprise them. Still they took no chances. Bows and arrows were used as they went out to hunt for food. The women busied themselves searching for coontie roots. Food had become their primary concern now.

There were no iron kettles of sofkee cooking over the fires now, and sometimes Bree found herself longing for its comforting fullness in her stomach. Many of the children grew thin and listless, but remained stoically uncomplaining. No child cried for more food at night, although Bree was sure some of the men and women had taken less food than their bodies had required in order to give the children more.

She was thankful that Cooee still nursed, although he'd begun to demand more substance. She chewed small bits of raw fish and meat when they had it and placed it in his mouth as she'd seen the other Indian women do with their babies. When the men brought in a lean carcass of a deer, so great was everyone's hunger they could barely wait until it had cooked properly and often ate their portion while it was still half raw. When their hunger had been assuaged, they carefully cut the remainder into strips and dried it for the rest of their journey.

As they had moved southward, Bree had been allowed to keep Cooee with her more and more and her mind was eased. She had found tiny scratch marks on his legs and knew Katcalani had made them. One evening as she retired to a

blanket away from the rest of the Seminoles, she
unwrapped the heavy blanket swaddled about
Cooee's legs. The evening air was balmy and she
wanted to allow him to roll and move about freely,
so his muscles might be properly exercised and
he might grow strong.

As she unwrapped the blanket she was horrified at what she saw. Long ugly scratches, red
and angry looking, covered his pink chubby legs.
With a cry of pain, Bree picked up her baby and
held him to her, while tears of pity gathered in
her eyes. He was so little and helpless. He depended on her to care for him and protect him
and she had failed.

Her gaze fell on Katcalani, who sat by the fire,
her eyes glittering with hate and spitefulness as
she watched Bree's face. Rage filled Bree's heart,
rage that the woman could vent her feelings on an
innocent baby. Carefully Bree lay Cooee back
against the blankets, bending to kiss and cuddle
him when he whimpered, then she rose, her heart
pounding in wild fury as she stalked across the
small camp toward Katcalani.

"How dare you do those things to my baby!"
she cried, barely able to speak in her anger. She
wanted to kill the Indian woman.

Katcalani looked up and grinned maliciously.
"Your baby bad. I punish him," she said self-
importantly, looking around the group of women.

"You are bad," Bree cried. "I punish you!"
Her hands slashed across the woman's smirking
face. Katcalani made no outcry but leaped to her
feet. Her hands flew to Bree's golden locks, pulling and tearing at her hair, while her nails raked
at Bree's face. The two women locked in furious
battle, falling to the ground, where they rolled
and shoved, each trying to land a telling blow on
the other.

"Bree, Katcalani," Shocaw cried, but the two

women paid him no heed. At Shocaw's direction, two warriors sprang forward to pull them apart.

"Why do you fight?" he demanded when the two women stood facing each other, their chests heaving, their eyes spitting messages of hatred at each other.

"She bad, she fight Katcalani," the Indian woman was quick to speak first.

"She's been scratching Cooee," Bree cried. "I won't let her do it."

Shocaw looked from one to the other of them. "It is the Seminole way," he told Bree. Katcalani flashed a victorious smile.

"Is it the Seminole way to punish as it is needed or to be cruel to the helpless?" Bree asked.

"Cooee bad baby," Katcalani cried. "He like mother. He cry, make noise, make soldiers find us. Has much evil spirits inside."

Once again Shocaw's eyes moved from Katcalani's face to Bree's. Around him the villagers listened to the argument. Everyone knew that in the old days such an argument would have been settled by a council, but there were not enough members for a council or the time for them to meet. Besides, the argument was between Shocaw's two wives and it was best left for him to decide what must be done.

"Where is Cooee?" Shocaw asked.

"Here, on the blankets." Bree led him to the blanket and Shocaw knelt beside his son. The baby stilled his whimpers and looked with black expectant eyes at his father. Shocaw lifted his son in his arms and cradled him against his chest, uttering soft Seminole words of love.

Listening to the gentleness of the fierce warrior, Bree's heart melted. Shocaw had not approached her during the nights since she'd rejoined his people and she'd lain awake in the dark many a night, wondering where he was and if he'd slept alone. Now hearing the soft caress of his voice, old memories came surging forth, sending a familiar tingle along her skin.

Shocaw examined the scratches on his son's legs and laid him back against the blankets. Cooee let out a cry of protest. What had happened to his world? Once it had been filled with soft loving touches and plenty of food. Many people had played with him and coaxed him to laughter. Now it was gone. He'd felt secure in the strong arms of the dark-eyed stranger. Bree knelt beside him on the blanket and gathered him into her arms. Cooee nestled his head into the familiar warm curve of her neck. Shocaw rose to his feet and looked about the gathering and then back at Katcalani.

"We are far enough away from the soldiers. Cooee will stay with his mother from now on," he said firmly. Katcalani opened her mouth as if to protest, then closed it, bowed her head slightly in acquiescence, and turned and walked back toward the fire. Only her stiff back had proclaimed her anger at this turn of events. Shocaw stayed where he was for a moment longer, staring down at the heads of his wife and child.

"Thank you," Bree murmured, looking up into his eyes.

"It is as it should be," Shocaw said stiffly. His gaze seemed hard and angry, yet his eyes held an expression the meaning of which she was unable to discern. Cooee moved restlessly against her throat and whimpered.

"He is hungry," Bree said. She didn't want Shocaw to think his son cried without reason.

"I understand." Shocaw knelt beside her again, his hands going out in a protective gesture to touch his son's arm and to hold the tiny hand. "Soon we will be far enough south to find more game and grow corn again and having cooking fires. Soon," Shocaw repeated, his dark eyes expressing his anguish at his son's hunger

He looked tired and his broad body seemed leaner and tougher. Instinctively she knew he was taking less food than he needed. Worry flooded through her. They all depended on him so much, this whole pitiful huddle of people. They depended on his strength and courage, just as she and Cooee did.

"We can make it," she said softly, her gaze level and reassuring as it met his. Shocaw's hand moved from Cooee's arm up to lightly touch her cheek and she remembered another time when he'd first touched her just so. She had been his captive and his touch had sought to reassure her just as it did now. That time seemed so long ago now.

From that day on, Cooee stayed with Bree and she was comforted to have him near her. Now, as they prepared to move southward, she and Cooee were placed in Shocaw's canoe. Billy Bolecks and his meager band of Seminoles joined them now and all together they made less than a hundred in number. The once-proud Seminole nation of nearly five thousand had been reduced to such pathetic numbers.

The faces of all the men and women were grim as they silently greeted one another. How many husbands and wives and children, parents and brothers had fallen in the seven-year war? But they were still not defeated; they would push on. Bree felt like weeping as she watched the ragtag band of courageous Seminoles. Proudly she held her son up so he could see the people about him, could feel their undaunted bravery and determination to remain free and on the soil of their homeland. There was little time now for mourning their lost ones or of celebrating their meager victory; they must move on. The great chief's face was weary from his struggles against the whites, yet he was undaunted as he moved his people southward.

The left the Caloosahatchee River behind them now, moving straight southward through the river of grass. The dugouts glided through the sawgrass over the shallow waters. The knobby cypress trees with their festoons of Spanish moss or parasitic clumps of wild orchids, gave way to open water-prairie with its marsh grasses. The Seminoles called it *pa-hay-okee*. It was, Bree decided, aptly named.

The flat-bottomed dugouts glided through the grassy waters where they were nearly hidden by the shoulder-high grass.

Now they were able to find more fish to eat and ducks and wild turkeys. At night they camped on hummocks that dotted the river of grass like raisins floating on the surface of a smooth pudding. They found hickory nuts and roasted them near the fire and once again dug the coontie plant, which God had given to the Seminoles so they might survive.

The mood of the people began to lighten somewhat. The sun was warm on their backs now and its golden light in the watery prairies of the swamp seemed a welcome change after the darkness of the forests they'd left.

Now the storytellers—newly appointed, for the old ones had been exiled to Oklahoma—told well remembered legends around the fires. It would be their job to keep these legends alive and pass them on to future generations. It was especially important in the years ahead as the Seminoles rebuilt their tribes.

One evening as Bree readied Cooee for bed Katcalani approached her pallet and knelt beside her. One hand reached out to touch the sleeping baby. Protectively, Bree moved closer to Cooee, shielding him with her body.

"Nice baby," Katcalani said, and smiled, her eyes guileless as she looked at Bree. Silently Bree waited for the Indian woman to go on. She didn't trust Katcalani.

"I am sorry," Katcalani said now, lowering her lashes in a meek manner. "Cooee firstborn." Bree looked at her in puzzlement. What did she mean? she wondered. There was no other child. Cooee was the only child. In sudden understanding her eyes flew to the hand pressed against the Indian woman's belly. Was Katcalani expecting a baby? Bree felt the blood leave her head at the thought.

"Are you with child?" she asked breathlessly. With a satisfied smile, Katcalani nodded her head.

"Is it Shocaw's baby?" Bree asked and again Katcalani smiled, her small brown hand rubbing against her belly.

"Soon Shocaw have two sons," Katcalani said, and with another smile rose and walked back toward the fire. Bree's troubled gaze followed her for a moment.

Once Shocaw had said that Katcalani would never share his sleeping mat, but for many months they'd been together in the swamp. Katcalani had been at his side while she, Bree, was at Greenwood, having his baby and writing the articles that she'd hoped would help end the war and free his people.

She could understand how it had been, could almost be glad Shocaw had had someone to give him comfort and love, but the angry tears rose to her eyes nonetheless and she couldn't deny the pain of betrayal she felt in her heart.

She'd always known Katcalani was his first wife and she his second, but she'd believed his vow that his marriage to Katcalani would be in name only. Could she go with Shocaw now, knowing she must share him in a polygamous marriage?

Resolutely she turned back to her sleeping son and covered his small body. How like his father he was beginning to look. One day when the chubbiness of babyhood was behind him and his bones were well defined, there would be little doubt who his father was. Bree lay beside him, her hands lightly touching the silky, fine raven-black hair that covered the little head. When she looked at her son, she remembered the love between Shocaw and herself when he'd been conceived. Now it seemed that love might be gone forever.

Troubled, she rose and walked a short distance through the trees to a secluded spot where she sat watching the moonlight on the rippling marsh grass. It seemed so large and bright in the midnight-blue star-studded sky.

"Bree." Her name was soft on his lips and she spun about to look at him. He was a dark silhouette in the moonlight, but she'd grown so familiar with the line of his shoulders, the curve of his waist, and his slim hips. She would have known who it was even if he hadn't spoken.

"I am here," she said softly, and rose to face him.

"It's unsafe to wander around in the dark," he said, and the words seemed commonplace enough, yet the air between them was thick with the things unsaid, with the feelings and emotions that had bound them since their first moment together. Suddenly Shocaw moved across the space that separated them and took her into his arms, burying his face in her hair.

"Bree, Bree," he whispered, and it was like a cry in her bloodstream, igniting tiny fires, calling to old passions to awaken once more. Her mate was here. Shocaw's mouth moved across the warm softness of her throat, her cheeks and mouth, and back again to her throat with an urgency that made her knees weak. She clung to him for support.

"I missed you so much," Shocaw whispered. "Those long nights without you, wondering what you were doing, remembering you, your warmth, the feel of your skin beneath my hands." His hands moved across her arms and under her blouse to the soft warmth of her waist and ribs and upward to the soft mounds of her breasts. As his hand closed eagerly, hungrily about her flesh, she moaned low in her throat, leaning into his body, her legs unable to support her. Gently Shocaw laid her back on the grass, removing her clothing with feverish haste, then his body was against hers. Smooth skin, made cool by the night air, sought warmth from the fire between them. Bree's cheeks were hot and flushed as she held Shocaw's face to hers, her nostrils drawing in the familiar musk of his body. Her own mouth, hungry now for his kiss, sought his.

There was no time for lingering touches, sensuous explorations that while away the night hours. Their need was too great. Greedily they drank from each other's passion, their mouths searing and demanding, their hands frantically touching, reassuring themselves that their beloved, at last, was there.

Shocaw's hands glided fiercely over her skin and her body sang a response to him. Above them the starry night seemed closer, closing them in a privacy of emotion that was theirs alone. Bree's own hands moved with urgent need over his broad shoulders, smoothing the tapering chest and hips and the surging, hardened manhood, guiding it home as she arched herself upward to receive him. Shocaw plunged downward against her, feeling her moist softness parting then cling-

ing as he withdrew only to repeat again and
again his movement of love and passion.

A roaring seemed to fill Bree's head as he
moved against her. A whimper escaped her lips
as she felt the tension mount within her and she
locked her long, slender legs around his hips,
plunging upward with him, hating the moment
of withdrawal before his next plunge, which
touched closer and closer to that tip of ecstasy
they'd shared before. Then with shuddering thor-
oughness they reached it together and clung to
each other in a surge of emotion that left them
breathless and trembling.

Bree's skin was wet and shining and every
part of her body was sensitive to the slightest
movement of Shocaw. Her nipples throbbed as
they came into contact with his chest with each
breath he took. Her fingertips tingled as she
brushed across his sweaty brow and stroked back
the thick, black locks. Her lips were tender as
she rubbed them lightly across his chin. She was
more alive with this man than she'd ever been in
her life.

The memory of Katcalani's words came back
to her and she thought of asking Shocaw about
the truth of them, but something held her back.
What if he said Katcalani had told the truth?
No, she wouldn't ask, she decided. Suddenly an
angry cry pierced the quiet night air, making her
leap to her feet.

"It's Cooee," she said, and pulled her clothes
back on hastily before rushing through the trees
to her blanket. Cooee had kicked his covers off
and grown cold. Now as she rocked him against
the warmth of her body, he closed his eyes and
went back to sleep.

Bree was aware that Shocaw stood behind her,
watching. At last Cooee was sound asleep and
she laid him back on the blanket and lay down

beside him, pulling him into the curve of her
body to keep him warm. Shocaw hesitated then
knelt down on the blanket in front of them. Bree
couldn't see the expression of his face in the
dark but she sensed his unspoken question. Without hesitation she pulled aside the cover for him
to join them. They lay side by side, their heads
pillowed on their arms, their son between them,
their hands clasped over the covers, and after a
while they slept, while the moon arched above
the sky.

When she awoke, Bree found that Cooee was
cradled on his father's shoulder, and both of them
were sound asleep. She sat and watched them
for a while, her heart filling with love. Her old
doubts nudged their way into the happy moment
and she sat thinking of Katcalani's claims. Could
she believe what the Indian woman said and did
it matter that much?

She loved Shocaw. She'd left her home and her
people to join him in whatever home he found
for them. She'd spoken the words of Ruth to
Naomi and she meant them just as surely now as
when she'd uttered them. She would accept
Katcalani as Shocaw's first wife and she would
accept Katcalani's child, for it would be Shocaw's
child too. She would love it as she did Cooee.

Shocaw would never know the pain she felt in
sharing the man she loved, but she knew it would
be a pain she would deal with for the rest of her
life. She blinked back the sting of tears in her
eyes and reached out a hand to touch the two
people she loved most in the world. At her touch
Shocaw opened his eyes and smiled at her and
her heart set up a beat of sudden joy. They were
alive and together. That was the most important
thing of all.

They traveled at a more leisurely pace now,
moving through the river of grass, the *pa-hay-*

okee. With the extra food they found, the men gained strength. Billy Bolecks led the group deeper and deeper into the Everglades. They must stay there for many years, perhaps for the rest of their lives, until the white man had forgotten about them. He wanted to be sure they would be safe.

Finally they reached a string of hummocks where all agreed they could begin to rebuild their homes. Shocaw and his people chose to build on the first set of hummocks, while some of the other clans decided to move onward. They stood on shore and watched as Billy Bolecks and his people moved farther south.

Now their work began in earnest. Land was cleared and crops quickly planted, for food was needed. Then the villagers set about rebuilding their homes. The warriors found suitable cypress trees and cut them down and stripped them for posts for chickees, the women and children began gathering palmetto leaves and cutting the low sawgrass for thatching the roofs. Everyone worked diligently, for they knew once the chickees were rebuilt they would once again feel at home. Holes were dug and the trees rolled into place. With ropes and everyone tugging and straining, each corner post was set for each chickee.

Since they would last for generation after generation the work was done carefully, with exactness. The fire pit, with its radial pattern of logs, was built in the center of the square and a kitchen chickee built nearby. A storage chickee was put up against the day when they would once again have enough food to store for the lean seasons.

Now it began to resemble the Indian village Bree had lived in before. Hope was growing within the breasts of the villagers. It was evident in the sparkle of their eyes. They had survived and the worst was over. They could get on with living.

During the day everyone worked long and hard, so they fell into bed at night tired and aching.

Cooee was nearly five months old now and was regaining his former chubbiness. His ready smile and peal of laughter made him a favorite with the older girls who helped tend the children. Now Bree felt safe to leave him with Callofonee, a young girl who reminded her of Sofangee, while she went to work in the fields or wove needed baskets. There was always work to be done. A feeling of contentment grew within Bree and she felt it in the others as well. An old familiar pattern was forming in their lives and gratefully they slipped into it.

Shocaw came every night to the chickee he'd built for Bree. Katcalani had been left to share a chickee with another woman whose husband had been killed in the last skirmish and was still in mourning.

A hammock was hung from the rafters of the chickee and each evening Shocaw placed Cooee in it and rocked him to sleep, cooing and talking to the baby as he rocked. Bree loved watching the tall fierce warrior with his small son. What gentleness, what tenderness he showed the tiny baby. Her heart filled to overflowing. So happy was she that she felt guilt for Katcalani, for it was obvious to everyone in the village that Bree and her son were the best loved by Shocaw.

Still, Bree felt a small core of unhappiness deep within herself. Some part of her would always be unable to accept sharing Shocaw with another woman. In his arms at night she was able to forget it and find reassurance in his hunger for her, but during the bright sunshine of the day, as she looked at Katcalani moving about the village, a small smile on her lips, she began to doubt again. Did Shocaw love Katcalani as well? Did he go to her when Bree was not around?

The village was nearly completed and the tender shoots of their carefully planted crops were pushing tentative heads from the soil. The men had gone hunting the day before and some of the women were tanning hides while others cut the meat into strips and hung it to dry in the sun. Still other women were engaged in the tedious business of grinding the coontie root into flour and putting it out to dry before sifting it. Bree was making cakes of coontie flour and putting them to cook on the hot stones.

Behind her in the village square, the children were playing, their voices rising slightly in glee. Even here in the broad expanse of swamp the old habits stayed with the people. Even the children learned to play quietly. The village was quiet and peaceful in the muggy heat.

Heavy clouds were moving across the sky, capturing the golden sunlight. Suddeny Bree was aware of the excited voices of the women as they began to gather up their things and put away the food on which they'd been working.

"Tallamee," Bree called to one of the women. "*Nock-a-tee?* What is it?"

"A bad storm comes," she answered in Muskogee. "See the grass pollen in the air?" She pointed out over the grass, swaying now in a slight breeze. Above the golden tips a haze of pollen filled the air, casting a soft glow over the grassy water.

"What about the men?" Bree asked fearfully. "They are in the dugouts, hunting."

"They will find high ground," Tallamee replied. "Put away the food and go to the other side of the hummock." Quickly Bree put away the cakes she'd been preparing. Carefully she wrapped them in palm leaves and placed them in a basket in the storage chickee. Food was too scarce for them to be careless with any of it.

When she was sure it was safely put away, she went to look for the children and collect Cooee.

The winds had picked up now and Cooee's hammock was swinging wildly from the ceiling of their chickee. Bree wanted to secure it better but decided she'd better get Cooee and move with the other women to the high side of the hummock. She walked to the area where the children had been playing such a short while before. They were nowhere in sight. They had already left for the high ground.

Callofonee must have taken Cooee with her, Bree thought, and hurried through the trees. Not only was the other end of the island higher, but there would be overhanging ridges where they could shelter from the storm. Rain began to pelt down on her as she hurried along and she was grateful Callofonee had taken Cooee there ahead of time.

The women and children were already settled into niches under the ridges when she arrived. The wind would blow over them and the overhang would keep the rain from them. They would be safe and dry. The rain was coming down harder now and the wind had begun to blow as Bree hurried from one ridge to another looking for her son.

"Callofonee," she cried with relief when she spotted the girl. "Give Cooee to me."

"Katcalani took him." Callofonee peered out at her.

"Do you know where she is?" Bree asked, pushing down the sense of dread that was rising in her.

"I saw her walk toward the river at the other end of the village," Callofonee answered.

"Are you sure?" Bree shouted. Dread was building in her, and as the girl shook her head Bree turned and raced away through the rain. It was falling so heavily now that she could barely find the path. Lightning streaked the sky, sometimes blinding her. The rain pelted down so hard her clothes clung to her skin and she shielded her eyes from its onslaught. The wind blew against her, threatening to pin her against one of the trees or to throw her to the ground. Still she pushed on, her heart hammering in her chest with fear for her son. Surely Katcalani meant him no harm.

Long before the village was in sight she began to call to Katcalani. At last she arrived back in the square. Palmetto fronds were blowing from the roofs and skittering across the square. The fire pit was black, only a little steam rising in the air as the rain quenched the flames and embers. Bree hurried through the village as she called frantically for Katcalani.

"Oh, please God," she prayed. She paused near her chickee and watched Cooee's sleeping hammock swinging wildly in the wind, and for some reason she was reminded of the day she'd seen the Indians hanged in another village.

"Katcalani," she screamed, but the sound of the rain only muffled her cry. Baskets rolled across the square and with a clatter the drying racks fell and began to blow about, landing finally at the base of a tree. The palms were bowing beneath the onslaught of the wind and dead branches and leaves pelted down. Behind her lightning crashed, hitting a tree. Bree heard it topple to the ground. Still she pushed forward, hurrying to the other end of the village and to the river.

"Katcalani," she screamed again, and almost missed the cry in the roar of the wind. Frantically she looked about. It had been Cooee crying. She was sure of it. She listened for the sound again and, when it came, hurried in that direction. She crawled over a fallen tree and almost stepped on Katcalani's outsprawled body. The woman lay pinned by the fallen tree, her hip and leg crushed beneath its weight.

Flung to one side Cooee lay in the mud and rain, squalling with fright. Bree hurried to him and, gathering him up, checked to see he was all right. He'd not been hurt. She held him to her, sobbing out words of love and endearment. Still he cried out his anger and fear to her. The world had once again turned awesome and frightening, and even with his mother there he felt threatened by it. He cried for the strong arms and protective shoulder of his father.

Trying to shush him, Bree rose and went to see about the fallen Indian woman. Her dark eyes were full of pain as she mutely looked up at Bree. Bree knelt beside the woman.

"Are you in pain?" Bree asked. Katcalani shook her head. There was no feeling in that side of her body, only in her chest, which the tree had hit first before sliding over to pin her leg and hip.

"I cannot free you, the tree is too large," Bree said, looking around frantically for some sign of help. There was no one else around but her. The others were on the other side of the island.

"I know," Katcalani said, and Bree recognized her resignation. She was going to die. Death was in the crushed chest and the speckle of blood on her lips. Helplessly Bree looked around her. What should she do? She must find some cover for Katcalani and for Cooee and herself. A sleeping mat came loose from its moorings in the rafters of one of the chickees and went tumbling across the square. Bree rose to her feet.

"Don't leave me," Katcalani cried fearfully.

"I won't," Bree reassured her and, laying her son beside the dying woman, hurried away to retrieve the sleeping mat. She brought it back and, lying down beside Katcalani and Cooee, pulled the thickly woven mat over them. It would keep the driving rain from them and protect them a little from the leaves and twigs that were blown about by the winds. They huddled against the tree trunk that pinned Katcalani and listened as the storm spent its fury on the land. It seemed that they lay like that for hours.

During a short lull Katcalani turned to Bree, her dark eyes bleak. One hand went to touch Cooee's rounded cheek. "He nice baby," she said softly, and not for the first time, Bree thought of the pain the other woman must have felt during the past few weeks. She could understand Katcalani's hatred of her. Until Bree returned, Shocaw had been hers. She didn't know what to say to lessen the woman's pain, but Katcalani spoke again.

"I take Cooee to the river," she said, "put him in river to drown, but wind come. I grow frightened. Ishtohollo not like this. I get Cooee. Bring him back to you."

Bree's heart turned cold as she listened to the disjointed words. How close she'd come to losing her precious son. She could barely stand to lie beside the woman who'd sought to murder her innocent child.

Katcalani spoke again, her voice gasping now with the pain. "I want Shocaw's baby, but"—she shook her head from side to side as one hand crept slowly to her flat stomach—"no baby."

"You aren't having a baby?" Bree asked.

Again Katcalani shook her head. "Shocaw not want Katcalani," she said. "Not share Katcalani's mat, only grieve, grieve for Bree." She paused, struggling to breathe through her injured lungs. "I tell lies. I say Bree take white man, lover. At first Shocaw not believe, then believe, angry. I think now he be husband to Katcalani, but"—again she shook her head—"He turn wild like the *Ko-wat-go-chee*. Kill many soldiers. Never sleep, eat." She paused. "You, Shocaw's *hoke-tee*." She uttered the final words on a long regretful sigh and said no more.

Bree lay beside the woman, listening to the rain pounding on the mat, thinking of all the words she'd said. So much death, she thought. So much hurt and misunderstanding. She felt sorry for Katcalani, but she remembered how the woman had tricked Shocaw into marrying her even when she'd known he had no wish to. She'd brought much of her misfortune on herself. Perhaps the Gods would deal kindly with her in the other world.

Where was Shocaw now? she wondered. Was he weathering the storm safely? She prayed he was safe. She cuddled Cooee's tiny body in her arms, grateful that Katcalani had been frightened out of her plan. Even while Bree had been struggling through the rain to reach her son, Katcalani had stood on the banks of the river preparing to kill him. The horror of that thought made her clutch her baby to her.

At last the rain abated and the storm moved on past the village. When the rain had halted altogether, she threw back the mat and sat up. Beside her Katcalani's face was still. Bree reached over and closed her eyes, then sat back to wait for the villagers to return. She could hear the trees dripping.

Katcalani's face had acquired a peacefulness in death it had never shown in life. There was a soft beauty to her. When the other women returned and found Bree with Katcalani, they gathered around to mourn for the fallen woman. Although in life they hadn't liked her a great deal, the passing of even one diminished their ranks and they wished her back among them.

The women put their shoulders to the tree trunk and moved it from Katcalani's body, then carried her back to the village square where they set about preparing her for burial. When the men returned, they would take her to the sacred burial ground. She would be the first of them to be taken there and they were saddened by the thought.

Somberly they worked, washing away the mud, arraying her in the best clothes they had left among them. At last Katcalani was ready for her final ceremony among her people. The women's voices rose in lamenting chants as they stood about. Some disarranged their hair in classic demonstration of mourning.

"The hunters are back," some called, and the children and some of the women hurried off to greet the returning men. Anxiously Bree hurried after them, Cooee on her hip. She prayed that none of the men had been hurt, but her main concern was for Shocaw. Her heart eased its hammering when she saw his tall, straight figure in the prow of the boat.

Suddenly hesitant about the news he must now hear, she hung back from the others, letting one of the other women tell him of Katcalani. She watched as one of the women stepped forward and began speaking to him, but her words were drowned out as Shocaw clasped his head between his hands and uttered a hoarse cry. Then his long legs were carrying him away from the riverbank through the village toward the platform where the body lay.

Bree stared after him in consternation. There had been such grief in his reaction. Had he loved Katcalani more than she'd realized? If so, perhaps it was best to leave him alone in his moment of grief. Slowly she made her way back to their chickee and placed Cooee in his swing. His lashes drooped over his eyes and he settled down for a nap. Confused, Bree sat in the chickee trying to sort out what she'd seen. Katcalani had admitted Shocaw hadn't shared her sleeping mat, yet he'd shown such grief at her death.

"Bree?" Shocaw's voice was hesitant as he spoke her name. Bree whirled around to look at him. He stood on the ground below the chickee, his face open and raw with pain and relief. Tears gathered in the corners of his eyes and suddenly she understood.

"I thought it was you," he whispered. "They said my wife was dead. I never thought of Katcalani." His voice cracked. "All I could think of was that I'd lost you after all," he ended on a whisper. Bree hurried down the steps and threw herself into his arms. They wrapped about her, crushing her against him. His wet cheek pressed against her brow.

"When I saw it was Katcalani, I was thankful it was she who had died and not you," he said raggedly.

"Shh, it's all right," Bree said. "She is out of pain this way. She was very unhappy." She wouldn't tell Shocaw about Katcalani's hatred for her and Cooee and what his first wife had tried to do to his son. It would do no good to speak of it now.

"Bree, I love you. I couldn't bear to lose you again," Shocaw said, and his words, spoken with such emotion, brought a rush of happiness to Bree's heart.

"Oh, Shocaw, I love you too," she whispered, meeting his kiss with one of her own. At last she and Shocaw were free to love each other as they wished, without secrets between them, without doubts and reservations. Katcalani had given them that final gift before she died when she'd told the truth. Now Bree meant to repay Katcalani. Stepping away from Shocaw's arms, she smiled briefly at him. "Katcalani was your wife, your first wife," she said softly, "and you are the chief of your village. She must be buried with honor."

"Yes," Shocaw said in agreement, straightening his proud head. "I will do her honor." He had been unable to love his first wife, but he would give her what he could. He turned and took a few steps back toward the square, then stopped and looked back at Bree.

"*He-a-maw, Cha-hi-e-waw,*" he said gently, holding out his hand. "Come, my wife." The words opened the heavens for Bree as she reached out to him. His hand closed about hers, pulling her close as together they walked back toward the village square. My wife, he had called her, and she cherished the words, but inside she would always think of herself as Shocaw's *hoke-tee*.

Epilogue

In the year 1855, government surveyors came upon a Seminole village in the swamps and, like many a white man before them, helped themselves to the ripe fruits and vegetables and destroyed the rest. The chief of the village, Billy Bolecks, demanded payment but his demands were ignored. Even here in their last stronghold they were not free of the white man's destruction. The next day Billy Bolecks and his warriors attacked and wounded the surveyors.

From this incident a series of small skirmishes occurred between Billy Bolecks (known among the white men as Billy Bowlegs) and the hunters, trappers, and soldiers. Chief Bolecks and his warriors made a last-ditch fight against removal from Florida. So great was their hatred and distrust of the white man that any Indian discovered communicating with the white men were put to death.

Finally, however, Billy Bolecks was persuaded by a group of Seminoles, brought back from the Indian Territory reservations for that purpose, to take the government's cash settlement and move his people to Oklahoma. He brought 165 of his people out of the Everglades. Two hundred Seminoles refused to leave the swamps and lived like hunted animals until the Civil War began and they were forgotten for the moment.

About the Author

Although Peggy Hanchar travels with her husband, Steve, they return often to their lake cottage in Delton, Michigan. She has four children, and in addition to writing romances, she quilts and sketches with pastels.